MARK OF THE

LAUGHING DEATH

AND OTHER STORIES

The **DANCING TUATARA PRESS**
Books from **RAMBLE HOUSE**

CLASSICS OF HORROR

CLASSICS OF SCIENCE FICTION AND FANTASY

DAY KEENE IN THE DETECTIVE PULPS

MARK OF THE LAUGHING DEATH

And Other Stories

Francis James

Edited and Introduced by
John Pelan

RAMBLE HOUSE

Mark of the Laughing Death, *Dime Mystery Magazine,* November 1936
Monster's Death Song, *Terror Tales,* December 1935
Slaves of the Midnight Caverns, *Dime Mystery Magazine,* July 1937
Arms of the Flame Goddess, *Dime Mystery Magazine,* April 1938
The Women Who Killed for Satan, *Horror Stories* June/July 1939
The Unwelcome Dead, *Terror Tales,* July 1935
Brides for the Half-Men, *Sinister Stories,* February 1940
Merry Christmas from the Dead, *Dime Mystery,* January 1937

ISBN 13: 978-1-60543-703-3

Edited by: John Pelan and Fender Tucker

Dancing Tuatara Press #24

MARK OF THE LAUGHING DEATH

THE FURIES OF FRANCIS JAMES

Hard to imagine that we've assembled over a dozen weird menace collections without touching on the works of an author who while forgotten by posterity was very high on editor Rogers Terrill's list of heavy hitters. In fact, so popular was Francis James that he is one of two authors whose absence from the pages of *Dime Mystery Magazine*, *Terror Tales*, and *Horror Stories* was deemed worthy of notice to the readership . . . "Francis James is back!" trumpeted the cover blurb; indicating that at least as far as Popular Publications was concerned, the appearance of James' by-line on the cover meant more sales. The only author accorded similar treatment was the indefatigable Arthur Leo Zagat, whose heart surgery caused editor Terrill to warn readers that they might have to muddle along for a few months without new Zagat stories while the author recovered (of course, no such shortage occurred as the prolific Zagat had ample inventory on file to cover his convalescence and by the time new material was needed he'd already turned in another 100,000 words or so of new work.)

We tend to think of Francis James as one of the second wave of weird menace authors along with writers such as Mary Dale Buckner (Donald Dale), Russell Gray, J.O. Quinliven and so on . . . While it's certainly true that his most productive run was after 1936, the fact is that James was on board and contributing major pieces as early as 1934 under the pseudonym of "James A. Goldthwaite". This by-line was quickly abandoned and James debuted under his own name in the first issue of *Horror Stories* with the lead novel *Music of the Damned*. Oddly enough, James is the only author not mentioned on the cover! Apparently, editor Rogers Terrill had yet to develop the confidence in James that he would have in just a short time. 1935 was hardly a banner year with only five stories published in the pages of *Horror Stories* and *Terror Tales* and one novelette in *Dime Mystery Magazine*. Another five pieces appeared in 1936, including the title piece of this collection and "The City Ruled by Death".

By this point James had established the style that would endear him to the editors and readers and the flaws that would cause critics to dismiss his work. James was a "gosh wow" writer; taking a cue from the "raw heads and bloody bones" school of the early British authors such as Dick Donovan and Clive Pemberton, a typical James plot introduced a horrifying situation, brought in an additional layer of menace in the second or third chapter and then piled additional horrors on until the penultimate chapter. This made for breakneck pacing and the literary equivalent of a roller-coaster ride to hell. In the final chapter, James would do his level best to tie all the loose ends together and resolve the mystery.

The downside to this structure is that James would often write himself into a corner and have to resort to a fairly preposterous *deux ex machina* ending. Great literature? Certainly not. Sloppy writing? Unquestionably. Entertaining reading? Here's where James' faults may be forgiven . . . Whatever else may be said of James plotting, his stories are a lot of fun to read. To an audience raised on the Saturday serials wherein inconsistencies from one week to the next were politely forgotten, James work had the same sense of fun about it, the pacing was so lively that any inconstancies or lapses in logic could be overlooked. I don't mean to suggest that James indulged in what critics James Blish and Damon Knight termed "the idiot plot", wherein it is necessary to the story that all characters behave like complete idiots in order to further the plot. (Seen to its best advantage in modern horror films such as *The Evil Dead* when playing the demonic chanting on the tape recorder apparently causes the ground to shake, lights to flash, and generally disturbing things to occur and no one thinks to turn the damn thing off . . .) I'm sure that the reader can think of dozens of other examples. No, these aren't the flaws that you'll see in Francis James; such flaws are pretty much limited to minor *faux pas*, rather than major insults to the reader's intelligence.

Looking at his work as an editor of some twenty-five years in practice, I can see where many of his stories can be improved, but were I reading for a horror anthology, the only reason I would ever have had for rejecting a Francis James story would be due to length. And here's another interesting facet of his writing . . . While most of modern colleagues would agree that the novelette to novella is the ideal length for the horror story (and editor Rogers Terrill seemed to agree as the majority of fiction that ran in his three magazines was of that length), no other authors of the Popular Publications stable other than Frederick Davis seem to have been quite so single-minded about writing at this length as was Francis James (and Davis wrote just a handful of pieces compared to James' tally of well over fifty pieces.)

Perhaps this, more than anything else, has been the root cause of Francis James being ignored by most anthologists. Certainly, the weird menace genre as a whole has received short shrift by most horror anthologists over the years, but short pieces by the likes of Arthur J. Burks and Hugh B. Cave turn up from time to time. However, once the 10,000 word count is reached, anthologists seem to think that more names on the contents page is always preferable and a lengthy piece (if included at all) need be by a very popular contemporary author or household name of the past, certainly not by a pulp author whose fiction has remained uncollected. Of course, Francis James almost never wrote anything under 12,000 words.

As mentioned, there are over fifty of these page-turners that, with the rare exception of a couple of stories reprinted years ago in small anthologies by Robert Weinberg and Sheldon Jaffrey, have remained unavailable to readers. With this and subsequent volumes on the drawing board, all we can say is to quote Rogers Terrill from the cover of the March/April 1939 issue of *Terror Tales*: *"Francis James is Back!"*

John Pelan
Midnight House
Gallup, NM
Winter Solstice

MARK OF THE LAUGHING DEATH

It's a queer thing, how terror that you don't dream of will jump out of a corner and leer at you, snarling. And often you don't realize, you don't understand the meaning of its first sinister signs and whisperings till it is too late.

My terror started with those three bottles in Jane's medicine closet. It had been two days before that hell had broken loose in the city. It's hard to tell you about that so that you will get the picture, see it as we saw it, panic and death in the very air—the red marks and the hell's laughter.

I saw the bottles there and I stared at them, wondering. Carbolic acid and a couple of other things, I wouldn't remember the names. Harsh, mordant fluids, used for cleaning, taking off unwanted marks and stains. I couldn't imagine what Jane had that she was so anxious to cleanse.

I dried my hands and went out into the living room, where I found her ready. And then there was another queer thing. She was dressed for the street, but differently than usual. Instead of one of the V-necked blouses that she commonly wore, she had garbed herself in a white linen suit that was buttoned up tight under her chin. I said:

"What's the idea of the uniform? Why don't you wear that little yellow blouse?"

I stared at her then, for she whitened and shrank away from me; her hand clutched the folds of cloth over her bosom.

"Why, Rancc, I—"

Just then the phone rang and she hurried to answer it. She put it down and turned around.

"Starbuck," she explained briefly. "He wants me to go after a story—"

Jane was a "sob sister" on the *Evening Star*, and Starbuck was her city editor.

"He says make it fast and get it while it's hot." she murmured as we hurried out and I jammed the bell for the elevator.

It took us maybe ten minutes by taxi up to the brownstone front on East Sixty-eighth. There was the usual crowd of morbid faces out on the sidewalks, but our badges got us through and we went upstairs into a chamber.

I took one look at the nude form on the bed and I turned away. God! I'd seen plenty of those sights in the last twenty hours, so many that their images wouldn't wash out of my mind in a thousand years . . . The woman had gone into convulsions before she died, the way they all did, her face was frozen in those frenzied contortions. And on her bosom midway between the breasts was the Mark.

I looked at that thing again and I felt that shock of numb incredulity that had hit me the first time I had seen it. That skull and crossed bones of death, incised into her skin in flaming red—

"Another one. Great God, where do they come from—how do they get there?" It was Mallory, one of my pals on the staff of Dowling's private detective agency, whose voice I heard over my shoulder. "They go to bed all right at night, in the morning they wake up and there it is. No one's gone near them. God knows they wouldn't put it on themselves—"

"Has the laboratory turned in a report on it yet?" I asked.

Mallory spat out of a window.

"Report, hell. A dozen big shot professors have had those stiffs down there to study and they've sent up a ream of opinions—and all they add up to is nothing. They've tried all kinds of chemicals to wash off those marks, and they don't wash. She even tried it herself. Give a look—"

Mallory pulled me across the hall into a bathroom. In the medicine closet over the bowl there were bottles—half a dozen varieties of cleaning fluids.

"She tried all of them on herself before—"

Mallory was talking and I heard his voice a mile away. For suddenly that picture of the bottles in Jane's cabinet flashed into my brain. *Those bottles of cleaning things—*

Back somewhere, I heard the medical examiner's voice.

"Something going on in this city that has never been heard of before in the world . . . A hundred persons killed . . . City swept by a red scourge . . . Scarlet marks on their bodies—and then sudden death . . ."

I paced those rooms in a ferment while Jane got what she wanted for her story. We got away at last and went back to the taxi. She crumpled down on the seat and she shivered.

"Rance—this horrible business—isn't it ever going to stop?" she half sobbed. "Who is doing it—who and why?"

"Looks like the work of some maniac," I muttered. "Someone who exults in sheer horror. But the starting point of it all is that mark. You looked at that woman back there—what did it seem like, something painted on, or branded, like tattooing?"

"I couldn't tell," she said. "It looked like a birthmark, like just part of the skin itself. But it isn't so much what it is as how it gets there. People put on their clothes in the morning and when they undress at night, it's there. How can they do it? How can anyone possibly—"

"Jane," I said. "Those bottles of cleaning stuff in your bathroom—what are they for?"

She glanced up quickly. She drew back into the shadow in the seat corner and laughed shakily.

"Why—to clean some things—some shoes and hats—"

I bent to look at her. She started to turn away. I took hold of her shoulders and pulled her around.

What I did next sounds crazy. I was close to that—half distracted with tension and fear. My fingers reached out and fumbled at the high neck of her dress.

"Jane," I muttered, "you've got to tell me. What did you put that on for? Why didn't you wear a blouse, the way you usually do? *Did you put it on to hide something—*"

She stared at me. "Rance!" She started to pull away.

A wave of stubbornness swept over me. I gripped her tighter.

"Jane! Open that dress!" I cried. "Open it and let me see—"

"Rance!" She whitened and her eyes flashed. "What do you mean—"

"Sorry," I mumbled. I swept her to me, strained her in my arms. "Jane! Jane, darling," I whispered. "Is everything—all right—"

She knew what I meant. She smiled wanly and she touched my face with her cool fingertips.

"Why, of course," she breathed. "I just put on this dress—for a change—"

I let her go and leaned back on the cushions. I didn't know whether she was telling the truth or not. She wasn't herself, her hands shook and her bosom heaved. Whether it was that I'd affronted her modesty, or because there was something there on her body—*a death's-head that she had been trying to hide under that high-necked dress; trying to wash off with those cleaning things the way that woman had who'd died laughing* . . . God!

It was Jane's night to work. She had to go out into the town and then do a column on what she saw—a city where death flew on sightless wings.

Rivers of faces flowed past us, white and staring-eyed. They were afraid to be alone—and they were afraid of one another, too. They bumped and collided and they jumped apart. Someone, something, was sowing death. Maybe that stranger whose elbow thumped in your ribs, maybe that sleek-looking youth or that flashy girl with the shining lip-stick and the sparkling eyes . . .

For half an hour we walked up and down. Then, gradually, I realized that someone was following us. Three times, over my shoulder, I'd glimpsed a weasel sharp face with pointed chin and black button eyes. Two of them, trailing us and drawing in closer . . .

I grabbed Jane's arm and started to run. A dozen yards along, the black mouth of an alley cut into the long line of house fronts.

I sidestepped in there. We fled on tiptoe, hugging the shadows. Half way through, I looked around. They were coming, dark, silent spectres flitting under the brick walls.

"Run, Jane, run!" I yelled. Up ahead we could see the opening at the other end of the passage. Another figure was coming, a stooped, ragged form that shambled uncertainly along.

I didn't know who he was, whether he brought death or was only a homeless wanderer . . . We brushed past him and he didn't look up. He was just a bum, ragged, unshaven.

The next instant we sped out of the other end of the alley into a lighted street. People and taxis were passing.

I drew Jane to one side, flattened myself against the wall and waited. Ten, twenty seconds, and nothing happened. I peered back around the edge of the house wall.

The two flitting shadows were gone. The old man we had met had turned, was coming back.

I saw the beard-matted countenance tilt upward, saw the white, jerking spasm that suddenly wrenched it.

He began to laugh. Laugh—my God! First a thin and crazy tittering and then peal after peal of mirthless screamings, laughter that he didn't want to laugh, that he couldn't stop, that held the wild terror of a soul burning in hell.

His legs started to twist, his arms flopped with the nerveless jerkings of a puppet dangled from cords. He tried to walk, to run away. His legs shambled and wrenched, they wound together and locked in convulsions.

He got those wildly twitching hands up to his face, crushed them across his lips as though he would jam those bursts of diabolical merriment back down his throat. But the laughter kept coming, it spurted through his locked fingers in ripping screams.

And now he was down on the ground. He thrashed there in spasms. His limbs tangled and twisted, they locked in convulsions like the writhings of snakes. He croaked out one last shriek and lay motionless.

My own hands were shaking as I stumbled over and knelt by his side. I knew what I'd find—those crossed bones and grinning skull, stamped midway of his nipples . . .

"What was it, Rance—oh, what made him do it?" Jane gripped my arm and her fingers burned through the cloth. "We were right by him—"

I put my arm around her and led her away from that thing on the ground.

"Some drug—there are half a dozen different ones that would throw a man into spasms of laughing," I muttered. "All the doctors are agreed on that."

"Those two men who followed us—they must have done it," she shivered. "But how could they? They didn't come within yards of him—"

I didn't say anything. Those men had been following us—*following Jane* before we got clear of them!

I'd had enough. I pressed Jane's arm.

"Let's get out of this," I muttered. "Let's go to your place—let's go home."

She smiled wistfully and shook her head.

"My story, Rance—I've got to go down there and write it—"

I flagged a taxi then. I put her in and sank down beside her. Somewhere behind us, a woman started to laugh. I looked at Jane and my brain was cold, as everything came crowding back.

Those bottles that I'd seen in her bath cabinet, and those identical ones in the closet of that woman who'd died . . . That mark on the woman's bosom that she had tried to wash off—and the, the laughter that we'd seen frozen on her fiend's-mask of a countenance . . .

Chapter Two

Scarlet Sign

We went on down to the *Star*, Jane filed her story, and then we dropped in at Dutch Joe's across the street. I saw my boss at one of the tables and we edged our way across the tightly-packed floor.

Buck Dowling was the head of the biggest private inquiry agency in the city and his name was known throughout the world. He was a husky blond with a tall forehead and eyes blue as chips of ice. He had a big mouth and granite chin and a heartwarming smile.

He took one look at Jane's face, pulled out a chair for her, and held two fingers in front of a waiter.

"Anything new?" he whispered to me.

I told him: "Just more of the same."

He shook his head and his big white fingers broke a dry fag in an ash tray.

"A hundred people killed and not a lead cracked," he muttered. "Those marks—how do they get them on there—how would I go to work to put a brand on your body while you were walking around with your clothes on, without your knowing till you undressed—or at night while you were asleep—"

"Regardless of how they are doing it, what they are trying to put across is a cinch." It was Starbuck, Jane's hardboiled and hatchet-jawed chief, across the table. "This raid is being staged by a gang who figure to stampede the town—drive every one away, clean the place out. They're after the banks. With the city emptied, they'll have time to crack the vaults with no one to stop them."

"Maybe so." It was Goddard, another private dick with a far-reaching practice. He was a big, swarthy man with a bulldog jaw. But now his face was yellow and beads of sweat stood on his puffed eyelids.

"But meanwhile, what's happening?" he demanded. "Death is everywhere, it's in the air. One of those killers may be right here in this room with us now." He beat his fist on his palm. "I called on the Governor to declare martial law. Stop every man, woman and child in the streets and search them—"

"The damn fool!" Dowling mutered. "As if the town wasn't rotten with panic right now. One little thing more and it's a stampede—"

I leaned over and told him about the pair whom Jane and I

had seen tailing us, and the old man in the alley.

"Whoever is doing it, that's how," he said. "He's got his killers out in the town. Wonder how Goddard guessed—remember, he said that those killers might be in here—"

"And maybe he is right," Starbuck muttered. "Maybe there's one of them at that table—"

Jane started up to her feet. She tugged at my sleeve.

"Rance—let's go! Let's get out of here!" she cried.

It was as though that cry of hers had reached every ear in the big dining room. Suddenly something got them all at once, some unreasoning mob-surge of panic. All over the place they were up on their feet, pushing and fighting to get to the doors. The cops and the dicks, the hard-boiled reporters, the good-time Johnnies and their flapper companions, white-faced and shivering, scrambling to get into the open and away from each other.

I beat my way through that bleating pack and outside. After a while I managed to get hold of a taxi and we started for Jane's place.

I went in and upstairs with her. We didn't talk, we were too weary and nerved up to talk. We went out into the kitchen and heated soup and made sandwiches and coffee. We turned on the radio and sat down to eat.

I lit a cigarette and tried to relax. Jane and I had no kith nor kin, we were alone in the world, and this little place of hers was what we called home. Over there in the corner, Goldie, her pet canary, was scolding because she had forgotten to put his cloth over his cage and the light got in his eyes. One of her dresses lay over a chair, and a couple of my pipes sat on the mantel.

Home—but it wasn't home. For if it had been, if we had been married, I wouldn't have to go off and leave her, I could stay by her side day and night. I could stand between her and that fear. And I would know, I wouldn't have to be guessing about that other thing—

Finally Jane got up. She came around beside me and kissed me.

"Rance—you've got to go," she whispered. "I know what you're thinking, but it isn't so. I'm—everything is all right." She smiled again, wanly. "Who would want to kill poor little me?"

I didn't say anything. I kissed her again and muttered goodnight. Who *would* want to kill her? But dozens of others had died.

My hands gripped and I whispered a curse. God, how could I protect her when all over the city people were dying in laughter . . .

Her door was locked, no killer could get at her through it. But around on the other side, where the fire escape which passed under her window came down to the ground—

Around there I went and under that black spider-work of steel bars I halted. Up those steps and in ten seconds I could be at her window. But—so could anyone else!

I sat down on the foot of that fire escape and I didn't move. Now and then footsteps scuffed at the mouth of the passage. I slid to my feet and ghosted back into the shadows. I could see them—dim, menacing forms that hovered there an instant and then melted away.

Down on the bottom rung of the steps I sank again and I waited. Waited for whom or what, I didn't know. For something that would come skulking through the dark, some unimaginable minister of hell.

It was just getting light when I finally dragged myself up from those punishing rungs and stumbled out to look for a taxi. I went back to my place and fell on the bed without taking my clothes off.

I tossed and dreamed for a couple of hours. Then I got up, went to the phone and called Jane. I thanked God when I heard her voice and made a date to meet her in an hour. There was a conference down at headquarters.

There was quite a crowd in the Commissioner's room when the doorman recognized us and let us through. The Commissioner himself; Morrissey, head of the G-men; Professor Stone, the big poison expert; young, suave Jim Fes-

senden, brains of the Seaboard Inquiry Company and I don't
know how many more.

A big, paunchy man whose once-fat face sagged as flabbily
as a pricked windbag, sat facing the group, and the Commissioner was just saying:

"Tell that over again, Mr. Holden."

Holden ran his tongue over his lips.

"Yesterday morning it was that I woke up and found one of
those marks on me. I did what so many other have done, I
suppose—I bought all the different kinds of cleaning liquids
I could think of and tried to wash it off. And at ten o'clock
yesterday morning I got this note in the mail—"

He held out a crumpled sheet of paper and we all craned
our heads at it. I won't give you the whole of it. It was extortion—they wanted money. The directions for paying it over
were all given.

"If you obey instructions and deliver the cash before
eleven tomorrow, your life wilt be spared," the screed wound
up. "And you will receive directions for removing the mark
from your body."

"As you know, I didn't pay," Holden went on. "I came
here and showed you letter and demanded protection. You
made up a dummy package and planted it. No one came for
it. And an hour ago I got this."

He held out another line of typed words. They said:

"Today at eleven."

The Commissioner's voice droned out the words and I
don't think there was an eye in the room that didn't jump to
the clock on the wall. The long minute hand was just crossing the vertical—eleven exactly.

"I want to know what this police department is good for!"
Holden's voice was jerky and queer. "I come to you for help,
and—"

Suddenly he stopped shouting. His mouth opened, his
breath caught and gagged. He snickered. Wildly he tried to
crush back the peals of mad merriment.

I won't paint any more of that picture. He went into convulsions and he died laughing.

Someone bent over Holden and opened his clothes. A mark was there, but it wasn't the one that we had seen before, it wasn't the skull and the crossed bones.

I won't even try to describe that mark to you. It was a scarlet symbol of disgrace, a mute and wordless thing that blazoned its own unmistakable message of sin. More than that—it was something individual and personal. It hinted at something in Holden's private life that he must have been keeping buried, a skeleton in the vaults of his secret soul. And yet some one had discovered it and branded its damnable confession on his naked flesh.

For an instant you could hear a pin drop in the room. It had struck them all dumb with sheer bewilderment. That other mark, that machine-made symbol of death, had been bad enough. But this—

I hooked my arm into Jane's and pulled her away.

"Let's get out of here," I growled.

We went out onto the sidewalk and we covered a morning of Jane's assignments.

The first was a house somewhere on the East Side. The woman had killed herself, fast enough. She had done it with scissors . . .

But first she had tried to cut something away from her bosom—cut it or burn it, I couldn't tell, in that mess. Another one of those marks. But this one wasn't identical with that which had been on Holden. It was a different thing, a picture that could have meant something referring to her alone. Something that she had rather die than have seen.

We saw others, three or four more, with new marks on them, and all different. They were all persons who had been ordered to pay money and hadn't. And there on their bodies death had left them with the tale of their life's secret in a crimson brand.

We went out and walked down Fifth Avenue. Rivers of faces flowed past us, eyes wolfish with fear. Terror that some one had delved into their lives and dragged out the dead and hidden things that they thought had been buried forever, and they walked here with their scarlet letters branded on them . . .

At 42nd Street the lights were against us. We stopped to wait. They changed, but we didn't go on. Nobody went on. Both ways of the cross streets, those hundreds of people and cars stood rooted to earth.

A man came walking down the avenue; he was walking in the middle of the street and he had that broad avenue all to himself. He came laughing, erupting burst of merriment from lips that twisted and jerked.

He shivered, his limbs shambled in palsy. His eyes rolled in their socket. Half way across the intersection, his knee crumpled. Down on the pavement he pitched and he thrashed there in convulsions.

In the last frenzy of his writhings, his hands ripped at his bosom. The mark was there, the private thing that unveiled his particular hidden skeleton to the world.

I steered Jane out of that hubbub of cursing men and led her down a side street. How had they found out—how could anyone have seen behind the veils into the secret vaults of these people's souls and dragged those horrors into the light? Was that why Jane had lied to me—if she had lied—about those things in her cabinet? Was that why she wouldn't open her dress and let me see? Because she had one of them on her—not just a warning of death—a scarlet symbol of sin . . .

We turned into an eating place and ordered something on plates—I didn't know what it was. For I didn't eat it, I sat there staring over at Jane. The orchestra was playing—a waltz that was our love song, for to its strains I'd asked her to marry me.

She smiled and she whispered: "Let's dance this, Rance—"

I took her in my arms and we moved over the floor. Her hair was in my eyes and the perfume of her was like a cock-tail made to be breathed, not to be tasted. I held her tighter. How I loved her—God, how I loved her . . .

We left and went down town to her office, and just as we got there her desk phone rang. It was a man's voice, that much I could tell. A voice that was vaguely familiar, one that I'd heard many times but didn't just place.

I watched her as she talked and I could see her eyes dilate. Her fingers tightened around the receiver.

"Yes—this afternoon. I'll be there," she said at last and then she hung up.

I reached over and touched her arm.

"Who was that? Where are you going?" I demanded.

She looked away.

"Rance—don't ask me," she murmured. "It isn't anything—for you to worry about."

I started to say something and then I saw Dowling beckoning to me. He and half a dozen more were gathered around Starbuck's desk. Professor Stone, big shot on criminology and poisons, was talking.

"Those marks—there is only one way to account for them. No matter what secrets there are in our lives, one or two persons probably know of them. And such persons will usually talk—if the money is big enough. Now, what classes of people have the best means of finding out things about private lives that aren't generally known? Newspaper men, police and detectives, of course. Gentlemen, if you want to lay hands on the brain behind this campaign, get after all the reporters, police officers and private detectives in the city."

"A smooth theory, professor." It was young Fessenden's voice, slightly sneering. "I'd rather put my money on some gang man. They could buy up this information and it would be more in their line. And no matter who has gotten wise to all this inside dirt, how do they go to work to stamp those marks on people's bodies without their knowing it?"

There was a lot more talk. One thing they all seemed to agree on, though—that there were two parts to the raid that was being staged. The first move, when all the marks had been the same, was merely against people picked out at random and killed to throw the town into a panic. The later victims, those with the special marks on them, were the ones from whom they were asking money. They probably figured that, with the whole city ragged with panic, these rich folks would fork over to save their skins in a hurry without trying to trace down those to whom they cashed up.

So that was it, extortion. Extortion by wholesale, murder-for-money on a scale that no one had ever dreamed of. A whole city sent frantic with the laughing scourge, so that those who got the special marks and the letters would put up colossal sums without talking, would hand over half of their fortunes to save themselves from that laughter.

Suddenly I looked around for Jane. She wasn't there. I stood in the middle of the floor and a cold hand clutched the back of my neck. For suddenly I realized whose voice it had been on that phone, talking to her.

The afternoon dragged away and I couldn't find her. I haunted her office, I phoned her apartment a dozen times. I went out and paced the streets.

It was after nine that night when she at last answered her door bell and told me to come up.

She was silent and white. She sat with her hands clenched in her lap, looking up at me, but she didn't speak.

"Where have you been?" I shot at her. My nerves were in tatters.

She sighed and shook her head. "I can't tell you," she said.

"You've been to see Fessenden!" I stormed. "It was he who called you there at the office. He was right there, but he went out into the hall and called you from the booth, so that no one would know. What did you go there for?"

She went pale at that, but again she shook her head.

"Rance, darling—please don't, don't ask me anything," she whispered. "I'm tired—terribly tired and I'm going to bed. I wish you would go—"

Gently she pushed me to the door.

"Don't worry—I'll be all right," she murmured. She kissed me goodnight and then suddenly she threw her arms around my neck.

"Rance—whatever happens, remember I love you!" she cried.

I went out of the building, but I didn't go home. Up and

down in front of the place I paced and I tried to think.

Down the deserted side street a figure came skulking, hugging the shadows. I slid back into the dark of the alley where the fire escape was.

He didn't see me at first, and step by step he crept closer. Now I could get his face, narrow and dark, with ratty eyes.

A taxi swung around the corner, throwing the beam of its light against me. He saw me crouching, tensed to jump at him. He spun around. Gravel crunched under his feet. By the time I got where he had been, he was just a racing huddle of black half way to the corner.

I wiped the sweat from my face and I turned back, cursing. For he had been going toward Jane's, creeping toward the foot of the fire escape.

Up and down that black cleft between the brick wails I paced for an hour—ten hours, I wouldn't know. And then at last I was creeping up those rusted rungs, crawling on my hands and knees and not making a sound.

For I had reached my limit at last. I had to end this suspense that was driving me mad. God would have to forgive me for what I was going to do—but I had to know!

Chapter Three

Finger of Death

The flight of steps came to an end at the edge of a platform of iron rungs which I knew ran along underneath Jane's bathroom window.

On hands and knees I crawled toward that shine of light that sprayed over the balcony. I knelt below the window and lifted an eye up over the edge of the sill. My fingers clutched those sharp and narrow slats till they cut into my flesh, yet I didn't feel.

For Jane had slipped off her underthings and she stood there, stark naked. The glow of the light bathed her white slimness, brought out the rounded curvings of her shoulders and breasts.

She was standing in front of the wash bowl. She had a bottle in her hand. She turned a fluid out of it onto a cloth and she scrubbed at her bosom!

She turned a little and I saw what was there. Between the ivory rounding's of her breasts was something that flamed scarlet—bright as though branded into her flesh. Not just that skull and crossed bones that warned of death. That other mark, a symbol whose utter vileness could mean only one thing . . .

She dropped the cloth. She buried her face in her hands and sobbed. She moved away and I saw her pick up a paper and read the words on it.

Over her shoulder I stared at the blurring lines while bewilderment blew in my brain. Jane was a poor girl. She had no money to hand over to an extortionist for the privilege of living. What was it that fiend was demanding, what was he ordering her to do . . .

I saw her tear up the letter and drop it in the drain. She turned and when she wheeled back again, she had things in her hand—long glistening blades of scissors, needle-pointed as swords . . . She lifted them, she held them pointed down at her bosom. "No! No, Jane! Put those things down! Jane, let me in—"

Crazily I was yelling, shouting at the top of my lungs. I swarmed across to the window and I beat on the glass. With my bare fist I smashed it above the lock, I heaved the frame upward and catapulted into the room.

I swept her into my arms. I crushed her to me, I wrenched the scissors out of her hand and flung them through the hole in the window.

"Jane—for God's sake!" I muttered brokenly.

"I wasn't, Rance—I wasn't going to," she sobbed. "I was thinking of it, but I wouldn't have, really I wouldn't."

Suddenly she realized how she was and her face crimsoned.

"Rance, how—what were you doing there—"

She caught up a towel and held it before her.

"I'm sorry, darling," I muttered. "But I had to—I had to know. You said it was all right, but I was afraid—"

"Wait a minute." She went into her bedroom and came back in a few moments, dressed.

We stood there and looked at each other. I crushed back the thought that hammered my brain, I didn't let my mind look at it. That scarlet sign on her, what it meant, I didn't care. All that mattered was that death wanted her.

"Now you know; I was hoping that you wouldn't have to, till afterward," her voice came hopeless and spent.

"Afterwards—there isn't going to be any afterward!" I cried. "We're going to fight this. I'm going to find the monster that's doing it, and—"

Sadly she smiled and she shook her head.

"It's too late, dear. How could you save me when dozens of others . . . I wish you would go, darling—please go. I don't want you here, when . . . I don't want you to see me—"

I turned from her and paced the floor. What I would have said or done next, I don't know. But suddenly there was a knock at the door.

She started to answer it, but I was before her. I unlocked it, opened it the small of an inch and canted one eye around crack.

It was a stranger, a man I'd never seen before in my life. A small, nattily dressed customer with sallow face and snaky eyes and a lighted cigarette in a long holder.

"Is Miss Jane Holland—" he started to say, and then I slammed the door in his face. I heard his curse as the panel banged into his eyes and then his feet beating a tattoo down the hall.

I swung around from the door and my knees were like water. I didn't get it, I didn't understand, but I knew that when I had looked into the face of that stranger I had been staring at death.

Jane came over and put her hands on my arm.

"Rance," she whispered. "I want you to go, dear. There isn't anything you can do . . ." She was sobbing, clinging to me. "I don't want you to see me. I want you remember me as . . . It may be any time now—"

I folded her in my arms and I ground out a curse of denial. I didn't know what this death was, where it was coming from, it wasn't magic, it wasn't supernatural, it was a thing done by men. The mark itself wouldn't bring on the laughing— because those who had received letters had been told that if they obeyed the orders to deliver the money their lives would be spared . . . So, no matter how that brand had been put on the flesh of the victims, *the killers must have a second contact with them before they died.*

I gripped Jane by the shoulders and shook her.

"We're getting out of here!" I cried. "We're going to Dowling's house. He'll take care of you. He'll have some kind of an idea what to do—"

At the mention of Dowling's name Jane gave me a strange look. Mutely she turned toward the door but I pulled her away.

"No, not that way," I muttered. I didn't dare take her down through those long and empty corridors with the corners and shadows where something, I didn't know what, could fly at her out of the darkness.

I pulled her back into the bathroom and through the opened window we climbed onto the fire escape. I led her along its slatted floor and guided her down the steep and creaking stairs with one hand back over my shoulder.

Dowling lived alone save for his servants in a big, old-fashioned house in the Twenties. I understood from him once that he had been disappointed in love—at any rate, he'd never married, and, having plenty of money, he had devoted his long life of bachelorhood to indulging his hobbies. He used to say that he preferred single loneliness to double cussedness.

The taxi pulled up in front of his number and I looked both ways before getting out and rushing Jane up the steps.

Peebles, the eagle-eyed little old butler, opened the door at my ring.

"Mr. Dowling isn't here, sir—I don't know where he is or when he'll be home," the old man said.

"Never mind, Peebles," I told him. "We'll wait. And listen—get a room ready for Miss Holland, will you—she'll be living here now until further notice."

If the old houseman was surprised, he didn't betray it by batting an eyelash. He gave me his best very-good-sir, and bowed himself out.

We stood in the little reception room, looking around. I knew that Dowling's front door was of steel, and there were bars on the windows. And two or three of his boys were always on guard around. It seemed safe. I looked at Jane and tried to grin.

She gave back a sad little wisp of a smile and shook her head.

"It isn't any use, Rance," she whispered. "The mark is on me, and—"

"And nothing!" I stormed. "You're safe here, nothing can get you—"

A figure stood in the doorway. It was Slim, one of the chief's house guards.

"Hello, Rance," he whispered. His right hand was in his coat pocket and his lips were tight. "You stepped into something—"

"What—" I began.

"Let me do the talking. There's some one in this house—who doesn't belong here—"

He took Jane and me each by an arm and steered us back to the door. On the way he stepped to the wall switch and snapped off the lights.

"There's a room upstairs without any windows," he muttered. "It's your best bet—"

We started upstairs. I didn't get it. What Slim said sounded lunatic. Some one here in Dowling's house . . . Jane had gone tense again. She was breathing in tight little gasps as she clung to me.

Half a dozen steps up, we halted. There wasn't any light up

there, either, but there were noises. Some one, more than one set of footsteps, was moving around, coming toward us.

"Who—" I started to whisper.

Slim gripped my arm. "Listen—"

Back behind, downstairs, some one had started to laugh. The next minute I knew it was Peebles. His cracked old voice jangled mad screamings through that deathly hush. He gasped for breath, with his strangling laughter he called to God . . . And then the rest of it—those hollow clatterings, thuddings of his heels and head against the floor.

"Go on up there, for God's sake get upstairs, both of you," Slim muttered. He turned away from me and I heard the click as he shoved back the safety catch of his gun.

I knew that I ought to stay there and help him, but I had Jane to guard. I pushed her ahead of me up the rest of the steps. Up here in the hall was darkness, too—pitch blackness thick with the breath of fear.

I listened and my heart stabbed me in the throat. There at my side, Jane was shivering, her teeth making terror-music like jittering castanets. Not a thing could I see, that aching darkness scalded my eyes with tears. That noise I had heard, where was it now . . .

I took a couple of steps and I stopped again. That noise was up here in the hall. Something that moved—

I reached for Jane's hand and we started along. A dozen feet more, and we came to the end of the corridor and a door.

It wasn't locked. I pushed Jane inside and followed her. Now I knew where I was—in the chief's office.

I snapped on my flashlight and twisted its white eye around the walls. There wasn't anyone here—nothing to catch the eye save a blur of color lying over there on one of the chairs.

Jane saw it, and gasped out a little cry as she flew toward it. I beat her there, I picked the thing up and held the light on it. I muttered and started to toss it down. It was a pair of women's underthings, soft silken unmentionables smelling faintly of perfume.

But I didn't drop it, for somehow that garment had a strangely familiar look. I turned it over and an oath jerked from my lips.

J.T.H.—Jane's own initials embroidered there on one brief little leg! Initials that I myself had had placed there when I had bought the thing for her on her last birthday!

She gasped out something and made a grab for them. I put them behind me. The light went out as my palsied thumb slipped from the button. Jane's most intimate underclothes in Dowling's office! And on her bosom that scarlet sign!

Chapter Four

When Death Laughed

Jane didn't move again, she didn't try to take them away from me. She whispered, "Rance—" and then was silent.

I lurched backward against the desk. I thumbed on my light again—I had to do something, think about getting away. My eyes lifted to a mirror against the wall. I saw my face there. My eyes were haggard, my lips twitched. And something else—down there on my bosom, where my shirt had been torn in climbing up the fire escape *the grinning skull and the crossed bones of death!*

I heard Jane exclaim and I wheeled around. Out in the hall someone was coming. Heavy, creaking tread that I knew— Dowling himself.

Back to that door through which we had come in I raced. There wasn't any key in the lock. I grabbed a chair and wedged its back under the knob. I wheeled and shot a fast look around the room.

Over on the other side were three doors. One after the other I jerked them open.

The first led into a bedroom, the second into a closet. The other one opened into a long vista of darkness, some kind of a passage, with the dim shine of a street lamp filtering in through a high window at its far end.

"Out here," I muttered. "A place to hide—"

I clutched Jane's hand and pulled her. There were noises,

Francis James

too. Slithering of feet, out there. Shadows thronging the place and creaking of floor boards. I strained my eyes into that hazy gloom. Where they were coming from, I couldn't tell. Maybe in front, maybe behind. Somewhere a voice chuckled. A door opened and shut with a muted squeak.

I pressed back against the wall and pulled Jane to me. Closer and closer came that shuffling sound. Those forms that came toward us, they had killed Peebles, they were coming for Jane . . .

And now I saw them, a trio of shapes blacker than the army of shadows. Close against the wall I pushed Jane and I stood in front of her. Closer and closer, they were coming with their hands outstretched, sweeping the walls. My eyes were glued to those hands. Did they hold something I couldn't see? Did their finger grip some fine instrument that would start that laughter screaming in Jane and me? For now that mark was on my bosom, too . . .

I slid a step farther in front of Jane. They heard me—and whirled.

The nearest one I caught with my butting head in the stomach. He let out a yell and reeled backward.

What happened after that was a nightmare. I was the core of a scramble of lashing and cursing forms. I pounded them with my fists, I butted and kneed them, I clawed at them.

I had put one of them away, and still there were two more. I was groggy and stumbling with the punishment I'd received, I couldn't duck as a fist lashed at me. I reeled backward, tripped, and crashed down in a corner.

Off somewhere behind me I heard Jane screaming, one tortured wail. Had they got her? Was that her death-cry?

In near-madness I battled, tried to drag my legs under me. The two figures were standing over me. Their hands went inside their coats and then flicked up to their faces.

A split-second dragged while I battled there to rise, and it was long as a century. Was it coming now? Would I hear my voice hiss out in those titterings, and then would that laughter of fiends rip at my vitals—

Then I croaked out a yell, for the door through which we

had come from the office burst open. A light shone over the threshold and an automatic crashed the tension with coughing barks.

Dowling—a gun in his hand. And something else that in the flash of a split-second told me how blind and wrong I had been.

For in the middle of his chest, between the tatters of his ribboned shirt, I saw the mark, the red symbol of the laughing death.

Dowling's gaze followed mine and he laughed curtly.

"Yes—they've got me, too." He looked at me and his jaw tightened. "You and me, both—"

He swept his hand across his face and cursed.

"They got in here, God knows how. They killed Peebles and Slim—"

For an instant we stood there without speaking. Suddenly I looked around.

"Jane !" I cried. "Jane, where are you—"

No one answered. Up and down the office and then over the whole house we hunted. We went back into the office and Dowling picked up the telephone. He gave one look at my putty-white face.

"God!" he muttered as his shaking finger clawed at the dial.

I don't remember going out of that house. I must have left Dowling without a word, for all at once I found myself on the sidewalk with the night breeze blowing against my face.

Up and down the pavement I raged and long rows of yellow lights danced in my brain. Houses and houses—miles upon miles of them, millions of people . . . Where should I hunt for her, how could I find her before that laughter came?

Suddenly an idea jumped at me. It been out of the back door of Dowling's house that I had run, I remembered, a door that I'd found unlocked.

Back down that alley I raced and in through the door and up that flight of back stairs. Down that long passage that led to the places where the fight had been.

Dowling wasn't in sight; I could hear his voice beyond in

the office; he was phoning headquarters. Figures lay crumpled against the wall—two that Dowling had shot, and the one that I'd knocked out with the smash to the stomach. He was coming back, just starting to sit up and peer around.

I stepped up to him, slugged him another one on the chin, and as he slumped over backward I grabbed one of his wrists, heaved him up and slung him over my shoulder. Dowling was still talking on the line when I carried him down stairs and out of the house.

In the taxi that I'd flagged out in the side street, I jammed a shot out of my pocket flask down the man's throat and massaged the back of his neck till he opened his eyes and stared at me.

I took out my pocket knife, opened it and let him see the blade. I gripped him with one hand around the throat and jammed his head back against the cushions. I held him there and jabbed the knifepoint into one of his cheekbones. He yelled and clapped a hand to the eye.

I smashed the hand away and belted him twice in the eye that was beginning to trickle blood.

I shoved my face up to him, and what he saw wasn't pretty.

"Ever see one of those blind men with a little tin cup?" I snarled. "That's what you're going to be. I'm bigger than you and I'm going to hold you there and carve your two eyes out of your head—unless—"

He cursed me and groveled against the seat of the car.

"What do you want? Give it a name," he whined. "I'll play ball—"

"We're going places," I bit back at him. "You're taking me wherever it is that your gang works out of—where your boss has his headquarters."

I jabbed the knife point at him again.

"And don't get the wrong number," I gritted. "Unless you want to peddle in hell with a tin cup—"

He cringed away from me, cursing.

"Don't!" he begged. "I'll take you there."

I told the taxi man to go where he ordered. It was a longish way, fifteen or twenty minutes, before the rat muttered for him to stop.

Down town and east we had traveled, into a district of warehouses and manufacturing lofts. A great bridge sprawled across the sky. A long, naked street with cold yellow lamps winking down at the shiny eyes of the windows.

My guide swung into an alley and I followed him with the snout of my gun—Dowling's gun, that I'd picked up from the floor of the little room where he'd left it—jammed into his back.

Where he took me I hadn't a notion. Up and down pitch black and stinking passages I trailed him till my brain was bemused.

And then suddenly he came to a stop. I saw a wooden door in the brick wall ahead. He reached in his pocket and a key rattled.

The door clicked behind us. It wasn't quite pitch dark in here, wherever it was; a haze of powdery light sifted down from a high window up in the roof. I had the feel of a big room, long, wide and lofty. Big and vague shapes, outlines of machines, were ranged down the floor. Smaller outlines that looked like baskets. And over all, a smell—a clean, slightly pungent odor of things being washed.

And then suddenly I realized. We were inside a laundry—one of the several big establishments ranged along the river front near this point. A laundry, the killer's headquarters!

I jabbed my gun into the fellow's ribs.

"Get going," I muttered. "Show me where they have taken my girl."

We started forward. I gripped his arm in a vise. For even with the gun in his back, I trusted him the same way I'd trust a coiled cobra.

We slid along through that blackness a dozen yards. And then I heard something, more of those shufflings, whispers of motion behind me.

Without moving my gun. I looked around. Some one was there, all right, trailing us, but I couldn't see him. One of the big mangles loomed beside me and I pulled my man over into its shadow. And now I could get it. Dim forms were gliding among the machines.

They flocked closer. They had heard us, were hunting us down. Men of the laughing death . . . Back up against the hard flank of the mangle I squeezed myself. Thronging shadows of death . . . And on my breast that mark burned.

Those footfalls drew nearer. I could feel my man tense, get ready to jump. He knew I couldn't use my gun in two places at once.

And then suddenly that light ray from the window fell on a face. The white and black-grooved face of Jim Fessenden!

Fessenden heard my muttered oath. He slid up to me and whispered: "Rance—"

Rage choked me, for suddenly I understood.

"Where's Jane—what have you done with her?" I snarled.

Fessenden stared at me. He cursed softly,

"Rance—you've got me wrong. This isn't my place. I came here to find out who—"

"You phoned Jane this afternoon," I accused. "You were right there in the office where she was and you went out to the booth in the hall to talk to her, so no one would know. She wouldn't tell me where she had gone—"

"She had called me before, she wanted to ask me a question—she had a lead," Fessenden said. "I went out to the booth to talk with her because she didn't want anyone else to get wise."

"She didn't tell me that she had a clue," I retorted.

"She didn't want you to know because she was afraid they would get you, too, you fool. She was trying to keep you out of it. She knew her number was up, but yours—"

I stared at him. Was he lying, or—God, if Jane had been bucking this horror alone!

"How did you find this place? How did you know where to come?" I muttered.

"I didn't know. I came here on spec. We were trying different ones, Jane and I. Dowling was working on it, too."

"I don't believe you," I muttered at last. "If you know so much, take me where she is."

Fessenden didn't say anything. He stood there staring into my face, and all at once he began to laugh. He stood there within a foot of me and those spasms gripped him. He crushed his hands to his face and the laughter screamed through them. He staggered back from me, flopped down to the floor. And then, in the darkness, those clatterings of his head and heels.

Back into the shadows I dodged. I sagged against the flank of that mangle and I was sick at my stomach . . . That other man that I'd made bring me here was gone—where or when I didn't know. And my gun was gone, too—he had plucked it out of my unresisting hand as I watched Fessenden's ravings, and I hadn't known.

Backward I slid from the contraption that had sheltered me. I dropped to my knees and started to creep. Maybe down here on the floor they wouldn't see me.

But I wasn't fooling them. They we closing in. Against the haze of light could see them gathering, ghostly vague shadows.

My fingers clawed at the oaken planks beneath me. They were going to kill me—why didn't they do it? Why were they torturing me with suspense? I felt my insides turn over, for an instant I thought that the laughter was coming. But it wasn't the laughing, it was only my vitals retching again with terror.

I squatted there on my hands and knees and I glared at them. God, why didn't they do it; I was waiting to die . . . And then suddenly I heard something, a thin and tortured wailing—Jane!

At the sound of that agonized moan, my brain blew its fuse. I cursed and started to lunge to my feet.

Back in the darkness, I heard running feet and a voice that shouted commands. Something hard crashed on my skull an everything went spinning away in purple stars.

I opened my eyes and looked around. I was sitting in a chair and my arms were lashed behind me, around its back. Two other persons were there. One was Jane. She sprawled on the floor in a corner. Her clothes were torn half off, face was swollen streaked with blood.

"Jane!" I yelled. "What have they done to you—"

She looked up then, her lips stirred, she whispered my name.

The other figure in there was a man; he stood back to me and he was packing things into a suitcase. Bundles and bundles of greenbacks. At the sound of my voice he swung around and I saw his face.

Dowling! Buck Dowling, my boss!

He saw the blank stare of amazement on my countenance and he laughed mockingly.

"Yes—me," he jeered. "You saw me every day and you never suspected—the hell of a dick you are!"

He finished stowing his loot and turned around again:

"My boys down there were going to slip you the laugh powder just now, but I stopped them. You wanted to get up here so bad that I decided to let you. Curiosity as hot as yours ought to be gratified."

He dropped down on the edge of a desk—the room was a small office—and lit a cigarette.

"How did I do it? Not so hard as it looked. The first thing was putting those marks on the suckers. Jane figured that out almost two days ago. Only she couldn't find out who was doing it.

"I bought up a lot of laundries—and those that I didn't buy outright I got some of my men into. We had some dies made with the pattern of the marks on them. We wet those dies in a certain chemical and stamped the design on underclothes just before ironing. The stuff dried out colorless. But when it came next to the skin when the clothes were worn, it branded that pattern right into the hide.

"That gew-gaw of Jane's that you found in my house, by the way—she brought it to show me what she thought she had discovered, and left it by accident. Later on, she told Fessenden, too, and we were all supposed to be working together.

"Of course the idea of the first marks, the skull and crossed bones, was to shoot the town full of panic, so that when we really started business, the millionaires would kick through without squealing. It didn't matter on whose clothes we stuck them. But when we came to the real showdown, we had to be careful to get the right marks on the right undies. And, of course, I had under-cover dope enough on a hundred of the best families to damn them black—I'd been filing it away for years.

"Then the laughing death—the profs had one thing right about that, too—it was caused by minute amounts of a drug introduced into the blood stream. What they couldn't imagine was how it was done. They never thought of this—"

Dowling reached around and picked up something from the desk. It was a cigarette holder, with what looked like a lighted fag stuck into it. But now I realized that the cigarette was a blind—it was made of some hard, white composition, and the light on the end of it was a spot of some kind of dye.

"This is a blow-gun," Dowling said. "There is a fine passage down the whole length of it. You load this dart into it—" Gingerly he lifted a needle—slim, glittering little thing about half an inch long from a cotton-lined case and slid it into the mouth of the affair—"and then you put the holder into your mouth. It will shoot twenty feet and shoot straight. The dart is made of a compound that melts the instant it strikes. There's no evidence left for the dicks to see—and who is going to dope it out that a gentleman strolling along with a cigarette holder in his mouth is a heat-number?"

He laid the thing down on the desk and swung back to me.

"I'm leaving this here where you can see it because in five minutes I'm going to let it go at you," he snarled. "And then I'm taking it on the lam—I mean *we* are getting out of town. I've got a yacht tied up to the wharf outside that will take me to South America or China. In that grip I've got a couple of millions that some of the wise ones forked over, and I'm pulling my bets before too many people start wondering."

He leered. He hauled his big form off the desk and turned

to Jane.

"I've wanted her for a long time—that's another thing that proves you're a fool, or you would have seen. I put the mark on her first to scare her into obeying that letter. It told her to go to a certain corner where no one one would be watching, and go alone. If she had done that you would be lining up for your ham and eggs tomorrow as usual. But she didn't. Then I thought for a while that I would have to put her away, she was finding out things. But when you brought her to my place, it was just ducky—I gave her to one of the lads to bring down here while I was phoning the cops. Peebles and Slim I had killed because they were beginning to notice, too . . ."

He laughed again and started toward Jane.

While he had gloated out his story of explanation, I hadn't spoken or moved, I'd listened in a daze of half stupefied horror. But when he turned toward Jane, I cursed him.

"Keep away from her!" I raged. "Don't put your hand on her—"

Dowling shot an arm down and pulled her up to her feet. He tried to clasp her in his arms. She beat at him with her tiny fists, she raked her fingernails over his face.

Blood spurted and he snarled an oath. He drew back and hit her.

She screamed and went sliding along the wall. He raced after her, jerked her up onto her feet, and hit her again.

She was down in the corner. She wailed thinly, and moaned my name.

"I'm coming, darling—I'm coming!" I screamed back shrilly. I cursed that monster with the fury of a forest ape. I fought with those ropes, I strained and wrench at them till I felt them like hot irons searing my flesh, but they were too strong—they wouldn't give.

Jane's resistance had made Dowling furious. He jumped at her. Wildly he cursed and he grabbed her by the throat. He pulled her up with her feet off the floor and he held her there dangling in air, a slender white pendulum that writhed and screamed with new torture.

He flung her down and she lay feebly stirring. He snatched up the whip that he'd been using before I came and lashed her again.

I raged at him hoarsely, I flung myself on the ropes and I felt the moist trickling of my own blood where they had cut into my wrists. Dowling jerked his head around at me.

"She wouldn't be nice to me, she was too good for me," he shrilled. "Well, we'll see. Now we're going to see—"

He stooped and caught her up in his arms. He started to carry her across the room. Over there was a big chair—

I was near to stark madness then. I shouted noises that weren't human words. For I knew what he was going to do.

He heard my wild ragings and he laughed back at me without turning his head.

"Take it easy, Rance—your time will come. Remember that little thing on the desk—or, on second thought, perhaps I'd better not wait. Maybe I'd better do it now and get rid of that noise of yours—"

He put Jane down and went back to the desk. He picked up the loaded cigarette holder and lifted it to his lips.

"One little puff now, and you're going to laugh, Rance— you're going to laugh yourself a round trip to hell!"

I sat there and stared at him, and my eyes were glazed. Numbness flowed over me; already those first grippings of laughter seemed to be wrenching my belly. Over beyond, Jane stirred feebly, she lifted her eyes and whispered my name.

I didn't realize what I was doing, in my frenzy I didn't more than half sense that I had got the balls of my feet down onto the floor, that I'd lifted myself, chair and all, a couple of inches.

For an instant I balanced there on my toes and then I lunged forward, carrying the chair with me. I felt myself catapulting through the air and then I hit him.

The force of the blow tripped him. He stumbled, waved his arms and went over backward. With that heavy chair still tied to my back, I sprawled on top of him.

I couldn't use my hands—I was helpless as a man paralyzed. Only my head.

That cigarette holder was still in his mouth. With the whole force of my neck I brought my forehead crashing down on it. Break it—crumple the thing so that he couldn't shoot, was the one desperate thought in my brain.

I felt the thin stalk splinter under the impact and I heard Dowling's gasp as the force of the butt drove the stem into his gullet.

I lifted my head to look at him and I felt my heart boil into my throat. *For Dowling was laughing!* First those maudlin titterings and then great belly gulpings that shook him from head to foot. He jerked himself out from under me, staggered up to his feet. Around the room he raced like a man driven by fiends. He crushed his hands to his face and those screams ripped through his locked fingers. At last he was down on the floor with his arms and legs tangling and knotting . . .

Never mind the rest of that picture. When the blow gun had shattered, the poison dart that was in it had been driven into his tongue . . .

I turned my eyes away, over toward Jane. She was getting her strength back now; she stumbled up to her feet and tottered toward me. From somewhere she got a knife at last and started cutting my ropes.

No one tried to stop us when we finally got some of her clothes onto Jane and started out of the place. At the door we met a squad of police; Fessenden had left word at his office where he was going. If they'd only come sooner . . .

The rewards that had been put up for the killer totaled two hundred thousand. Jane and I split it with Fessenden's widow. We got married and we went away—ten thousand miles away—to forget . . .

MONSTER'S DEATH SONG

Marian had heard the noise twice, before little old Mrs. Sherburne dropped her knitting and looked up. The noise that brought back the dark, dread legends of doom whose menace she had been trying for weeks to sweep out of her mind. The log fire crackling on the open hearth made the cozy little living room oppressively warm. Yet at the sound, a flush of cold had tingled over her. She shivered, as though icy fingertips had raked across her flesh.

"What was that noise?" Mrs. Sherburne burst out in her cracked, rasping voice. "It sounded to me like a chain rattling. There it is again!"

Nobody spoke for a moment. The seven guests in Marian and Ralph Holden's little summer hotel sat motionless, holding their breaths as they listened. It was an hour past sunset of a chilly October evening. After dinner, they had flocked together in front of the open fire while they chatted and loafed.

Now the noise sounded again—the gritting metallic clank of a chain being dragged over a floor. Where it came from, no one could tell—maybe upstairs, maybe outside the house on the long piazza.

"You don't mean to tell us you don't know what that is?" another of the guests laughed. She was Miss Wilcox, a middle-aged schoolteacher down for the weekend. She shivered deliciously. "That was the ghost. The house is haunted by the ghost of the man who was hung out there in the front yard."

Miss Wilcox looked around at Marian.

"That's so, isn't it, Mrs. Holden?" she inquired archly. "There was a man hung out there—a pirate or something?"

Marian started. She had been standing straining her ears,

listening. The guests weren't frightened yet; they were amused, puzzled, half uncertain what to think. But if they had known what she knew—if they had lived there, listening day after day for the sound of that chain, hoping, praying that it would never come—if they knew the dark warning of fate that called out to her in its clanking . . .

"Yes, a man was put to death out there, a hundred and sixty years ago," she answered absently. "He was a pirate of sorts; he stole my husband's great great-grand father's wife away from him."

"They sure had the right idea about love-pirates back in those days, didn't they?" Holloway, the speaker, was an artist who had come down for the autumn foliage. "Strung 'em up in the front dooryard . . ."

He got up and went over to a window, lifted the shade and looked out.

Some hundred yards away, a gaunt black outline—a tall upright beam with a smaller one running out from it at right angles—stood on the summit of a little knoll at one side of the yard. Down from the crosspiece hung the gaudy scarlet and gold sign of the hotel—Ye Gallows Hill House.

"That's the very same gallows, isn't it—the one you've got your sign hanging from—" he commenced, then stopped short.

Instead, he swung around. Through the dull undertone of voices and cracklings logs, sounds were coming from the outside of the house—feet ascending the front steps. Now the feet were crossing the piazza toward the door. Heavy, slow, dragging step, scuffing over the boards . . .

The footsteps ceased. The jangling peal of the doorbell shrilled out in the sudden silence.

Holloway looked at Marian. She crossed the living room and went out in the little front hall. The bell shrilled again as she reached for the knob and swung open the door.

In the light shining over her shoulder from the living room she could see the figure that stood there looking down at her.

Huge, towering form, with massive arms and legs, shoulders broad as a giant's, clad in worn, shining garments of sepulchral black . . . the head globe round and monstrous, the face yellow as old parchment . . . great, slack-lipped mouth around broken, jutting fangs of teeth . . . gloating jet-black eyes above red, rheumy lids . . . oily black snake-eyes pinned on hers . . . Long, grey-white hands that shimmered with a ghoulish glow as they jutted out of the ragged sleeves . . . And reeking out from the giant an odor that swept sudden nausea through her—the rank, stale fetor of a tomb—the smell of unclean death . . .

For an instant that seemed a century, the thing stood there, grinning down at her. It took a step forward. Its ghostly grey hand came reaching out for the doorknob.

"This is a public hotel—I want a room," a voice mumbled out of its shaggy, loose-skinned throat. "I am your newest guest!"

With a stifled cry, Marian slammed the door shut, knocking back the foot which had already crept in across the threshold. She shot the safety bolt and stood leaning against the door, panting.

Frantically, Marian was fighting to pull herself together as she crouched, suddenly faint, against the door. The others in there—the guests—mustn't know, mustn't even suspect. One glimpse of that horrible face and they would all go, and she and Ralph would be ruined . . .

She dragged her legs into motion and turned back to the living room. In the doorway, she forced a smile.

"A man—he wanted a room. I told him we were full up," she said.

Old Mrs. Sherburne was looking hard at her. She had noticed the whiteness of Marian's cheeks, the huskiness of her voice, which she had tried to make casual—and couldn't . . .

Marian turned her back on them. She went over to a table and started to arrange some magazines. Her hands were trembling as she fussed with the papers. Her fingers were cold—as cold as death. This thing that had come to her door, demanding to be taken in—this mad, incredible shape of clanking death—what it was, she had no idea. Bewildered amazement still gripped her, made her brain whirl. If she hadn't seen it with own eyes, she would have said it was impossible—it couldn't exist . . .

But what it meant, what it promised them, she knew—the fate that they, that she and Ralph, had been waiting for, dreading and praying that it might not come, as they waited . . . The doom that had killed four of Ralph's ancestors there in that very house . . . Doom of Holdens that they, in the foolhardy confidence of youth, had shut their eyes to and shoved aside in their last desperate try for success and happiness; shoved away and tried to forget, while in their secret hearts they had trembled under shadow of that ghastly fate . . .

She caught her breath and spun around. So close that it seemed to come from right there in the room, the loud, gritting clank of a chain rang out again.

"That's Holden's ghost, all right," Holloway laughed. "He's hired him to walk out there and clank for us, to give local color—sort of prove that his gallows isn't a fake, so to speak."

"Well, I wish you would find your husband and tell him to send it way," Mrs. Sherburne said tartly. "I've had enough of his music."

Marian forced a laugh. "You're scaring Mr. Holloway, Mrs. Sherburne. That must be Ralph himself. He probably got back from town sooner than he expected. He's doing some work around somewhere."

Mrs. Sherburne sniffed, while Marian crossed the room and slipped around behind the little office desk in the corner. She couldn't look at them; she couldn't face the battery of those curious, probing eyes. She couldn't let them see how her hands were trembling, how her knees were shaking under her thin evening frock . . .

She busied herself with papers and bills, sorted them and put them away without seeing them, without knowing what she was doing. Blind-eyed, she was listening—straining her ears for the chattering roar of Ralph's ancient flivver climbing the grade back from town. She had known it couldn't be

Ralph, when she had told them that it was. He had a lot of errands to do down in the village, and he couldn't have gotten back.

. . .But if he would only come now! If he would only come and stand there beside her, and tell her what to do!

She turned a swift look around at the guests. Still they hadn't started to be really frightened. They didn't know— they didn't guess what voice of doom had called to her in that clanking chain . . .

Doom that she had known of, shuddered at before, without ever clearly understanding . . . Ever since the day of its building back in old Colonial times, the house had been in Ralph's family, an heirloom of tragedy, shunned and cursed by the generations who had tried in vain to dwell in its death-cursed rooms.

By inheritance, the empty, abandoned old place had come at last into Ralph's name, the sole tangible asset remaining to him at the end of four disastrous years of depression and idleness and failure. It was the old house or nothing. Steeling their hearts against the curse, they had borrowed a little money—enough to remodel a small part of the huge, rambling structure. A dozen rooms that had been fixed up into a small summer hotel. Standing on the crest of a rocky bluff at the very edge of the sea, the place had a magnificent view, splendid bathing beach, isolation and solitude for those who wished their vacationing removed from the busy turmoil of life. Open only a few days, they were already filled to capacity. Everything was going well. In their happiness, they had almost forgotten the curse. And now . . .

Suddenly tense, Marian straightened, letting the sheaf of papers riffle down on to the desk out of her limp fingers. That sound out there, outside the house . . . It wasn't Ralph coming back; it wasn't the clanking of chains, either. It might be the crooning of the wind around the eaves of the old house; it might be the swishing whisper of the leaves of the old elm tree against the roof . . .

She stole over to the corner of the desk and peeked out into the room. The guests—were they hearing it, too; were they beginning to wonder. . .?

But they hadn't heard anything yet. They were sitting around peacefully, knitting and chatting . . .

Crunch—click! The snapping of sticks—and slow, dragging sounds, like the tread of heavy feet . . .

Marian clenched her hands. The people out there had heard it. They were sitting up, their books and knitting in their laps, listening.

She slipped back behind the desk again, where they couldn't see her as she wiped the cold sweat from her face. If they called to her, asked her what it was, what should she say? Suppose it wasn't the wind and the big tree; suppose it was something alive, something insane and horrible. . .?

Scrape—scrape . . . From outside the house, right on the other side of the wall at her elbow, the coarse, heavy rustling sounded, like a big body moving there, rubbing its shoulders against the boarding.

Wildly Marian looked around. She felt as though she must scream, must run away somewhere and hide. But she mustn't scream. She must keep cool. In a minute the guests would call out and ask her what that noise was. Her voice mustn't tremble when she told them was only the tree scraping against house . . . If Ralph were only there! Why didn't he come. . .?

She took a long breath. Her tense body relaxed. Now the sound had stopped. Nothing but the soft, muffled rustling of the surf down on the beach . . .

Marian stole across and looked out of the window at the end of the office. Nothing out there to see, save the white moonlight shining aslant the old gallows—on which she and Ralph had found a length of iron chain swaying and clanking in the wind, the day they had first come, crusted and overlain with a horrible brown stain that was not rust . . .

In vain she had begged Ralph to tear the thing down; Grimly, stubbornly defiant of the curse, he had kept it there—and on it he had hung the gaily painted sign of the hotel . . .

She could see the sign now, swinging back and forth in the wind. Swinging from the gallows tree in whose horrible embrace Ralph's ancestors, generation by generation, had been found strangled. And, so ran the stories, the sign of the return of the curse that had put them there was the echo of a clanking chain . . .

Marian caught her breath. Now she was hearing something else—the wheezing roar of a car ploughing through the loose sand on the road over the dunes. Out of sight from where she stood, it came rattling into the back yard and stopped. A door opened and shut, out in the kitchen. Steps pounded down the long passage.

The next instant, Ralph came around the corner into the office. He stopped, stood staring an instant, and then hurried up to her.

She flung herself into his arms. Half laughing, half crying, she buried her face on his shoulder.

"Oh, Ralph darling, I'm so glad you're back—I'm so glad," she sobbed.

"Not half as glad as I am, at that." Ralph kissed her and patted her shoulder. "Great Scott, what's the matter? You're trembling like a leaf!"

She put her lips to his ear. "Ralph—come out in the kitchen a minute. I want to tell you—" she started to say.

They both turned. Miss Wilcox, the schoolteacher, had called to them from the living room.

"Now that everything has quieted down, couldn't we have some of those wonderful apples that you treated us to yesterday, Mrs. Holden?"

"Sure thing. I'll go right down and get some," Ralph said.

Marian gripped his arm. "No—let me go," she whispered. "I'll tell you afterwards."

She stepped around Ralph and turned down the passage that led back to the kitchen. She lighted a candle—they had not been able to afford having electric lights put in the cellar as yet—and took a small basket from a hook. She was glad of a chance to get the apples, grateful for a few minutes alone in which to pull herself together before anyone saw her.

She crossed the kitchen and opened the cellar door.

On the top step Marian halted. For an instant she stood peering down. When she had said she would come, she had not realized how thick and cold the blackness would be down there—so darkly heavy that it seemed to penetrate her clothing and permeate her very body with an eerie unmoving motion . . .

Biting her lips, she started down. Creak-creak . . . The old dried boards squealed and snapped like rifle shots under her weight. The dank reek of mouldy earth stung in her nostrils.

At last she was down on the dirt floor at the foot of the stairs. The wooden bin with the apples was right ahead, ten feet away across the floor. She could smell the pungent tang of the ripe fruit over the reek of mouldy earth.

Holding the candle high in one hand, Marian stood looking around. Now the flickerings of the candlelight against the wall held her eyes fascinated. Movements of shadow and light like huge, malformed faces—yellow, globe-round countenances like that of the thing which had looked into the window; faces of gargoyle monsters grimacing and gibbering and mocking at her—swayed and danced, eddied toward her and billowed away again . . .

She leaned forward to set the basket down while she filled it. She picked up half a dozen apples and stopped. Something cold was stealing over her—sly, gelid fingers stroking her flesh . . .

She held her breath. Was it real sound she was hearing, or was it only her fancy? Was it her ears rebelling from the bottomless hush, chiming fantastic brain-images of things that were not; or was something actually moving behind her, scraping and whispering in the maze of crisscrossing alleys?

She flicked a drop of sweat from her forehead and leaned over the apples again. Now she was hurrying—snatching and grabbing at the round red slippery fruit—racing to fill up the basket and go, before she heard that sound again. And all the while she was calling herself a little fool to let panic get her so. There wasn't anything down there; the thing she had seen was outside the house. It couldn't get in through locked doors . . .

Something behind Marian was pulling—dragging her head around, trying to make her eyes twist back over her shoulder. She gritted her teeth and kept her eyes on the apples. She knew there wasn't anything there, yet she couldn't look—not for her life could she look around . . .

Her hand poised half way to the basket, she froze. What was that new sound—that faint, muted clicking of something solid and fleshy that rubbed over the floor?

Swish—swish . . . Or was it the husking wheeze of her own breathing? Swish—swish—grit—grit . . .

Inch by inch, Marian turned. She screamed, but the shriek never broke into sound through the strangled muscles of her terror-locked jaws.

One of the yellow gargoyle faces had stopped wavering and swaying. It had materialized into something solid and fleshy. Huge, globe-round face, yellow as old parchment; great, slack-lipped mouth around broken, jutting fangs of teeth—oily black eyes leering into hers . . .

Now the thing was stealing out of the shadows. She could see the great sloping shoulders and gorilla-long arms, which were slowly rising over its head as it started to glide toward her . . .

Marian couldn't scream again—only husky strangled sobs through her numb jerking lips. Back behind, the thing croaked a snarl. She heard its feet start to rush over the dirt bottom.

Now she was running—racing and plunging across the half dozen feet and up the stairs. The thing was catching up with her. She could feel the stairs sag under its weight as it started up . . .

She wheezed out a cry—a breathless, sobbing moan through a throat so numb and horror-tight that it could scream more. Something had touched her—a cold hand that had come darting up and closed around her leg. Through the thin silk of her stockings she could feel the dank, slimy slithering of the hand as it gripped her leg and then slid down the ankle.

Her feet jerked from under her, Marian went down on hands and knees, Savagely she kicked back. The hand slipped off her ankle. The basket upset as she fell and the apples went thudding and tumbling back down the stairs . . .

She did not take time to get up to her feet. On hands and knees she was racing, scrambling up the steps—clawing her way like a wild thing over the rough, splintery boards . . . Now the door was in front of her. Up on the landing she gathered her feet under her. Through the half open door she staggered into the kitchen. Whirling, she slammed the door shut. She twisted the key in the lock. Across the room she stumbled and stood leaning against the wall.

On the other side of the door, the floor-treads were creaking. Now the thing had got clear of the rolling apples that had tripped him, and come to the top. It was standing there, right on the other side of the flimsy, half rotted old door, listening to find out if she were still there, before it crashed the panels down and came through . . .

Chapter Two

The Clanking Dead

Marian stumbled over to a chair and sat down. Her brain was spinning. Only a couple of minutes before she had gone down in the cellar, she had heard the thing outside. How had it gotten into the house?

She knew—it must have stolen in behind Ralph, through the back door which he had left unlocked . . .

Back there beyond the cellar door, it was quiet now. Little by little, Marian's wild pantings died away. Her ears focused on the sound of Ralph's voice coming out of the living room. He was telling the guests the story of the house and the hanging out on the gallows—how the first owner, his great-great-grandfather, had been a smuggler and the owner of a priva-

teer in the Revolutionary War; how his next neighbor, half a
mile away, was a royalist, loyal to England. This neighbor
had owned a schooner, which he used to carry supplies to the
British in Boston. One dark night when the vessel happened
to be lying becalmed in a fog a few miles off shore, old Holden had crept alongside with his privateer and captured her.
She was carrying a lot of valuables consigned to the British,
among other things about twenty thousand dollars in gold,
which the old patriot confiscated and divided among his
crew. His neighbor, the owner of the schooner—Jenkins by
name—had escaped.

"And what became of your great-great-grandfather's share
of the money, Mr. Holden?" the voice of one of the women
guests broke in.

"That is what a lot of people would have liked to find out,"
Ralph said. "There were no banks that people trusted much
in those days, and the stories are that my ancestor hid his
treasure somewhere around this house. But if he did, he
made a good job of it. The place has been gone over with a
fine comb about ten thousand times and no one has ever
found a trace of it."

"Well, is that the end of the story, Mr. Holden?" a voice
asked. "You say this royalist was a neighbor of your ancestor's. I should think that would have stirred up some local
unpleasantness, to say the least."

"It stirred up plenty of it," Ralph answered dryly. "This fellow Jenkins, a fascinating sort of devil, according to the
tales, had a great way with the ladies. He got even with my
great-great-grandfather by stealing his wife away from him.
Old Holden squared things up by chasing the man down,
catching him, having him tried and sentenced to death by the
local authorities—and then by securing their permission to
hang him in his front dooryard. That gallows out there is the
very one on which the Tory, who ruined my ancestor's
home, was strangled in chains."

"And the rest of the yarn is that the ghost of the old Romeo
still haunts the place, I suppose?" the artist, Holloway, said
as Ralph finished the story.

Marian did not hear Ralph's reply. He had told as much of
the story as he wanted the guests to know, she realized. But
he had not told the grim, dreadful sequel to the romantic tale
of a century and a half ago. How a few months after his
great-great-grandfather had caused his enemy to be hung in
his front yard, his own body had been found dangling in the
selfsame chains; how, according to the stories, not only he
but his son and his son's son had died there, too, and how
Ralph himself, coming home one night five years ago had
found his own father lying strangled on the doorstep of the
house . . .

Marian stumbled up to her feet. The curse of the Holdens—
the doom of five generations that she and Ralph had dreamed
they had put behind them—had come back. The sound of the
chain had been no silly ghost frolic; it had been the grim
warning that the fate which had taken four of his family was
reaching out for one more. The thing that had come to the
door, which had chased her up the cellar stairs . . . The mad,
impossible incarnation of that doom—the vengeful spirit of
old Jenkins come back to life . . .
    She crushed her hands against her heart. Wild, incredible
the legend sounded—yes. But there had been nothing
ephemeral, nothing ghostly about the lewd, clammy touch of
the hand that had slithered down her leg. She could still feel
her flesh chilled and numb, as though at the gelid gripping of
a snake's folds. The hand had been solid, fleshy—the hand
of a corpse!
    Marian stumbled across to a table. She pulled open a
drawer and fumbled for a compact that she had left in
there . . . The hotel—all hers and Ralph's hopes were bound
up in its success. The guests mustn't know . . . She must
smile when she went back there into the living room—not let
them see the tear-streaks, the ghastly whiteness of her face.
She mustn't even let them guess at the truth that would send
them away, in sudden panic-stricken flight.
    In front of a wall mirror she fumbled color on her pasty
cheeks and lips, dabbed powder over the tear channels. It

was a crude job that she did, her hands were trembling so—trembling and shaking so that the powder scattered down over her dress . . . While she worked, she was thinking: She must find help; someone to come and help her catch the thing, before it was too late . . .

But who? Out here on the lonely, sparsely settled foreshore of the New England coast, there was no one she knew— nobody save one . . .

Marian's heart gave a throb; and a flush of color stung her lips. Nobody save Kane Hammond . . .

She paused, her pulses racing. Kane Hammond—dare she phone to him? He, another late summer vacationist and their nearest neighbor, lived alone in a little cottage which he had rented, some half mile away, on the edge of the dunes. Kane Hammond—the older, wickedly attractive sophisticated man—whose dangerous liking for her she had felt the instant his eyes had rested on her, weeks ago . . . For a time, the three of them, he, she and Ralph, had been good friends. Then Ralph, developing a dislike of the man, had told her not to ask him there any more. But now, in an emergency of life and death . . . Hammond was experienced and cool. He could tell her what to do.

Marian lifted the telephone receiver off the hook and whispered Kane Hammond's number. Back behind, beyond the cellar door, something creaked—the scrape of a big body shouldering against the wall!

Silence now, while she waited for her connection. In the dead hush of the kitchen, the splat-splat of water from the sink faucet plunked in her ears, loud as hammer strokes . . .

Frantically she jiggled the hook. "Oh, hurry—please hurry!" she cried. What if Hammond wasn't there—if she couldn't get help. . .?

She caught her breath in relief. It was Hammond's calm, cheerful baritone, sounding so close that he might have been at her side.

"This is Marian Holden," she burst out into the mouthpiece. "Please come over here as quick as you—"

She cried out, spun around, and dropped the receiver. A

step had sounded behind her. Ralph stood in the doorway at the end of the passage that led back from the living room.

For an instant, Ralph stood there staring at her. His brow darkened. His glance shifted from her white face to the receiver dangling at the end of the cord, and from that to the basket, with the three lone apples that had stayed in it when the rest spilled out, lying tipped over on top of the table.

"What's the idea of getting only three apples?" he said at last. "Whom have you been phoning?"

Marian swayed toward him. She reached out her hands.

"Ralph, I—"

He strode over and picked up the basket.

"Never mind. I'll get the apples," he said. He took a step toward the cellar door.

Marian rushed past him. She flattened her back against the door and stood there with her arms outstretched, barring his way.

"No! No! You mustn't go down there!" She was panting, breathless as she stared up into his face.

Puzzled, Ralph frowned at her. He could see how frightened she was. But was still angry. He had heard her talking to Hammond and it burned him up.

He reached around behind her and tried the door. He shook it, then felt for key. It was not in the lock.

"Give me that key!" he exclaimed.

Marian clung to him. He could feel her body trembling against his. Sobbing, she was trying to push him away from the door.

"Darling, you mustn't go down there!" she cried. "There's something . . . It chased me—!"

Holding her in his arms now, Ralph pushed her back so that he could look in her face.

"Why, Marian—" he started to say.

His voice broke off. From somewhere upstairs, the sound of a scream had come ringing through the house. Just one heart-breaking shriek of agony and terror in a man's voice. It died away, with a hoarse guttural croaking. And then the pounding of feet—hammering of great dragging feet, and the clanking of iron chain echoing down from up above.

Ralph whirled toward the door. He took a step and froze. Suddenly, every light in the house had gone out.

Feeling his way through the dark, Ralph was running back, down the passage toward the front of the house, dragging Marian behind him. He pushed through the swinging doors, came out from behind the office desk into the living room, and stopped.

The fire in the grate had died down to a few glowing coals—not enough to spread any light through the room. In here, no one was making a sound—the vague, frozen shadows in the gloom. Marian could make them out—the figures of the guests standing rigid, holding their breaths as they listened and waited.

The guests—and something else, too, was there in the room. There was noise there—noise that the motionless men and women didn't make. Confused, vague rustling that came from nowhere and everywhere . . . Shuffling of sly footsteps . . . The puffing sigh of heavy breathing . . . The sound of laughter—soft, sardonic, chuckling, so faint and muffled that it might have been only a dream created by her screaming nerves.

Marian felt for Ralph's hand, clutched it in hers. Her hand was cold—clammy cold like the hand of a corpse, yet sweat slimed her fingers as she wound them around his, making them slip and slither in his grip. Now she saw something that wasn't her fancy. Just for an instant, in the red glow reflected from the dying coals in the fireplace, a great, black, hunchbacked form—the arms huge as an ape's, the head globe-round and hairless—had appeared.

It was gone. It had passed out of the fire glow, and she couldn't see it. But she could hear it. Everyone in the room could hear its sly footfalls whispering over the rug—its soft, guttural chuckling.

Nobody was moving or speaking. Marian knew why they were all keeping so still, why they were standing there like statues in the aching dark. . . because they were too frozen, too congealed with terror to move; because they were trying to hide from the thing—bury themselves in the silence and blackness, out of the sight of death . . .

Marian gripped Ralph's arm. Outside the house, footsteps were pounding up the walk, then racing across the piazza. The front door burst open. Somebody came hammering into the hall.

The steps froze into silence. The next instant a match crackled. In the dazzling glow of the tiny yellow flame, Marian could see the face and figure of a man in a dark suit outlined in the doorway.

For a moment, the newcomer didn't speak. He appeared to be well acquainted with the arrangement of things in the Holden's living room. Guiding himself by the light of the match, he sidled along the wall till he came to a candle in a brass holder on top of a bookcase. He touched the match to it and turned around.

"Don't be afraid—it's only me—Kane Hammond," he said.

In the candlelight, Hammond appeared to be a thickset, athletic-looking individual with a broad, good-natured face and shrewd black eyes which traveled everywhere and took in everything at once.

"I was going past, down on the shore road, and all at once I saw every light up here go out," he said after an instant. "And then I thought I heard a scream. What's happened? Is there anything I can do?"

Marian's lips curved in a little inward smile. She knew why he had explained his being there like that. He wasn't going to give her away. . . not let them know she had phoned him.

"There seems to be something peculiar going on around here," Ralph replied guardedly. "We've heard noises— footsteps and rattling chains. Upstairs somebody shouted for help, and then the lights went out. There was somebody in this room just now. He cleared out when he heard you coming . . ."

"Looks as though some practical joker was at work," Hammond said. "Disturbing, of course, especially to the ladies, but nothing to worry about—nothing really dangerous, of course. That shouting for help was probably part of the act."

Marian held out her hand for the match box which Hammond still carried. She moved around the room, lighting the other candles in their tall holders. As the flames flared up, the guests were turning to look at one another, peering white-eyed into the corners.

"Mr. Holloway's gone!" Little old Mrs. Sherburne's cracked voice burst out suddenly. "He went upstairs for a handkerchief just before that screaming began, and he didn't come back."

"Probably heard the commotion and decided to lie low till he found out what was happening," Hammond said. "He'll be right down in a minute."

He stepped out into the hall at the foot of the stairs. He shouted up: "Oh, Mr. Holloway! Everything's all right now. Come on down."

Nobody answered. But somewhere up there, the clank of iron sounded, and a burst of cracked, jeering laughter echoed down the hall.

Hammond fell back a step, his face puzzled, his cheeks whitening. In the living room, Mrs. Sherburne stumbled up out of the chair where she had sunk down a moment before.

"That's enough for me!" she cried. "I'm getting out of here this very minute. It's got Mr. Holloway—it'll get the rest of us if we stay here." She looked around. "If any of you others haven't got cars and want to come with me in mine, you're welcome . . ."

The guests flocked toward the old lady, en masse.

"We're going—we're all going!" they gasped.

The old lady in the lead, they rushed out of the room into the hall. None of them stopped to look for hats, coats or luggage.

Marian looked up into Ralph's face. Tears were trickling down her cheeks.

"If they go, we lose everything—we lose all our hopes," she sobbed.

Ralph patted her shoulder.

"Brace up, sweetheart," he whispered. "We've still got each other. And you're all I want . . ."

Slipping around the knot of scrambling figures, Hammond was hurrying out to the door ahead of them.

"Just a minute. Better let me take a look outside first," he said. "Just in case—"

Hammond opened the door and went out. The others trooped after him. Following behind, Marian and Ralph saw them push past him and start running across the lawn, heading toward the little garage over at one side of the drive.

Suddenly they all stopped. They were standing motionless, gazing up at something over their heads . . .

Chapter Three

Fruit of the Gallows Tree

The people fleeing from Holden's were looking up at the gallows. Something was hanging down from the cross-piece—something long and dark that swayed slowly back and forth in the wind, with a soft, muted clanking of the length of iron chain that dangled loose from it . . .

It was not the scarlet and gold sign. That had been ripped away. It was a six-foot pendulum body, tolling dismal rhythm at the end of the chain. The moonlight shone down on it, spotlighting its face in demoniac fantasy of black and green. The eyes bulged from the purple face. The man's inch-thick tongue swelled from between his grinning teeth as though he were out-thrusting it in maniac derision of the dirty, cheese-colored moon overhead.

The man on the gallows was Holloway!

For a long moment nobody moved. Huddled together, the men and women who stood there clung close, bunched tight for the comfort of physical contact. Their ashen-white faces turned to one another and jerked apart again. Their eyes darted shuddering glances under the trees where hulks of green shadows crouched and coiled like lurking beasts.

"I'm afraid—I'm afraid," little Miss Wilcox was sobbing. "There—something under that bush—I saw it move!"

"It's coming—look! Around the corner of the house!" another woman cried.

"Nonsense! It's only a shadow," Mrs. Sherburne snapped. "Come along—"

Her voice husked away into a gasp. Something was coming now, racing toward them over the grass. Something silent and black—a thick jet figure that traveled on the ground and in the air.

The wind had started to blow, setting the pendulum to swinging, sending its shadow leaping down at them. The black figure brushed across a woman's face. She jumped away. She started to scream shriek after shriek of guttering horror.

As though driven apart by a bomb, the knot of figures burst open. Screaming, bent backward by shudders that coursed their bodies they fled from the long swart semaphore of death that seemed to pursue them in demoniac hunger as they ran from its ghastly touch.

Out in the open, in the midst of the yellow-green moonlight, Marian, Hammond and Ralph stood watching. In stumbling, tripping runs, the guests were stampeding for the garage. The doors slammed open. From inside came the roar of motors starting up. One after another three cars backed into the yard. They turned, shot into gear and went tearing off down the driveway which led to the main road running along the top of the bluff.

In a moment, the last of them had disappeared. Now it was dead silent again in front of the house—silent save for the soft clanking of the grim pendulum on the gallows tree . . .

Marian looked up at Ralph. She was sobbing.

"They're gone! she whispered. "They're gone—!"

Hammond's voice spoke up.

"Look here, Holden—how many people did you have staying here?" he asked.

"Seven," Ralph answered. "Why?"

"Holloway was killed—that left six," Hammond pondered. "But only five persons went away in those cars."

Ralph nodded.

"I noticed that, too. Mr. Trask wasn't there." Ralph wet his lips. "He probably decided not to go. He must have stayed in the house."

Nobody spoke for an instant. Nobody wanted to say what was in the minds of all three of them . . . If Trask had stayed in the house, it wasn't because had decided not to go . . .

Marian gritted her teeth, to keep from chattering as she clung to Ralph. The sightless, motionless wind was blowing through her again, freezing her blood—spectral wind of death that moved through the green moonlight . . .

"We've got to find Trask," Hammond said after an instant. "Also we've got to catch that—that madman or thing whatever it is that's inside there. Here's what I've been thinking, Holden. This is no place for your wife. Over at my shack I've got a rifle and an automatic. Why don't we take your car, drive her over there, leave her where she'll be safe, get my shooting things and then come back here and see this through—the two of us?"

And that was the way it was settled. Fifteen minutes later, Marian was standing alone in the cozy little living room of Hammond's cottage, listening to the purr of Ralph's engine dying away up the road. The two men were armed, now—Ralph with the rifle and Hammond with the automatic. They carried a couple of high-powered flashlights. There was no reason for her to worry about them. Whatever it was that had been doing the things, they could have nothing to fear from it now . . .

Nothing to fear, her reason told her. And yet . . . She picked up a magazine, glanced at it and threw it down. Nervously she got up and started pacing the floor. It wasn't late—only half past ten by the clock over the fireplace—but it seemed as though she had lived through a lifetime since she had cleared the dinner dishes off the table. She went to look of the window. Half a mile away, she could see the twin white arms of Ralph's headlights just climbing back up the bluff to the house.

She wrung her hands. Ralph, her husband, whom she loved more than life, gone back into that house of dreadful doom— the house where death had stalked his kin for five generations—and she had not stopped him . . . she had let him go.

She went to the mirror to powder her cheeks. With a choking cry, she snapped the case shut and flung it down. Her fingers were trembling, shaking and quivering so that she couldn't hold on to the powder puff. Sweat on her face caked the sweet-smelling stuff into gummy muck . . .

Marian whirled and ran into the hall. Something was driving her—some wild, throbbing instinct of terror. She couldn't stand it. She couldn't stay here and do nothing while Ralph was there in the house of doom. Guns or no guns, something was waiting for him there—death was waiting . . . Death that would reach out and snatch him unless she came. No matter what happened to her, she had to go. She had to go back there and find him—before it was too late.

Too late—too late . . . The words tolled dreadful cacophony in Marian's ears while she toiled over the soft, shifting ground. She was not stopping to go around by the road. Straight across country she was running, over the rolling tops of the sand dunes which were treacherously slithering under her feet, toward the spot of yellow light that showed where her house was.

Now at last she had come to the foot of the hill where it stood. Slower and slower she plodded, crept on hands and knees up the shelving, slippery face of the bluff, where the sand slid out from under her, plucked and dragged at her, milling her backward. Panting, she crawled up the final punishing yards and came out on the level top. She stood an instant looking around.

Down on the beach a hundred feet below, the moonlight splashed green and blackly coiling dragons over the sand. Glassily it shimmered and glinted on the surface of the quicksand marsh, up at the far end of the cove. The heaving, churning slough of stinking slime made her think of the bosom of some demon lying there, spreading its filthy maw to suck down any victim that might come too near. Ghastly, soul sickening were the tales of the things which had happened there in the quicksand bog—happened to strangers who had not been warned . . .

Marian swung around and started toward the house . . . Now she was up at the foot of the steps. A wind was blowing through the house—a wind of emptiness and cold. It set the candles in the living room swaying and guttering in their holders, waving in the air their pale yellow hands of ghosts . . .

Marian stopped and slipped off her shoes—the narrow, high-heeled little slippers which, full of the sand, were gritting, rubbing, blistering her feet so cruelly. Soundlessly she started up the steps. On stocking feet she glided across the piazza and in through the door.

In the entryway she stood listening again. Listening with her clenched fists crushed to her heart. Nothing here—nothing but the slow, labored breathing and sighing of the old house in travail. . . the creaking of boards, the rattling of loose shingles on the roof. . . the swish and moan of the wind driving through the vacant rooms.

Marian was crying softly as she stumbled from room to room. Their house, which she and Ralph had laughed, worked, and hoped over for so long—now murdered and desolate, with the wind of terror blowing down its empty halls . . .

One after another, she looked into all the rooms on the first floor. Nobody there . . . She stood in the middle of the hall and called softly.

"Ralph! Ralph, darling, where are you?"

The wind caught up the words and flung them back at her, snatched them up and sent them echoing in garbled, mocking echoes up and down all the long spaces . . .

Marian was climbing the stairs, creeping step by step up over the dried, creaking tread-boards.

On the second floor, she went from room to room, halting in each to throw the light of the candle around and call Ralph's name. Wonder, amazement, was growing over her as she crept along. Hammond and Ralph—where on earth could they be? What became of them? They couldn't have gone anywhere else—they must be somewhere in the house.

She went back to the old, unused part of the house—the empty, dust-mantled rooms whose dread barrenness had depressed and frightened her so that she had never visited them after the tour of inspection that she and Ralph had made on their first day there. From door to door she hurried, half running, her haste making the candle's flame stream out behind her. A new kind of terror was traveling beside her now— terror of the cold, empty loneliness and the echoing void of the barren rooms. Loneliness that chattered and clicked, chuckled and whispered—garbled, rustling echoes flocking behind her in the dancing shadows of the candle flame. Cold, stealthy fingers came stealing out of the corners, brushing her flesh, creeping into her bosom where they lay like leaden ice against her pounding heart.

She stopped. She held her breath listening.

Thump—swish . . . Footfalls trailing after her—the brush of a big ungainly body against the walls . . . Or was it only the clattering rush of the regiments of rats that went thundering and squealing across their parade ground up on the attic floor?

Marian spun around, holding the candle at arm's length over her head. Nothing to see save the mob-scene of yellow shadows jostling and elbowing one another up and down the walls. She caught her breath. For an instant she thought she had heard a voice. Could it have been Ralph's voice calling her—or was it a throaty, guttural chuckling of sardonic mockery that came out of the gloom. . .?

At the end of the long hall, the grey oblong of a window blocked itself out of the pitch darkness. Marian scratched a space in the opaque frosting of dust that covered it and looked out.

Down below she could see the knoll with the black right
angle of the gallows tree with its black, tolling pendulum of
death, on the little hill. Beyond, the moonlight glinted on the
white crests of curling breakers as they riffled against the
beach. Off at one side was the treacherous slick of the quicksand heaving and churning like the vast, sucking mouth of a
thing alive as the incoming tide lifted it from underneath.

Shuddering, Marian turned from the window. Half a dozen
feet away she noticed another door. She stepped over to it,
pressed down the old-fashioned latch, swung the door open
and stepped into the room.

As she passed through the portal, a gust of wind from
somewhere blew out the candle. For an instant she stood
there motionless in the darkness. Yet it was not quite pitch-
black, for the moonlight, filtering in through the dust-
covered windows, filled the place with a gibbous haze of eerie green luminance. The room was larger than any other she
had seen. As her eyes grew adjusted to the dim glow, she
could make out the shapes of furniture that covered the floor.
A storeroom, crammed from wall to wall with ancient hulks
of tables and chairs, couches and bureaus . . .

She took a step and paused. Midway of the room, a flat
white oblong was slowly taking form out of the powdery
murk. Then she discerned what it was—a bed . . .

There was something queer about the bed. Something long
that stretched up and down its middle, marring the dingy
sweep of its flatness—something darker than the dusty grey
of the soiled sheets . . .

Marian was shivering now, with horrible understanding as
she crept toward the bed. That long dark shape—someone
lying there—someone stark and motionless, who did not stir.

At the side of the figure, she stumbled down to her knees.
She couldn't see . . . Out of her numbed, wooden hand, the
unlighted candle had slipped to the floor . . . Through the
dark she stretched out her hands—fingers cold, shrinking.

A face . . . She bit her lips to keep from screaming as her
fingers felt it—a face with mouth jerked apart in mad laughter from the grinning teeth . . . Her fingers trailed downward

till they shuddered over the throat—touched it and leaped away as warm, bubbling wetness slimed their tips.

Sobbing Marian dashed the tears from her eyes. Who was it, lying there horribly dead in the darkness? Was it Ralph or someone else? She had to know. She had to have one look at that poor, ravaged face that lay there, laughing at death, and know . . .!

On her knees, she swept her hands over the floor. The candle—the candle that she had dropped. She must find it—and light it again and see . . .

Blindly she groped through the blackness. Straining, panicky fingers sweeping over the rough boards whose splinters knifed her skin—fingers slithering and clutching in the inch thick dust—clutching in the darkness and emptiness, while eternities dragged on . . .

She gave it up. The candle was gone. But she had the matches. As she had left the living room, she had picked up a paper pack of them and thrust it down into the top of her stocking. The candle might go out in the wind, she had thought . . .

Still on her knees, she fumbled for the bottom of her skirt and twitched it up. The little cardboard folder was still there.

She pulled it out and felt for a match. She couldn't get one loose. Her fingers were all thumbs. Cold, quivering, sweats limed fingers, blundering and twitching at the inch-long, flimsy things . . . Seconds passed. Why couldn't she get hold of a match? There were matches there, but she couldn't feel them. Dozens of them, slipping and sliding under her fingers . . .

Between her ice-slivers of dead digits Marian clutched a little paper strip at last. Clumsily, awkwardly, she dragged it over the roughened end of the card. A little dagger of yellow light spurted into the gloom, and she leaned forward, holding the flame over the bed.

The man on the bed was not Ralph. He was Trask, the one who had disappeared while the others were running out of the house. His purple, ghastly face grinned up at her over the ragged hole in his throat, while the flame ate its way up the paper stalk, bit at her fingers, and then died.

Inch by inch, Marian got up from her knees and, legs palsied, pushed herself back onto her feet. Little sobbing prayers of thankfulness to God were husking through her jerking lips. It wasn't Ralph—God was good—it wasn't Ralph . . .

She pulled herself around, turned back toward the door. Now she was trying to make herself think; striving to calm her plunging nerves, and figure things out. Where could they be, Hammond and Ralph? She had been all over the house—everywhere but the cellar—and they weren't there . . .

Suddenly she froze, her heart leaping. Out in the hall, just the other side of the door, there had been a sound—the snapping creak of the old floor. The latch rattled once, twice, and then was silent . . .

Chapter Four

Into Horror's Reeking Maw

Marian couldn't move for a moment as she stood there frozen by fear. Her body seemed gone—congealed to ice in the dank, clammy folds of darkness.

Click—click . . . There it was again—the latch being moved . . . Now she was turning her head, straining her eyes into the shadows . . . Over there in the far corner, the dark bulk of a bureau looming in the green murk . . . Inch by inch she dragged herself around, lifted her numbed, ton-weight feet and stumbled across to it. She squeezed around behind it and sank down to the floor.

With the dusty back of the bureau scraping against her face, she couldn't see anything now, but she could hear. The latch was rattling again, clanking anvil strokes in the choked hush. She shifted her position, peered out around the edge of the bureau. She could see the door starting to open. Something was shouldering in—something monstrous and huge in the green light. Vast sloping shoulders, globe-round head, face yellow and wrinkled as old parchment, huge grinning mouth and shattered fangs of teeth . . .

Now the looming form was inside the room. It pushed the door shut behind it and started scuffing around between the pieces of old furniture. Methodically it was setting to work to hunt for her!

Piece after piece, it felt behind tables and chairs, and then pushed them to one side. Back and forth it was progressing across the room. It was coming on fast. In a minute now it would be up to her corner . . .

Marian's brain swam in a haze—her poor, half-mad brain that had endured so much it couldn't think any more. Dully, over and over, the thoughts turned in her mind: It was coming for her, coming to get her and kill her—before she had found Ralph . . .

On hands and knees, Marian was starting to creep out of the corner. Where she was going, she didn't know. She just crept inch by maddening inch along the foot of the wall where the moon glow didn't come, where the shadows were thickest. The dust that swirled up under her scuffing choked her, blew itching torment into her nostrils. She bit her lips to strangle the hot sneezes that surged up for release—bit her lips till the teeth met in the flesh, to crush down the wild sobbings of terror, while she crept and crawled through the darkness, pressing her shuddering body to the floor— hugging her face to the filth and dust as she groveled away from the hellish, searching creature . . .

Over her shoulder she was watching the thing. It picked up a chair and shoved it aside. It bent, swept its hands over the floor and muttered low snarls of rage. It stood irresolute a moment, then turned to peer around the room, as if thinking where to look next.

Faster! Faster! She must go faster! It hadn't spotted her yet. But any minute now . . .

Faster and faster!

But if she went any faster she would make a noise . . .

Hugging the foot of the wall, creeping inch by furtive inch behind tables and chairs, digging her bleeding fingers into floor whose splinters raked and ribboned her flesh, she got to within about ten feet of the door. Ten mile-long ghastly feet to crawl on her hands and knees while the thing shoved and tore at the furniture behind her . . .

Over her shoulder she saw that it had come to the corner. It gripped the big bureau, yanked it aside, stooped, and swept its hand down into the darkness.

Crouched double, Marian was up on her feet now. Up on her poor, blistered half naked feet, tottering and stumbling to the door. Stumbling and running while the board splinters caught in her stockings and ripped the sheer silk from her flesh . . .

Now she was up to the door, her hands thrust out, feeling for the latch.

Quietly—quietly—not a sound . . . She jerked a look over her shoulder. The thing was standing with its back to her, feeling around in the corner . . .

The door started to move as she found the latch and pressed it down. Thank God, the hinges didn't squeak . . . The door was opening, inch by torturing inch . . . Now she was shuddering through, gliding out . . .

She didn't try to latch the door again—only pushed it to, without closing it, behind her. Now back down the hall again—racing and stumbling, fleeing through the long, whispering corridors away from the room, away from the gibbous grey-green sheen of the moonlight . . .

Now she was back in the new part of the house, clutching the stair railing as she crept down through the empty, creaking house where the black wind of terror was blowing again . . . Back through the living room, with the candle ghosts waving their pallid yellow hands in mournful welcome . . . She stepped over and took one of the candlesticks off the table . . . Now out through the passage into the kitchen . . .

Marian gasped raspingly above her labored pantings. The cellar door stood ajar! Something had opened it since she had locked it—opened it and gone down there . . .!

She tiptoed up to it, stepped through onto the landing at the top of the stairs.

For a long time she stood there, holding her breath, peering down. Below there was the eerie, silent blackness, heavy, seemingly tangible and cold as death . . .

Step by step, she started down the stairs. She had to go—she must find Ralph . . .

Now she was down all the steps, with the sour reek of wet earth and mold stinging her throat. She took a step and froze.

Out ahead there, in the coiling gloom, she thought she had heard something—a little clicking creak about as loud as the snap of a match . . . With a sigh, she let her taut muscles relax. There wasn't anything there; she must have imagined it . . .

Mechanically she started along. Where she was going, she didn't know. Going to find Ralph . . .

Rows upon rows of stone posts, crisscrossing, stretching away into the darkness . . . Walls with great dust-mantled stones jutting out at her . . . Underneath, the dank chill of the wet floor striking through the thin, tattered silk of her stockings, making her feet ache with the cold.

On and on . . . Slower and slower Marian was going now. The darkness around her was alive with rustlings and whisperings. She didn't know how it was that she was moving at all—what it was that was making her go along. Her body felt numb, dead. Only her will power was alive—will power that flogged her dragging legs and feet forward . . .

Creak—snap! Somewhere, something was moving—something following her . . . A long way off, Marian heard the peculiar clicking sound. Her teeth chattered, and she shuddered and quaked while her heart beat a wild tattoo . . .

Another half dozen steps—or maybe a hundred—she didn't know . . . Suddenly she stopped. By the light of the guttering candle in her trembling hand she could see something now in the middle of the cellar floor—an oblong spot darker than the surrounding gloom.

A step nearer, and she saw what it was. A hole in the floor, where a big flagstone had been pried up and shoved to one side.

She crept up to the hole. Holding the candle low, she

peered down at a flight of rough stone steps . . .

Marian stooped and started feeling her way down the stairs—into a reeking maw of horror to find Ralph . . . Slime of decades beneath her feet sent her slipping and staggering, clutching at the dripping walls.

Now she was at the bottom, standing in a passage some six or eight feet wide. Under her bare feet, the floor was sodden and clammy with foul ooze. Long tentacles of viscid grey fungus trailed from the walls. There was a choking, sickening stench of corruption, of fetid putrescence that drew retching gasps up from the pit of her stomach.

The passage sloped down quite steeply as it led off into jet darkness. Her bare feet skidding and slithering in the clammy cold muck, she pushed ahead.

Marian knew where she was, now—down in the secret passage which Ralph's old ancestor, the smuggler, had built as a store-house for his illicit stock in trade. All through the years there had been a legend of such a passage under the house, but none of old Holden's descendents had ever been able to find out where the entrance was.

Her brain was racing now, wild with excitement. Somebody had discovered the secret of the ancient hide. What had he been doing down here? And Ralph—all over the house she had searched for him. This was the only place left. It might be down here in this old dungeon that the thing had caught him, and . . .

Marian lifted her slime-daubed hand to sweep the cold sweat out of her eyes. But Hammond? Where had Hammond been when Ralph disappeared? Where was he now?

Every few steps, Marian stopped and stood listening. At first she heard nothing, save the echoes of her breathing between the muck-slimed walls.

But now there was a sound—the click of feet following her from behind—feet which slithered and swished as they skidded in the ooze. Now the crunch of a big body banging into the wall . . . A clattering thud as it fell down. The gritting of feet as it struggled up again . . .

Wildly Marian was running now, slipping and sliding through the viscid, filthy muck. Down here she had thought to escape from the thing, to find Ralph. But it wasn't Ralph who was coming—it was the thing! She could hear the whuff of its pursy breathing, the clanking of iron. It had trailed her down from upstairs—trailed her through the cellar, watching for the chance to get her in a trap . . .

With mad, frantic little blows Marian was beating her clenched fists against her breast. The thing was coming, and Ralph wasn't there! For dear God's love, where was Ralph?

Now the sounds were up closer . . . The other end—there must be another end to the passage! The stories had been that Ralph's great-great-grandfather had used it to bring up his contraband from the beach, where it had been landed in the dead of night from the ships. No one had ever been able to find this underground tunnel, but there must be an opening! If she kept on she would come to it. She could get out that way. She gulped down a cry. That was what Ralph had done—gone through the tunnel and out of the other end . . .

She swung around a corner of stone whose slime-tentacles a foot long swished gelid snakes in her face—and stopped. Motionless she stood while her heart turned to iron in her breast.

Chapter Five

The Eyes Inside the Monster

Marian had come to the end of the passage—and suddenly she understood why no one had ever found it before. Straight ahead, a big half-circle of sky and stars showed the opening into the tunnel. A piled-up barrier of great rocks choked and filled it almost to the roof of the passage.

Looking through the chinks in the boulders, she could see a flat, green-black surface churning and heaving beyond the stones, as the moonlight winked up off its rolling bosom like twinkling demoniac eyes.

On Marian's side of the barrier there was a ten-yard pool of the stuff, and long, clotted tentacles of slime came rushing up through the clefts in the rocks and lapped at her feet. They seethed up around her legs, tugging at her ankles like coiling snakes . . .

Gasping, Marian jumped back. Now she understood. No one had ever found the mouth of the old tunnel because it came out through the face of the bluff on the edge of the quicksand marsh. Back in the days of old Holden, there were doubtless stepping-stones at intervals through the swamp by which a man who knew their location could enter and leave the cave safely. She had read of such things. . .

But Marian did not know the way. And Ralph would not know the way, either . . .

She caught her breath and stepped forward, holding the candle low. There was something that wasn't a rock in the black, surging kettle of slime—something that glimmered ghastly white as the little swart billows surged over it . . . The sucking blacksnakes writhed away backward and she could see it more clearly.

A hand, the hand of a man, fingers tight-clenched in agony, thrusting up out of the glutinous mass of this writhing cauldron!

And now his face came into view—grey, grinning, staring up open-eyed as the streamers of slime washed over it and ebbed away . . .

Marian was deathly sick. Numbly she pulled her eyes away, swung around up the passage. For one soul scorching instant she had thought that the face was Ralph's. But it wasn't. It was the ugly, sin-graven face of a man she had never seen before.

Now the thing was almost up to her. She could hear it around the next corner, muttering and grunting as it churned through the passage. Step by step she moved backward, shivering in terror. Now she was close to the wall, against the greasy slime whose fetid putrescence made her reel with nausea. Her hand—the hand that was not holding the candle—was fisted over her mouth, and she ground the knuckles with her teeth till they were pink with blood. She could feel herself fainting—feel the strength melting from her like water. Slip—crunch . . . Only a few yards more now—just around the last corner—that hideous creature was coming . . .

Wonder dilating her eyes, Marian shot her gaze down to the floor.

As she cringed back along the rock, she had stubbed her foot against something which tinkled. Now she saw what it was—a knife with a long, shimmering blade!

Amazement pounded at Marian's brain as she stooped and reached for the handle. A weapon—a thing with which to protect herself. How did that knife happen to be lying there? Thank God that it was . . .!

But there was no time now to figure it out. She snatched for the handle and twitched the knife up out of the slime. She pressed its dripping steel against her bosom. She sucked down a sob of savage joy as she felt the hard edge gouge the soft tenderness of her breast.

Around the corner, the footsteps were louder. The bestial creature was almost upon her . . .

Into a chink between two stones Marian wedged the base of the candle. Back into the black shadows of a big rock at the end of the passage she shrank, out of sight. The next instant she saw the *thing!*

Around the slime-fringed angle of the wall, a face edged into the candle-glow—the globe-round visage with the hideously twisting lips snarling back from the shattered teeth. The great sloping shoulders, the mammoth arms swinging gorilla-like at the sides . . .

Now it was close to her—only a couple of yards away. She could hear its hoarse, stifled breathing. In the middle of the circle of candle-light it halted and stood looking around.

The sweat on Marian's hand slimed the knife handle under her fingers as she swung it up. She winced and gasped from the pain of her teeth biting her lips so that she wouldn't scream—ravaging the pretty mouth till trickling blood salted the saliva that drooled from its corners.

SLAVES OF THE MIDNIGHT CAVERNS

Chapter One

It Breeds in Darkness

The fear that I'd felt vaguely for weeks sharpened and leaped at me as I unfolded the note. Before I looked at its message I knew that I had lingered too long in this place, trifling with death . . .

It was around dusk, so dark, in fact, that I had to light a match and hold it over the few scribbled lines to see the words. Old Anton, the humpbacked man of all work, had come running with it the half mile from the house. I could hear his tight, frightened breathing as he stood behind me waiting for me to read it.

The note was from Phil Morrison, another one of the engineers who worked at the mine with me. I had left him at the house with Karol, my wife, and the three other girls when I had started out on a check-up job two hours before.

That message was queer for a man to write. It was the sort of thing that a terrified woman might have penned. It only said:

Jim, for God's sake, come back here as quick as you can.

The match flame bit at my fingers. I muttered and flung it away. Get back to the house—why? What sudden menace had put that strain of hysteria into the summons of the usually calm and phlegmatic Morrison?

I swung around to where Anton was waiting. In the west, the sunset gashed a bloody wound across leaden clouds. The jagged slag-piles around the mouth of the mine zigzagged the sky like the saw-edged teeth of a snarling beast.

"What's wrong? Has anything happened to Mrs. West?" I gripped his arm. "Is it my wife?"

The bearded old laborer looked at me sidewise. He muttered:

"Your wife and Miss' Evarts go to walk an hour ago and dey don' come back. Mist' Morrison say you better hurry."

I motioned Anton ahead of me and swung behind him into the narrow path that wound in and out around the bottoms of the huge waste-cones.

Mrs. Evarts—that was the wife of Fred Evarts, another one of the four engineers responsible for the operation of Clyde Harkins' big gold mine. We all lived together in the cottage at the edge of the grounds. She and Karol gone and not come back? Where could they have gone? Nowhere—for the gates of the great steel fence that surrounded the entire property were closed now and impassable save on special permission from Harkins himself.

Closed now—and within them where I ran, the dark seemed to be crawling with drear, dismal shadows. Things had been happening around here during the past weeks to chill one with horror, but so far they had all hit at the workers, the mine laborers. That any danger could turn toward us, the privileged group of engineering experts and our wives, had not really been brought home to me. I had sensed the onmarch of that eerily unnatural menace, but I had temporized, postponed action. And now in that note of Morrison's—in what he *didn't say*—lurked something that shot a knife of foreboding through me. Karol gone and not returned! Gone where? . . .

Suddenly old Anton checked his advance. He stopped short, trod backward so sharply that he stepped on my toes. His head jerked around. His face, sunken between his misshapen shoulders, was a blob of pallid white.

"Mist' West—dat noise!" he husked. Back in the shadows that bulked on the road, some one was talking. There were words, so blurred together that I couldn't understand them.

But the voice wasn't that of a man. It was a hair-lifting sound. Thin, eldritch, unearthly! Like the piping of birds or the thin stridences of little night insects! Only here there were no birds, no twittering night insects.

The noises were drawing closer. They warbled they trilled in bubbling gurgles.

The short hairs on the back of my neck were lifting. I strained my eyes into the darkness and I couldn't see any thing—not anything of which I was sure. The blue-brown shadows of afterglow coiled and interlaced like writhing dragons. And then, melded among them, it seemed as though there was something white. A shapeless and formless blot, wavering and pale as a ghost, was swaying there.

For an instant I thought it was just my overwrought nerves tricking me with hallucinations. And then a sound was audible over the wheeze of Anton's thick breathing—the click of a rolling stone. Those things were walking! And in the sound of their footfalls was something that slid a shiver of cold down my spine. For their feet didn't lift, man-like, from the ground. They dragged in irregular and nerveless, unnatural jerkings.

Old Anton was beside me, his gnarled fists clutched at my sleeve, while his eyes bulged, white-rimmed. "Don't go dere, Mist' West!" he gasped. "Before God, don' go near dose t'ings ! Dey are de walking dead! Dey mak you lak dem—"

Ghosts of the walking dead! That superstitious cry of the old man's had been nonsense, of course. And yet those voices and those spectral white forms were part and parcel of the horrors that swarmed this place.

In the last two months, almost a dozen of the laborers had been killed in mysterious and ghastly ways, Killed—and worse. Later I'll tell you more about that, how some of them had been murdered outright, others infected with a virus of creeping death that caused their bodies to rot away inch by inch. And others still, who had come back from the depths of the diggings with the shadow of madness in their eyes, gibber and grovel at the sight of the sun!

Horrors unspeakable, without explanation! Yet in some way, I knew, there was connection with these spectral forms that squeaked in the rock-piles at dusk. And out there, into that menace-packed gloom, Karol had gone and hadn't returned!

I shoved Anton ahead of me into the path. "Faster! Faster!" I shouted.

We were travelling swiftly now, through the village where Harkins housed his laborers, several streets filled with the hovels in which they lived. They spilled out of their doors, they and their women, to glower at us as we passed. Gaunt, suffering-stamped faces in which all hope had died. Terror had done something indefinable to these people, something that spoke out of the dark depths of their cavernous eyes. Dull, hopeless eyes that yet seemed to glow with a mad, fanatical fire that suggested things unthinkable.

I remembered how I'd seen them looking at Karol, how they had licked their lewd lips as she tripped past, short skirt swinging, and something clutched at my heart. I knew now that I never should have brought her to this place where evil leered at her with snarling fangs.

I pawed at old Anton's arm.

"Hurry! Hurry!" I muttered

Five minutes later I ran up the steps of the cottage. The little house in which Coleman, Morrison, Evarts and I, we four engineers, lived with our wives, stood off to one side close against the base of the twenty-foot high steel fence that encircled the whole hundred aces of mine property.

Morrison flung open the door as I raced up to it.

"What about Karol—" I started to shout. And then she ran out from behind Morrison and threw herself into my arms.

I bent to kiss her. "I thought you were gone!" I exclaimed. "What—"

Paula Morrison stood there with her husband's arm around her. Further back I could see Coleman's wife. Morrison's face was white and the girls had been crying,

"Where's Sally?" I questioned.

"We don't know," Karol shivered. "She and I went to walk. We were coming back through the slag heaps, we were almost here, when something chased us. It—it didn't seem to run, it sounded like something *crawling*. I was a little ahead. I heard Sally scream. I went back to look for her and she wasn't there—"

Something chased them—something that seemed to crawl—and got Sally! Only God's mercy that it hadn't been Karol! Those twittering things with their shuffling feet that I'd heard there . . .

I went out into the kitchen, got a handful of flashlights and handed them around. "Let's look some more," I muttered. "She's got to be here. She couldn't have got past the fence—"

For an hour or more we hunted up and down through the slag piles and we didn't find her. A wind had come up with the sunset. It crooned and sobbed in drear moanings. It swept the gravel down the flanks of the waste cones with thin hissings. We walked huddled together, our fingertips clutching and the spirit of unearthly terror crept into the marrow of our bones.

Karol stumbled, halted. She screamed, and tugged at my arm.

"Jim—the light! There's something here—" Her voice died on a note of stark horror.

The white eye of the torch showed a little cave, a cranny in the rocks. The light slanted down to disclose a dark, irregular heap of something strewn over the ground. They were a woman's clothes, and over them dark stainings were splashed.

Karol stooped, reached for a garment and held it up. She whispered: "Sally's dress. Her blue one; she wore it this afternoon." Her lips sagged slack, her eyes were enormous staring pools. "Sally—"

Her stifled sobbing came to me through a fog. For my eyes had lighted on something else. In a little hollow among the rocks a few feet to one side, rested a dish with curved, outflaring sides. It was a common mixing bowl taken out of some kitchen.

The beam of the light shafted down to a gleam on the surface of the thick, syrupy looking fluid that almost filled the bowl. The reflection of the light cast up from it held a rich carmine sheen.

I heard Helen Coleman's voice burst in a choking cry. And then we were all there on our knees, clutching at one another while we stared at the ruddy, throbbing richness of that stuff in the bowl.

The light in my hand twitched with the horror that flogged at my nerves. Its motion slanted the beam into a corner of the cave of whose existence we hadn't been aware.

Morrison let out a curse. Karol shrieked, "Sally!"

For over there, in the white frame of the flashlight, a head stared at us over the top of a rock. And then her naked white shoulders and her crooked arms were visible, as though, prone on her face, she had been trying to drag herself up over that barrier when death had struck her down. Her wide-open eyes stared at us, moon-round pools of blind horror. The blaze of the torch beat on her face, ashen whiteness of a carved cameo medallion.

Unnaturally sunken and thin that face seemed, with its flattened cheeks. And that arm, too, which lay over the top of the rock! Sally Evarts had been plump and deliciously rounded, but that lifeless member was flaccid and shrunken, drained empty of the juices of life as the limb of a witch.

Drained, flaccid and shrunken—yet, in my daze at the sight of that ghastliness, I still didn't realize, I didn't plumb the full depths of the awfulness here.

Despite the noisesome rush of my horror, I found myself in motion, crawling over there to her side. I threw the light on her throat. For an instant I held it there, while my own body seemed to grow gelid and lifeless.

For in Sally's throat another mouth with thick and blood-scarlet lips grinned up at me. Lengthwise this mouth was planted—the gash where her neck had been ripped from bosom to chin. A throat cut lengthwise instead of across!

Such cuts I had seen before—in the throats of animals that had been slaughtered, their jugular veins severed so that they could be bled! And that was why Sally's nude body was so shrunken, so unnaturally withered and pinched—because the stuff in the white kitchen mixing bowl was her blood which had been drawn from her and caught in that vessel!

Morrison and I got Sally's body out of that cave and carried it back to the house. We took her into the spare bedroom down stairs and shut the door on her horror.

Out in the front room, we stood staring at one another—till Karol wilted into a chair, buried her face in her hands and burst out in wild sobbing.

I stuck a cigarette between my teeth and tried to smoke the thing without lighting it. I paced across to a window and stood staring out while I tried to hammer my spinning brain and make it think.

Those things that I thought I had seen, which Anton had called the walking dead—they could have been the ones who had got Sally. It was a mad thought! With all the force of my trained and logical mind I pushed back the crazily impossible idea. Such things couldn't be! Yet in the same breath I knew that they must be, for I had seen.

A rush of pure horror chilled me. Sally's blood in that mixing bowl! Put there in sheer maniac impishness or later to serve some unthinkable loathsome end? Such a purpose as the walking and hungry dead might conceive of . . .

Out where I was looking, the iron frame of the hoist over the mine shaft etched black tracings against the moon, a gibbet shape. A loose iron girder, swinging in the wind, clanked ghoulish laughter against the beams.

I jammed my fists into my pockets and that spot of cold on my spine crept nearer my heart. Sally! And it might have been Karol instead who lay there in that silent room! She had escaped this time, but the next . . . For I knew that this wasn't the end, these horrors that had leaped at us weren't over; it was only the beginning.

Over to Karol I went. I took her into my arms. I strained her tight to me; through tight lips I whispered her name while fear sickened me.

Chapter Two

The Dead Want Blood

I set Karol back in her chair, turned around to speak to Morrison.

"I'm going up to see Peterson," I said. "I won't be long. You stay with the girls."

This Peterson was one of the foremen. Although he lived in the laborers' village, he was many degrees superior in intelligence to the rank and file of the pick and shovel crew. In his manners and some of his ways of speech I thought I detected traces of a better past. He had always been friendly to me. If anyone had a rational idea of what was going on here, he was the one.

My thoughts were busy as I stumbled over the dark and rutted road, going over what I knew of Clyde Harkins and his mine and trying once more to see some reason behind the tangle of horrors.

Isolated as it was far in the depths of the badlands, Harkins had still further cut his property off from the world with the twenty-foot high steel fence which enclosed every foot of its area.

And inside that barrier he had built up a little community, self-contained. His half hundred foremen, clerks and machinists he had hired on the condition that they should live inside the fence, whose gate was always kept locked, and not leave it more often than once a month and then only with his special permission.

Strange conditions indeed they were—warnings, had I but sensed it, of the horrors that were to enmesh us here. Puzzled and suspicious, indeed, Karol and I had hesitated long when Harkins laid before us his terms of taking me on as one of his managing engineers. But it had been two years since I had had a regular job, years in which the world had showed us how cruel could be its fangs, and at last we had decided to take it on.

Harkins had quartered us here in the cottage where we had found Evarts, Morrison and Coleman, with their wives, already installed.

We were all young people of about the same age and condition of life, and for a while we had made quite a gay and carefree group. Laughingly we had made a joke of our virtual imprisonment. Harkins paid good wages and our bank balances grew, for save on our monthly sprees to the nearest town, fifty miles away, we had no opportunity to fritter our money.

And then, little by little, the chill of that malignant and strangely horrible shadow started creeping over us. Harkins himself was affable and smooth-spoken. He explained the fence around the place:

"I've got some bad enemies—parties that would give their right arms to get hold of this property, or wreck it, if they couldn't do that. They've sued me over the title, tried every dodge there is. They wouldn't be above sending a gang of bad actors to raid us if that fence wasn't there. And then these badlands are full of bandits. Plenty of folks know that I often have a hundred thousand in gold in my safe."

Plausible enough—till one looked at the mine diggers, the two hundred pick and shovel hands. Somewhere and somehow—I never asked—Harkins had had them rounded up and smuggled into this country, ignorant Czecks and Slovacks and Poles, scum and sweepings of Europe. No free labor was this but near-peon stuff. Life-time jobs were theirs. In virtual slavery they lived behind the steel fence.

Men too stupid and too brutalized by their sufferings in the old countries these were to realize what was being done to them or to care much, as long as their primitive hungerings for food and women were satisfied. Harkins knew well the cruder verities of human nature; he had provided for this last—the "housekeepers". And that was an angle of our existence here from which our wives turned their eyes away—and in the dead of night, their ears as well.

The trouble started when the laborers began to disappear. A squad of forty would go down into the shaft for a day's work and only thirty-nine of them would return, Some accident in the workings—wandered off and fell down a shaft or got hit on the head by a falling rock, were the easy and quick guesses. Nobody cared.

And then, after a few days, they would mysteriously show up again. They seemed dazed, they couldn't tell where they had been. But it had been somewhere that fingers of hell had laid hold of them. For in little slivers and ribbons, the flesh had been torn from their faces.

Others had been pitched out on the ground dead, their throats shredded into grisly pulp.

But still this wasn't the worst. Some had been sent back alive. But alive in a horror that was worse than death. For a ghastly skin disease had fastened itself on to them. Their dry flesh flaked off in yellowish scales. Whole areas sloughed away as though by the ravages of galloping gangrene.

Then was when the wildness of unearthly fear began to blaze in the eyes of the pick-men. Abysmally ignorant, they believed all the age-old superstitions poured into their childhood ears in their peasant villages of the old country. They blamed the deaths and the disease not on anything mortal and tangible, but on the curse of a menace from another world.

Huddled in tight-faced knots they whispered about the bird-like voices that shrilled at them out of the rock crannies. They told of the flitting white shapes. The mine was dug too deep, they said, too close to the roof of hell. Up through that too-thin covering pierced the walking dead who tortured and killed them.

Day after day I watched those men. Dull and insensate they had seemed, but of late there had been something different about them. Did I say that all hope had died in their eyes? It hadn't quite—or if it had; something terrible had taken its place. Down there beneath the inscrutable surface of their faces blazed the fanatical glare of hope fused with madness. Something that clutched at my heart as I watched those eyes fixed on Karol . . .

I had felt all that, and while I shivered at the menace of this thing primitive and blackly horrible, my college-bred mind rebelled at their talk of the walking dead. Just crazy fancies of peasant louts, I said. There was some reasonable explanation. And whatever the curse on them was, it couldn't come near Karol and me. And as for their hurting her, they simply wouldn't dare. So, in my self-sufficiency I had trifled with death!

Finally, Harkins had called a conference of us four engineers. The square jawed owner had ridiculed our insistence that he call in the police.

"Some bohunk has gone nuts and hid out down in the mine," he pronounced in his autocratic way. "He's having one hell a time grabbing the men and carving them up. I'm looking to you four to take care of this. Go on down there and dig this gorilla out."

"Maybe. But how about those others, the ones with the skin disease?" Morrison asked. "Flesh rotting off their faces by handfuls! What's happened to them?"

Harkins shrugged. He shoved a cigarette into his poker face.

"How could I know? Something they get into down there. The doctor (Harkins maintained a physician on the premises) is working on it. Let him worry about that. All you men have to think about is the killings."

That had been five or six days ago. We four had made several trips into the mine when we could spare the time from our other duties, and we hadn't found anything. A couple more of the diggers came back to the surface with their faces hanging in tatters. Up in the workers' village, those sullen, hate-filled eyes glowed more vindictively, their fanatical lights danced crazily.

And with all this going on, I still hadn't taken Karol away! Blind in my fancied security of our position, I had allowed her to stay here—till I had turned my flashlight on to that bowl of Sally's blood, and had seen her moon-eyes staring at me over the top of that rock!

Peterson himself opened the door when I knocked at his cottage. In the background I caught a glimpse of the dark face and startled eyes of Nettie, his "housekeeper".

He invited me in, but I beckoned him outside. When I'd finished talking, he shivered and wet his lips.

"Mr. West, dere's hell goin' on in dis place," he muttered. "W'at it is exactly, I dunno. But—"

He pointed at a knot of the miners clustered in the street a little way off. "Dose men say de walking dead get hold of our boys down in de mine, rip deir t'roats. Dose dead feller, dey hate de living! Dey want us to be lak dem. Dey give us dat disease, we die little by little, inch a day."

So earnest was the old man, so fiercely did his beady black eyes hold me that for one second a crazy conviction stormed in my brain. The living dead, whose thin voices I'd heard twittering there!

That thought importuned me while in my conventional and educated mind I dismissed it as madness. "That blood in the mixing bowl, that woman they killed?" I muttered.

"I not know, Mr. West, before God I can't guess!" Nils shuddered. "Dose spirits out of de mine, maybe dey want dat blood—"

The old man's whisper died on a stark note of horror. For an instant there was silence between us. The wind freshened, it sobbed past us in moaning streams. The loose beam on the mine scaffold dinned on the framework with the measured clanging of a toll-bell of doom.

"What's that? What are those men doing?" I muttered.

Up the street, the group at which I had been looking were gathered around a fire of sticks. The leaping flames carved their faces in frenzied exultings. It shone on their gleaming eyes, their bared teeth.

One of them had a stick, curved in twistings that suggested writhings of a body in torment. Another man approached with something that did writhe and lunge as he held it firmly by two ends.

Gripping the serpent this way—for I now saw that the squirming object was a yard-long rattlesnake—he coiled it around and around the stick. While he held it there, others bound it with wire.

Through the flames he now passed it rapidly back and forth. Crazed by its torture, the snake hissed and writhed, frenziedly it struck with its fangs.

At that eerie spectacle something crawled on my spine. I gripped Nils' arm. I half shouted: "What are they doing? Why are they doing that to that snake?"

"It is a charm," Nils muttered. "A charm of Bohemia—"

"Charm?" I echoed.

"Dat stick wit' de snake, she charmed now. And man w'at carry it, he can't be touched by de ghosts." The old man clutched my arm. "Look, dey finish de charm—"

The snake's torture was over, its writhings had ceased. Through the ring a figure came carrying a white bowl. He held it while into it the other dipped alternately the two ends of the stick bearing the dead snake.

Into that white bowl they dipped it and it came out dripping with something that flowed in sluggish and syrupy tricklings! Something on which the fireglow shone darkly red!

The ring had opened. The men were scattering back from the fire. Madly they laughed. They brandished the dripping stick through the air. They wheeled, saw me, turned toward me fanatical, wild eyes of savage glee.

Now they were jabbering together in a tongue that I didn't understand.

"What is it, what are they saying?" I cried to Nils.

Nils licked his lips. He cast a look of pity upon me. "Dey say, not enough blood. Dey got to have more blood. It must be de blood of a young woman, a beautiful woman to make de charm stronger."

"More blood—blood of a beautiful woman!" I echoed his words in thick mumblings. I clawed at his arm, I started to cry out again in my horror, but he shook his head, imperatively he shushed me to silence.

For the ring had broken up and the miners came streaming past. In crazy excitement they chattered, their eyes leer at me, tauntingly insolent. They shook their fists, their hooked fingers clawed air in lewd symbols.

Nils gripped my arms and his fingers burned through the cloth.

"Go home, Mr. West! If you love your wife, go back an' don' leave her!" he cried.

Over the rutted and stony road I raced and a specter of ghastliness ran at my side, gibbering. I'd been a miler at college, but this was a different race from any I had ever run before. Up ahead I could see those dark figures spread out, humping against the moon. Wildly I pumped, my feet skidded and slewed over the loose rocks. Snail-like my progress as I overhauled them. Whether they would let me by, I didn't know. They were going for Karol; they knew I was her husband.

One by one I caught up with them and pounded past. They looked around, they snarled with bared teeth, but they didn't interfere with me. More and yet more of them . . . Around the flanks of the waste-piles that endless road wound and unwound, and at every turn I'd see another knot of those ghouls racing ahead of me. The moon was sinking, its yellow eye leered at me over the peaks of the slagheaps, serrated fangs of a cosmic monster.

Now I was getting winded. I stumbled and tripped, a haze swam in my eyes. Thickly I moaned Karol's name. Karol, my darling! Could I do it, could I keep going, could I get there in time . . .

Chapter Three

The Hand on the Door

The door of the cottage opened as I barged up the steps. I'd out-distanced them, they were all behind me. Karol was there. She fell into my arms.

I rushed her inside, slammed the door locked and stood sagging against it. I held her and kissed her till she struggled and pushed herself back, breathless.

"What happened, Jim? What's the matter?" they all cried.

"I saw Nils, he doesn't know anything," I panted. I kept the hideous truth of what I had seen to myself. "Something down in the mine is stampeding the men. They say they're spooks, come up out of hell."

I stumbled past them into the living room. I didn't want their probing eyes to rest on the terror that whitened my face. I knew now who had killed Sally, and in that revelation I had grazed on something that was loathsome, unthinkable. The miners! Killed her to get her blood to make their charm against the ghosts!

Here inside of Clyde Harkins' fence murder stalked— something unspeakably more hideous than simple death, the mob hunger of superstitious fools, gone crazy for blood!

And they were coming for Karol, around this house they were gathering now! I spun around to the others, standing silent and white-faced behind me.

"I'm getting out of here, right now this minute!" I cried. "I'm going to Harkins and make him open the gate. We're all getting out—"

Morrison shook his head. "Harkins isn't here. I went up to get him when the girls didn't come back. He's gone to town, he won't be back till morning. And you know he's got the only set of keys there is in his pocket."

I stared at him, I swung around without speaking. The only set of keys! Well I knew vehemently our boss guarded the entrance and exit from his property, how he would allow keys in no hand save his own. Gone till morning! And to-night we were trapped there inside of that fence with its horrors!

None of us had had any supper yet. After a while the three girls got something on and we sat down to it. But we didn't eat. Our stomachs were tight, they revolted at food.

We got up, drifted back into the front room and sat around, making a bluff at talking. We couldn't talk either. It was ten o'clock and Coleman and Evarts hadn't come back from their afternoon trip into the mine. We knew that they wouldn't ever come back. I started going around, making sure that the doors and windows were locked. It was an empty gesture, I knew. So far, those mad miners hadn't come. Perhaps the knowledge that there were two men in the house now was keeping them back. But when they got ready to come . . .

It had been a hot day and a thunderstorm was making off toward the north. We sat listening to the long rolls of the thunder and the dead, aching silence-claps that fell in between. The lightning was lashing long, vicious sheets along the horizon, snarling fangs of a cosmic beast.

We were all deathly tired and before long we went to bed. The Morrisons and Karol and I had one another. But Helen Coleman was alone in her room. The picture of her white wanness and her sick eyes haunted me. I could hear her pacing the floor, up and down, sobbing.

Karol and I lay down on the bed without undressing. Neither of us wanted to take off our clothes, for the night seemed alive with crawling things waiting to touch our naked skins. She crept into my arms, cowered there shivering.

Hours passed. I dozed off and then I was awake again. The storm was almost on top of us. The air was sultry and breathless. Its weight stifled me like a leaden pall.

I shoved up from the bed and went over to a window for a breath of air. The knock on the door behind me made me jump. I saw Karol's startled face and staring eyes start up from the bed as I went over and opened it.

It was Paula Morrison. She stood shivering in the sultry heat, clutching the folds of a dressing gown to her throat.

"Phil!" she choked. "He went down stairs—hours ago—he hasn't come back—"

I pulled her into the room. "Where's Helen Coleman?" I asked.

She shook her head. "I don't know. She isn't in her room—"

"You and Karol stay here," I muttered. I went out into the hall.

The last thunder roll grumbled away and silence lay like a held breath on the face of the night. And in that hush a noise became audible, a sly and stealthy creeping, down stairs.

"Phil!" I half shouted. And then again, "Phil—"

Phil didn't answer. A thunderbolt split on the house-roof. Silence clapped down again and against its dead tenseness I heard something else. It was a ghoulish sound, heart-stopping in the night! A voice groaned. It gurgled through bubbling blood. Its location I couldn't fix, for in the tight hollowness of the house the echoes came garbled and distant.

And then I found myself stumbling down those stairs, feeling my way in the darkness from tread to tread. That gasping and tortured wail! Where it came from, what I was going to find down there, I didn't dare to think.

Behind me I heard a noise. The girls hadn't obeyed me, they were coming, too. "Jim! Jim, don't leave me!" Karol moaned. I fumbled behind me till I felt her hand. It was a hand of ice. I twisted my arm around her and kept going.

No one was in sight at the foot of the stairs. Thunder was blasting TNT off the ridge-pole and lightning boiled through the place in a vibrating flood. We should be alone in that house, for Phil hadn't answered. But I knew that something else was there, a presence. An invisible, eerie something whose nearness made my skin tingle with racing chills.

Stealthily I crept forward, step by step. Half way across the hall . . .

The door into the living room stood right in front of me, and before it, on the floor, lay a vivid white line from the lightning that seethed through the windows on the other side. And that line was starting to widen! Seconds dragged by while it grew into a streak and the streak into a lane and upon that lane came a blot that slowly resolved itself into the shadows of something that stood on the other side.

Something, some one—but not Phil Morrison, or he would have answered me, I knew. I licked my lips, for the fear of something unspeakable was upon me. I whispered to Karol, "Get back!" I pushed her behind me and took a step toward that door.

She wound her fingers into my sleeve. She screamed: "Jim, look!" Her voice died in a stark whisper of terror.

For there on the side of that door, a hand had suddenly become visible, reaching around from the other side. The fingers curved, they clawed and clutched at the edge of the wood.

And that hand was the hand of a corpse! Its fingers were fleshless digit bones spectral blue with sulphurous fire that seemed to drip from them in trickling blobs.

I heard my breath hiss in outrush of horror. Against the wall the three of us stood, clutching at one another, while we stared at that hand.

The thing was moving, it opened and closed like a hand of life. It slid down the edge of the door and its dried bones rattled like wooden sticks.

Somewhere back in the dark, Morrison's wife was being sick on the floor. I heard Karol's teeth chattering under my ear where she had crushed her face to my shoulder. Her fingernails dug into my hand till I felt the blood trickling.

Backward I was groveling away from that thing. In the superior sureness of my book-learning I had scoffed at the tales of the miners—the walking dead. But that thing there on the other side of that door, whose fleshless claw was slowly pushing it open—what in God's name was that?

And then we relaxed. Spent and shivering, we sagged against the wall.

For that hand was gone. Without coming through into the hall, the thing that belonged to it had retreated.

I waited a minute till my legs had stopped shaking and then I made myself go over and look into that living room. What I'd find there, I didn't know . . .

The place was empty. Whatever had been in there was gone. Departed by the open window on the other side . . .

I found myself back in the hall with the two girls clinging to me.

"Phil!" Paula Morrison chattered. She hammered her hands on my chest. "We've got to find Phil—"

Phil, yes . . . I pulled myself around and stared on down the hall. All the rooms on that floor I visited, one after another. But I knew that I wouldn't find Morrison. If he had been in the house he'd have answered.

Nothing in any of those rooms . . . And then I found myself back in the hall again with Karol and Paula whimpering as they clung to my arm. "Phil! Phil!" Morrison's wife couldn't control her hysterical sobbing.

Suddenly Karol cried, her voice reedily thin and unnatural. "Jim, listen—"

There was another calm spot in the storm's tumult and out of it sobbed that moaning again, that gurgling wail. The wings of the wind whipped it away before I could even guess its location.

Another blast flogged the house with shrilling whips. The back door, right in front of us, burst open. As though pushed by an invisible hand it came swinging inward.

All the demons of hades were loose in the shrieking gale that lashed in my face. With bowed shoulders I staggered on toward the door, thinking that at least I would close it. I put out my hand to force it shut and then in the glare of the blue-white cauldron outside I caught sight of the figure there on the piazza boards.

Wind and rain blasted me, snatched the breath from my lungs as I braced myself and pushed out there. And then I was down on my knees beside that form.

The blinding glare disclosed the ashen face, the throat spurting blood through severed arteries.

I gripped that bowed face in my hands, turned it up where I could look at it again. Helen Coleman . . . She tried once to speak. A convulsive shiver racked her and she died as I lifted her and dragged her inside.

I shut the door and locked it and got a light going. My hands were shaking, my fingers all fumbling thumbs. I turned to see my wife staring down at the dead girl, her lips parted, her eyes glazed, enormous with terror.

"What did it? Who could have that to her?" she sobbed.

"No man—no human thing—"

No human thing . . . I gripped my fists and the crazy thought reeled in my brain. Ghosts, the workers had said, and I'd laughed at them. But now I had seen that hand on the door. I had seen its blue white bones stripped of flesh. I had seen that hand move!

What ghoul or what thing from beyond the grace had got in here and killed Helen? Killed her and taken Morrison away? For all over the house I searched again and he wasn't there.

At last I gave it up. I took Paula and Karol up to our room and the two girls stayed there together. I hunted around the house till I found an iron fireplace poker. Not much of a weapon to stand between us and what was out there, but still better than nothing.

Up and down the house I patrolled. Two terrors bewildered me now. The miners, without question, were the ones who had killed Sally. Terror-mad at the things that were cursing them, they had fanatically sought aid from the supernatural power of her blood to protect them. But none of those laborers had been here tonight. That hand on the door told me that it had been one of those things that had got into this house.

Those things . . . Again I pounded my brain with questions that a sane mind couldn't answer. What things? In God's name, what kind of a creature, coming from where, could have stretched that grisly claw of death out at us, and then silently withdrawn?

From room to room I paced. Every few moments I would stop and stand listening, trying to sort out the chaos of bangings and shriekings. The wind howled eerie death-song through the harp-strings of fence wire, the loose beam in the mine hoist clanked tempo to the mad orchestration.

That chaos of noises—I couldn't tell which of them were outside and which inside the house. Doors creaked, blinds slammed. Up stairs, the two girls were sobbing. Through the dark I guided myself with my hands against the walls. My fingers scraped with thin hissings. God, this darkness, these crowding walls! These hunched, swart forms that seemed to be gliding past me, intent on stealing up to Karol's room!

This night of horror that would never end!

At last I went up and sat down on the top step of the stairs outside my wife's room. For centuries it seemed I sat there, listening and waiting. My heart stabbed with its beating and cold sweat ran over my back.

Chapter Four

Madman's Loot

That night dragged past at last and a grey and aching dawn stole through the windows. I went down stairs and cooked up some breakfast and then called the girls. While we were sitting there, trying to make ourselves eat, Nils Peterson came. He hadn't any light to throw. Finally I left him with the girls while I went up to see Harkins.

The boss hadn't gone to his office yet. I found him still at his house. There was a look on his face that I didn't get as he listened to me. The man was obviously puzzled and frightened. But there was something else. Almost a gleam of sadistlike triumph, I fancied.

He bit on the shank of an unlighted cigar.

"Here's what I think is going on," he said at last. "I told you that certain parties have tried to run me out of here and get hold of this property. They haven't succeeded and this is their last try. In some way they have found out how to get into the mine without going down through the shaft—some of the caves around in the hills lead right back into the workings. They have put some thugs in there to kill the men, to dress up like ghosts, talk in those thin twitterings and all the rest. They know that those laborers are ignorant and superstitious. They are playing on their fears, trying to panic them and ruin me that way."

I pitched my cigarette into a corner.

"Whether they are or whether they're not doesn't interest me," I grated. "What I'm thinking about is that three of us four engineers have disappeared and that two of our wives were murdered last night. I'm getting out of here. Here's my resignation and I'll thank you to unlock that gate."

My employer looked at me. He shook his head.

"No, I don't think you are, West," he said.

"What do you mean, you don't think!" I exclaimed. "This isn't a prison—"

"No, it isn't a prison," Harkins said slowly. "But right now I don't want anyone leaving here and telling stories outside. Frankly, I can't afford to have those other parties get an idea of how hard they are hitting me. I'm sorry, West, but I'm afraid that you will have to stay here till this business blows over."

I felt my face tighten.

"You're telling me that I've got to stay in this place when the next person to be killed may be my wife!" I half shouted. "You're crazy. Give me the keys to that gate or I'll take them away from you."

Harkins smiled thinly. "I wouldn't advise you to try it," he said. His hand slipped into the top of his half-open desk drawer and I saw the blue snout of a big automatic.

I stood there and cursed him while he smiled that thin mockery again.

"But let me assure you," he said. "I'm going to work on this right now myself. I'm going to take a picked crew and go down and ransack that mine from end to end. I'm sure that we will find whoever is responsible for this before night."

And there wasn't any more. I realized the futility of trying to argue with ten inches of cold steel and I left him.

I went back to my house and I was sick with terror of a menace uglier than any that I'd yet felt. For in that sinister gleam of Harkins' eyes I had read treachery. Not because was afraid of what we might broadcast on the outside, but because for some reason of his own, he wanted to keep Karol and me there inside of that fence.

Karol! And now I remembered how I'd seen him looking at her. Time after time with a flame of coveting hunger in his oily gaze. Was that why he wanted us there, because he knew that I would be killed, and then that he and she . . .

God, I had to get her away from here before another night came! Somehow, some way . . . I racked my brains and my thought beat themselves against the bars of my prison. I wanted to fling myself on that fence, rend it apart with my naked hands. And I had another idea, that I would take Karol away from the house, carry her out in the dunes and hide her among those tangled hills, where she would be safe.

And then I realized how hopeless that was, how hopeless anything was. Safe? Where could she be safe? Where inside of this fence did safety lie for her, for me?

The day dragged past. I saw Harkins and his special gang start down into the mine. Karol and Paula and I pottered around the house. There was nothing to do but wait for night and what it might bring, whether of madness or death.

As I look back on that now, I think that perhaps I was wrong to have let Harkins best me so easily. Maybe I ought to have jumped him there in his house, despite his gun, and put up a fight for those keys. But if he had shot me, Karol wouldn't have had anyone.

Hell, what's the use of thinking what I might have done? In situations like that, when death leers at you from a dozen angles, you don't know which play is the wisest to make—until afterwards.

The searching party came back from the mine just before dark. On his way to his house, Nils stopped in. They had hunted the mine over, he said, and they hadn't found a thing. There was no creature there, living or dead.

It had grown dark while I stood outside the house talking to Nils. I went back inside again and locked the door. From room to room, all through the cottage, I travelled, lighting the oil lamps. Karol stood watching me, her eyes enormous with dread. Paula Morrison sat crouched in a chair, talking to herself and slowly tearing a handkerchief into shreds.

The evening wore on and we waited. Waited for what, we didn't know. We stayed close together; we couldn't bear to have one another out of our sights. The old dried floors creaked under our feet. The dim kerosene lamps spread only pale halos of light. Shadows crouched in the corners. Beyond half open doors the angular darkness seemed crowded with lurking forms. A big cottonwood tree with overhanging branches grew close to the house. The scouring of its leaves on the roof as the wind stirred them was like something crawling up there . . .

Close to ten o'clock it must have been when a knock came at the door. The face I saw outside as I opened it belonged to one of the clerks up at the office. White-faced, he stood with both hands clutching the door-frame.

"Harkins wants to see you up at the office, quick!" he burst out. "He's going to let you go. He's going to open the gate!

"I'll stay with your wife," he said, as he saw me hesitate. "He told me to. It won't take only a minute—"

I didn't stop for my hat. I said to Karol: "Keep the doors locked," and ran out of the house.

Just about two minutes it took me to get over to Harkins' house. He gazed at me, blank-faced, as I half-shouted my inquiry at him.

He shook his head. "I didn't send that man. I'm not going to let you out—"

I didn't stop to question him. I spun around and stormed out of his house with the door left wide open behind me, and I ran as I had never run before. It had been a trick—a ruse to get me out of the house and get Karol there alone! And that messenger had been one of Harkins' clerks. He must have sent him!

Lungs bursting, I raced up the steps of the cottage four at a time.

The front door was open. Beyond, I could see the lamp flames wavering in the breeze. And out of that empty house there blew toward me a breath of horror beyond words to describe.

I ran inside and I stormed through those rooms. Wildly I called Karol's name. Echoes answered me. That wind that blew wasn't a breeze of the air, it was a gale of coldness within my brain that froze it in utter and elemental fear.

Out of the house I stumbled at last. In the roadway in front of it I stood, gazing around. Near-madness must have touched me then, for I seemed to see her. Every shadow and jutting rock took on human form. From one to another I raced. I snatched at them, I felt their ridges under my hands as I choked out her name. They weren't Karol, those stones and shadow blots didn't answer me.

And then I found myself racing over that curving and rutted road that led to the workers' village. Those beasts who had killed Sally and Helen were the ones who would want Karol's blood.

From house to house of that village I ran, shoving the doors open without knocking and bursting inside. I visited a dozen of them before at last I halted, amazed.

For those houses were empty! Not one of the miners was left in the place. Not only the men, but their women, too. Every one of those companions whom Harkins had put there under the thin euphemism of "housekeepers" was gone.

I got myself out of that ghost-town of echoing hovels and back down the road I went stumbling. The night was thick and choking around me, in its black loneliness an errant wind crooned as it wandered among the dunes.

Karol gone! The words hammered a death-knell in my brain. Horror that seemed impossible, too hideous to be true! Sally Evarts' dead body, that bowl of blood! Morrison gone . . . Helen Coleman's pulped throat, and now Karol . . . Those women, too—where had they taken them all, in the dead of night? Taken them where and for what unspeakable purpose!

Out of the shadows, Nils Peterson came running toward me.

"Your wife—I know where she is!" he panted. "Dey have taken her down into de mine!" He whirled, dragging me after him.

I raced at his side. I didn't try to talk. I was past talking. With every discovery horror grew thicker. Karol taken down into the mine! Taken down there for what?

Swiftly the distance slipped away. Six thousand feet we had
to go down, more than a mile into the bowels of the earth.

Soon I was aware of the heat, the humid and stifling,
breath-taking pressure that made working the mine so peril-
ous. It was this more than the greed for cheap labor that had
driven Harkins to import his jackal help for jobs where no
ordinary workman would risk his life.

A red light glowed in the wall and the car came to rest.

I snapped on my electric torch. The white beam showed
that we stood in the middle of a big circular cavity hewn
from solid rock. At intervals, openings of side openings of
side passages cut into the walls, crookedly leering mouths in
the skull of a stone monster.

With held breath I listened. Karol was here—somewhere
here. Close enough that I might hear her voice, maybe her
death cry? No—only the heart-beats that drummed in my
ears and the silence which pressed me with the weight of
tangible force.

Beckoning to Nils and me, Harkins turned into one of the
side passages. Twisting and turning, the damp and slippery
floor sloped under our feet. There were angles and corners,
holes where other tunnels came in, heaps of rock and rubble
piled in confusion.

A vast labyrinthine maze was this ancient mine. Here one
might wander for days. But Harkins seemed sure of himself.
Did he know where he was going, did he know where Karol
was?

Deeper and deeper we pressed into the gut of the earth-
bowel. The heat became oven-like, the weight of the air was
a ton-heavy hand. Sweat streamed from me, the steaming
vacuum sucked the breath from my lungs till I panted emp-
tily.

"Where are we going? Where are you taking me?" I gasped
to Harkins. "Karol isn't here. No one could live here—"

Over his shoulder he muttered: "Shut up and keep going.
You'll find your wife—"

Down and still down . . . Wilder, more sinister, grew the
way. Towering black cliffs glistened with water. Over the

rim of the yard-wide shelf where we walked I peered into bottomless depths. Mad, ghoulish place! The crazy thought surged in me. Close down now we must be to the roof of hell. It should be easy for those things to crawl up through the crevices . . .

Suddenly I checked my stumbling advance. I stood motionless, jaws a-gape. For I had heard it, Karol's voice! And it hadn't sounded from ahead, the way we were going, but back behind.

"Harkins!" I shouted. "I heard my wife! You're taking us wrong! She's back the other way—"

My yell brought Harkins whirling around. "The other way! Turn around!" I started to cry again, and then I jumped away. For Harkins came toward me in a flying leap. Murderous rage knotted his face and in his hand a club whirled aloft.

The rush caught me off balance, cold by surprise. I tried to duck under his swing while with both knotted fists I swung for his vitals.

The blows landed, but they weren't enough. I felt the stabbing agony of the club crashing against my skull. Harkins' foot kicked me in the mouth as he jumped over my prostrate form. I heard Nils' cry of fear, cut off in a gasping moan as the club fell again. And then crimson blackness swallowed me.

Whether it was minutes or centuries before I opened my eyes again, I couldn't guess. I drew my hand over my splitting skull. Groaning, I rolled over and shoved up on my hands and knees.

For an instant I rested there, swaying from side to side while nausea surged in me. Nils . . . A painful yard I crawled to the spot where I had seen him go down. He wasn't there. Dully I reasoned—Harkins must have taken him away.

Harkins! So Harkins himself was the boss of this horror! The owner of the mine, doing these things that were ruining his business, stopping his production and that at the end would certainly bring him afoul of the law—why?

That was a question that no sane man could answer. But I

believed that at last I knew the answer—because Harkins himself was mad. Mad, undoubtedly, nothing else would account for the facts. But not too mad to bring Nils and me down into these depths to get rid of us . . .

On my hands and knees I squatted there in the darkness and a specter of terror sat by me, gibbering. Karol! Karol and Harkins! My darling somewhere there alone, free to the will of those beasts! Just as he had struck, I had heard her scream. God, that tortured and desperate wail! Where it had come from, I couldn't guess save in a general way, for it had rung garbled and echoing through the maze.

I spat from my fire-hot lips and essayed to push myself up to my feet. I was a little stronger, I struggled upright and stood sagging against the wall. In frantic hope I listened again. If I could only hear her once more, just one little sound to tell me which way!

Karol I didn't hear, but another sound came throbbing from far away. In that dead of night it was a weird, a spine-tingling noise! The measured thumping, rhythmic metallic clanking of the stamp mill! The huge contrivance with its grinding rolls into which the quartz rock was fed to crush it into smaller bits—running now at midnight, when the work of the mine was stopped!

Working, why? Gnashing its blunted steel teeth together to crush what?

Chapter Five

Spoil of the Walking Dead

The macabre thuds of that machine guided my steps as I flew up those twisting ways. Louder it swelled as I approached, till its slogging roar deafened me in its beating against the walls.

At last I swung around an angle of rock. I swayed one more step in advance and halted, transfixed.

I stood at the entrance of a cave, a big and high-roofed opening carved in the rock by the forces of time. In the glare of torches stuck into niches in the walls, the dark bulk of the stamp mill loomed gaunt and sinister.

As a background to that grinding monster there was a sea of wild and half-mad faces and staring eyes—eyes that glared with hatred and flamed with fear. More than fifty men, all the pick and shovel hands who lived in the miners' village, gathered in a half circle around the walls.

My gaze whipped from them to the knot of white figures who stood between them and the machine. A madhouse I had come to, for those were the women of that same village, the "housekeepers." Stark naked they had been stripped and tied hand and foot, tied and gagged. Motionless they huddled there. Now and then one of them lifted a shuddering glance, only to drop it the next instant while she grovelled in terror.

For up on the platform built around the mouth of the chute stood two figures. Near-naked, streaming sweat, their muscles bulged in the torch light. Fanatical light of sadist-ecstasy convulsed their faces, madly they laughed.

A cinema of the Inferno! For now two other men down below picked up one of the nude women and passed her up to them. A human log, they shoved her, kicking, into the mouth of the hopper.

Down the steep slide she went. One last shriek rang from her as her gag slipped away and the steel teeth caught her between their revolving drums. And from that clanking Moloch came awful cracking noises that raised the hair on the back of my neck!

Down at the other end of that chute, where the broken stones were supposed to emerge . . . Something else was coming out there, a ruddy stream like the yield of a wine press. A wine press of human grapes! A tub stood there, into it that crimson trickling flowed.

I covered my eyes with my hand to shut out that loathsome sight. And then I snatched them away again, to sweep my gaze more closely around that circle of faces, over the naked white forms in the middle. Karol! God, if Karol were here!

And then my eyes seemed to sear with the horror of what I saw, for she was there! Not standing in the middle with the rest of the women, but alone, by herself over against the wall. They had taken her clothes away, too, trussed her and gagged her. Nude before the profanation of those lusting eyes, she sat gazing at the crimson harvest trickling from the mouth of the chute.

Savagely I cursed, my heart seemed to turn to a clod of ice. For an instant, a wild impulse surged in me to spring out into that circle, sweep those monsters aside and snatch her into my arms. But I knew how hopeless that was—how hopeless anything was now. One against that throng, I would be overwhelmed, torn limb from limb before I could touch her.

A moment, I say, I stood wavering. And then I stiffened, in amazement I stared.

For another figure had sprung into the midst of the circle—Nils! Like a master-demon in hell, he stood with the sleeves of his open-necked shirt rolled back over his bulging muscles, his eyes glittering as he watched that clanking mill.

He waved his arms. "Kill! Kill! Kill all your women, and by the sacrifice of their blood you will be saved!" he thundered at the wild-eyed mob. "Kill men, kill women! Kill all those who have been your oppressors! Kill Harkins and all his crew! Bathe in their blood and you shall be free! The dead ghosts fear the fresh blood of the living. They will go and leave you alone!"

Bewilderment stunned me. Nils! Nils himself the fiend of this horror! Nils whom I trusted, while in my blindness I deemed Harkins the villain!

The old man's voice rose again over the grind of the crushers. His beard jutted, through his parted lips his teeth glistened with spittle.

"And here is the one whom I have saved for myself, the youngest and prettiest!" he roared. "Her blood is the freshest, its charm will be strongest—"

I saw him turn then toward Karol, saw his red hands reach toward her. He seized her, he crushed her nakedness in his arms.

Something blew its fuse then in my brain. I let out a yell and through that door I went lunging.

And even as Nils heard my voice and spun around, they were on me from all sides. Savage faces loomed in the murky glare. Heavy fists swung at me, pounded against my face, my head, my chest.

Twice I went down beneath those blows. Twice I managed to wriggle out of that bone-crushing embrace. They piled on top of me and held me down by sheer strength of numbers,

Once again I kicked them off and lunged to my feet. I hammered and pummeled them, I butted and kneed them, I sent my fists and then my knees crashing into their vitals. I dug my thumbs into their eyes. A black-browed ape came whirling at me with a blazing torch. I snatched it out of his hand and I used that on his head till it was gone.

And it wasn't enough. They were too many; too strong for me. At the end half a dozen of them were sitting on me. I felt rough, cruel hands pick me up, carry me and at last fling me against the wall.

I sagged there, bruised and panting with the hands of those giants holding me, and it was Nils who leaned over me, savagely laughing. I noticed again that the thickness of speech that had contributed to his appearance of ignorance had vanished.

"You are an educated man, but you were as big a fool as the others," he grated down at me. "You thought that I was a common laborer. I am not. I am a college graduate, a trained mining engineer like yourself."

His sweat-glistening face jerked in uncontrollable fury, his words poured insanely.

"I had a son, a mining engineer also. Harkins hired him to survey this mine before he bought it. My son discovered that lost lode of virgin gold down in the depths—something that you, with all your cleverness, never found out about.

"My boy had a bride. Harkins wanted her. Also he didn't want anyone alive but himself to know of that lode, the richest part of the mine. He framed an accident down here, my boy was killed by a falling rock. Alter that Harkins married Stella. He married her and abused her so that she killed herself in a year.

"Harkins had never seen me, he didn't know that I existed. I got a job here, I made myself useful and got promoted to foreman. It was I who got hold of those miners, ripped them to pieces and sent them back to the top to panic the others. It was I who forced Harkins' clerk under threat of death, to go and tell you that Harkins wanted to see you. Harkins had begun to suspect me. He led us into a remote part of the mine, intending to kill us both. But I got the best of him in the fight after he had knocked you unconscious and brought him here. I killed those friends of yours, Evarts and Coleman and Morrison. I didn't have anything against them you say? No—only that they were Harkins' tools, they kept his mine running. And I had sworn to destroy him, him and everything that he touched."

The madman straightened, drew back from me.

"Destroy—as I am going to destroy you and your woman!" He turned to Karol, he swept her into his arm. He held her there while he caressed her. God, before my eyes he slid his hands over her soft nudeness! "But before I kill her, I am going to have her, do you understand, I'm going to have her for my wife! You will stand there and watch me and then you will die. You and she and Harkins there—" (—for the first time now I espied the form of the mine owner sitting trussed hand and foot against the wall—) "—you will all die in my wine-press, and your blood—"

What else he said I didn't hear, for terror sickened me. I yelled curses at him, madly I fought against the huge figures that gripped me. He laughed again and smashed me across the mouth.

I looked over at Karol. She met my gaze and her eyes smiled at me, smiled to say that she loved me. In my anguish I sobbed, I strained my wrists at those gripping fingers till I felt the sticky wetness of trickling blood.

Suddenly the mob's chorus of shoutings died like a candle flame pinched between finger and thumb. And against the background of that million-volt stillness I heard a sound—

that voice which I'd heard once before in the dusk by the slag pile! Some one—something—was talking out of sight there in the tunnel. And it talked in the thin and treble twitterings of a bird!

And then there were two of the voices. Across the black and velvet emptiness of the terror there they crawled like wavering threads of light.

No one was moving or speaking now in the cave. Only that the miners shuffled and huddled closer together around the wall. With fear-stiffened faces they gazed into the shadows beyond the door. Someone had shut off the motor and even the clanking of the stamp mill was stilled.

And out of that aching hush came the husking of footsteps. Grit, grit . . . Not feet of normal men, those same unnatural jerkings and draggings that I'd heard before, scouring rasp of a snake's coils! Those footsteps and those same reedy chirpings!

Closer and closer—And now, faces, two countenances that peered in around the mouth of the cave. Stiff and glassy those faces, the skin tight as parchment stretched over skulls! Yellow scales matted that skin. Its flesh was half eaten away, it hung in patches from skeleton bones that glowed yellow green with phosphorescence of decay.

Step by step those two things advanced, they were coming into the cave. Their hands stretched toward the miners. Hands that were fleshless bones aglow with spectral radiance.

A sigh of terror breathed around the mob. Livid, eyes bulged to the whites, the miners were shrinking away. Their voices guttered hoarse cursings, imprecations of utter and inchoate fear.

But over me, Nils was bending down, laughing slyly, muting his whispers so that no others should hear.

"Frightened, mister college graduate?" he sneered. "I'm surprised that you haven't guessed. Those things are not ghosts, they are lepers! Harkins kidnapped them from the Cold Mountain colony five hundred miles away. He brought them here and put them down in the deeps where the virgin gold vein is, almost another thousand feet below where we are. It is so deathly hot down there that not even the bohunks can stick it. But the lepers do. That's why Harkins got them. Their sensation-nerves are gone, they can't feel anything. Down there in that furnace they sleep, eat, work—and die. Slaves. No one ever sees them except me and one other inside man that Harkins trusted.

"Those two out there now are a couple that I let out to wander around and play ghosts for the miners. That pair up there on the top were the same. It was a perfect set-up for me to convince the men that they were cursed by ghosts and then work on their fears till they were ready to kill for me. Those men who were gone for months and went back to the top with the sores—I kept them down here and gave them something in their drinking water to make them break out that way. Of course a real case of leprosy takes years to develop—"

The Lepers were coming into the cave, three of them now. Three swaying skeletons, to all outward appearances, a trio of emissaries sent up from hell, ghosts of the walking dead. Backward and still further back from them the miners groveled. Their eyes were gaunt caverns of animal terror, spittle drooled from their sagging lips. The grip of something hideous held the very air in the place, gibbering panic of men before horrors from another world.

And then suddenly the suspense burst in a mad outburst. "The young one! The young woman! Her blood is stronger, it will protect us!" Shouts rang through the cave. The mob whirled. Bunched together, they came rushing toward Karol.

One desperate effort Nils made to turn back that revenging horde and keep Karol out of their hands—keep his particular prize for himself. In a screaming surge they overbore him, hurled him out of their path. A dozen grimy hands snatched out for Karol. High over their heads she was lifted. The murky glare of the torches shone on her nakedness, a victim of old Carthage born aloft to the statue of Moloch.

That was all that I saw consciously. And then another part

of me that had nothing to do with saneness or reason took possession, sent me lunging against the grip of that pair who held me with the fury of madness. I wasn't sane then, I was a screaming and cursing primitive who fought with nature's savage weapons. With a power of fury that wasn't my own, I flung those two mighty men stumbling. And then I was out in the midst of that pack, fighting to get there to Karol.

The mob was thick in front of me, their figures blocked me away from her. I grabbed them by the hair of the head and yanked them back; when they wheeled to stare at me I drove in short and deadly blows that crumpled them, gasping. Some of them essayed to fight. With my thumbs in their eyes I sent them screaming and pawing.

But it wasn't enough. There were too many of them. Closer up to the stamp mill those who held Karol were rushing her. I heard the rolls clanking again, I saw the black faces of the two on the scaffold grin in fanatical exulting as they reached down for her.

And then I was aware of another form in that whirlpool of frenzy. Nils, dark faced with rage, pounding his way in toward me. I left off from the others, I whirled to meet him. We closed, and my outlashing fist crashed on his bared throat, sent him reeling and gasping.

Before his sagging form hit the ground, I was bending over him. My hands wrenched at his clothes, seeking the pistol whose butt I had seen gleaming under his coat as we talked. My fingers closed over it, I yanked it out and spun around as the rearward part of the mob suddenly swooped in descent on me.

The nearest of them I killed with my first shots. A yammering ring opened around me. I whirled back toward that roaring sound where the stamp mill was grinding its teeth.

I didn't wait to use the pistol against those on the ground again. For Karol was up there. The two naked feed-tenders held her limp whiteness in their arms. They were bending forward, shoving her head into the chute.

I was panting, trembling and out of breath. I whispered a prayer as I swung the gun up toward them, a prayer that God would guide my aim . . .

The gun roared twice and two hairy forms came pitching down onto the floor. And then I was running and hurdling, climbing and pawing my way over their shoulders, their heads, to get there. I vaulted up on to that platform, I snatched Karol's knees. Out of that passage down which she was starting to slide I pulled her free.

I won't take the time to tell you all the rest of what happened that night. How with my now empty gun I cowed those men, kept them off, finally drove them out of the cave. How I went over and set Harkins free and how at last we got back to the top.

How I backed my boss against a wall and took his keys from him . . . How I locked him up a prisoner in his own office while I got on the telephone and talked with the sheriff . . .

And how later, the Law came and together we explored the hidden deeps of the mine till we found the den of those lepers and took them back where they belonged.

And how at the very last, Karol and I drew out our bank account and took a vacation—traveled as far as our money could take us from Harkins' mine and its horrors.

ARMS OF THE FLAME GODDESS

The Precursors of horror are sometimes strangely innocuous. Just a string of dancing dolls was the thing that brought the cold fire to kill five of our friends and send Helen behind madhouse bars. Paper dolls such as children scissor out of folded newspapers . . .

None of us had expected to meet death that day when we went out for a late afternoon stroll in the woods around Monmouth mountain. Just a summer day's jaunt—but it was an outing that was to lead us into the valley of hell!

After rambling for an hour or so, laughing and chatting, the six of us came out of the trees on to the crest of a little knoll. And then, at the sight which suddenly leaped at us, we came to a standstill and I for one felt my very spine go cold.

Fifty yards away a man stood with whips of thorns in his hands. Save for a dirty rag twisted about his loins, he was stark naked. He was lashing himself with the whips. The blows brought rivulet of blood trickling over his pipestem limbs and at each stroke he leaped high in the air. Foam spattered his face and his eyes blazed with a maniacal glare.

He was muttering some unintelligible gibberish under his breath. What he seemed to be saying, in a hoarse, hysterical croak, was:

"Blood! Blood and fire to wash me from sin!"

It was a revolting spectacle. We had all heard that this remote region of mountain valleys was a hotbed of the Penitentes, a cult of self-torturers who had imported their weird beliefs from Mexico—religious fanatics who sought hope of forgiveness of sins through punishment of the body here upon earth. But this was the first evidence we had had that the tales contained an element of truth.

We all stood spellbound an instant and then I broke away

from the others. Anger at sight of such human beastliness needled me. I rushed up to him, gripped him by a naked, sweat-glistening shoulder and spun him around.

"You fool!" I yelled. "What are you doing!"

He whirled to snarl through bared teeth. He brought his thorn whip slashing across my face. As I stumbled away, he jerked from my clutch and went galloping into the bushes.

The others came up and we all ran after him. There was no sane reason for this, for we knew the danger of meddling in the affairs of the clannish and hate-ridden folk of these valleys. It was some urge of horrified curiosity that sent us beating through the underbrush on his heels.

A dip in the ground shut him from our view. A moment later we came into the open again at the edge of a little glade. We rushed a step forward and then froze in our tracks. Ed Bradshaw's voice came in gagged husking:

"Great God, what is that?"

The man we had been chasing lay motionless on the ground in the midst of the grassy plot. He was dead. But as we stole forward, we knew that it wasn't the flogging that had killed him. He had been burned to death! His body was charred to a blackened husk crusted over with a queer hard shell that flaked off in crackling fragments as Ed poked at with his foot.

For a long instant then there wasn't a sound save the eerie croon of the wind in the trees and our tightened breathings. This was incredible. Two minutes before we had seen him running—and now his carcass lay charred to a cinder as though it had been exposed to the blast of a holocaust!

Helen—my wife—slid her hand into mine. It was a hand of ice. George Thornton's voice came thick with bewilderment:

"He's done to a crisp. But there isn't any fire. The grass around him isn't even burned."

We stared from the dead man to one another's whitened faces. No human hand, it seemed, could have killed him, only a power conjured from sorcery's depths. He had burned to death there where he lay—but the grass stems around him still waving and green! In vain I told myself that I was a fool, tried to use reason to convince myself that it was some kind of a grisly hoax. Educated man though I was, I couldn't, for this was beyond reason.

It was the voice of Nathalie, Thornton's wife that snapped us out of our horrified staring and brought us wheeling around. Nathalie was a carefree and jolly sort, buxom, blue-eyed and always laughing. But now she stood queerly white, staring down at the ground. Fear was in her face.

"Look! Oh, look at that!" she cried.

It was because they were so small that in our excitement we hadn't noticed the line of figures half buried in weeds and grass. We saw now that they were dancing dolls, long strings of six-inch high cutouts linked arm in arm. From their nests of green stems they peered up with pert impish faces of sprites evoked from the nether world. Such things as evil-minded children might have scissored and left to enclose the form of the dead man in a magic ring. But no children had been here—no one had been here.

Mary Bradshaw let out a cry, her voice reedily thin and unnatural.

"Don, let's go! Let's get out of here. I'm afraid!"

We were all afraid. Horror rode on the cold that flowed out of the mountain caves to tingle at the roots of our spines. "Yes, we'll go," I muttered. I slid my arm around Helen's slim waist, started to turn her away and then stiffened. For the undergrowth around us had suddenly come alive. Hunched squatting forms could be seen, with gnome-like faces, as though a vent from hell had poured a horde of its denizens up onto the earth. Their hands clutched sticks and clubs. The bushes rustled as they crept forward. Still sheer terror held us transfixed till a cry suddenly tocsinned:

"Kill! Kill! Burn them to death!"

We turned then and fled—fled from the picture of a dead man inside a ring of paper dolls, from the yells of those who wanted to do likewise to us. I don't know how we managed to keep ahead of them through the half mile of wood road

out to the place where we had parked our car on the highway, for terror of nightmare seemed rooting our feet to the
ground. The last hundred yards, I snatched Helen up into my
arms and carried her and Thornton and Bradshaw did the
same with their wives.

The sun was close to setting as we dashed out to see the
machine standing at the edge of the road. Yet there was light
enough to show us the addition that had been made to it
since we had left it there—a string of paper dolls looped
across the front of the windshield.

I yanked the things off and flung them on to the ground.
We piled into the car without a word. Sweat clammed the
palm of my shaking hand as I fumbled the key into the lock
of the ignition.

I tramped on the gas and sent the car lurching and skidding
around the sharp turns of the narrow road. Fast as I drove, it
wasn't swiftly enough to shake us free of the terror that raced
at our sides, that seemed to snatch at us from the shadow
blots rolling down from the hills like swollen carcasses of
octopi.

We were returning to the house of one of the natives where
we had engaged accommodations for the week or so that we
had expected to be here. The business that had brought us to
Monmouth Valley had started when Helen and I had been
induced to join the other four friends who were with us in
buying as a speculation a large tract of woodland property.
That had been some years before. I knew that the timber
standing on our land was of considerable value. But I had
opposed their suggestions to cut and market it. I knew this
region hereabouts and I hated the dark solitudes of the ridges
and gloomy ravines. I feared the ignorance and sullen cruelty
of its natives.

But when there came to us a report of an engineer that
signs of oil were apparent in several places, the importunities
of my wife and the others became too insistent to stand
against. My first suggestion had been for the other two men
to come with me to investigate the truth of the reports. But

the girls vetoed the idea of being left out. "I'm an owner as much as you are, and I'm going, too!" Helen had exclaimed, her eyes sparkling.

That was like Helen. Petite, brown eyed and vivacious, she was a live-wire of eager vitality. For the five years of our marriage she had been my partner in everything—mind, soul and body. I loved her with respect for her fine brain, devotion to her loyalty and a hunger for her lush, perfect womanhood that held still a lover's ardent heat.

The other wives too had insisted on coming and so we had made up the party. We had arrived three days before and from the information we had so far gathered, the prediction of buried riches seemed to have something. It looked as though we might be in for a clean-up.

But I couldn't be easy in mind. The natives hated us, strangers coming to disturb the vice-ridden isolation in which they delighted. In the squalid little village which formed their metropolis, something foul and obscene seemed to breathe in the very air. When I saw the sin-bitten countenances and piggy eyes of its inhabitants fastened on Helen, I would have given a million if she hadn't come.

And now the dead man in the woods, and the paper dolls. And those dolls, too, across the front of our car . . . What sense in that macabre mingling of childish toys and hideous death? It was the revolting prank of a ghoul. I looked down to meet Helen's eyes turned up to mine, and I knew that the smile I strove to make reassuring was twisted and white.

The house to which we were returning was the home of Frank Leadbetter and his wife, who had been recommended by our only friend in town, lawyer Emery Paave. Supper was ready when we had garaged the car in the barn and gone into the house, with our two hosts awaiting our arrival in the kitchen.

Leadbetter was a gangling bean-pole of a countryman, with tallow-white face that sloped, chinless, into the open neck of his faded blue shirt. He had a shock of slicked-down red hair and pale blue parrot eyes above a hooked beak of a nose. Big as he was, he was dominated into cringing subservience by his acid-tongued little shrew of a wife. Maria Leadbetter could have served as a pattern of womanhood at its most re-pellent—a face dark and forbidding as a tomahawk, with ro-dent black eyes under greasy tangles of hair that looked as though it had never known the ministrations of a comb.

We ate without much conversation, for the memory of what had happened lay like something dead in our stomachs. Finally I leaned toward the farmer and suddenly asked:

"Did you ever hear of a man being burned to death without any fire?"

The man's fork dropped clattering to the table. He shot me a glassy-eyed stare. He lifted a big white hand, matted with reddish hairs, to paw at the wattled flesh under his gullet.

"He didn't pay up," he managed to mutter at last. "They hexed him to burn."

"Whom didn't he pay?" I exclaimed. "Pay what?"

For a long moment, while Leadbetter stared at me, there wasn't a word spoken. Bradshaw sat motionless, his square heavy face with the mop of black hair tensely alert. Thorn-ton's lean, intellectual countenance with the brilliant blue eyes was sharp as a hound's on the scent.

Whether the farmer would have told us more, I do not know. But his wife, standing behind at the stove, half turned to rasp out a cry discordant as a raven's croak. Leadbetter flinched as though he had been lashed by a whip. And after that he wouldn't utter another word.

The meal was finished in silence. Rising from the table, I left the house and went out on the piazza. I wanted a chance to try to focus my thoughts, to try to figure some sense out of these fantasies. In a moment Helen joined me, to wrap both of her arms around one of mine and huddle against me.

It might have been five or six minutes that we stood there, staring at the black wall of the forest only a short distance away. And then I heard my wife's breath in a swift indraw-ing as her grip tightened around my arm.

Out there among the trees, lights were moving, pale will-o'-the-wisps that flitted through the gloom like torches of

ethereal fire. And then came something more inedible yet.
For the fire seemed to take on the shapes of girls dancing—
linked hand in hand like the paper dolls! Slim nude shapes
that swayed in spectral minuet. And now they seemed to be
beckoning to me, luring, taunting, with an invitation of
Circe-like wantonness.

Foul, unclean things were whispering, I felt their snaky
crawling across my brain. For I was aware of an amazing
emotion, a longing to go there to those girls!

I knew a cold clutching of incredulous fear. I as an educated man, couldn't believe in any rot of supernatural powers
as was driving the Leadbetters cold with fear. But what could
have happened to me to make me so unlike myself, to make
me sweat with unnatural desire to clutch those naked girls in
my clasp? It was as though the hex sign of the dolls on my
car, despite my disbelief in them, had distilled a subtle poison into my soul.

What dreadful thing might have taken place the next instant I don't dare to think. I was tugging impatiently at
Helen's hands to free myself when steps sounded behind and
Bradshaw's voice came in a gagging shout from the doorway. What he husked out in terror was:

"Collier, come in here! For God's sake, come into the
house!"

His voice sounded insane devoid of meaning, it rose from a
strangled sobbing to lash the air in dull iterations.

Chapter Two

They Kill Without Hands

A scream tocsinned from inside as we turned to run after
him. It came from a room up at the head of the stairs. We
saw Mary Bradshaw's face peering down over her husband's
shoulder, and the next moment we were up on the landing
too.

A few minutes before, it seemed, Thornton had excused

himself to come up here. Wondering what had kept him when he didn't return, Nathalie had come to see. She had found—what we saw there in the middle of the floor.

We knew that it must be Thornton, the platinum wrist watch on his arm told us that. But the face that looked up at us wasn't his. It wasn't—human. It was a jet cinder, a shrunken and blackened skull burned hard as iron with rows of white teeth in sardonic grinning between what was left of the lips. The rest of him hadn't been touched, his clothes were unscorched. And no fire had been there, for the bare boards around him weren't even singed.

I stood there with my fingernails biting into my palms and I wanted to yell out my horror. Helen's mouth opened to speak, but the rasped croakings that came from it conveyed nothing save utter terror. She threw herself into my arms, shaking hysterically, her hands clawing my shoulders.

"Oh, what did it? What killed him like that, without any-one's hearing?" she finally managed to gasp.

I didn't answer her. I was just a common man, as well in-formed as the average, as open to reason. But this—I put it out of my mind. I wouldn't allow myself to think what I would have to if I thought at all.

Steps became audible on the stairs and the face of Maria Leadbetter showed in the doorway. Her huge husband scuffed dog-like at her heels. He took one look at what lay on the floor and went green. His mouth made gulping mo-tions like those of a fish and then he gasped:

"It's *them!* They've been here! Been in the house—"

His wife didn't utter a word. She shot a glance at Thornton and then she whirled and went clattering down stairs. She was muttering some unintelligible farrago under her breath. What she seemed to be croaking was a rigmarole of dis-jointed phrases, over and over like a charm.

I pulled Helen out of the room and then they were all get-ting out of there. We didn't even lift Thornton to lay him on the bed. None of us could endure the thought of touching that twisted thing that we knew would squirm and crackle under our touch.

There was only one thing to be done now, and we all knew what it was. But Helen voiced it first. She moaned:

"Don, take me away from here! Get me out of this place!"

I looked at Bradshaw. He said:

"I'll get one of the cars. You folks get busy and pack what you will need for overnight."

He hurried down stairs. I stayed with the girls while Helen and Mary packed for themselves and Nathalie, too. Thornton's wife was on the verge of a crack-up. She sagged down on the edge of Mary's bed and sat swaying to and fro, racking out those horrible tearless sobs.

It took Helen maybe two minutes to fling a few necessaries into a couple of bags. When the suitcases were ready I picked them up and preceded the girls down stairs. The front door was open. Maria Leadbetter was outside working feverishly with a shovel. She was digging a hole in front of the step. Just as we came into sight she dropped into it a freshly killed chicken. And with it was silver—a handful of trinkets and cheap jewelry—and a wisp of hairs from the tail of a horse.

"What are those for?" I said.

She looked up at me, face contorted, wild-eyed.

"The hexes can't git over 'em," she panted. "I'm a-goin' to put some more at the back door an' lay knives on the winder sills."

The spot of cold on my spine slid to my scalp. Where were we? In twentieth century America or back in the Dark Ages?

There wasn't long to think about that, for suddenly Bradshaw appeared around the side of the house. He barged up to the door and stood gripping its frame, face sweat-beaded and whiter than wax.

"We can't make it!" he gasped. "They've ruined the cars. Tires slashed, ignition ripped out, gas tanks split open—it will take hours in a repair shop to get them rolling."

For an instant no word was spoken. Something sightless and cold seemed to pass over us, the shadow of death. Then Mary Bradshaw screamed:

"We're too late! They're going to kill us! We're all going

to burn to death!"

Finally we hauled ourselves around back into the house
and into the grubby little sitting room. We stood there and
tried to think what to do. Walking was out of the question,
we were twenty miles from the nearest town. There was only
one man in the place to whom we could appeal—lawyer
Emery Paave. And he was down in the village a couple of
miles away.

Finally it was decided that one of us—it chanced to be me
who was picked by the fall of a coin—should try to get there
and see him and also the sheriff. It was agreed that the three
girls and Bradshaw should all sit together down stairs and
that he should have Leadbetter's loaded shotgun.

We didn't know how much time we had—if we had any
time. No one knew how Thornton had burned. But if he had
died, why not Brad, or Mary—or Helen? Anyone of us, at
any moment now, turning black the way he had! Somehow I
felt, I think we all knew that whatever we did would be helpless and futile. How could we, with puny human means,
thwart the unseen menace of those who had twice killed with
a power that must come from hell? I took Helen into my
arms to kiss her goodbye, and my soul was cold.

The village houses were like skulls of long dead colossi with
blinking yellow eyes, lining the road. A brighter cluster of
illumination marked the location of the store. Through dust-
grimed windows I saw the place half filled with a motley
crowd. Worm-eaten boards creaked under my feet and then I
swung open the door and paused on the threshold, looking
around.

For a moment none of the score of slouched figures
seemed to have noticed my entrance. In that instant before a
word was said I noticed again a fact that had puzzled me
more than once before, that many of them wore in the lapels
of their coats small buttons as though marking membership
in some order. The design of the emblem was a face of scarlet against a black background. And what a face! A miniature
replica of a Satan, with beady green eyes and sprouting

horns.

I raised my voice.

"Can anyone tell me where to find Emery Paave?"

A few heads turned to cast black glances back at me but save for that my inquiry elicited no response. One pimply-faced youth stood slouched against a wall, eyeing me. I approached him, money displayed in my half-opened hand.

"Want to make five dollars?" I said.

The lad's eyes lighted greedily as he pocketed the bill.

"Doin' what?" he said in a high treble.

"I'm after a little information." I stepped closer and lowered my voice. "Did you ever hear of men that go around in the woods with whips, flogging people?"

The paucky-looking youth stiffened. His eyes narrowed to wary slits. His mumbling reply was too ready, too facile:

"Me? I never heard of 'em."

I reached out to touch the devil button in his coat.

"What's that?" I said. "Some society that you belong to?"

His eyes flickered sidewise. A vulpine look came over his face. He mumbled:

"Hit's nawthin'. Jest suthin' I found." I ought to have known that I had said enough, for the others had turned to come flocking around us, a cluster of pale, menacing eyes. A wizened old ruffian with trickles of tobacco juice leaking from the angles of his toothless gums shoved up to me and rasped in a strident falsetto:

"You ever hear o' folk getting' into trouble by askin' questions that didn't concern 'em? Git out o'here and go along o' your own business."

Common sense should have told me my danger then and warned me to clear out while they would still let me go. But foolhardily I asked one more thing, for I thought that some one might let go of a hint to indicate who was behind the outrages that were taking place, and I still didn't really believe that they would dare harm me. What I said was:

"I found a man dead in the woods this afternoon. He must have been burned to death by children, for there were paper dolls—"

The moment those words left my lips I knew I had done it. Hunger for murder had lain like a mine in that crowd, only awaiting a spark to set it off, and my remark was the spark. An animal growl rasped around the ring. I saw upraised hands gripping clubs. Hunched figures surged toward me, a circle of hate-twisted faces. Hatred founded on the primitive unreasoning ignorance of beasts.

Terror snatched at me then. I started backing away from them toward the door. I had just managed to get outside when some one threw a stone. A shower of missiles pelted me and the next moment I was pinned in the center of a cursing and milling pack.

For an instant it was slug, smash and punch with my fear-needled muscles endowed with a strength that wasn't my own. I had been a middle-weight boxer in college and for a short time I held my ground with them. My jabs drove them back holding their jaws and clutching their stomachs. They surged closer and I grunted grim relish as I felt faces cave under my full swings.

But this couldn't last. They yammered fury and came on afresh. I knew stabbing agony as their sticks bludgeoned my skull. Some one tripped me and I was down. They were using their feet on me now. With insensate cruelty of a wolf-pack rending a fallen one, they pounded my head and my vitals. I rolled on to my face and tried to protect my brain with my folded arms. Their blows ripped them away. The most terrible of all sounds upon earth, the death roar of a mob, rolled over me while shrill voices skyrocketed:

"Kill the damned rich 'un! Pound the damned spy to death!"

Only feebly now could I strive to cover myself, for my numbed muscles were almost done. I knew they were killing me. I sobbed prayers for mercy and I heard them laughing in mockery as my senses slipped into oblivion.

Chapter Three

The Punished Of God

I came back from unconsciousness—from death as I at first thought in my dazed bewilderment—to find myself lying on a couch with a huge figure standing and looking down at me in the light of an oil lamp. My forehead was wet and the raw taste of whisky burned my lips.

I blinked, grunted and pushed myself up to sitting. Seeing me at last coming around, the big man set the lamp down on a table and with a sigh of relief pulled a chair up to my side. He was the man I had come to see, lawyer Paave, a mountainous Dutchman with a mane of yellow hair and a face round and red as a balloon.

"You haf had a narrow esgape, my friendt Collier, a fery narrow esgape," he said in his thickened guttural. "Those maniacs out there would haf gilled you if I had not come along yust in time and driven them off. What happened—from de beginning?"

I told him the story, commencing with the flogging man in the woods and ending with Thornton's death and the crippling of our cars. He shook his head as I finished. Deeply troubled, his voice rumbled back:

"It iss even worse than I feared. I do nod need to tell you of the dreadful ignorance and superstitions of de people in this valley, how they are believers in witchcraft. This may seem ingoncievable in these days of progress, but you haf only to read in de newspapers to know of de hex murders that take place around here.

"But this iss nod all. There are de Penitentes, those fools who haf gone mad pondering on their sins. They commit horrible deeds to gain salvation through punishment of de flesh. And it iss believed—though no one iss sure—that the man who is at de head of de Penitentes is also de hex boss who through his supposed power to cast charms and bewitch his enemies forces efery man, woman and child to obey his gommands. He plays a double part. From time to time he kills some one in a terrible way to terrify de others and keep them obedient. And he has goot reason for wanting you out of de way. If you find oil, it will mean the coming of business, of progress, everything which will end his gontrol which iss based fear and ignorance."

"Have you any idea how he does it?" I said. "How he kills them without any fire?"

Paave got out a silk handkerchief and mopped the sweat from his bald head. He looked at me strangely.

"Hexes," he muttered. "They are bewitched. He puts a charm on them so that they burn."

I stared at him.

"You believe that, too?" I exclaimed. "You, an educated man—"

"When I first came here, I would haf said the same as you," the blue-eyed giant muttered. "But now, my friendt Collier, I haf seen—Gott knows what I haf seen!"

I got myself up from the bed to pace the floor. The fear of this unimaginative Dutchman, his acceptance as fact of the things that I had tried to tell myself were sheer madness, frightened me more, actually, than Thornton's death and the thing in the woods.

"Who is this man?" I said after a moment. "Where can I find him?"

"His name iss Hans Ludlam. He iss another Dutchman," Paave answered. "He lives in a shack in de woods."

"I'm going to see him," I said. "I'm going to have the truth out of him. Will you take me—or are you afraid?"

Paave knocked the ashes out of his long pipe and rose slowly. He said heavily:

"I am nod afraid of him, but you must nod go there—nod now." He held up his hand. "Listen out there, to the mob. The town iss crazy tonight with hate against you and yours. When I wass bringing you in here I heard them talking about going out to get the rest of your friends. You haf a lovely wife, and—"

The big man's voice dropped to a fear-tightened husking.

"But it iss nod those out there with the clubs whom you should fear most, for they kill only the body. It iss the others who slay body and soul too with their fires—fires from hell kindled without human hands." The grip of his powerful fingers bit into my arm. "This afternoon they put the hex on you—and her, too. No one who has ever received that has lived, not ever one. If you have one little chance to see her alive before dot burning come to her—"

Still talking rapidly he steered me across the room toward a door.

"Go by the back way out and get home to her. Go as fast as you can, and then faster. I will go to the sheriff. He and I will get Ludlam and the two of us will take him to Leadbetter's. You can talk with him and then we still stay with you the rest of the night."

I gripped his hand silently. Through the moment's silence voices in the street rose in hubbub of curses. Lantern lights glinted on waving clubs.

"Come on! Let's go and get them!" the gathering cry rang.

Paave pushed me swiftly out of the room and pointed my way along a darkened rear passage. I followed it to a back door opening into a yard.

Outside, I halted an instant to listen to the growl that rolled over the housetops and then I started to run. The two miles of rutty, mud-plastered going seemed long as eternity. I raced through patches of forest and then between overhanging cliffs where the wind came freighted with cold and voices of things unseen crooned from the rock crannies. My panting breaths tugged my lungs out by the roots while terror, gibbering at my heels, flogged me faster and faster still. If God would only let me find Helen there, find her alive . . .

When at last I pounded into the yard, I took one look at the house and my heart dropped like a lump of lead into my stomach. The front door sagged awry on shattered hinges, the windows gaped with splintered panes. The mud in the yard was chewed into quagmire by milling of many feet.

I raced up to the door and there I stood rigid an instant before I could move or speak. At last I wet my lips and managed to gasp: "Helen! Helen, where are you?"

There was no answer. A ribboned window shade slatted back and forth. A vagrant wind was wandering through the dark hallways. It swayed the flame of the single candle that stood on a table as though tugging at it with spectral fingers. Somewhere a dog howled.

I stumbled in over the threshold and caught up the candle. From room to room I stormed. I cast wild-eyed glances into dark corners, from time to time I halted to sob out her name.

And then suddenly I heard her answer, a far-away shrilling: "Don! Don, I'm here!"

I beat my way toward that wailing, my hands pawing the dark as though they would tear open a passage through which I could fly to her. As I rounded a corner, there was a pattering of feet and a slim little figure rushed to throw itself into my arms. She clung to me in hysterical reaction and I could feel her body throb in the tremors that racked it. She lifted her tear-streaked face to mine and I couldn't stop kissing her.

"What happened?" I whispered at last. "Was it the mob from the village?"

"No—some of those men that we saw in the woods, with the whips. They broke down the door. I ran up into the attic and hid under a bed."

"And the others?" I said. "Thornton and Brad and Mary—"

Her answer came in sobbed moaning. "They got them, they took them away. Not the Leadbetter's, though; they ran into the woods."

My heart beats checked with a sudden sick feeling. All our friends gone. And only God's mercy that Helen, too . . .

I blew out the candle and for a long minute we stood motionless, clinging to one another and listening. Outside, the night was alive with noises, whisperings and clickings and rustlings. Whether those ghouls had departed or were still hanging around there was no way to tell. If those noises out there were men, they would realize that there was one whom they hadn't got and return.

Then, little by little, a small wooden sound became audible, rhythmic, persistent, like tapping of spectral drumsticks out of the night's immensity. I listened a moment longer and then I slid my arm around Helen while I laughed shakily.

"That's the loose spoke in Paave's buggy," I said. "He and the sheriff are coming. And the boss of the Penitentes."

A couple of minutes later the ancient horse-drawn vehicle turned into the yard. Paave and the big flaxen-haired sheriff got out and came forward. Helen and I met them on the steps and I told them what had taken place.

"They've got all of our friends," I concluded savagely. "And if that man there is Hans Ludlam, he knows where they are."

Paave turned to the figure which up to this time had stood half concealed in the shadows.

"Dere iss Hans Ludlam," he said.

I stepped closer to Ludlam. Big as Paave was, the boss of the Penitentes loomed shoulders above him. A huge white beard rippling like burnished silver from the blue, intensely penetrating eyes clear to the man's wrist gave him a patriarchal appearance. He had a swelling dome of a bald head over high corrugated forehead, a nose massive and rapacious as a hawk's beak. The mouth under the bushy moustache was a pair of lips thin, white, incredibly cruel.

"Is it true that you are the leader of a sect known as the Punished of God?" I asked.

The big shining head nodded indifferently.

"I am the pastor of those of us who are aware of the power of sin," a deep voice rumbled sonorously.

"And your adherents torture themselves and one another by voluntary floggings?" I continued.

"Christ was flogged with a whip of thorns before He died on the cross," the patriarch intoned. "Can we wretched mortals do less than accept punishment for our sins in the same way?"

"And you practice witchcraft as a side line," I went on. "You keep this valley of ignorant people in slavery by working on their superstitions. You kill men and women to keep them subservient to you."

The man's voice came with the bellow of an angry bull.

"That is a lie! I do not deny that such things go on. But they are the doings of—others. We are just a company of poor struggling souls trying to purify ourselves so that in the day of judgment we may be received at the heavenly gates. We harm no others and what we do among ourselves is our own affair."

"My friends and I saw a man flogging himself in the woods this afternoon," I retorted. "When we got to him, he had been burned to death, but no fire was near him. Men with whips—some of your men—were there and chased us. There was a hex sign of paper dolls there, and one on our car. Later, one of our party was killed in this house in the same way. Those men of yours did it all. They took our friends away an hour ago. Where are they now?"

For a long moment the man stared at me in such frozen silence that I thought he had not understood what I said. Then suddenly he leaped at me, clubbed fists beating like pile drivers. They came down on my shoulders and one smash of them beat me to my knees. I tried to jump backward, but they found me again. They pounded my head and the back of my neck. Their blows rang on my cranium till they filled it with shooting stars.

Paave and the sheriff were after him now. He drove his great knotted hands into their faces like rocks at the ends of piston rods. They staggered back, gasping through spurting blood. They rallied and charged him again and he beat them like puppets.

They were gone now, taken to flight, and he whirled to where I was just staggering up to my feet. He blasted me down again. His fists were hammers of Thor beating the life out of a squirming pigmy of mortal man who twisted and grovelled this way and that to escape from their punishment.

Finally he paused to get breath. Like a mouse fleeing a torturing cat, I dragged myself, half crawling, half running, into some bushes. He didn't follow me. I heard him muttering under his breath as he turned and went stamping out of the yard and off down the road.

I got myself up on my feet and stood leaning against a tree, panting and spitting blood. I felt as though I had been pummeled by the hoofs of a horse. I wiped tears and sweat from my eyes and looked around for Paave and the sheriff. I couldn't see either of them, or the buggy. And then the spine-tingling realization came that they had fled. Terrified at Ludlam's berserker onslaught, they had left Helen and me to his mercy. Helen—what had become of her? I looked wildly around, gasped her name.

Footsteps sounded and she was there, shivering against my side. I slid my arm around her yielding softness and I thanked God for one mercy, that she was alive. She clung to me, she sobbed through chattering teeth:

"What are we going to do now, Don? Where can we go?"

"Try to get back to town, I guess," I said. "Get to Paave's. He's a coward, but he'll take us in."

I thought that, then—I dreamed that in this night of fear there could be one place of safety for us!

Helen and I groped our way to the road. For five or ten minutes we plodded along, clinging to one another's hands and not talking. The darkness was thronged with armies of shadows that scuttled forward, skipped sidewise, rolled backward again. Shadows of rocks and trees, or ... We couldn't tell. We slid past them, cringing, and the leaping of their swart arms at us brought showers of gooseflesh tingling our spines.

And little by little I was convinced that they weren't shadows of inanimate things. The croaking of frogs in the marshes had been the only sounds for a while. Then from behind came rustlings and grittings, squashing of feet, rumble of gutteral whispers. The roadway was clogged with jumble of forms whose whiplashes zigzagged against the stars.

"There they are! They're coming for us!" Helen's cry spurted. And then we were running, stumbling and tripping, slewing through mud, racing as we had never fled before. I pulled Helen along by one hand and visions of Thornton's cindered face and the circle of paper dolls twisted an iron hand in my vitals.

How long or how far we ran I wouldn't know. Finally came the time when I knew it was over, for we couldn't go any more. Helen's knees had melted beneath her, I had swept her up into my arms. Now I too was winded, retching for breath and spitting blood.

Her voice came half strangled from where her face was crushed into my shoulder.

"Kill me, Don! Kill me now with your pocket knife! Don't let them get me!" she sobbed. "Not to die the way Thornton did. Do it now, quickly, while I am kissing you!"

Chapter Four

Fingers Of Doom

With my free hand I fumbled for the knife in my pocket. She was right. Better death at my loving hands than the tortures of those sadist beasts. And that was something for which the Almighty would forgive me on judgment day.

Wildly I groaned as I kissed her. I would have done it the next instant, had I not suddenly caught sight of a light in a house window. And perhaps, even so, it would have been better. Perhaps she would be happier now; perhaps I would be spared the nightmares that are slowly driving me mad, if I had opened a vein in her little white throat.

But the house was there, just a short distance ahead, and I flogged my legs in a frantic sprint. Sagging piazza boards creaked under my weight as I rushed up to the door. I didn't pause to knock. I pawed for the latch, burst open the door and threw myself over the threshold. Before looking to see who was there or explain to them, I spun around to find the bolt and throw it across.

I set Helen down on her feet. White fires where searing my

inwards and for a long minute I sprawled against the wall gasping before I could utter a sound.

"The floggers are after us!" I finally managed to pant.

There were two of them in the poverty bare kitchen, a woman and man. The poorest type of the most ignorant inhabitants of the valley, ill-clad, ill-nourished, vacant-eyed. At my words the woman let out a moan. The man's jaw went limp.

"They—ye say they're out there?" His voice rasped in a scream. "They'll git me! They've come to kill me!"

"We'll fight them off," I said. "Haven't you got something, a gun or an axe or some clubs, anything we can fight with?"

He shook his head. "Wouldn't do no good. I didn't pay in, didn't hev no money to pay."

"You didn't have money to pay what?" I said.

He looked at me curiously. "You're strange in these parts, ain't ye? We couldn't pay fer our button. They come high—twenty dollars. And now—"

He turned to point at one of the windows. Against the outside of the glass had been pasted a string of the dancing dolls. His finger jerked with his trembling, beads of sweat rolled over his face.

"They put 'em up three days ago," he slathered. "That means he hexed me. Means that I got to die."

I stared at him. It couldn't actually be true, that in these modern days I was watching a man gibbering in terror because some one had pasted paper dolls on his window pane! Yet when I remembered those other two men, my heart seemed to turn over. Explain it or not, call those fears madness of fools, that pair had died in a way that no sophistry of the effete civilized world could begin to account for. Something hideous and stark and primitive was here.

"Who is this man you say hexes you because you didn't buy one of his buttons?" I said at last.

The farmer shook his head.

"I dunno. Nobody does. He never shows up himself, jest sends around one of the boys that works for him. Some of the men tried stringin' up one of them boys to make him talk. He didn't—but every last one in the crowd that did it was dead inside of a month. Burned to death."

I understood now the meaning of those emblems that I had seen in the village. Some mind with a hellish genius that cast that of a New York racketeer into eclipse had figured out this way to capitalize the superstitions of these besotted country folk and wax fat on their sacrifices. If they bought a button and wore it—paid for "protection"—they weren't bewitched. If they didn't . . .

"Anyhow, it's all nonsense." I gripped the man's arm and shook him to jolt his bovine mind out of its daze. "There is no such thing as witchcraft. It's all a—"

He wasn't listening. He was staring past me at something over my shoulder. I saw his jaw drop and then a strange light that I can only describe as hunger stab through the apathy of his eyes. His lips grew slack and wet and a gurgling sound broke from his throat.

I turned to follow his gaze. I heard Helen's gasp and then I felt my own pulses spurt with amazement.

A window opened from the kitchen onto the piazza. And through this, against the awful blackness of the night, a figure was visible. It was that of a young girl, utterly nude save for a gauzy scarf around her slim loins. She was of a witching, Circe-like beauty. Her gaze fastened on us—on both of us men—and I for one couldn't withdraw my eyes. Her look held a pagan allure, knowledge of age old power of things beyond words, of the stark and primitive instincts that call from woman to man.

She stepped back from the window so that her whole figure was visible. Her arms rose over her head. Her slender body taut and standing on tip-toe, she seemed to be reaching to draw down the tide of white light to her bosom. Like a naiad of ethereal and inhuman beauty she stood there, quivering, breasts hardened and throbbing—a thing not of this world, thrilling to the call of something born of the night and the moon's radiance.

Her arms dropped. Lascivious ripplings passed through her, writhings of a cat in throes of desire. She lifted her breasts in her cupped hands, holding them toward us.

A choked cry burst from the farmer. And then I saw him rush past me to claw at the bolt securing the door. Sweat stood on his face, it was the passion-gripped face of an animal. His wife let out a scream. She ran after him to pound at his hands, trying to beat them down from the latch. Failing in that, she flung herself on him, battling with all her frenzied strength to drive him away.

He shoved her angrily one side. He shot back the bolt, wrenched the door open and dashed out.

And I ran behind him! I didn't at that time understand what prompted me to do that. If I had used any reason at all to account for my action, I would have told myself that I wanted to find out what was happening, who was behind it. For those who had been chasing us were no longer in evidence. They seemed to have been drawn elsewhere to a fresh victim.

I would have told myself that. But my eyes had devoured the seduction of that naked girl and heat fired my brain. Again that strange impulse that I had felt once before was urging me, too, in pursuit of the evasive figure that eluded the farmer's wild rush and went pirouetting across the yard.

She didn't pause for him to overtake her. She ran swiftly to the opening of a path that led into the woods. Down this she sped, a lambent white flame in the darkness, and behind her lumbered the ungainly form of the rustic.

I turned in there to rush after them. But Helen had had enough. She brought me back to my sense with a stinging slap the face.

"What are you doing, Don?" she cried. "What is the matter with you?"

I halted, blinked and passed my hand over my eyes. I had a queerly dazed feeling.

"I don't know," I muttered. "I must have been bewitched."

I had said that, not of course meaning it literally, but as a thoughtless form of words to convey that something had taken place which I couldn't explain. And then my voice broke as a cold hand leaped to the back of my neck. The farmer claimed to have been bewitched, and I had scoffed at the notion. But some unholy compulsion had drawn him from his wife's side to follow the girl to what he must have realized would be his death. And for the second time tonight I too had known that same unearthly, almost uncontrollable temptation!

I groaned and swept Helen into my arms. Hexes, witchcraft—phantoms whose power lives only in the minds of damned, those slaves of fear, or vital of evil? In that moment of terror I didn't know, for I had lost the faculty of reasoning. I only knew that I had just experienced an invisible magnetism of sin against which no will power could struggle. If Helen had not been here to save me . . .

Sweat stood on the palms of my hands as we turned and started back toward the road. Still we saw nothing of our late pursuers. They had gone into the woods where the girl had been leading the farmer. From deep in the forest came cracking of whips and a tocsin of agony. A voice rose in gagged screechings to lash the dead air. A sudden light flared briefly and died. Wafting of breeze brought aroma of roasting flesh. I grabbed Helen's arm and husked through clenched teeth:

"Come on, let's run! Let's get out of this!"

We came to the highway and started once more in the direction of town. For perhaps ten minutes we plodded along when we were overtaken by a buggy which came lurching over the road at a gallop. It drew down to a halt and the face that peered from around the side curtains was that of lawyer Paave. He waited for us and exclaimed as we came up:

"I haf been looking eferywhere for you. Ludlam knocked me out senseless into some bushes, that must be the reason you did not see me. The horse took fright at de fighting and ran away and then de sheriff is scared too and he goes. After you two haf left, I come to my senses back. I catch de horse half a mile down the road and start to search for you."

He made room on the seat.

"Get in. I take you back to my house where you will be safe. De sheriff is out with a posse looking for Ludlam. In de morning everything will be all right."

There was nothing else to be done. I dreaded going back to the village. I feared to stay in Paave's house. For his story of that last half hour sounded fishy. Between him and Ludlam I had seemed to sense some unspoken understanding. Suppose he himself were in with the bearded giant—was the boss of the hex business! But we had to go somewhere. The lawyer's house seemed the only hope.

If I had realized then that there was no hope—not any at all!

Paave arrived at his back door by side streets avoiding the crowd that still milled in the main thoroughfare. The first faces I saw when we got inside were those of Leadbetter and his wife.

"They came here to get taken care of, too," Paave explained.

I went up to my erstwhile host and said:

"Have you got one of those buttons?"

He stared at me for an instant as though tempted to say he didn't know what I meant. Then his face twisted as he said:

"No, I hain't got one. Maria won't let me. Says it's all nonsense to pay twenty dollars fer a hunk o' glass."

I said: "Are you afraid—really afraid?"

He licked his parched lips. He darted a look back at his wife, her narrow face alive with a vulpine ferocity.

"I'll say I'm afeared," he husked. "Maria wants fer me to git killed, That's why she won't give me no money fer to pay up. She wants 'em to hex me."

The farmer produced a flask from his hip pocket and held it out. The liquor was the vilest of rot-gut, but its raw scorching against the walls of my stomach gave me a synthetic courage that I badly needed. I took two drinks, long ones.

It was late, long after midnight. Paave came, proffering beds, but I declined for Helen and myself. This was one night that I didn't dare close my eyes. The Leadbetters, however, accepted and departed to leave Helen and me alone in the small sitting room.

She stretched out on a couch while I pulled a big chair up to her side. Hands linked, we listened to the buzz of excitement now dying away in the village. The place seemed to be quieting down. Yet I couldn't relax. Visions of terror rocketed through my brain. Thornton's face with the grinning white teeth—the demoniacal power that radiated from that patriarch of sin, Hans Ludlam—our four friends gone where, suffering what, God only knew.

We two had so far escaped. But would they leave us in peace now? Was Paave himself the boss of the hexers, and had he brought us under his roof to make the rest of it easy to arrange? Minutes dragged into eternities while terror sat the night watches with me.

Chapter Five

Love Of The Damned

I don't know when it was that I closed my eyes and allowed slumber to overtake me—that night of all nights when with hell meshing closer I should have fought off the demons of weariness and kept awake at no matter what cost.

Then presently I was conscious again, lying sprawled in a stupor of half waking, half sleeping. The moon was higher now, spilling a rectangle of misty light through a window. I watched it, trying to focus my thoughts. The picture of those two dead men, the circle of paper dolls, the elfin forms of the dancing girls in the woods . . . Was I mad or had uncanny and supernatural things really been taking place around me tonight?

My eyes slid away from the spot of light in the effort to shake off those bewildering thoughts. They moved toward the window and there they stopped. My breath caught in my lungs. A strange incredulous terror prickled me with icy needlings. There in the moonlight was the girl! She wore only the same diaphanous scarf about her lithe hips and her hair was a tossed mass of gold above the ivory mask of her face. Her eyes, deep with that knowledge or unnamable, timeless things, clung fixedly to mine. For a second she stood there in suddenly arrested motion and then she was gliding toward me.

She halted at the side of the chair, stooping over me, and her perfect body was an alabaster white statute sculptured from moonlight. Her hands reached down to glide over my face. Cool firm fingers stroked my temples.

There was a tingling passion in the touch of those finger-tips that thrilled me over my whole body. She smiled, slowly, languorously; her voice came like an echo from far away. What she was whispering I couldn't tell, but the cadence of her voice vibrated answering strings in my brain. Half conscious, half stupified, I groped to seize those pale hands and crush them against my lips.

She trilled a laugh and moved swiftly out of my reach. Then I was conscious of rising to my feet and stumbling toward her. My throat seemed to be bursting with the hammering of my heart which had flown up to lodge there. And the fear that gripped me sprang from my knowledge that it had happened to me now, as it had to those others. Having bewitched me with longing for her beauty, she came to claim me, to make me another one her victims.

And yet for all that terror, I was glad with a fiercely reckless exulting that dried my mouth and brought sweat to the palms of my hands. I was a damned soul, cursed by her beauty to follow her to my death in the fire, yet the blood hissed on my ear drums as I mumbled wildly:

"Wait for me. I'm coming. I'm coming!"

I rushed another step toward her. She pirouetted away and stood in the moonlight close to the window. She waited there, smiling. She lifted her breasts in her cupped hands and held them toward me, a maddening offering.

I started to run to her, and then some deep-buried and almost forgotten memory prompted me to halt and direct a glance toward the couch where Helen had been. One faint tugging of loyalty to her, still alive in the quicksand that was sucking me down!

Again I looked and a cry broke from my lungs. She wasn't there. Helen was gone. While I had forgotten her in swinish sleep, they had come and taken her.

For an instant longer I stood there transfixed, while grief-stricken terror rolled over me in a flood that made me oblivious to the girl and her temptings. I turned my back on her and rushed out of the room. Through the house I went storming, shouting Helen's name. Only echoes beat my cries back to me, for she wasn't there. Paave, the Leadbetters—no one was in the house.

At last I found myself out of doors. I must have been half demented, for the triangles of the hills hunched over me like squatting beasts and the wind from their caves brought voices of night and bottomless sin. I stood there alone with the stars and my agony.

And then at last I was aware of the girl again. She stood near me, swaying slightly, a wind-blown lily against the dark, waiting and beckoning.

Her call surged over me once more with a longing that obliterated all other thoughts. Fires swept through my parched throat and filled my brain. I dashed after her, arms straining. God forgive me, with my wife carried away to torture and death, I raced after that naked woman and choked cries burst from me, imploring her to come to me, to wait till I could catch up.

She didn't pause. She ran scarcely seeming to touch the ground with her twinkling white feet. By deserted back roads she led me out of the village. And now she had turned into another narrow way into the woods. Down this she sped, whirling, spinning, gyrating, her nude body like a woodland sylph in the moonlight.

No words can possibly portray the weird, uncanny loveliness of that spectacle. Her slim white body against the dark boles of the pines; her blood-red hair spreading and billowing till it seemed an aureole of fire against which her torso and limbs stood outlined in gleaming ivory. Then suddenly she vanished—rather she seemed to turn wholly into a flame, for her body disappeared and there was only a fire, an errant pointed flame that flitted in ghostly dippings against the black tree trunks.

Whether that fire was human or animal, material or only a hallucination of my maddened brain, I didn't know. It was a will-o'-the-wisp that led me sweating and panting through bogs and across fallen trees, gasping incoherent cries while I fought to get near enough to clutch its flickerings into my arms. Stark terror twisted my soul, but I couldn't help myself. Honor, my duty to Helen, my love for her, all seemed windy words without meaning. The only thing that mattered was that leaping, gyrating figure of passion incarnate—passion whose attainment would bring my death as Thornton had died . . .

Suddenly the girl vanished completely, blotted out as though by a veil of enveloping gloom. And the fire, too. I came to a sudden standstill and stood breathless, staring while my figure went rigid as stone.

As my eyes focused to take in my surroundings, I became aware that I stood at one side of an open space among towering trees. The area was half filled with raggedly clad figures—some in Mexican costumes—clutching whips. The flames of a bonfire in the midst of the circle etched their faces in crimson and black, countenances inhuman in fanatical cruelty. They could have been imps of hell cavorting around a furnace-mouth in its infernal depths!

But those furies weren't alone there. My horrified eyes counted other faces—Bradshaw and Mary, Nathalie Thornton. And Helen . . . Brad and his wife and Nathalie they had stripped naked and tied to stakes. The Penitentes pranced around them in a march, bearing whips pointed with steel barbs. They whooped in glee as they laid on the flagellations. Garment by garment they ripped off their own clothes till they were stark naked. They lashed themselves, too. They leaped high in the air at the pain, grotesque, plunging figures that seemed to have been whelped from earth's hidden horrors.

The rout grew frenetic. Their shrieks held wild ecstasy of devotees approaching ultimate frenzy of pain-rapture. I tried to identify some of the faces, for I told myself that if ever I got out of this alive, I would invoke the help of the Governor to wipe out this unspeakable cult. In the uncertain firelight, I couldn't be sure. Of only one individual was I positive, of a huge white bearded form that I suddenly spied standing behind a screen of bushes and watching proceedings—Hans Ludlam!

My hand groped over the ground, seeking a club. If I could find a weapon and creep around in the rear of this Satan, I would strike one blow to bring an end to his racket with the dashing out of his brains.

I hadn't crawled more than a few steps in my search when I froze to crouch staring into the circle. A curse sprang to my lips. For they had taken Helen down from her stake and brought her into the ring. She was still clothed and for an instant they contented themselves with disrobing her. I had to kneel there, helpless, and watch that! Fingers hooked into the neck of her dress. A rip shredded it to the waist, bringing her white shoulders and arms into view. Then they went after her underclothes. In a moment it was all over. Before those gibbering satyrs she stood utterly nude.

They fell in behind her and drove her around and around while their whips rose and fell. Crooked red fingers leaped in zigzaggings over her skin. Her face in the firelight was a twisted white cameo chiseled from torture.

I felt every one of those whip strokes as though it were falling on my naked skin. I cursed in meaningless snarlings, my fingers clawed at the ground as I went scrambling on all fours, still in search of a club. I stopped to spin around as Helen's moans rang again. Some one had brought a bridle and jammed the steel bar between her teeth. They forced her down on her hands and knees and they were driving her like a horse. Flogging her and sawing the reins till the foam on her lips dripped crimson.

I lunged up to my feet and the yell that burst from my

throat was a sound wholly animal. I hadn't been able to find any weapon. But I couldn't wait any longer. The way I felt then I could tear them all limb from limb with my naked hands.

I surged a step forward and then to a standstill again at an incredible sight. The gang had suddenly wheeled from Helen to flock in a group around Nathalie, still tied to her high stake. Exactly what happened—whether they did anything at all to her or not—I couldn't tell. But suddenly her body seemed to burst into flame, a spurting glare of yellowish-pink light. It was an outlashing of heat terrific in its intensity, for it sent the crowd spilling backward and even there where I stood I could feel its torrid wave in my eyes.

The fire went out as swiftly as it had come. It had been, in fact, more of an explosion than a flame. As it ebbed away. I saw Nathalie's body glowing all over red as a great coal drawn from a furnace. Swiftly it cooled to a black cinder. It twisted in spasmodic convulsions of muscular reflexes.

I stood there spellbound while gooseflesh of an unspeakable horror rolled on my spine. In my smug assurance of twelve hours before, I had mocked at witchcraft and all its works. But now I had stood and watched that girl burned to death when no fire was within yards of her. What hope did I have, what hope could there ever be, of saving Helen from those who killed with a power that could only be evoked from hell?

The knot of forms moved rapidly to stand before Bradshaw. And while he writhed and screamed in his ropes, the same thing took place again. And then there were two blackened things, grotesque and curled-up as foetuses snatched in untimely birth that crackled with thin gritting noises as they swayed in the breeze.

Mary Bradshaw was next. One of the Penitentes seemed to throw something invisible toward her. The light sprang in a blinding surge and then the breeze brought the stench of roasting meat.

All this time I hadn't moved. Sheer fascination of horror rooted me to the ground. And then came the thing which blew the fuse in my brain. As in a moving picture of doom, I saw them seizing Helen and dragging her toward another stake, as yet untenanted. Their shouts rang:

"The next! She is the next! The fire god wants a new bride!"

I saw them hustle her up there, tie her by her uplifted arms to the vertical shaft. Saw her white nudeness against the pines, her eyes upturned to her Maker, while before her the pack stood motionless, waiting . . .

Chapter Six

Damnation's Picnic

I had no weapon of any kind, only my naked hands, as I smashed through the undergrowth into the open. Neither had I any real hope of fighting off that mob single handed and rescuing her. I was only a berserker primate who had slid backward ten millenniums in evolution in as many seconds, in whose brain just one red emotion surged—to get to her side and gouge and rip and tear, to kill as many of them as a man, fighting by the side of his woman, may kill before he himself dies.

It was the fury of my unexpected onslaught that took them off balance and scattered them for an instant. I fell upon the ring from behind and I had dropped four of them with smashes to the nerve centers of their necks before they were aware of my presence. Two who halted to spin around at me I felled with clubbings that broke their jaws. And then I was through and running to Helen.

I had got out my pocket knife as I ran. I had thought to cut her down, at least get her away from that stake where death leaped out of nothing. But there wasn't time. They came swarming over me, dragging me back. Pinned inside of a ring, I lashed at them with loathing of terror giving me a maniac's strength. I used my fists and my feet on them, then my fingernails and my teeth. And suddenly then the ring parted to let through another figure.

I saw a leather-brown face, contorted and foam-spattered, with glaring black eyes of a maniac. Long hair tossing against the stars told me that I had to do with a woman. But no qualms of chivalry need have kept me from slugging her, for she fought with the ferocity of a she panther.

With a screech she flung herself on me. Her hands, equipped with fanged claws, lashed at my face. Long dirt-clogged nails dug into my eyeballs. Horror-thrilled, I recoiled from her fury. Such a face as hers could have been whelped from no mortal mother, only from womb of witches and midnight hags.

Some one tripped me with a kick from behind and I was down. She caterwauled and came flying knees first, medusa locks, streaming. I retched with nausea at the smash in my vitals while she knelt there ripping and scratching.

She was killing me, tearing my face into ribbons. Needled by pain, my hand lashed out. It caught her in the front of her dress, rending it to the waist and bearing her withered brown breasts. I jolted another blow to her face as I got my breath and lunged up to sitting. She yowled like a rabid cat and drove her thumbs into my eyeballs. All compunction swept away now; I drove out a short jab that took her flush on her scrawny throat. She slumped onto hands and knees, gagging, her larynx shattered.

Somewhere in the maelstrom that seethed around me, Helen screamed. I gathered myself for a leap back to my feet, but the mob surged in and their clubs beat me down again. I was crawling on hands and knees while their whips found me. Helen sobbed again and the sound of that tortured wailing seemed to burst something inside of me. God, I had to get my feet and go to her, before there came another puff of that pink fire and her body swung there, a blackened pendulum.

But I couldn't rise, they were too many for me. I clenched my teeth through bleeding lips and dug my fingers into the ground as I clawed myself forward.

Suddenly I stumbled over something that impeded my progress. It was a wooden box half filled with a greyish powder. In frenzy I snatched it up and whirled to throw its contents over my shoulder into the faces and eyes of my tormentors.

It blinded them for an instant and as they stumbled back, I attained my objective, the edge of the bonfire. Long heavy sticks, only partially burned, projected around its rim. I snatched up one of them and with the thing in my hands I leaped to my feet.

Armed now, I rushed at them. With the blazing end of the brand I belabored their bodies and faces. And suddenly something took place which caused me to let the stick and stand gaping in amazement.

Where sparks flew from the stick to light upon the irregular patches in which the powder had landed on the men and adhered, there burst out those explosions of incredible heat.

Some with faces half burned away, others with cindered cavities where eyes had been, still others wearing jagged black shawls draped over their chests, they shrank from me to throw themselves on the ground and lie rolling and shrieking in agony. The foul horrible smell of burning flesh filled my nostrils, and a fierce tumultuous joy swept me. At last my friends were being avenged. I left them yammering there and stumbled around to the stake from which Helen's choked screams were coming.

I didn't wait to get out my knife. With bare hands I wrenched at the cords that pinioned her crossed wrists. They parted and her limp figure came tumbling down into my arms. I clutched her in the crook of one arm and wheeled back to face the pack. For I hadn't disposed of all of them. There were still enough of them left to do their will on us. Teeth bared like an ape, I gripped the end of my club and stood waiting.

They didn't come. And when my blurred vision cleared so that I could see again, I stared transfixed with amazement. For another battle was in progress there now. A second group of men armed with long flails had come dashing out of the trees. They fell upon those of the torturers whom I hadn't

disposed of and were engaged in bashing their brains in with
their six-foot wagon stakes. The leader of the new-comers
was the white bearded boss of the Penitentes, Hans Ludlam!
And at his side, bellowing vengeance, stormed lawyer Emery
Paave.

A sound of sobbing brought my eyes back to Helen. She
hung limp in my clasp. Her eyes lifted to meet mine, but she
didn't recognize me. Through the blood-flecked foam on her
lips she was moaning dull, toneless screams, over and over
and over. I groaned with agony drawn from my own tortured
soul. Fast as I had tried to come, it hadn't been soon enough.
The pain and terror had been too much for her gentle mind.
She had gone mad.

I was still holding her crushed to me, kissing her poor
twisted face and begging her to speak, when feet sounded at
my side. The fight was over. Paave and Ludlam paused an
instant and then without speaking strode forward to shaft the
light of a lantern into the face of the woman I had hit in the
throat and of the man lying next to her, his face half obliterated by the strange burning. The revelation of their features
didn't tell me anything new. For already I had divined that
they were Frank Leadbetter and his wife.

"It was those two who was doing it," Paave's voice rumbled at last. "They was the ones who have been collecting
twenty dollars for buttons from eferyone on pain of hexing
and death. They fixed up t'ings to make it look like de Penitentes, so that Ludlam would get the blame. I myself thought
he was doing it till he came to me an hour ago and asked for
my help. Their men with whips was all fakes. Those men
you saw in the woods the first time was some of theirs. Ludlam and his people never hurt anyone. They yust whipped
one another and minded their own business. The Leadbetters
did not want you here because they knew that sooner or later
it would mean the end of their business. They must have collected thousands of dollars. They must have been terrible
rich."

I stared at him and even now that I understood I was cold

with the horror or it all. What a racket! And one possible only in a community whose members believed so implicitly in the power of witchcraft that they never questioned the genuineness of the things that seemed to be taking place.

"And the girl who led the men into the woods to their deaths?" I said at last.

"She wass my little Ella, my niece who keeps house for me," the big Dutchman groaned. "I did not know it, I had no suspicions. The Leadbetter woman got her to do that, she must haf given her money—and drugs. Many times I haf seen her acting not herself and I haf wondered what iss wrong. Those other girls that you saw from the house, dancing, are probably more that she used in the same way."

"The men on whom the Leadbetters put the sign of the dancing dolls—without the victims knowing it, some of their men must have got them to eat or drink something containing a drug that made them insanely sex-hungry," Ludlam went on as Paave halted, overcome by grief. "And then when the naked girls came, they could not help themselves, the instinct was too strong. They would follow them anywhere, even to death, believing all the time that they had been bewitched!"

"Leadbetter gave me a drink of whiskey in your house, Paave," I exclaimed. "That was how be got me. And the first time, back at the house, it was in the food. When I thought that I saw the girls turning into flames, it was hallucinations brought on by the drug."

"When the girl came to you, you could not help from following her," Ludlam said. "But when you arrived at the place where they were torturing your wife, you came to your senses. The drug had not been strong enough."

The big man took a turn up and down.

"But what I do not yet understand," he muttered after a moment, "is how they did it with the burning. How one could be burned without any fire."

"I can explain that now," I said. I remembered the box of grey powder which I had hurled into the men's faces and which had later burst into flame. "There is a certain chemical—thermite—which can be ignited with a match and burns with a terrifically hot fire, hot enough to melt iron. It is used for welding together broken pieces of metal. If this thermite were mixed with a little grease to make it adhere, and the paste smeared over a person's body, it could be set going with just a match and he would roast to a crisp in five seconds."

Paave and Ludlam both stared at me, open-mouthed.

"Then that is the way it was done," came the deep voice of the bearded giant. "In some way, Leadbetter, ignorant as he was, learned of that chemical and got a supply of it. Those men you saw in the woods had already spread the body of the self-flogging one with it before he started whipping himself. During the few moments when he was out of your sight, they set him on fire and then placed the circle of paper dolls around his body. The man who died in your house—"

"Leadbetter did that himself!" I exclaimed. "He must have got Thornton upstairs alone, knocked him senseless with a club and then in only a few seconds, spread the stuff over his head and touched it off."

For another long moment nobody spoke. Now that we knew the truth of the horrors, it didn't seem to make them any less dreadful, rather more soul-sickening. And the sight of Helen's nude body, dribbling blood while those meaningless noises rasped from her throat.

I picked her up in my arms and carried her out of there while the two big men were tieing up the Leadbetters who by this time had recovered consciousness. Buggies were waiting in the highway at the end of the wood road. Some one brought blankets to wrap around Helen and we started the twenty mile drive to the nearest town where there was a doctor.

It was noon of the next day before I finally got her into a hospital. She was there for two months before she knew me again and they said it would be better for her to go away somewhere with me.

That was two years ago. There wasn't any oil on our property in Monmouth Valley. I sold the timber right to a syndicate and tried to forget it all. Little by little, those memories are fading from Helen, too. But when the flame of lighted match suddenly spurting in her eyes sends her to fly shivering into my arms, I know that she is seeing again the form of Nathalie Thornton bursting into red fire—and hearing the croon of whips hissing against her naked skin.

THE WOMEN WHO KILLED FOR SATAN

Chapter One

The Beggar of Doom

Carols have always given me a feeling of sadness. So, although Sibyl and I had been married less than six months, I was glad we were not alone that Christmas Eve. Prescott Denham, one of our oldest friends, had dropped in, to find Sibyl up to her pretty elbows in a last minute whirl of red paper and ribbons. We had insisted on his staying awhile. We had a few drinks, which made us quite gay. Gay? If only I could have known that it was to be the last moment of gaiety of my life—the last minute in which my brain would be free from the spectres of Madness!

The radio was going, and we were listening to *God Rest You Merry Gentlemen.* And then all at once Sibyl froze with a half-wrapped parcel in her lively bare arms. And I saw Denham's face arrested in astonishment as he turned with a half-raised cocktail.

Cutting into the holy music came the sound of a voice so unbridled in savage fury that it brought a chill to our nerves. I can't remember the incredible words exactly—but they were something like this:

"Woe to the wicked! Woe to a nation of hypocrites and blasphemers! Thieves, lechers and murderers—ye shall die! For tonight fire will come from heaven and burn you to ashes even as we destroyed Sodom and Gomorrah."

The voice ceased as abruptly as it had come. The carolers chimed to their conclusion. A suave voice intoned: "You have been listening to a program of Christmas music sent to from the Cathedral of the Redeemer. We now return you to the supper room of the Hotel Mirador . . .”

For a moment none of us found words. We just stood there staring at one another. Then Denham laughed. A big corporation lawyer, he was tall, clean-cut and slim; cynical and effete, a man of the world. Sibyl laughed too. But there was a forced sound to her laughter. She turned oddly white.

“For heaven’s sake, where did that come from?” Denham finally exclaimed. “It sounded as though some maniac was on the air!”

“Yes—how perfectly ridiculous!” Sibyl echoed. “Such a horrible thing to have on a Christmas program!” She let the parcel fall to the table. She stood there, pensive, one slim hand stealing to her throat. Her gaze seemed arrested in a far away look, eyes strangely darkened by what might have been fear.

“The world is pretty wicked, isn’t it—when you stop to think?” she said slowly. “The wars and the greed and the cruelty—somehow it does seem all wrong—as that voice said. I think that if I were God I might really be tempted to destroy it and start all over again.”

I was amazed. My wife was the last woman in the world to have taken such stuff seriously. Sibyl was tall and willowy, lithe as a birch wand, with slim tapering hips and perfect legs; shoulders that would have been a sculptor’s joy, and full breasts swelling in her low dinner gown.

Sibyl had a Slavic cast of countenance, broad cheek bones in the upper half of a face narrowing to a triangle. Her eyes were tawny yellow. Fire would dance in them when I took her into my arms. When I held her soft body it seemed as though I were holding not a woman of mortal mould, but some elemental creature whose love I had somehow captured. And now it was strange to see her agitated by that super-moral gibberish.

Then she came gliding toward me, white hands reaching for mine.

"Paul!" she whispered in awe. "Could God do that—could He destroy us all if He wanted to? Do you believe that there is any power that—"

Bewildered by an indefinable apprehension, I stroked her tawny rebellious hair, stooped to kiss her reassuringly. I whispered that of course there wasn't any such power. It was all nonsense. And meanwhile I experienced the growing perplexity that was mirrored in Denham's face as to how such a crazy outburst could have interrupted such a well-known station.

I realized that our caller had gone to the radio and turned it up louder. A routine news announcement was coming through. There were half a dozen miscellaneous items—and then these clipped syllables chopping off lengths of sound:

"Police are investigating the manner in which death came a short time ago to two men found in an alley off Center Avenue.

They had apparently been burned to death, although no traces of fire were to be found in their vicinity. Persons in the neighborhood are reported to have testified to have seen falling illuminated rain resembling drops of fire, though at the time the sky was entirely cloudless . . ."

Abruptly Denham snapped off the current. His emotionless face bore a queer whiteness as he turned to the little cabinet where drinks were set out. "What the hell—" I heard him muttering under his breath.

Sibyl gasped. She seized my arm and I felt her fear heightened as his fingers pressed harder into my flesh.

"The voice said that people would be burned by fire from heaven!" she whispered.

I stared at her. It was the craziest thought that sane people had ever been asked to entertain! "Just a coincidence," I muttered. "What's got into you anyhow, Sibyl? This is Christmas Eve. Snap out of it!"

Denham took his departure soon after. Sibyl and I finished tieing up the rest of our packages without talking much. When we had gone to bed she snuggled into my -arms, crushed her loveliness against me as though she couldn't ever get close enough. "Hug me tight, Paul!" she whispered. "Oh, darling, never let go of me! I'm afraid!"

Afraid of what? I told myself that such bizarreness was food for mad minds! But just the same, I'd have given a million if we hadn't had that radio going.

Morning came with sunshine winking diamonds from raindrops against the trees. Here in our far southern city, Christmas was even warmer than usual. The whole world seemed to have been scrubbed spotless for the Holy Day. The night's shadows were gone. We were young, alive, in love—and living was grand!

We dawdled through breakfast, sitting side by side, opening our presents, exclaiming and giggling like a couple of kids. Sibyl was up to her trick of flinging her lovely bare arms around my neck and smothering me with kisses till I couldn't breathe. "Oh, Paul, my own—I love you!" she whispered.

It wasn't till after more than an hour that I finally got around to unfolding the morning paper. The business that had jolted us the night before had stirred up a sensation. The general reaction was that of amused bewilderment as to how the thing could have taken place. Officials at the broadcasting station denied that anyone there had uttered the words. How the voice could have managed to crash the wavelength was, they professed, something that had them stopped.

The station's denial of responsibility failed of conviction in most quarters. The impression seemed to be that some wag in the outfit had pulled a practical joke, and now the responsible heads were trying to crawl out from under.

One commentator said that the business of bad-taste radio gags had gone far enough; it was time for government censorship . . . A lot of people had been gullible enough to get badly frightened. Midnight services at the churches had been packed as never before. Scores of calls had come through to police headquarters from panicked listeners begging protection. Out in the country, a farmer had been found behind a woodpile with a shotgun waiting for the destroyers to come with the burning rain . . . A quippish feature writer put in a column comparing the wickedness of the world today with that at the time of the Biblical flood when Noah and his family alone of all mankind had escaped in the Ark. And so on . . .

Sibyl was leaning over my shoulder, her fragrant hair brushing my cheek, her bare white shoulder close to my lips as I read through the pages. She was the loveliest thing!

"What utter nonsense!" she murmured. "To think that educated people could be such fools—"

And then I heard her voice catch, saw her face slowly stiffen as her eyes fixed on an item in small print tucked away at the foot of a column.

The police, it said, were continuing their investigation of the strange fates of no less than seven men whose bodies had been picked up in dark alleys. Through some as yet mysterious means they had been burned almost entirely to a crisp. Only enough of them remained for identification. They were known to have been in the company of women earlier in the evening, but no traces of their companions as yet had been found.

And in a still more inconspicuous place under a column of ads I noticed the following:

Shortly after midnight last night a demented woman was found wandering nude in an alley. She was taken in custody by officers in a patrol car. From her rambling talk it was evident that her mind had been affected by certain parts of a radio broadcast. She muttered continually about having seen drops of fire falling from the sky. She has been sent to the psychopathic hospital for observation . . .

Sibyl made odd, gasping sounds. Her little head with its tangle of copper ringlets twisted around to me.

"Seven!" she whispered. "Last night it was two! That voice we heard said that—" She shivered, again gripped by that eerie terror that I couldn't comprehend, her eyes dark wells against her cheeks' pallor. She sobbed: "Those men were burned to death—on Christmas Eve! Could that happen—to us?"

I kissed her and patted her shoulder. "Forget it!" I muttered. "Just newspaper sensationalism—and rank coincidence. Go get ready while I bring the car out. We still have a lot of presents to deliver."

We got through that Christmas Day much the same as any newly married and prosperous couple with a gang of friends, calling around at numberless parties, dancing and downing cocktails in polite merriment. And secretly thankful in our minds for the uproar that kept us from thinking.

By evening we were paired with Laura and Chris Archimbault. Laura was Sib's particular girlhood chum, a grave, quiet girl demurely lovely in a way hard to put into words. Chris was a rising young engineer.

We dropped in at several night clubs and finally about midnight decided to call it enough and started for home. It had turned warmer. The light was grey all over the city and fog hung in the windless trees. The street lights were blurred misty blobs.

We suddenly found Denham and Emil Mowray with us, and several others. Mowray was Denham's law partner. He was short and stocky and important appearing. His face was a granite-grey deadpan with searching blue eyes. We four younger ones were a little ashamed of having drunk so much.

We turned at random down a side street and all at once were aware of a small crowd knotted around the head of an alley. "Oh, what's happening?" Sibyl exclaimed. She started running, pulling me after her. We came up on the outside of the ring. And then we were all six standing there spellbound staring.

On a box a few yards down into the alley there stood a figure dressed in unspeakable beggar's rags. So tall that his stooped shoulders seemed to lend him even greater height, he had a long face green-white in hue and aglow with the eerie light that plays over the countenances of the dead. A fuzz of mold overspread his hairless cranium. A goatish black beard straggled down from lips that were writhing blue worms. He posed there gruesome and heart-stopping as though a corpse had broken its cerements to curse the earth on Christ's Birthday.

We stood chilled before that revolting macabre spectacle. And then the creature's voice rose harsh as a raven's cawing:

"Nation of lechers, drunkards and thieves! Ye who worship Mammon and have forgotten God!"

From the outskirts of the crowd a mawkish voice jeered, "That's right, old timer! Give 'em hell! Where will you be at the millennium? I'm goin' to Florida—"

A ripple of vapid laughter rose uncertainly and then died. With a scream fanatical in its intensity, the man raked hooked talons across the air. "Bibbers of wine and chasers of women! Ye shall be burned tonight by fire from heaven!"

And then suddenly silence fell; not one sound was heard, not even a whisper. For they all had the same thought that came when Sibyl finally gasped, "That is the man we heard on the radio! And those people—seven of them—burned to death!"

"Not seven—twenty-two, now," Mowray muttered. "They've been picking them up all the evening. The police won't let it get into the papers—"

"Twenty-two! Dear God!" Sibyl wheeled to stare at him, lips draining bloodless. For in some way what Mowray had said had stricken her with a terror infinitely sharper than my own incredulous horror. Sibyl had always seemed a more primitive creature than most women. And now the swift thought came to me. With her uncanny feminine intuition, had she sensed the presence of something dark and cataclysmic at which my duller mind could only wonder? Were there really such things upon earth?

Then she came pressing against me. I felt her taut quivering and it infected me too with her fear. "Paul!" she whispered. "Take me away from here! I want to go home!"

"Yes," I muttered. "We'll go." I had half turned to work our way out of the crowd when from behind the voice sounded again.

"I am God's vengeance. But He did not mean for man to labor alone. I must have a helpmate to work at my side—"

The beggar paused and those eyes that seemed like festering sores once more swept the circle around. "Men lust for women's flesh. In their lust they shall perish," he was muttering.

And now I saw that the creature's gaze had ceased its wild slow roving to focus on the upturned face of Chris Archimbault's wife. He leaned from the box, pointing toward her, and his hooked finger beckoned.

"Come! Come here to me!" His call had fallen to a whisper vibrantly compelling.

I had expected that Laura would laugh at him. I turned to look at her—and stood petrified. I felt the hair on my back bristling like that on the spine of a terrified dog.

Chapter Two

Death—Girl

Laura didn't laugh! Instead, she started to move toward that noisome figure! Her lips parted, her eyes searched his eyes. Her face was deathly pale, rapt in an expression of terror—and of ghastly attraction!

She had moved two or three steps away from her husband before he awoke to the truth. "Laura, what are you doing!" he shouted. He seized her arm to pull her back but she brushed his hand down. She uttered a sound that was more like a mewing that anything human, and started running.

"Laura, for God's sake!" Chris made another grab for her but the pack wedged between them, shutting him off. "Let her go! Let's see what's going to happen!" voices cried. There were men in the crowd too intoxicated to realize what they were doing—others, too callous to care as long as they saw something exciting.

Chris and I both went after her then—Mowray and Denham, too. We were frightened to death—of what, we didn't yet know. But a tight surging line shut us off from her by that time and we couldn't break through.

Over the shoulders in front of us we got glimpses of Laura. She stood at the beggar's feet, gazing up at him, conscious of nothing else in the world! He leaned down to whisper. What he was saying no one could hear. But slowly her hands rose to loosen the fur-collared evening coat around her neck. It fell to the ground. Her white shoulders blossomed against the dark. Her hands rose again and then the evening dress had followed the coat. Daintily she slid her fingers under the straps of her underthings and they came rippling away. Save for her high-heeled silver slippers and stockings, Laura's rosy-white form stood utterly nude!

I heard Archimbault's crazed yelling as he flung himself against the wall of people. But even now they wouldn't let him go through—for they wanted to see! They grinned lewdly. A woman so drunk that she was undressing before a bum in an alley!

Laura swayed slightly, her whole figure seeming to reach toward the monster. Then from head to foot she was quivering. She held out her hands toward him, smiling invitation!

I heard Sibyl's sobbing beside me. I turned to look at her. And then there assailed me such a shock of terror as stopped my heart.

For my wife's face didn't register fear or repulsion now—but rather, a hideous longing! A desire that was making her thirst to do as Sibyl was doing! I saw her hands flutter up to her bosom—as though she too experienced an irresistible hunger to bare her own body to that satyr's gaze.

"Sibyl, for God's sake!" I shouted. I grabbed her hands and yanked them away.

That was enough to have made me pick my wife up and carve my way with her out of this place! But the crowd pinned us there—and beyond, the beggar was whispering to Laura again. Obediently she turned to go past him into the blackness that clogged the rear of the alley.

Their animal desires stampeded by what they had seen, a knot of young thugs went flocking after her, shouting. For a minute there was wild confusion. Sibyl and I and our friends were carried along with the mob into the narrow passage. We came to the corner around which Laura had disappeared. Turned—and then we saw!

In a dark angle Laura stood with shoulders swaying, hips moving rhythmically. I knew her as a shy girl almost painfully modest. But now! Passion rippled down her slim body. From head to foot she was vibrating, gyrating, in a muscle dance that was eerily beautiful—lasciviously suggestive.

The men yelled and surged around her. I saw one rat-faced ruffian grab her arm and jerk her toward him. She shrieked—*in crazed delight!* Then others were tugging at her, dragging her back. They battled over her with the insensate lust of a pack of wolves.

Over her head Laura's arms rose to weave in swift serpentine motions. She crooned bestially—with clawed fingers she seemed to be invoking the aid of unearthly powers. And then came incredible horror!

The knot of men exploded away from her as though burst apart by a bomb. They staggered against the walls of the alley and then fell to the ground. They lay there rolling and thrashing in agony, squealing like dying animals. Convulsions overtook them and their hands tore at their clothing, ripping themselves nearly naked, exposing flesh . . .

Flesh that in a space of seconds turned from white to yellow, from yellow to brown . . . and then to black—save where their frenzied fingers clawed furrows of crimson.

While we all stood there stricken, unable to speak, unable to breathe—they were all dead. Six of them lay there, their bodies the cindery black of overdone roasts of beef, crackling as they slowly writhed in reflex contortions. In the air hung the sickeningly sweetish odor of cooked meat.

Laura, too . . . Scraping against the wall of a house as she sagged downward, her body twisted and shrivelled like a husk of burned paper . . . folded into a crinkling mass . . .

I stared at the faces around me, ashen terror-masks, the eyes haggard, things that crawled in the whiteness. Sibyl flung herself into my arms and clung to me, small fisted hands pounding my back. The noises that came from her were sounds utterly insane, wholly devoid of meaning.

"He did it! He made Laura kill them with fire from heaven!" her gagged retchings came. "And then it killed her! On Christmas Day! Christmas isn't for death! It's for parties and laughing and happiness. Oh, merciful God!"

I got my arm around my wife and crushed her against me while gooseflesh of animal terror rolled on my spine. If that had happened to Laura, it could happen to Sibyl! It could happen to all of us!

The beggar had vanished during the excitement. Wild confusion seethed then. Police whistles were shrilling. Blue uniforms came beating through the mob. I looked around for Chris Archimbault and the other men and couldn't find them. Finally out in the open with Sibyl, I located a taxi and bundled her into it. I told the driver to break every law to get us home.

Back in our apartment at last, Sibyl stood staring at me, paler than death. Her clenched hands crushed to her bosom which rose and fell under her hysterical breathing.

"He did what he said he was going to do!" my wife whispered over and over. "He burned them to death without any fire! He took Laura away from us and burned her, just like that!" She seized my hands, clutched them half crazily. "Paul—can such things happen? Is there a power that men can use to do things that are impossible?"

I shook my head. "I don't know," I muttered. "A thousand years ago men believed in forces wielded by devils. We thought that those ideas were discredited—dead. If civilization is wrong—if they can come back to life . . ."

I was bewildered.

To think of such a thing was horror enough! But it wasn't the worst. I had a vision of Sibyl's face with that look as though she too had wanted to strip herself before that monster, and my skin was clammy. Laura had done that—and died!

Sibyl went over and poured herself a drink, spilling most of it on the table. She muttered and went jerkily to switch on the radio. We both stood with our glasses half raised, listening. Again, in that inhumanly emotionless tone, the words issued forth:

"Five more men have been found strangely burned to death since the similar destruction of six in an alley back of the Lazy Cat Club half an hour ago. This raises the total to forty-nine in the last twenty-four hours. Professor Latham, pathologist of State University, has been hastily summoned to examine the bodies in the hope of determining the cause of the deaths. Authorities are at a loss to explain the weird occurrences. It is extremely dangerous to venture into the streets . . ."

The program switched into a fanfare of swing music. I strode across the room and shut off the radio. Sibyl clutched at my hands. "Paul—could that happen to us?" she said hoarsely. "Could it get us in here?"

In the moment before I could find words with which to answer her, the sudden hush of the apartment was pierced by the whir of the doorbell. Thankful for any diversion, I hurried out into the hall.

Our caller was Everett Noble, a friend of Sibyl's and mine for some time. He had been with us when Laura had succumbed to the mad beggar's power. Noble was big and white-skinned with Scandinavian blue eyes and flaxen hair. Almost contemptuously self-assured, he seemed to radiate the animal virility of a bull. His eyes held lights that penetrated one's brain with the flaming quality of an electric arc. He had the reputation of exercising an uncanny fascination over women—one that had always made me vaguely resentful of his presence in my wife's company. But now I welcomed the arrival of anyone!

There was only one thing about which to talk. We discussed the sensational occurrences for a few moments and then Noble exclaimed:

"Did you know that Laura Archimbault wasn't the first girl

to go haywire like that? Seven or eight young women have been reported missing in the last couple of weeks."

"There are always a lot of disappearances," I said. "You're not trying to tell me that those girls could have had anything to do with the burnings, are you?"

Noble shrugged. "We all saw what happened there, didn't we?" He smiled strangely, his electric eyes swerving to fasten on Sibyl. "You must know that there are men who *do* possess a queer power over women. There was that Russian monk, Rasputin. He was hideous, but they fell for him in droves. They would commit the most ghastly deeds if he told them to." Noble took a stride down the rug. "I tell you, Adams, there are forces loose in the world that civilization hasn't explained . . . that sanity is afraid even to question."

I stared back at him without answering. A sense of irritation assailed me, to think that I had admitted him, to increase Sibyl's nervous terror by such crazy talk. Then I was conscious that his curiously penetrating gaze was traveling past me again to fix on my wife.

Sibyl stood there staring at Noble while her lovely pale face drained bloodless—while over it stole an expression that no words can describe. The same ghastly attraction that had been in Laura's eyes the instant before she had started discarding her clothing! Sibyl didn't actually move from the spot where she stood—yet in some intangible way she seemed to sway toward Noble, reaching out to him with her whole being.

I spun around, rage needling me. Noble was going too far with his woman-charming! I opened my mouth to order him out of my house—and then froze under the most weirdly gruesome thought that had ever come to my brain.

For as I looked at Everett Noble, it seemed as though I were seeing not him, but the ragged fanatic in the alley! It is a baffling thing to try to describe, for their features were utterly different. Yet I had the grisly conviction that the two shared not only the same soul—but that they were the same flesh and blood. Different incarnations of the same physical substance—as though some magic had altered the death's head of the beggar into virile manhood to come here and weave its spell over my wife! The spell that had taken Laura Archimbault to her death!

I cursed behind my locked teeth. I must be going insane! The resemblance must be only a fancied one, bred of my terror-fraught nerves.

Yet something was here in the room with us three. It was nothing that I could see or touch or hear, nothing that I could put my finger on. But I could feel it, leering and hideous and cold.

Chapter Three

Satan's Understudy

Sibyl glided toward Noble. Now she stood at his side, trembling with some dreadful excitement—lips falling open, bosom heaving. And then once again her hands rose to fumble at the front of her dress. I could almost feel the effort of will that it cost her to keep from baring her breasts to his gaze in the same way that Laura had done under the beggar's eyes! Her voice came awed, breathless.

"Tell me, Mr. Noble—this influence that you say some men have over women. How can such a thing be? How could one human soul enslave another?"

"A woman's function in life is to reproduce life." Noble smiled with the tolerant superiority of one instructing a child. "For her, all existence interprets itself in terms of sex and nothing else. The sex impulse is like an electric current passing from man to woman. Usually this passing is hindered by the checks and inhibitions impressed upon us moderns by what we call civilization. But in rare cases the man's impulse is so overwhelming—his sex-voltage is so high, if one may use the expression—that it crashes down the resistance that a modern woman instinctively sets up between herself and her genuine instincts. She is swept off her feet. She becomes his slave."

"Yes—I understand," Sibyl whispered. She licked her lips that curved sensuously, her eyes crazily brilliant. "And if there were such a man here today, he could make women work for him? He could make them slaves for his killings? And they would love to kill—even if they died themselves?"

Noble smiled at her—lewdly, possessively. "A woman mastered by sex-consciousness will do anything for her master," he whispered. "Beautiful and refined as you are, you too would—"

And then I snapped out of my horror trance to lunge at him, fists swinging. "Get out!" I cursed hoarsely. "If you ever look at my wife again I'm going to kill you!"

He smiled mockingly, shrugged and turned to pick up his coat from the hall table. I heard the door click behind him, heard his departing steps—and then there was only the sound of Sibyl's thin breathing.

I turned numbly to reach out for her. But my wife wouldn't allow me to touch her! She jerked away from me. "Don't come near me!" she muttered. She darted a look that was almost hatred.

"Sibyl, for heaven's sake!" I gasped. "What is it—what have I done?"

She didn't answer. I stared at her while black maggots of hideous surmise crawled on my brain. Before Noble's coming, she had been all sweet, yielding passion. She had looked at him with eyes of desire. And now she snarled at me like a she-cat that has found a new mate. I licked my cold lips. Would the next step be for her to do as those other women had done?

For another instant we stood there staring at one another, not speaking—scarcely breathing. And then I heard my wife's voice exclaiming: "That box! He must have left it! But I didn't see him bring it in!"

Sibyl was pointing at a sizable paper wrapped parcel that stood in shadows near the end of the couch where Noble had for a moment sat after he had arrived. Curious noises came from it. It rocked back and forth, as though some living thing inside were moving.

I went over, lifted the thing to the seat of the couch and cut the cords. As I pulled up the cardboard flaps of the carton there leaped onto the floor a huge black cat. With a snarl he sprang to the middle of the rug where he crouched, with ears flattened against his hideous sloping skull, tail lashing, eyes glaring—yowling insanely.

I was assailed by a stab of nervous anger. I had always hated cats—their smug arrogance, their inscrutable malevolent ways. In the middle ages they had been deemed agents of infernal powers!

Suddenly the creature stopped growling and trotted over to Sibyl. It purred at her fingers, rubbed sensuously around her legs. Its blackness against her white skin made me think of an evil spirit nuzzling and fondling, whispering temptation— as though Noble, departing, had left behind his *familiar* of unholy power to carry on in his absence!

Then it galloped across to the door. It paused, looking back, mewing. I was glad enough that it wanted to go! I hurried over to open the door but it wouldn't depart. It stood half way over the threshold, gazing back at Sibyl with its lustful yellow eyes. It seemed to be—saying something to her!

"It wants us to go with it!" she cried suddenly. She sprang up to run for her coat. "Paul, that cat wants to take us somewhere!"

"What are you talking about!" I shouted. This was the craziest yet! I would have kicked the thing into the corridor and had done with it. But I saw that for some wild reason Sibyl was determined to follow it.

I dragged my coat off the hook and ran after my wife as she passed through the door. The cat led us out of the apartment house, and down the street we went, following the black tail that stuck up rigidly as a flagpole . . .

The bizarreness of that trip was something that I'll never forget! For that jet imp led us through streets and alleys, seldom pausing, never at a loss which way to go. The surroundings became darker, more fearsome and sinister. Stalls of shabby tenements closed around us. From corner saloons came the blaring of tinny music, maudlin voices roaring in song.

At length the cat turned into an alley more forbidding than all the rest. Noisome smells issued from pitch blackness. I thought of what I had seen take place in that other alley and the gelid miasma of night slid on my scalp.

At length worm-eaten boards creaked under our feet and then I was pushing at a door that sagged from one rusted hinge. The cat had already scuttled through into whatever in the devil's name might lie there beyond.

We found a rear hall out of which rickety stairs crooked up into gloom. At the top of the third flight was a gas jet like a wavering yellow mouth without any face. And in front of another door stood the cat, gazing up at us from its slitted green eyes.

I pushed softly against the door—pushed again . . .

The room on the other side of the door disclosed itself as an attic den truncated across one corner by the sloping roof. Mismated pieces of furniture stood amidst squalor. A pair of peaked gable windows stared like blind eyes from behind veilings of cobwebs. And squatted down in a corner was the man we had seen in the alley! The beggar who had called Laura Archimbault from her husband's side!

I heard Sibyl's tight, frightened gasp. She came surging against me, fingers clasping my arm. And then the repulsive form had arisen to come scuffing toward us. He smiled in ogre-like welcome. I cursed and pushed Sibyl behind me. I had another vision of those blasted men in the alley and black terror-worms started writhing out of my brain and along my nerves to my finger ends. That devil wasn't even going to look at her—not if I knew it!

"Welcome, my beautiful one," he purred. He was addressing Sibyl! "I knew you would come to me. I need you to work for me. That was why I left Niger there in your house—to bring you here to me."

"You left the cat!" I yelled hoarsely. "It wasn't you. It was

Noble—"

Then came such gripping horror that I couldn't breathe. In my house I thought I had recognized Noble as the fiend of the alley. And now, facing the beggar, I knew the grisly conviction that he was Everett Noble! To be sure, the emaciated figure, the raven croaking, the corpse-head mildewed with bluish mold, were not Noble's. Nor was there any possibility of cheap deception through theatrical makeup. They were two different men. Yet in some infinitely deeper and more hideous reality they were the same blood, bone and tissue—identical bodies.

I told myself that imagination was running away with me. Such things didn't happen! Then while I stood staring, the ragged man pointed at a small object upon the table.

"Your cigarette case—I picked it up in your house by mistake," he smiled mockingly.

I let out a gulping noise; for an instant I couldn't think sanely—my mind was a blank. I had the crazy idea that Noble had indeed changed into this creature. And then I wondered where Noble was now—if his mortal body had disappeared or if he were taking his turn at death while his *were-self* masqueraded in the guise of this monster! A mad notion! But I knew that there was something damnable here.

And then I heard the cracked voice addressing me again. "Now that you have brought the woman I wanted, you may go."

"You swine!" The yell burst from me and I leaped at him. His hand rose and I froze in my tracks, my brain jellied.

He stood there, rags swaying, eyes inhumanly lurid with sulphurous flames. And from his beard, his cadaver's cheeks, his unspeakable garments—and from his upraised hooked fingers—there bubbled and flowed streams of dazzling luminance. Rivers of fire!

"You saw the men in the alley!" his rasping voice came. "Lay a finger on me, and it will be your wife who will bring the fire upon you. For her soul is *mine*, now. And her body will be mine—soon."

I saw his gaze whip aside to fasten on Sibyl's dear blood-drained face—transfigured in ghastliness. Her eyes locked on his, lips parted, her features were stamped with the awful subservience of a slave for her master. She stumbled toward him, slim body quivering, hands trembling out.

I knew that if he told her to kill me—she would obey!

Chapter Four

"Kiss Me—and Die!"

That moment of suspense was as long as eternity!

And then I had snatched my wife by the hand and I was dragging her out of there, tripping and stumbling down the steep flights of stairs. Whether we would live to get out, I didn't know! We hit the alley and I didn't stop running till we were back in a broad thoroughfare with lights and crowds.

I stopped the first policeman we met and panted out an incoherent tale of what had occurred. But when he eyed me disbelievingly to ask the address of the house, I could only shake my head. I muttered that a cat led us there. The officer grunted something about everyone going screwy these days, and turned away.

A taxi cruised past and I hailed it. Inside, I put my arm around Sibyl and drew her close. Her fingers in mine were clammy, colder than death. I tried to say something to her but an iron hand had me by the throat.

I had to accept it at last. In spite of my education and intelligence I accepted it—the existence of a power wielded by dual souls from an unseen half-world. Under my very eyes I had seen it meshing around my darling as those death-women had been enslaved. How far away was the hour when I would see the girl I loved naked, enticing sex-stampeded men into an alley—to kill them? To die with them as Laura had died?

I didn't try to reason with Sibyl when we finally arrived back home. I was past reasoning! I had had a look through

windows of hell into an infernal world! And she was hysterical, unable to say anything rational. I undressed her, put her
to bed and gave her a powder to make her sleep.

When I bent to kiss her goodnight, she shuddered and
again drew away from me.

"No, Paul—don't touch me!" she almost screamed.

My heart lay like something dead as I left her. I went to the
telephone and asked my friend Denham to come over. I had
to have some one to talk to!

Denham sat fingering his highball glass and his thin dark
face became tensely motionless as I recounted the events of
the last couple of hours. "Tell me I'm crazy!" I finished. "To
think that Noble and that beggar have the same body in different forms! That one or both of them could enslave the
wills of those girls and make them kill for him!"

He shook his head pensively. "Crazy—not at all," his answer astonished me. "The human soul—the will—is a baffling thing. I believe that under stress of terrific emotion a
stronger mind can establish its power over a weaker one.
And then the subservient one will reflect the personality of
its master. That beggar is a crazy fanatic and Noble is undoubtedly tied up with him in this business. That is why you
thought they looked alike. The police ought to know about
this."

"Leaving that angle out for a moment, how about the rest
of it—what he called fire from heaven?" I said. "Those people really are being burned to death, you know."

My caller's deepset eyes gazed at me strangely. "Fire from
heaven—Sodom and Gomorrah!" he murmured. "Are you
one of those who take the Bible literally, Adams?"

I stared back at him and I shivered. The room was stiflingly
hot—it was the wind of fear that fanned my brain.

After a moment Denham leaned over to switch on the radio. That ghastly voice that I had come to dread rose from
vague mutterings as the tubes heated:

". . . eleven more bodies have been found in the last hour,
bringing the total to seventy-nine . . . Ten thousand dollars

reward offered for apprehension of a character known as "the Beggar" . . . All persons again warned to remain in their homes except on matters of utmost urgency . . . Scenes throughout the city unparalleled since the days of the Black Death . . . Tonight a million men and women are learning the meaning of fear . . . Annihilation is apparently striking from the skies, but mysterious, unclothed and demented women are in some way concerned . . . The committee of public safety announces the following places of refuge in the event of a mass attack . . ."

"Great God!" I muttered.

Denham left soon after that. I went in where Sibyl lay sleeping under the influence of the sedative. She couldn't repulse me now! I knelt by her bed to draw her into my arms. I kissed her forehead, her eyes, her soft neck.

How I adored her! It was her dear body that lay there; but inside she didn't belong to me any more. Her soul was struggling to go where she had heard the compelling whispering of that monster!

Finally I undressed and got into the other twin bed. For what seemed centuries I twisted and turned while the whole grisly parade of the horrors marched through my brain. My throat parched, I finally drained the glass of water that stood on the side table. I drifted into heavy slumber . . .

The sun was shining when I awoke. I stumbled to the floor, rubbing my eyes, wincing, puzzled at the headache that throbbed in my skull. Sibyl was already up. I heard the water splashing in the bath tub.

I made my way out into the living room. I started to go out into the hall to get the morning paper—and halted as my gaze focused on something on the floor in front of the outer door. I saw the mark of a foot; a bare sole that had walked through water and mud.

For another instant I blinked at it without comprehending. Then all at once I stiffened in full realization—starkly awake now, apprehensive. For that wasn't my footprint; it was narrow and dainty. A woman's. Sibyl's!

I whirled toward the bathroom. I jerked open the door and

stood stock-still, my brain frozen, my nerves congealing into ice.

Sibyl had just stepped out of the tub. She stood there, rosy nude figure dappled with water drops, a Dryad of enchanting curves and pearly hollows. She was gazing intently into the mirror, scrutinizing her shoulders and bosom.

The water in the tub was dark with grime that had come from my wife's feet. And over her rounded creamy arms, her breasts, were deep scratches. Gouges that could have been left there only by men's lusting fingers!

Something snapped in my brain. I knew now the secret of my heavy slumber, my headache. Sibyl had switched the glass in which I had administered her sleeping potion, for the one on my table. She had drugged me! And while I slept she had wakened and . . .

A strangled cry broke from me. I seized her wet shoulders and shook her.

"Where did you go? What did you do?" I cried. "Where did those marks come from?"

She didn't speak. She cowered there in my grip, shrinking back from me. Drop by drop the blood ebbed from her face. Her eyes stared madly.

I groaned in my agony. She didn't need to confess to me. I knew that she had gone out to meet the creature who had twined his noisome power around her soul. And if she had obeyed his commands . . .

Then I was aware that her supple form had started twisting under my hands, an indescribably lewd rippling of shoulders and hips. And then with a cat-like writhing she came pressing against me, till I felt her breasts crushed to my chest— felt the surge of her flesh welded to mine. Her arms flew to twine around my neck. Her voice was hoarse:

"Kiss me, my lover! Paul, take me and kiss me!"

In spite of horror, flesh and blood couldn't withstand her. I stooped to kiss her. The lips that she crushed to mine were the slack lips of a wanton! Her eyes drooped sensually.

Then while I still held her, I saw her arms rising over my

head. They moved with that curious stiff jerking, hooked fingers clawed downward, that I had seen that other girl use on the men who kissed her the instant before they died screaming in fire. And into her eyes darted a gleam that was utterly fiendish.

"Paul—kiss me again!" she whispered through twisted lips.

"Heavenly God!" I let out the cry as I leaped away from her. This was hideousness to blast the soul! Sibyl enticing me into her arms to kill me while our lips clung with the power that she had learned from her master!

It was stark terror of death that sent my fist driving out to the tip of her chin, dropping her in a limp heap at my feet.

The rest of that day passed in a blur. After I had revived Sibyl she locked herself in the spare bedroom. She wouldn't open the door, even when I prepared something to eat at noon and again at night, and called softly through the panel.

I paced the rooms, dizzy, half crazed. I didn't dare let my mind dwell on what she had done during the night—in that direction madness lay! There was only one thing to think about now! How I could save her—if any mortal could find ways to battle powers dispatched from hell!

But I had to try—I had to do something!

A thousand detectives were searching the town for the beggar—without success. Then along in the afternoon a news broadcast stated that the monster had been seen. But when pursued into a vacant house, no one was found there save Everett Noble, a well-known young attorney, who professed to have been hunting for the beggar himself.

That meant little to the authorities. But for me it had a stunning significance that snaked cold things along my spine. I thought of that wild idea I had had in the attic when I had wondered if Noble had changed into the beggar. And now the insane fancy was whispering again. Was the reason that the monster couldn't be caught because when in danger he altered himself into Noble?

I knew that thought must be madness! But what about that cat? And Sibyl had manifested the identical unholy attraction toward both of those figures. For a time I considered going to the police. But if I should tell them that Noble and the beggar were one and the same, it would be me whom they would put behind bars.

All I could plan in the end was to try again to find the beggar and kill him. If I did that, would it be enough? Would Noble die at the same time? Or would he live to go on with the awfulness? And if I did at last find him, would I have time to tear out his heart before I felt the fire leap over me . . . before I smelled the aroma of my own roasting meat?

I got Denham on the phone and asked if he and his wife would come over and stay with Sibyl while I was gone. I wouldn't have left her alone for a million!

"We'll be over right after dinner," he said instantly. "I'll guarantee that she won't go out anywhere. And if that devil shows up at your place—well, I'm bringing my automatic!"

Shortly after dark Sibyl opened her door. She was calm now, her beautiful face pale as death, scored with cruel lines. While she ate sandwiches and sipped coffee, I told her about the plans for the night.

She looked at me startled, eyes filling with tears. She swayed from her chair—and the next instant she was held tight in my arms.

"No, Paul! Oh, dearest, don't leave me; never let go of me!" her sobbed moaning came. "Last night—I don't know what happened." She could scarcely choke out her piteous words. "I seem to remember—oh, terrible dreams! Don't ask me to tell you—don't ever ask me. Just keep me with you every minute, my darling."

I held her tight and breathed thankfulness to God. That malign spell had passed from her soul. She was her dear normal self again.

"You're all right now," I murmured. I stroked her hair as she nestled her head on my shoulder. "But he isn't through with you yet. He'll never stop trying to get you as long as he lives. I've got to finish it up tonight—end it so we can quit worrying."

"No! No!" she cried again. She clung to me like a terrified

child, clutching my shoulders. "Don't go away from me to-night—not *this* night!" she pleaded desperately. "I'm so horribly afraid! But nothing can hurt me if you just hold me in your arms, tight!"

The Denhams came and I left her with them. They could protect her as well as I could, I reasoned. And I had to finish this thing.

I believed then that I was doing right. If God will ever forgive me for that! If any remorse of mine now, or a lifetime of service to my poor wife can in some measure atone for my blindness when with hell meshing around her I left her alone! When I forgot the unearthly powers that could summon her through thin air!

Chapter Five

Sibyl Kills!

Out in the streets terror's dark wings were whispering. All knew their danger, yet the sidewalks were jammed by throngs drawn by macabre curiosity—watching and waiting like gladiatorial crowds for the appearance of another of those nude figures whose coming meant death.

I left the crowds and went alone—I deemed my chances better in the dark corners and alleys. Hours—centuries—passed and I didn't see the man for whom I was searching.

Then finally I found myself ringing the bell at the door of the apartment where Everett Noble lived in bachelorhood. He admitted me and I didn't pause to use tact. I gripped him by the throat and banged his head against the wall till his protruding tongue grew purple and his eyes squirted out of his head.

"Talk!" I gritted. "Tell me what you have to do with this or I'll kill you!"

He swept out his hand for a vase that stood on a table to crash it down on my head. But I beat him there and it was my blow that smashed him. There was a jangle of splintering pottery and I felt the man wilt through my hands to sag on the floor. I went out and left him there, alive but unconscious, with blood gushing from a long cut over his temple.

I was back in the streets again—baffled, bewildered, my terror a strangling web. But still darker horrors were swiftly to follow!

I came up to the fringe of another throng spellbound by one of the news bulletins now being issued every ten minutes. I wasn't going to listen—I was fed up with the awfulness. But in hastening past I heard a voice that I recognized.

The beggar was on the air again!

That brought me to a standstill—while a slow frigid rolling of horror congealed me from heels to heart. For this time he wasn't preaching hell fire. *He was talking to Sibyl!* To her alone of all the hundreds of thousands in the city! His tones came in those vibrations charged with unearthly authority before which she had once before quailed in obedience.

"Sibyl, kill Denham! Kill the man and woman who are keeping you away from me! Last night you became my slave. Do what I showed you how to do. Bring the fire from heaven upon that rich man. Do it now, while you hear me! And then come to me—"

I whirled from the doorway and started running as I had never run in my life. In the macabre onrush of terror sweat gushed over me and I shivered under it as though it were ice. I had thought that by leaving Sybil with some one to watch her I had shut her away from the monster's power. One thing I had overlooked in my blindness—the radio. His voice could go to her through that modern magic—and she would obey!

But she wasn't in sight when I ran panting into the house. Only Denham and his wife were there. Mrs. Denham lay on the rug, her naked body charred to a cinder. Denham had been burned, though not killed. I found him at the telephone, clothes hanging in ribbons, arms and torso raked with livid weals, bleating for the police.

He jerked around at the sound of my steps. His face was

the hue of raw veal, his eyes were glassy marbles against the white.

"She lifted her arms and it came!" he muttered. "And then she ran. She got away—"

I left him yammering there and got myself out of the place. How many more hours passed while I prowled the dark places, I'll never know. Madness walked hand in hand with me. I knew it was too late to save Sibyl now. One prayer was left in my heart, that I might just see her long enough to beg her forgiveness—to hold her in my arms and kiss her as I died.

But I didn't find her. The night waned. And then suddenly as I emerged from an alley into a back yard even darker and more menacingly shadow-thronged, I saw the beggar!

He was alone. All my muscles taut, my fingers hooked, I stalked toward him.

"My wife!" I cried. "Give me my wife or I'll kill you!"

The figure laughed. "If you could! But you can't. And if you did get her back, what good would it do you? She's my slave. If you kill me, I'll take her away with me—"

I gathered my feet under me to spring at him—and then my gaze suddenly focused on something that struck me motionless in my tracks.

Two hours before I had hit Everett Noble with a vase and opened a six-inch gash on the side of his head. And now across the skull of the beggar I saw a long diagonal cut in that identical spot—freshly made and wet with trickling blood.

I had smashed one man with a vase and another one bore the wound!

I sagged against the side of a fence, stricken, partly unable to utter a sound. All along I had been convinced of hellish duality between the two men, yet my common sense had told me it was because of terror-fraught nerves. But this! . . .

The next moment a police whistle shrilled from the street close behind. I saw burly figures come running. And when I jerked my gaze back to the spot where the beggar had been, he wasn't there.

I stumbled around to meet the sergeant at the head of the squad. "He went in that way!" I muttered, pointing. Behind the officers a knot of figures came running. In the lead I saw my two friends, Denham and Mowray. Denham's face and body were swathed in bandages.

I got them out of the confusion into a corner where we could talk. I told them about my fight with Noble and the wound on the beggar. "When I told you that I thought those two men were one—that they had the same bodies—you said it was a fancied resemblance, Denham. But I tell you, when I hit Noble, the beggar bled too!" My teeth were chattering, my fists clenched till my fingernails cut into the flesh.

Mowray stared at me in contemptuous incredulity. But Denham's face whitened, his voice came in awed thickness. "A thousand years ago they believed in warlocks—if you shot one of a pair the other died. But today—here—"

"Snap out of it, you two!" Mowray exclaimed. "This business is driving you crazy. You both really know that when we get to the bottom of it, we are going to find that everything—even the fire from heaven—was caused by perfectly scientific means and was done for a perfectly material and sordid purpose—money. Some one is using this to clean up."

"Who? Clean up how?" I exclaimed.

"Well, take the beggar," Mowray replied. "With half the police force on a terror strike and the other half hunting him, gangs of outside thugs have taken over the city. They are breaking into houses and stores, looting, raping—killing. They've got away with hundreds of thousands in cash. Suppose all this is just a buildup to give his gang of imported toughs a chance to go looting?"

That made more sense than anything I had heard. But it didn't bring Sibyl back! I muttered something and turned away. I was past reasoning now. Which one I was trying to find—Noble or the beggar—I didn't know. If I should catch one and take him to the police, he might change to the other before my eyes! I only knew that black forces out of another world were running wild and that my darling had forsaken me to join them. To become one of those sylphs of hellish allure whose kiss was the touch of death . . .

Most of the city's lights had been smashed. A pall of smoke-laden fog brooded over the housetops, lighted from beneath by lurid flashes like flames from infernal pits.

Streams of the beggars paraded past stores with shattered windows and goods strewn over the sidewalks. Their sin-bitten faces leered defiantly as they elbowed me into the gutters. They dragged screaming girls into alleys. Unafraid, they whooped and caroused in shadows where the fire-death had touched—as though they now felt secure in a partnership with the killers that would save them from harm.

I passed the railroad station, and bus terminals where cursing and sobbing throngs fought for a chance at the doors. Uncertainty, grim mother of fear, was driving the people in flight as though before a plague. Through wide-open doors of churches could be seen ranks of bowed worshippers. The sonorous tones of the organs rumbled over moaned prayers. Figures brushed past me running—pale faces upturned, eyes glassy, ashen lips jerking. Mothers clutched little ones to their bosoms—men openly carried pistols and knives.

I sobbed in my torment. Dear God, where was Sibyl? What was she doing now? What ghastliness had she been learning all these long hours?

New hallucinations were coming to unseat my mind. It seemed as though every swaying light shadow, every moonbeam, were the nude form of my darling.

And then all at once I knew that it wasn't fancy. That white shape that had gone gliding into an alley was real! It was Sibyl! And behind her clattered three uniformed figures—police.

I raced after her. If they should catch her and give her to the law—she would be the first upon whom they would pour out their vengeance!

The four passed from sight around an angle. And when I had reached the corner I saw her standing there—her slim, naked figure swaying, eerily beautiful as a half-creature out of another world. Her body glistened as though covered with oil, her satiny breasts throbbing. Slowly her hips rotated in those lewd undulations, inviting love! Her hands clutched at her breasts, fingernails piercing to drag at them till blood trickled—as though some insupportable hunger were flogging her.

And then horror came!

The officers rushed to close in on her. Her arms shot up, fingers hooked downward. From them dripped the same blobs of fire that had flowed from the beggar! And then on the brick pavement before her ... You don't want the details again—those men writhing there while they tore at their clothes and gave off the aroma of a Sunday roast ...

Words are vain things with which to convey the ghastliness that overwhelmed me as I stood there with brain petrified, limbs frozen. Here at last, before my eyes, I had seen ...

This was what had happened because I had left Sibyl, had ignored her frantic pleading to stay with her! If I could have given my life then to recall that blindness ...

For yet anther instant I crouched there as though palsied. And then my head jerked around. From behind had come confused noises. Into the mouth of the alley poured a solid mass of white faces—men brandishing knives, fists and clubs! They had seen what had happened! They were after Sibyl! I had a vision of her sweet flesh trampled under their feet ...

"Sibyl, run!" I gasped. And then I was rushing toward her, forgetting my own peril, forgetting that once she had threatened to kill me—probably would again! "Run somewhere! I'll keep them away!"

What she did, I never knew. For on reaching her side I whirled to confront the pack. Their noise rolled over me before their onslaught arrived—that sinister deep snarling, mob-cry of blood-hunger, which is the most terrible sound upon earth.

A piece of wood lay on the ground. I snatched it up and then the vanguard was on me. For a few seconds I held them at bay in that narrow space in a wild battle that could have but one ending. I hammered and flailed them. I crashed my bludgeon down on their skulls again and again.

A filthy ruffian snatched my weapon and then I was reduced to elementals. I clawed my fingernails over their faces till they were stuffed with shredded pulp—raked at their eyes. I used my knees in their bellies and then I used my teeth on their throats.

In less time than it takes to tell it, it was all over. They swept me up like chaff. They seized me and, lifting me up, passed me from hand to hand over their heads. I expected to be torn apart, for their eyes were not the eyes of men, but of animals.

The solid mass parted and they dropped me onto the ground. A boot came driving into my skull. And then they were all kicking me. They stood in a ring driving their feet into my vitals. I felt as though my ribs were splintering; jagged fires lanced through me. Weakly I rolled on my face, trying to get my arms up to cover my head. They kicked them away and the blows came in drumfire, endlessly. I moaned in my torture. With the insensate fury of brutes they laughed as they sought to kick me to death.

I seemed to sink into the shadows then, and they were dark—dark. The shadows gibbered around me; mocked me with their phantom substances. I knew I was dying. And somewhere near, Sibyl, my darling . . .

Chapter Six

Where Madness Dwells . . .

The cellar in which I found myself when I opened my eyes had been dug deep down toward hell, for into it penetrated no sound from the outer world. I tried to move and found myself lashed by wrists and ankles on top of a table.

The beggar was there and besides him two robed and masked figures. A dozen or more of the girls could be seen standing in groups. Their bodies glistened with a bluish unguent that gave off the same ethereal light that I had seen on the beggar and Sibyl.

And then a groan broke from me. I gave a spasmodic lunge against my ropes. For my darling was there! Utterly nude like the others, she stood rubbing the ointment over her body.

From some hidden source music was coming. Horns wailed and cymbals clashed. A pipe skirled obscene laughter and the girls filed before a black background. Their arms, raised over their heads, twined and interlaced, weaved bewildering patterns against the black-ground. Their arms, raised over their heads, twined and interlaced, weaved bewildering patterns against the black—*raining drops of fire.* Then they moved more swiftly, rippling, darting, coiling—a medley of indescribable weird beauty.

In and out among them moved the beggar. His hand clutched a whip. The tongue rose and fell, cutting at their flesh till they shrieked in crazed ecstasy.

Sibyl he lashed more cruelly than the others. She cowered back whimpering. She crouched in a corner, trying to cover herself with her clasped arms. Yet still on her face was that light of awful rapture! The adoration of a slave girl for the master who flogs her!

I cursed through clenched teeth. With all my strength I strained at the ropes that held me fast. The thin cords cut into my flesh till blood trickled. I fell back panting and desperate. I had to get out of here! I had to get over there and stop that hellishness. But how? The cords were like wire.

The uproar I raised accomplished one thing—it brought the two robed forms across to my side. Their hands rose to slip down their masks.

I looked up into the faces of—Denham and Noble!

For an instant I could only stare up at them witlessly.

"You two!" I muttered at last. "Denham—I thought you were my friend—"

"If you hadn't been an utter fool you would have learned long ago that there is one thing that friendship doesn't recognize—and that's money." Denham's eyes were glazed obsidian discs. "This business is getting us millions. All over the city people are dumping their property for what it will bring. We've got straw men buying it in for us. We'll corner the real estate. And then when it's over, and business comes back—"

"You did this to Sibyl and me—to thousands of people—for money!" I whispered. "God, what kind of a thing are you? But still I don't understand. That beggar—where does he come in?"

"I suppose we might call him the brains of the business," Denham grunted. "We heard him preaching one of his harangues about hell fire and it gave me an idea. Scare everyone half to death and clean up while they aren't bothering about money. We just took him over and organized his campaign."

"But the fire?" I whispered. "He did burn them—"

"That was done with powder that has the same effect on the skin as poison gas. It spreads over the body—burns—kills—in a few seconds. It was invented in—well, in a country of Europe—"

"The girls did that?" I gasped.

"They didn't do any killing themselves," Denham said. "They were just lures to get the men into the alleys and dark places. I've got the keys to any number of vacant houses. Either Noble or the beggar or I would go into one of them. We would have taken a girl in there, dressed, some time before. Then we would send her out to gather a crowd. When they followed her into the alley, we would throw the powder on them out of a window. The girls are covered with a counteracting oil to protect them. That was what made them and the beggar seem to drip fire. But we didn't have time to grease Laura Archimbault."

I stared at him, incredulous.

Across the room the whip crooned around Sibyl. It coiled like a black arm about her breasts and then leaped to snip away bits of her flesh while her thin screams shrilled.

"Stop it, damn you!" I foamed. "She is yours now, she'll kill for you. What more do you want? Are you such a swine that you just enjoy seeing that?"

Denham stood looking down, sneering crookedly.

"Squirm!" his thickened cursing rang. "I've been waiting years to see you like this—yelling in torture! The mob left you for dead and it gave me my chance—I brought you here. The money was only half of it. The first time I saw Sibyl I wanted her—made up my mind to have her. God, how I've hated you, seeing you kissing her." He smashed me across the face and sadistic triumph blazed in his eyes as blood spurted.

"You knew that she would never go to you in her right mind so you are driving her insane!" I snarled, understanding.

"She's half gone now, it won't take long to finish," my tormentor muttered.

He turned to beckon behind him. Steps sounded—and then above me I saw Sibyl's face! Her ivory shoulders and red lips, copper-gold hair streaming over her bosom—beautiful as a dream. But still in some way not Sibyl's face, not the dear wife that I loved. Rather, it was a mask of such loveliness as to break a man's heart—of a cruelty to drive him mad.

Then I saw that in one hand she held a small metal box while in the other she grasped a tiny scoop. She scraped up a pinch of the powder in the box and scattered it over my ankles.

Fangs of liquid fire gushed at me. Pinioned under the ropes I thrashed in convulsions while a yell of uncontrollable agony tore from my lungs. "Sibyl, what are you doing?" I panted. "Sibyl—don't put that stuff on me—"

I gritted my teeth in my anguish. Then I observed that Noble had left my side to go over and speak to the beggar.

"I never did understand Noble," Denham muttered. "There are things about him that aren't human. He started working with me and then that beggar got him under his spell—or whatever you call it. Those two have secrets they don't let me in on. Sometimes I think you were right—they are two men with one soul between them. And that one soul belongs to the devil . . ."

The nude girl scattered more of the powder. Inch by inch the fire was creeping upward—from my feet to my ankles, to my legs and my knees. I felt all my blood cooking me. And it was Sibyl, my darling, who was killing me!

"Sibyl, for God's sake!" my screaming rang. "Don't you know what you're doing? I'm Paul—I'm your husband! Sibyl darling, you don't want to kill me! You love me! Oh, heavenly God—"

To those mad cries she paid no slightest heed. That waxen unliving countenance seemed incapable of any human emotion! And then, thrashing in my convulsions, I looked toward a corner—and understood. For over there Sibyl was standing! While the sylph who tortured me wore a mask to look like her!

My wife stood gazing at my tormentor, her dear face wrung with perplexity, piteous. I comprehended the hideous ingenuity that had schemed this even before I heard Denham's sardonic voice in explanation:

"Quite a little while ago Noble and I started drugging her with stuff dropped in her cocktail whenever we called at your house. An aphrodesiac that weakens the will power. Laura got it, too. That was why they fell for the beggar— why Sibyl went to him when she heard him calling her over the radio."

He nodded toward a big transmitter in a corner. "We broadcasted from here, on the same wave length as the station, with a power strong enough to penetrate their beam." He looked at the beggar and laughed oddly. "That old devil certainly has got some power over women that is supernatural. Of course, the girls are all drugged. But it's more than that. When he flogs them into a frenzy they will do anything he tells them."

"Then Sibyl didn't kill your wife, didn't burn you!" I muttered as fresh revelation dawned on me. "You had some of that powder with you in my house. You murdered your wife because you were tired of her. You put a little of the powder on yourself to divert suspicion. Sibyl didn't kill those men in the alley, either. You sent her out and then made her think that she had!"

"Yes—she believes that!" Denham said. "Thinks that she is a killer and that she has been untrue to you. She is almost crazy now. And when she is, I will have her! I'll have her kisses and her white body while you're rotting in your grave!"

I looked at Sibyl while I cursed Denham with blasphemies reserved for the damned. Driven already to the point of breakdown, her poor dimmed mind unable to distinguish between fact and shadow, she thought that she saw herself killing me! The ghastliness of that would finish her. All her life she would live in a daze, believing herself my murderess.

My teeth met in the pulp of my lips. The noises that retched from me were the snarls of an animal as I flung myself against the ropes again, straining, twisting—battling. I had to be up on my feet, going to Sibyl—doing something to save her!

Denham's voice came again, mocking now not me but the beggar.

"He's mad as a bedbug! He really believes fire from heaven is killing those people! He is God's chosen agent on earth to wipe out the wicked! If the poor fool only knew that he's just the hired loud-speaker! Not even hired—"

Hell knows no demon like fanatical sincerity victimized and then ridiculed. Denham's contempt had caused him to ignore the fact that the man about whom he was speaking had come up behind him—and overheard. Beyond his shoulder I saw the beggar's features constricted in amazement, then jerking into a mask of utter fiendishness.

And the next instant he charged in a leap that brought him down on top of Denham, fingers clutching his throat.

I didn't see the rest of the battle, for Denham went down under the onslaught and then they were both out of my sight on the floor. I only heard Denham's cries and the thwack of his skull on the stones, as the madman battered it. Battered and battered till the noise sounded more like ripe tomatoes being smashed . . .

The uproar had caused the masked woman to wheel around to look. And suddenly I realized that the ropes around my legs had fallen free. The fire with which she was burning me had eaten them through!

The lower half of my body folded at the hips in frantic jack-knifing. The force of my lunges slipped the ropes from my shoulders.

And the next instant I hurled myself onto the floor.

My legs pained as though I were wading in liquid fire . . . Through the torment I saw two enraged and astonished faces lunging toward me—the beggar's and Noble's.

I had no weapon in my hands, nothing with which to fight. I had another glimpse of Sibyl sagging against the grey stones, and I needed no weapons save those God had given me. I flung myself at the ragged man and for a time I ceased being a human being. I was a jungle primate, snarling, screeching—ripping and gouging till my fingers dripped crimson. I seized the beggar by the throat and flung him across the room. I was on top of him when he came down and I hammered his head against the stones, tearing at his face till it wasn't a face any more.

I crooned thin squeals of murder lust. And back there in the corner I heard Sibyl, jabbering like a mad-woman.

There follows an interval when memory is blank. Somehow, I suppose, I must have got Sibyl and myself out of there, but the next lucid moment I recall is when I came to in a hospital.

I stayed there six months while the doctors grafted skin on my legs. They say Sibyl is nearly cured, and will be completely normal in time. I am not sure.

Sometimes I see traces of that spell of madness. After all, I have seen what I have seen . . .

I have seen the cat that Noble left to take us to the beggar. The detectives explained that by saying that Noble had oil of asafetida on his shoes, went to the beggar's from our place, and the cat followed his scent. Maybe so . . . They explained

the cut on the beggar's head by claiming that it was a coincidence—he must have fallen and cut himself in that identical
spot. Perhaps that is true, too.

You can believe those explanations if you want to. But
then—tell me why in all the months that have passed, the
police have been unable to find Everett Noble! Or why Sibyl,
once in a great while, looks at a stray black cat with a
strange, momentary yearning in her eyes.

Is it possible that Noble still has some hold on my wife's
soul, some communion for which a black cat is the go-
between?

I do not know . . .

THE UNWELCOME DEAD

With the sweat of terror wetting his cheeks, Wayne Peters jammed the gas-pedal down to the floorboards. He darted a glance wildly at the endless ranks of dark, towering hemlocks that crept at snail's pace past the car. A muttered prayer and curse, co-mingled, was on his lips . . .

It seemed to Peters in his agony that he was moving at a torturing snail's pace, though, in fact, the ramshackle little runabout was clattering and banging along the stony mountain road at a pace which threatened every instant to send it skidding off into a bottomless chasm.

But the speed was too slow—too maddeningly, torturingly slow—to escape from the thing that pursued him—the grim, sightless Presence that rode, unseen, with him there in the little car . . .

Peters steered with one hand on the wheel, the other clasped around the passenger at his side. It was a strange, heart stopping passenger riding with him here into the wilderness of darkening hills. . . . For Peters clutched the white-faced corpse of a girl, easing her body from the jabbing springs that poked through the tattered upholstery as the car lurched and see-sawed. Limp, still soft and yielding, her body bumped and thudded against him as the car careened through the rutted curves. Still warm and poignantly alluring was the curve of his wife's breast under his fingers. Her lips, brushing against his cheek, thrilled his blood with their spiced fragrance . . .

Peters fought with the throttle and spark, cursing the laggard speed of the ancient machine. Second by second, terror was flogging him with searing whips. Closer and closer he crushed his wife to him in his despair. Too late, too late! . . .

Wilder and madder grew the speed of the car as it fled like

a live thing around the beetling flanks of the hills. Over his shoulder, terror was screaming: Faster, faster! Too late, too late!

Dusk was closing in as Wayne Peters had left the broad, traveled highway and turned off into the hills. It was growing dark rapidly now. The mountains were looming higher and grimmer, heaving up their black, tree-covered flanks, leaning over him, menacing him with their vast, mysterious, shawl-covered shoulders. They seemed grim, silent presences, standing sentinel before the dread secrets of things more terrible than death itself . . .

Suddenly, Wayne pulled the car to the side of the road and shut off the engine. Whirling to the figure beside him, he snatched her into his arms. In agony, he strained her to him, kissing her lips, her cheeks, her eyes.

"Nancy! Nancy, darling! For God's sake, speak to me!" he moaned. "Nancy! You are not dead. I can't have you dead—"

The girl did not move. From under the dark caverns of the hemlocks, Wayne's cry came whispering back in hushed, taunting echoes.

Wayne pushed her away from him, held up her drooping chin with one hand while he supported her body with the other. Winging away the tears that half-blinded him, he peered into her face.

Dead . . . Nancy dead . . . The words tolled in his brain. Her blue eyes closed; the color fled from her cheeks; her lithe, joyous body limp in his arms . . .

Peters laughed—wild, mocking laughter that was flung back in sardonic echoings from the cliff walls that hemmed in the road.

Dead . . . dead! . . . and what man in heaven or hell could undo death . . .?

Peters was driving like a man insane, sending the little car bounding and clattering along the road that zigzagged into the black, yawning maw of the hills. With him rode stark, utter loneliness and the desolation of hell. There was no sight of the thing Wayne had come to find—no sign of house or human form . . . And in the crook of his arm, Nancy's limp body jostled and thudded against him . . .

The evening was growing chill now. Wayne muttered a curse through his clicking teeth. It was not the wholesome tang of oncoming dusk. No, it was the dank, soul-numbing chill wafting from tombs . . .

He swerved the car sharply. Someone was standing beside the road—a farmer or workman in rough, tattered clothes. The man's hard, furrowed face was matted with a week's beard. A double-barreled shotgun rested easily in the crook of his arm.

Wayne leaned out of the car. "I wonder if you could tell me—?" he began. But the words slid away into breathlessness on his tongue. The rustic had shuffled closer, had darted a look into the car.

The man took one glance at Nancy's body, wilting against Wayne—one look at her deathly white face and parted his lips. His eyes shot up to Wayne's face. A curse snarled in his throat. White-faced, his eyes bulging, he shrank back.

"For God's sake, come here!" Wayne cried. "I'm not going to hurt you. I only wanted to ask you the way to—"

The man did not wait to hear what Wayne was going to say. He jumped back, whirled the shotgun up to his shoulder. Murder was in his eyes—and mad, witless terror that lashed out savagely, blindly at the mere vision and picture of the thing it feared.

Crouching low in the seat, pulling Nancy down beside him, Wayne threw in the gears and stamped on the gas pedal. Behind him, as the car went streaking along the road, the echoes of the gun boomed, and heavy, reverberating echoes came from among the hills. A hail of birdshot rattled and hissed against the back and sides of the tonneau.

On and on, further and further into the darkening maw of the hills, terror rode with Wayne now—terror of the things that had gibbered and leered in the farmer's white-rimmed eyes as he looked in at Nancy. Thicker and denser grew the spell of something diabolical and inhuman that brooded in the dank, bottomless silence of the hills . . .

Suddenly Wayne throttled down. As he swung around the last curve, the steep grade had flattened out. A hundred yards ahead lay the end of the road. The lights of the car glinted on the steel bars of a tall gate. To right and left, on both sides, he could see long lines of a towering fence running off into the gloom of the woods.

Wayne sat motionless, his heart pounding loud above the vibration of the engine. Through the bars of the gate, he could see the road climbing up the steep hill between ranks of ancient, mammoth trees. Dark, inky shadows lay under the matted evergreens, save where the beams of the full moon splashed halos of pale, spectral white amidst the gloom.

And now a figure was moving in one of the lighted spots. The man had stepped out of a little house—a sort of porter's lodge—that stood back a few yards from the gate. Keys jangled. The gate opened. The man was coming down the road toward the car.

As he passed through the beams of the headlights, Wayne got a good look at him. In face and figure, he was a man. He had the body, arms, legs, head and face of a man. And yet it was such a face as no human being ever had. Mouth, eyes, nose and all the rest were there—and yet something was lacking . . .

For a full ten seconds, Wayne sat staring at the face, puzzled—wondering why the sight of it should have laid a clutch of gelid fear around his heart . . .

Now the figure had come up to the car, looked inside. The eyes lighted on Nancy, slumped motionless in the curve of Wayne's arm. The man did not speak. No flicker of expression stirred on his face. He merely stepped back from the car, nodded, waved his hand toward the gate . . .

The wheezing and laboring of the ancient car sent echoes rocketing up to the black, feathery fronds of the hemlocks—like wings of vast, brooding night birds—as Wayne drove in through the gate and started up the narrow road that climbed the sharp grade of the hillside.

He was moving slowly between black, towering ranks of evergreens. Suddenly he half-turned to look into the woods, He had caught sight of something peering at him from behind a tree: a face—the white-meat face of a man who was not a man—a human being in outward form, yet lacking something within . . .

The face was gone as quickly as it had appeared. In a moment, Wayne saw that figure was moving along between the trees, keeping pace with the car as it rattled and panted up the heavy grade.

And now the creature swerved out from under the trees and came over to the car. He was peering in at Nancy and Wayne as he ran.

In a minute more, there was another one. Then two more! In a few seconds, a dozen or more of the things were trotting alongside!

Their eyes were big and round. They had the dull, stolid, lackluster, eyes of oxen. Not a flicker of expression stirred the lines of their faces.

Wayne sucked an oath between his gritting teeth. It was a fantasy out of a mad-man's dream—the towering, black trees with their masses of jet dragon wings; the corpse of his dead wife jostling and thudding in his arms; the crowd of white-faced creatures running beside him like soulless demons out of a—

That was it! *They were men without souls!* They were men whose bodies were perfect, whose muscles and brains could work, but whose souls had been stripped from them, dissipated into thin air, lost . . .

With savage, primitive fierceness, Wayne gripped Nancy closer to him. For the last hour he had felt the shadows of darkness closing around him and his dead. But not yet had he braced his mind for the terrible, sardonic horror of this—of seeing things once human turned into clods of flesh—men in God's image changed into things without souls. What powers of hell owned this land here and worked in it? What demoniac lore had its master delved up out of Satan's pit to teach him how to jeer at death—to keep bodies alive while he killed their souls? . . .

Now the creatures were becoming still more numerous. They were getting bolder, more curious. They were commencing to jump up on the running board of the car. They stared in at Nancy with their round, wide-bulging eyes—eyes like the unwinking orbs of great vultures . . .

They were beginning to stretch out their hands. One of them plucked cautiously at Wayne's coat-sleeve. Another reached out and started to move its fingers across Nancy's face.

Savagely, Wayne hurled the hand away. The thing looked at him and not a ray of expression stirred its face. Woodenly, stolidly, it put its hand back again—this time on the girl's bosom.

Wayne gritted an oath. His fist shot out, striking the thing between the eyes. It went tumbling backward off the running board onto the ground. It picked itself up and came trotting along again.

On the other side, three or four of the creatures were crowding around Wayne as they perched on the running board. Their hands were clawing him, pulling him, reaching into his pockets, jabbing his face. He whirled and sent them flying with a shower of blows. And as he looked around again, the first one came climbing back onto the running board to reach for Nancy.

Now the things were gathering in front of the car. They were standing and pushing against it. By sheer force of their numbers, they were overcoming what little extra power the engine had after climbing the grade.

Wayne shut off the engine and set the brake. In an instant, the car was surrounded by a pack of them, twenty or thirty in all. They came running up from the black shadows under the trees—strange, wooden-faced creatures with round owlish eyes—things of the night, hideous, unholy—things from beyond the grave, denizens of the dark, demoniac world along the rim of hell where Wayne had come with his dead wife . . .

Now there was a solid ring of them around him. Their arms

were lifting up into the air—a forest of white-taloned fingers straining, clutching in the green moonlight They were chattering and gibbering thin, ghostly cries as they started to crowd around the car.

Chapter Two

Men Without Souls

Wayne stooped, pulled up one of the floor boards and yanked out a monkey-wrench. He whirled, brought it crashing down on the head of the nearest of the things.

Howling and yammering, the creature slunk away. Wayne flung open the door of the car. He picked Nancy up in his arms and lifted her to his shoulder.

The things swung around and came trooping and crowding in front of him. Beating a path through them with the wrench, he started on up the road on foot.

Till he had arrived here he had had a glimmering of hope. Now he knew the truth—and it was a hundred times more terrible than his wildest fancies.

He recalled the incredible story he had heard from the lips of a newspaper detective friend half a dozen hours ago— such a yarn as only a man in the depths of mortal despair would have believed. It was the story of a mysterious scientist who could bring the dead back to life . . .

Frantic hope had brought him here with the one dearer than life itself clasped in his arms. All along the road he had told himself that it was impossible, insane . . .Yet, mad as it had sounded, it was true. These creatures around him, that came pushing their inhuman, expressionless faces into his, peering at him with their dead, lifeless eyes—all these were undoubtedly things from beyond the grave. They had been brought back from death into life . . .

Some part of them had been brought back while the rest of them had stayed in some far place . . . their bodies—muscles and brains—had been made alive again. *But their souls had been lost!* The process of infusing physical life into their stark bodies had succeeded. But the fleeting, insubstantial portion, the invisible, intangible thing called the soul—the spiritual light which separates men from beasts—that had been beyond the cunning of the master fiend to reproduce.

He had made hideous, ghastly caricature humans of them . . . Empty, lonely things, accursed, doomed to wander the dark, wild places of the earth like gibbering phantoms, thinking nothing, feeling nothing, forever seeking their lost souls . . .

Midway of the road, Wayne halted to lash out with his monkey-wrench. Half a dozen swings scattered the pack. But not so quickly now as the first time. They kept pressing in, closer and closer. Wayne spewed a curse through his file-dry lips. If the creatures would only speak—shout, curse or howl—if only some flash of expression would show on their features. If he could feel that he was fighting humans, instead of soulless clods of flesh . . .

Savagely, Wayne beat open a way before him. He was losing time—time more precious to him than life. And now he saw that the creatures had picked up clubs and stones. They were throwing the stones and shaking the clubs in his face. A stone hit him, cutting his forehead and sending the blood trickling down his face. The sight of the red fluid seemed to infuriate the things.

With one arm, Wayne held his dead wife clutched tight against his breast. Nancy, limp and cold, her lips like chilled rose petals as they brushed across his face was strained to his bosom while he stood fighting specters—battling ashen faced phantoms from beyond the grave who were trying to kill him because he was different from them . . .

Two of the creatures gripped the arm that held the monkey-wrench and clung like bulldogs. With sheer weight they were dragging him down! Their waxy white faces were filled with a sort of dull wonder as they hammered at him with the clubs.

Wayne husked an oath between his teeth. While he was battling those on one side, some of the others had grabbed hold of Nancy. They were prying her loose. They were pulling her away from him . . .!

It was no use. He was down on his back. Nancy was gone—he could not even see where. Dully, stolidly, with dogged, pitiless, animal persistence, the things were slugging him with clubs and stones.

Wayne cursed in wild terror. Nancy—what would become of her when he was dead? Her soft, white helplessness at their mercy—at the mercy of soulless ghouls . . .!

Frantically, Wayne pushed himself up, fighting to hurl off the meat-faced, blank eyed things that swarmed over him. A stunning blow from a rock crashed on his head. Everything melted away in an ocean of reeling blackness . . .

Wayne opened his eyes. Somewhere a car was coming, its tires gritting and plopping over the stones of the roadway. The car stopped. Now he heard a sound like the crackling of rifle shots . . .

Painfully he pushed himself up on his elbow. Engine still running, the car stood a few yards away out in the road. A dozen feet nearer, a figure stood in the midst of the things.

A big, broad-shouldered man stood there with the green moonlight shining into his face. For an instant, Wayne thought he was still unconscious, dreaming in a nightmare of soul-tingling horror . . .

It was the face of Satan—long, tallow-white face with deep-set green eyes and a black, pointed beard. Long, jet tapering eyebrows up-turned over the temples. The big, tight-lipped mouth was sneering in a grimmace of demoniac glee . . .

In one hand, the figure gripped a thick, long-lashed whip. He was whirling the lash, sending it hissing at the faces and backs of the creatures.

Wayne rubbed his eyes. He muttered an oath. Cringing, whimpering, the things were running away. In a moment they had all disappeared.

The huge figure tossed the whip back into the car. He came striding over to where Wayne lay on the ground. Unsteadily,

Wayne pushed himself up. He wiped the blood from his face with the back of his hand. "That was just in the nick of time," he muttered. "In one more minute, they would have finished me."

The big man did not speak for a moment. He stood looking down at Wayne. A sardonic sneer was twisting his lip corners.

"They knew you were different and they didn't like you," he said at last. Gloating, purring mockery of a fiend dripped from his curling lips. "Ever see a flock of ducklings pick on the ugly one? The same idea. You're the ugly one. I'll take you up to the house. Then you can talk. Get up."

Wayne stumbled up to his feet. Half a dozen yards away, he saw Nancy lying under a bush at the side of the road. He staggered over and picked her up. He carried her over to the car, lifted her into the back seat and got in beside her.

Wayne got a glimpse of a low, rambling building covering quite a plot of ground in a cleared spot under the trees as the car rolled up the last few rods of the road. The big man stopped, got out and let the way inside. Passing down a long corridor, he took Wayne into a small office with desk, shelves of books and tables of medical apparatus standing around.

Laying Nancy down on a couch, Wayne sank into a chair. The big man poured out a stiff shot of whiskey and handed it to him. Wayne tossed off the burning fluid in a couple of gulps. He lay back in his chair, letting his gaze drift around.

At one end of the office, he could see an open door leading into what looked like a laboratory. Tables of shining glass and metal apparatus half-filled the place.

Over in one corner of the room, he got a glimpse of something else that was half-hidden by the open door. A sudden chill like an icy hand flushed down his spine. Grim, hideous, sinister as the yawning door of a tomb, the thing stood there, a shadow of brooding death amidst the shining porcelain and metal . . .

The thing was a right-angled wooden frame, rising up to a height of eight or nine feet from the floor. Down from the horizontal projecting beam of the frame-work hung a rope with a sliding noose at the end.

The thing in the corner of the laboratory was a hangman's gallows . . .!

The big man was standing, watching Wayne. He was laughing with soft gloating.

Suddenly Wayne heard the gritting of feet. He looked around.

A corridor with glass windows ran along the outside of the office. A face was peering in through the window—another one of the meat-white faces of the things, with round, black, bulging eyes. Now another and then four more, till half a dozen of them were staring into the room, noses pressed to the glass panes.

The big man laughed again.

"Don't be afraid, my friend," he purred. "They are all around the place—my children, I call them. My children of hell . . .They are harmless as rabbits—usually—"

He tossed off the rest of his drink and set down his glass. "And now, if you feel able, it might be a good idea to tell me who you are and what you are doing here," he snapped with an abrupt change of mood. "And make it a good story. I can't remember that I ever invited you to call—"

"My name is Wayne Peters," Wayne told him. "I am a newspaper reporter. I suppose you are Doctor Crains." Wayne licked his lips. "It sounded like a mad thing to say, but I've seen mad things happen the last hour . . . Somebody told me that you could bring the dead back to life—"

The big man laughed once more, The laughter sounded to Wayne like the hissing of the great black whip as it fell on the faces of the gibbering things in the woods . . .

"I am Doctor Crains. I suppose I should be honored that you heard of me," he sneered. "And it is true that I can bring the dead back to life." He waved his hand. "All these creatures that you see around here I have created—out of cold corpses. You might say that I am their father—and that hell was their mother . . .!"

Wayne ran his tongue over his parched lips. "But it can't be—it's impossible!" he heard himself muttering. "When a man is dead, he is dead—"

Doctor Crains laughed again. "You are behind the times, my very rash friend," he purred. "You ought to know that in the big medical colleges, the scientists have been doing that very thing for years. In one institution, they have a pair of dogs which they have killed and then brought back to life again so many times that I have lost count. There have been a lot of cases recently—you must have read about them in the papers—where human beings on the operating table have died—have remained dead for as long as half an hour—and then have been brought back to life again by the use of adrenalin.

"All I have done is to carry the idea a little further than anyone else has yet done. I can bring men back to life provided they have not been dead more than three hours. When I started, the best I could do was ten minutes."

The doctor was pacing the floor. His green eyes blazed. His face twitched with the mad, unholy exulting of a fiend. "Ah, my crazy friend, death used to be the one thing in the world that was sure, permanent!" he exclaimed. "I am going to make it about as lasting as a morning hangover! But for the present as I told you, I have to use freshly killed subjects for my experiments."

An icy wind seemed to be blowing through Wayne's brain. He was looking past Crains at the shape that stood in the corner of the laboratory. The gallows with the dangling rope—

"Then your corpses to work on—you don't get them out of the morgues—" he mumbled, wetting his lips.

Crains purred a mocking laugh.

"Will you tell me how I am going to get fresh corpses to work with if I don't make them myself, right on the spot, you fool?" he growled. "All these creatures that you see here are—or were once—badly wanted by the bureaus of missing persons. I go out and get them myself as I need them." The doctor chuckled as he poured out another drink. "I have a wonderful system, my friend. It has never failed. But never before has anyone come here without my asking—to save me the trouble of going after them. So I feel that I owe you my thanks—"

Chapter Three

Corpses to Order

Ashy-faced, Wayne sat jammed back in his chair, staring up at the doctor. In this place of sin incarnate, the sacredness of human life meant no more than the squeal of a dying guinea-pig ... And the partner of the fiend who stood sneering down at him was the gallows-noose hanging behind the door in the laboratory . . .

Wayne licked his file-dry lips. "These—these children of yours, as you call them," he muttered. "You have only partly brought them back. Their bodies are alive, but their souls are dead."

Crains nodded. "There you have hit the problem that I am facing right now," he mused. "There is something wrong with my method. Something I have missed—"

Crains had turned to look at Nancy as he spoke. Suddenly he spun around and almost ran to her side. He knelt on the floor by the couch, twitched a stethoscope out of his pocket and held it to her heart.

He listened an instant. He jumped up and whirled back to Wayne. "That girl isn't dead!" he exclaimed. "She's in a trance—suffering a cataleptic seizure of some kind—"

Wayne nodded. He jumped to his feet and paced the floor. "She came down with it months ago," he said. "I had a procession of doctors. Nobody could understand it. It's some kind of a brain condition. That's all they would say. Day after day I have sat and watched her sinking, sinking. Now she is at death's door. Any day, any hour—any minute, almost— And then I heard of you. I brought her here. I had a wild hope that you might be able to—"

Crains' green eyes were aflame with excitement. His face twisted and writhed as he strode up and down the floor.

"My friend, you have brought me the very thing that I have been praying a whole year for," he exclaimed. "As you say, all these others have lost their souls in returning from death into life. She is just on the borderline; she is not alive und she is not dead. When I bring her back, she may have her soul—"

Crains whirled back to Wayne. Demoniac glee curled and twisted his long, evil lips. "I can bring her back, but I am not sure of the result," he said. "It is about an even chance, whether she will have her soul or not. You are her husband—suppose you decide. Would you rather have her die as she is—would you rather carry the picture with you of her as you knew her and loved her—or would you rather have her live again and take the chance of her being like these creatures around here?"

Wayne stood motionless in the middle of the floor. His thoughts were whirling in a millrace of dizzying horror.

He was looking at Nancy—Nancy lying there so sweet, so beautiful, even in death . . . Lovely as on her bridal night, in his arms, her face on his shoulder, her lips pressed to his . . .

A cry of choking agony—a prayer and a groan comingled—husked from Wayne's twitching lips. Nancy. To have her alive once more, to be able to see her walking around, to clasp her in his arms—or to lay her away in the black ground, never to see her again . . .?

But if she lost her soul when she lived again . . .? Would he rather have her alive, and like them—would he rather see her walking and eating and looking at him—her blue eyes wooden and cold, never knowing him, never answering? Could he stand to see the lips that he loved frozen and smileless, her face the dead expressionless face of a body without a soul? Or would he rather lay her away, never to see her again?

"God! God help me!" Wayne muttered.

And still another question! The doctor had said he could bring her back. Had he a right to refuse that offer? Would he not be a murderer himself if he refused the chance and doomed her to death?

But if he had her brought back to life and her soul was dead—he would have killed that. Which was the greater sin? To kill the body or murder the soul? . . .

White-faced, Wayne went over and dropped on his knees at Nancy's side. He gathered her into his arms and pressed agonized, tear-moistened kisses against her lips.

"Nancy! Oh, Nancy darling!" he moaned. "Nancy! Nancy, my sweetheart—!"

At last Wayne pushed back from her and stood up, facing the doctor. "I have decided," he said through lips that moved like numbed, frozen things. "I will not have it done. I will let her die. I will kill her body and save her soul. I cannot take the chance—"

Crains' purring laughter mocked through the silence as Wayne stopped talking. "I was just wondering how you would figure that out, my white-souled Sir Galahad," he sneered. "It was really a nice little problem in human emotions . . ."

Suddenly the big man's face jerked into snarling savagery. "Of course I am going to bring her back, you fool," he snapped. "Didn't I tell you this was the case I had been waiting a year for? I wouldn't pass it up for a million. Whichever way it turns out, it will probably give me exactly the knowledge I need to correct my whole process . . . And another thing, you idiot—where did you get the pretty idea that I would ever let you leave here after what you've seen? I am going to give you the kind of a party you never expected to have. I am going to stake you to a free ride to hell and back again."

For an instant, neither of the men spoke nor moved. Wayne and the doctor stood crouched, tense, their eyes glaring at one another. A great number of the soulless creatures were peering in through the windows. Dimly, Wayne saw the figures of two big, white-coated men approaching down the corridor.

Wayne's lips jerked back from his teeth. Gritting a curse, he hurled himself at the doctor. He took one step, and then a pair of hands crashed down from behind him. They gripped him around the throat. He felt himself jerked backward and flung head over heels across the room.

Dizzily, he pushed himself up to his feet. Between him and the doctor stood a pair of huge, white-uniformed orderlies. Crains nodded to the two men. "Bring him in here," he snapped.

The two orderlies gripped Wayne by the arms and started hauling him toward the door which opened into the laboratory. Crains went over, picked Nancy up and followed them.

In the laboratory, the orderlies threw Wayne down into a chair in one corner of the room. "Stay there and keep quiet if you know what's healthy," one of them growled.

The doctor laid Nancy down on a couch and turned to Wayne. His smile was the Satanic leer.

"In return for your effort to thwart me, my friend, I am going to show you just what is going to happen to you. You can be thinking how it is going to feel while you watch—how it is going to feel to die by inches and minutes and seconds with a rope around your neck . . . But you can have one comfort while you're watching," he gloated. "You are not going to stay dead. I promise to bring you back to life in exactly two hours. And then, for the rest of your life, you will be a human ox—"

The doctor muttered a few words to one of his assistants. While the second one stood guard over Wayne, the man left the room. In a moment he returned. He was shoving and pushing along a man whose hands were tied behind him.

At sight of the gallows, the man gasped out a scream. He whirled. Still bound as he was, he rushed at the big orderly, butting him with his head, snapping and ripping at his throat with his teeth.

For a couple of minutes a wild battle raged in the room. Wayne was biting his lips till the blood crimsoned the saliva that dribbled out of his mouth corners. Get up and help him! Don't sit there and let him die like a dog! You'll be the next!

The words screamed through his brain. But he did not move. Cold, heart-stopping terror was freezing his blood. He was waiting, holding himself back, saving his strength for the battle for his own life that was to come . . .

With clubs, Crains and the orderly beat the man into a stupor. Now on his knees he was sobbing, screaming curses and prayers.

While the orderly held him up, Crains pulled down the noose and fitted it around his neck.

The other end of the rope ran up over a pulley in the horizontal beam of the gallows. The orderly grabbed the free end and began to pull steadily.

Wayne shut his eyes to crush out the picture of the writhing, twisting thing that was pulled up from the floor. The man was uttering choked, strangling screams. Now the rope was shutting off his wind. The screams grew fainter, slobbered and croaked into silence . . . Mutely now, the dangling shape flopped convulsively . . .

Wayne's eyes were glazed, his fingernails bit into his flesh. He jerked his eyes away from the ghastly, grinning pendulum and turned them toward Nancy.

He could have screamed in frenzy at the thing that he had done. Playing that last, desperate hope, he had brought her helpless loveliness into the lair of a fiend. Crains was a double murderer—first he slaughtered the body and then he killed the soul—!

Wayne lifted his numb hand to dash off the beads of sweat which wet his face. God had said: Thou shalt not kill. The body thou shalt not kill . . . What of the man who killed the soul? What everlasting torture could be fit for him? For in a few hours more, Nancy would have been dead, her soul in heaven . . . Now in a few minutes, she would be alive again, but her soul forever lost. And he, Wayne, who loved her more than his own life, had done that to her . . .

He groaned. He did not ask to have Nancy live again now . . . All he wanted was to have her die—to die with that tender smile on her face, her sweet soul lingering in her smile as she passed away . . .

A mirthless laugh of raging mockery bubbled through Wayne's jaws. On the wings of frantic speed he had brought her here to have her live again. Now in his agony, he beseeched God that she might die—!

Chapter Four

Life "Worse Than Death"

The white-coated orderly had hoisted the body of the murdered man to a wheeled table. He was trundling it out of the room. In a moment he came back. Another figure was on the table now—a different man from the one he had carried out.

The man was dead. He lay flat on his back, his wide-open eyes staring straight upward. His face was knotted in the last spasm of terror that had branded his soul.

Crains turned to Wayne. "Now I am going to give you another treat. I'm showing you quite unusual attention, I assure you," he grinned derisively. "I am going to show you how I bring them back to life again. So that you will be able to see what is going to happen to you . . .

"This man here has been dead almost three hours. Now watch—"

On the other side of the room, another piece of apparatus stood on a table. It was a long, oval shaped glass tube—something like a glass oven, with flat bottom and curving wall and top. It was long and wide enough to hold a man's body. At one end was a hinged door of shining metal with wires and hoses running into it. A complicated array of valves and wheels covered most of the surface of the door. Wires passed through the glass at the other end of the cell, ending in a bunch of dull-colored electrodes. The two sets of wires ran up to an intricate set of electrical coils and tubes mounted on a raised shelf under the ceiling.

The assistant unlocked some bolts and swung open the metal door. The doctor yanked the sheet off the dead man and tossed it on a chair.

The corpse was nude. It lay there cold and uncovered, pitifully exposed to the driving, mocking blaze of the electric lights.

"He has to be naked for the treatment," Crains purred over his shoulder to Wayne. He picked up a hypodermic needle with a long, glistening tip. He plunged the needle deep into the man's chest and squeezed down the plunger.

"I am injecting a dose of my super adrenalin hormone into his heart," he explained to Wayne. "Adrenalin is a substance secreted in the ductless glands of the living body. An infinitely tiny amount of it has a tremendously stimulating effect on the heart. If there is any such thing as an elixir of life, this is it. What I am using here is a hundred times as powerful as the natural adrenalin."

Together, the doctor and the white coated man pushed the dead man off the wheeled table into the cell and shut the door.

Crains started working the switches and knobs. A zigzagging blue flame crackled out from the coils up on the shelf. A glow of pale light spread through the inside of the tube, bathing the stark, white body of the man in eerie radiance.

"The cell is now filled with oxygen," Gains said. "I am passing high-voltage electric rays through it—"

For five minutes, there was no sound in the room save the faint humming of the electric spark. Crains and the orderly stood watching. Through the windows, Wayne could see the white-meat faces of the things peering in—round, vacant eyes of oxen in the dead faces of corpses . . . Animal curiosity was all that stirred them as they watched another like themselves being created out of lifeless flesh in the glass cell . . .

Now the man in the cell was beginning to move. Spasmodic jerkings set him twitching and shivering. Wayne watched his face through the glass wall. The strained, terror-jerked features were beginning to relax. The bulging eyes sank back into their sockets. The writhing lips softened, flowed back smoothly over the grinning teeth. The black-graven lines that harrowed the cheeks melted away . . .

Now the man was struggling and kicking in the cell, trying to sit up. Crains opened the door. Gripping him by the shoulders he and the orderly pulled him out. Half carrying, half leading him, they took him across the room and sat him down in a chair.

For a minute or two, the man sat there, his chest rising and falling with his fast, labored breathing. He was alive, all right—alive with a life a thousand times more terrible than the death that had held him ten minutes before. In his dead-white, frozen face was no light of expression. His big, round eyes were dull as a beast's. He was a creature without a soul . . .

Wayne's blood ran cold. He clutched the arms of the chair with fingers whose tips oozed drops of blood. About death there was something beautiful, sacred, holy. Death was dignified, unhurried, eternal. Something about a corpse suggested the calm and peaceful, everlasting majesty of God . . .

Crains had tried to play God. He had laid blasphemous hands on human life. Out of dead clay, he had manufactured a thing that breathed and moved. With his tubes and needles and electric wires, he had created a demoniacal, lewd mockery of God's image . . .

In a few minutes now, Nancy would be in there, her sacred nakedness helpless before the foul gaze of the doctor and his two thugs! Nancy, his wife, whose body and soul belonged to him, to be twisted and wrenched and worked on by the necromancy of hell—altered and miscreated into a thing of horror . . .

Crains walked over to Nancy. He bent down. He began to tear off her clothes. His white face, upturned brows and curling lips made him look like a fiend of the pit exulting over a virgin.

"Purely a scientific necessity, my dear Peters," he mocked back over his shoulder. "She has to be naked for the rays to take effect—"

Wayne's teeth snarled between his curled-back lips as he sat glaring at the man. He was breathing in shrill, whistling gasps. His fingers itched and burned to clutch around the doctor's throat.

Crains motioned to the orderly. The big man looked over his shoulder at Wayne and grinned as he lifted the girl's nude figure in his arms. He carried her over and laid her down on the table.

"Since she is not really dead, I am going to try it with just the rays, without the adrenalin injection," Crains said. "I have an idea that they will be enough—"

Crains broke off what he was saying with a startled grunt. He whirled around. The door of the laboratory had opened behind him. Half a dozen of the soulless creatures that had been hanging around, looking in through the windows, had come inside.

Paying no attention to anyone, they walked up to the table where Nancy lay. They stood in a ring, looking down at her. Crains was standing staring at them. They were crowding closer around Nancy. They were bending down to peer at her . . .

Red spots splashed the centers of their white cheeks. Their eyes were blazing. Their mouths gaped open. *Expression was dawning over their faces—!*

Crains whirled around to his two assistants. His eyes glowed with excitement. "Look at that! Look at their faces!" he shouted. "Never before in their lives have they had an atom of feeling about anything except their food. And now they're—!"

Crains was pacing the room, his lips twitching.

"Maybe that will do it!" he was muttering to himself. "Maybe a woman will bring back their souls. It's a wonder I never thought of it before! I've been keeping women out of here on purpose—to avoid complications—"

For an instant, Crains stood looking around, thinking.

On the further side of the room, a big hook stood in the wall. The doctor stepped back to the table and lifted Nancy off it. He carried her across the room. With the assistant holding her drooping form up half erect, he tied her to the hook with ropes under her shoulders.

Like a virgin crucified before a ribald mob Nancy hung there, her head down on her bosom, her legs bent at the knees, the soft swelling curves of her breasts and limbs etched in a statue of limp, fainting marble . . .

Crains went over to the door, flung it wide. Another half-dozen of the creatures were hanging around out in the corridor. Herding them like sheep, he drove them into the room.

He muttered something to the orderly. The white-coated giant went from one to another of the things, pulling off the rough shirt which formed the sole covering above the waist. Now the fifteen of them stood half-naked.

"Make them get down on their hands and knees, facing her," Crains said.

Docile as sheep, the things obeyed the curt orders growled at them by the assistant. In a moment, they were all kneeling on the floor, their faces toward Nancy.

Crains picked up a whip from the corner. He looked back toward Wayne.

"Of course you know there is really no such thing as a soul, Peters," his sardonically sneering voice drawled out. "What most people call the soul is just the mechanical working of an infinitely complicated system of nerves and cells in the brain. When these creatures here were brought back to life, something failed to click—some adjustment of personality did not take place. These nerves and brain cells were sort of short-circuited, if you get the idea. Now what I am hoping is that a shock will do the trick—some violent emotion will jar these pieces of brain machinery back into their places again. With the kind assistance of your wife, I am going to give them a dose of the two greatest stimuli in the world—sex excitement and pain, both at once. It ought to start something—"

The whip rose and went swishing through the air. It cracked on the back of one of the kneeling things. The creature winced and howled. A purple welt leaped out on the white skin. Back the lash whirled and came hissing down again. Again and again . . .

Rigid, Wayne sat crouched on the edge of his chair. It was a picture out of an inferno that his scalding eyes gazed on while he croaked curses through his blood-caked lips.

A herd of bare-backed human beasts on hands and knees before a towering white-faced satyr who snarled grunts of mad excitement as he sent the great whip hissing and biting into their bodies, Foot by foot on their hands and knees he was driving them toward the limp, white figure of the naked girl, lashing and flogging them, torturing their brute bodies with the maddening allure of sex and the merciless pain of the whip . . .

And the woman crucified on the cross there in front of them, the woman whom their lewd gaze clung to and devoured, was Nancy—his wife . . .!

Screeching wild curses through his jerking lips, Wayne lunged up out of his chair. "You fiend—you spawn of hell!" he screamed. He dropped his head, rushed at Crains.

Wayne took only a couple of steps. Behind he heard the grunting snarl of the orderly who stood guard over him. A stunning pain shot through his head as the man's club came crashing down. Dizzily, Wayne felt the giant pick him up by the collar, drag him back and fling him down into the chair . . .

Now Crains was whirling the whip faster. His eyes blazed. His teeth snarled between his drawn-back lips. The creatures were beginning to creep forward. Their eyes were commencing to blaze as they drank in the seductive loveliness of Nancy's white form.

Now they were jumping up to their feet, starting to rush toward her. Wayne saw their faces and snarled another curse through the blood-flecked foam that dribbled off his lips. They were not the faces of cattle now. They were the faces of men, hot with lewd hunger . . .

Crains was trying to stop the creatures now. Jumping around in front of them, he was yelling to them to get back, and lashing the whip in their faces.

But they did not go back. They were snarling at the doctor,

spitting hoarse animal sounds, whirling their fists. Three or four of them started to duck around him, fighting, digging each other with their elbows as they rushed toward the girl.

Crains' face was dripping sweat as he stood pouring whip-blows over the pack. There was no stopping them now that they had got started. They were snarling at the doctor, shoving him one side, raging and growling as they fought to advance. Beyond him was the thing they were on fire to get to—the naked, white form of the first woman they had ever seen since their rebirth.

Chapter Five

Valley of Hell

The big orderly who had been helping Crains grabbed up his club. From the rear, he made a dive at the pack. The long nightstick rose and came crashing down, bringing the blood spurting where it ripped away skin and flesh. The orderly beat a path through the mob up to Crains' side.

Little by little, the creatures fell back from before the club. Snarling and cowering, Crains and the orderly at last drove them out of the room. The doctor shut the door and locked it.

Crains was pacing the floor. He was panting and pale. For a minute, he himself had been looking into the eyes of death.

"That's it! That will do it!" he was muttering. "A woman will bring back their souls. So far, they're only like beasts about her. But it's a beginning. I've jolted them out of their sleep. The rest will come—"

He stood thinking out loud. "I'll bring her back to life and give her to them. Maybe she will have her soul—maybe she won't. If she doesn't, she will be the way they were at first. If she does—"

Crains swung around to Wayne. He was himself now, purring fiendishly sardonic laughter. "I'm going to kill you, too, you know, and then bring you back, friend Peters. That will make you like them—without a soul. Your wife is going to live again, too. She will have plenty of men to choose from. Which one do you think she will take—you, or one of them? Suppose you don't have any soul and she does! What chance will you have?"

Cursing, Wayne lunged to his feet. Through the windows, the faces of the creatures were peering in. Faces of half men, blazing with hunger! Nancy was to be turned into one of them—his sweetheart to be brought back to life and given over to them while he looked on! Nancy, not knowing him, chosing another to be her mate—

Savagely, Wayne crashed his shoulder into the orderly as the man started to jump for him. The assistant went stumbling and staggering across the room;

A wild, roaring tide of frenzy boiled in Wayne's brain. Nancy's soul—he must save it! Not save her body—save her soul! Kill her! Kill her body and save it from them—Kill her body and save her soul . . .!

He groaned in mad despair. No—he could not simply kill her—because Crains could undo that. He could bring people back from the dead. He must kill her—mutilate her—so that no one could restore her!

On the table with the glass cell lay a big monkey-wrench. Crains had used it to tighten the nuts on the machine. Kill Nancy with that! Hammer her head to pieces! Hammer the sweet, holy loveliness that he loved into a pulp! Break the bones and spill out the brain! Set her soul free and winging straight up to heaven, where he, God willing, would find it one day . . .!

Wayne heard feet gritting behind. He whirled. The big orderly was right on top of him. The club swished through the air . . .

Snarling like a wolf through his grinding teeth, Wayne ducked under the blow. His head crashed into the pit of the man's stomach. Belching agony, the assistant went tumbling backward. Another two yards for Wayne's rushing feet to cover now, in order to get the monkey wrench. The way was open. No one was in front of him—

Now he was there. Now the long, deadly wrench was in his

fingers! He turned. Voices were clamoring in his brain: Grab it and beat in her face—you won't even have time to kiss her once more—strike those eyes that have smiled into yours! Burst her brain open and watch the blood gush over the lips that have whispered, "I love you!" Kill her—smash her to pieces—let out her soul before they stop you—!

Wayne felt the cold butt of the wrench under his hands. He snatched it up and spun around. Crains' face was jerking in demoniac rage as he came lunging across the room. At sight of the face, something clicked back into place in Wayne's brain. A curse of mad laughter screamed in his palsied throat.

"No! Don't kill Nancy, you fool! You don't have to kill her. Kill Crains. Kill the doctor. He's the one to kill! He is Satan! Beat out *his* brains—and then let's see him bring himself back to life!

Teeth bared, lips snarling back like a dog's, Wayne sent the heavy iron spinning through the air at Crains' face. But his brain was still dizzy from the blows of the club. It missed. He saw the wrench sail past Crains' head and smash against the wall.

Over his shoulder, Wayne caught a quick glimpse of the orderly's club come hurtling down. He tried to duck the swing. Too late—!

A burst of dizzy pain exploded in his head. Reeling nausea flooded over him. Half out, he knew that big, brutal hands were gripping him, dragging him backward . . .

~ ~ ~

As Wayne lay on the floor, stunned, one of the orderlies brought a pail of water and dashed it into his face. Choking and panting, he pushed himself up.

Crains and the two men were standing and looking down at him. They had unfastened Nancy from the hook and laid her out on the wheeled table. Behind them, the black noose at the end of the rope on the gallows was swaying to and fro . . .

The doctor's thin lips twitched like a cat's. He nodded to

the two men. One on each side of him, they yanked Wayne to his feet.

While one of them held him, the other tied his hands behind him. Gripping him by the arms, they half led, half dragged him across the room.

The noose on the gallows was not fastened to a hook. The rope went up over a pulley in the horizontal beam and the other end hung loose.

With the two white-coated men holding him, Crains fitted the noose around Wayne's neck. He pulled it up to take out the slack, but not yet drawing it tight.

He handed the rope to one of the orderlies. He and the other one went back to Nancy. They wheeled the table up to the glass cell, opened the door and slid her inside.

Crains was purring sardonic laughter as he turned back to Wayne.

"Now you are going to die, Peters—and I don't have to tell you how! As you feel the rope squeezing your life out, you will see her living again. In two hours more, you will join her—alive. But you will be just that much too late. You will see her belong to somebody else. But you won't care. You will be a human ox, without a soul—!"

Cursing, Wayne strained his wrists against the rope. To die and then to live again, a human ox! To look at Nancy and pass her woodenly—to see Crains give her to the creatures . . .To look on and not to care, because he would have no soul . . . As though the noose were already gripping it, his throat was palsied, numb. Thin croaking oaths wheezed through his knotted lips.

Just a minute now—a little handful of seconds more to live. He fixed his eyes on Nancy's face. With his dying gaze he would carry her picture with him into hell . . .

The creatures outside the door were growing impatient. They were crowding closer around the windows. Their faces were gripped with expression now—aflame with desire . . .They were rattling the locked door. More and more of them were coming up and joining the crowd.

Crains was darting quick glances over his shoulder as he worked at the cell. The big orderlies were growing white. The one who was helping the doctor carried his club gripped under his arm.

The doctor turned a switch. A humming sound filled the room. Pink light vibrated and trembled from end to end of the cell.

Crains spat out a curse, jerked his head around. The jangle of smashing glass had clattered through the humming sound.

One of the creatures had put his fist through a window. Snarling and muttering, half a dozen heads jammed around the hole.

Crains pulled out his handkerchief and mopped the sweat from his face. His little, green eyes were lighted with terror.

"We'll have to hurry this," he muttered to the others. "I'll bring her back fast and give her to them."

He nodded to the one holding the free end of the rope. "Pull him up," he grunted.

Wayne saw the orderly's arms start to move. He felt the rope biting around his neck. The next instant he swung up off his feet and hung in the air.

He gritted his teeth and gripped his fists till the nails cut into the flesh. Now—now it was coming! Death, in the scorching clutch of the rope . . . death in the agony of choking that was welding a ring of white-hot flame around his neck . . .

The laboratory was now dead silent, save for the purring of the electric spark. Inside the cell, Nancy's body swam in a trembling river of rosy light. In a few seconds now, as he died, he would see her sit up and look around. Back into life again, but not to be his—!

Savage screams of despair puffed the bloody froth that spewed from Wayne's mouth. With black, writhing lips he was calling on God—calling on Him to stop it—to strike the grinning fiend dead in his tracks . . .

A vast, molten weight of fire was crushing Wayne's chest. Through the crimson haze that reeled in his brain, he could see the creatures swarming around the door, fighting to get in.

Crains and the two orderlies were ashy faced now. The doctor was clutching his whip, the assistants gripped their long clubs.

The door was crashing—it was starting to crumble inward . . .

Chapter Six

Kill Her to Save Her Soul!

As though from miles away, the sound of crashing glass and rending wood cut through the red ocean of torture that flooded Wayne's brain. His eyes, glazed and bulging, saw the laboratory door crack open in splinters. Over the threshold poured a stampede of big, wild-eyed things.

Dimly, Wayne felt himself go plunging downward. His feet hit on the floor. He was down on his hands and knees now, the rope dangling as the orderly had dropped it. Gasps of air like liquid fire sucked into his throat. In a daze, he saw the man who had been hanging him snatch up his club from a corner and rush over beside Crains and the other orderly.

The room was full of the creatures. Backed into a corner, Crains and his two men were fighting for life. The doctor's whip snarled and cracked a fiend's song as it hissed and gouged into the white faces. The clubs of the assistants whirled and crashed, rose and fell again.

Half a dozen of the creatures were down, lying senseless on the floor. But the others kept crowding in. Their faces were not the mute, white masks of oxen now. They were the red, twitching faces of men gripped by murderous hatred.

Suddenly Wayne understood. The creatures were getting their souls back. The sight of Nancy had done that for them. And as they recovered, they realized that they had been changed from men into brutes—and they knew who had done it to them! Like doomed souls gazing up from the pit of hell at their fiend-master, they were aflame with a terrible blood rage of revenge.

But not all of the creatures were going after Crains and his orderlies. A dozen or more of them had rushed straight toward the cell where Nancy lay. They were beating on the glass, clawing at the handles and valves in a wild frenzy to get at her.

Now Wayne was on his feet. He was still gasping down bloody froth as he fought for air, but his head was clear.

Beside the cell, one of the loathesome things had picked up a club which one of the orderlies had dropped and was hammering the glass with it. The curved, specially made glass was strong, but any second now, it would break. And then . . . !

One of the windows in the wall of the laboratory was directly behind Wayne. He lunged backward, lifting his hands as high as he could and shoving hard against the glass.

There was a jangling smash. Darts of pain stung his wrists. Laughing with mad frenzy, he pushed his hands harder, sawing the ropes back and forth against the jagged edges of the broken glass . . .

In the corner, all three of the white coated men were down now, under the pack of yelling, ravening things whom they themselves had created out of dead meat . . . !

Crains and the two men were screaming—screaming in terror of death—while huge, wolfish hands were clutching their throats, gouging their eyes, ripping their cheeks . . .

Wayne sucked an oath through his teeth. The rope was gone. His hands were free.

He took a couple of steps toward the cell. He was waving his fists, yelling at the crowd of figures clustered around it trying to break the glass.

He froze in his tracks. The mob in the corner had finished its work. On the floor lay bloody, motionless things, riven and ripped and torn out of likeness to human flesh. And at the sound of Wayne's voice, the pack whirled toward him, snarling and brandishing their red dripping hands in the air.

Despair froze Wayne. Go on! Go get her! Beat them down. Tear them to pieces! Get her out of that cell! Get her out of that hellish river of light that is bringing her back to life, changing her into a beast! She must not live—she must die!

Thicker and thicker the pack was closing in between him and the table with the cell on it. One big satyr grabbed Wayne but the blood on his fingers made his grasp slippery. The next instant, two more of them lunged forward.

Wildly, Wayne cast his eyes around the room. Alone! Alone against the mob of half-souled savages, while Nancy lay there in the pink river of hellish light, coming back to life to be a beast . . .!

A couple of yards from where Wayne stood, he saw a shelf of big bottles containing chemicals. The label on one of them read: "ALCOHOL."

Wayne reached over and snatched the bottle off the shelf. He whirled and flung it at the tiled floor at the feet of the line of snarling things.

The bottle burst with a shatter of jangling glass. The colorless, inflammable liquid darted out over the floor. As he threw the bottle, Wayne had darted his other hand into his coat pocket. He pulled out a box of matches. He gripped one of the slender pieces of wood and scratched it frantically against the box.

A little yellow flame spurted. He stepped forward, tossed the blazing match into the alcohol.

Swift as the flick of a snake's fang, the faintly blue and yellow flame shot up. Yammering terror, the things fled from the sudden, intense heat.

In an instant, the gallon of blazing fluid had spread over the floor. It was everywhere about the creatures, searing their feet, running up the legs of their trousers, scorching their knees, darting into their faces.

In mad terror, they forgot Nancy and Wayne. Yelling, they jammed the door in a mad stampede to escape.

Wayne held his breath as he dashed across the lake of flame that boiled between him and the life-cell. The heat beat into his face; the fumes half-strangled him. Now his feet were searing as his shoes caught fire. His trousers were beginning to burn. He paused an instant to rip off the blazing garments and to fling them away. Now the fire was scorching his legs—he could smell the reek of burning hair.

All around the table, the floor was a small sea of yellow and blue flame. Fiery pain bit and tore at Wayne's naked skin as he whirled the handle that he had seen Crains use to open the cell.

Get it open! Get that cell open! Pull her out and take her away! Get her out of that river of rosy hell which is changing her into a beast!

Now the metal door of the cell swung open. Wayne gripped Nancy by the shoulders, pulled her out. Now she was in his arms. Holding her clutched against him, he raced, head down, half-blind, through the lake of dancing hell toward the door . . .!

Wayne went staggering and stumbling down the long corridor toward the door. He did not see any of the things. Only vaguely he heard the clatter of racing steps, the yells and cries of voices in agony . . .

Now he was out of the house, out in the cool, blessed night air, with the stars shining over his head and the breeze flushing against his feverish face.

He was running down the road along which Crains had driven him. He looked around. Nobody was in sight. He and Nancy were alone . . .

Wayne stepped to the side of the road. He pushed through the bushes. Now he was standing in the middle of a little open glade among the trees. The moonlight shone down quiet and calm.

Stooping, he laid Nancy down on a carpet of downy moss. He knelt at her side, peering into her face. He bent, held his ear to her heart. It was beating. She was breathing. She was still alive!

Wayne sat back on his knees, watching her. She was alive. He had saved her from Crains, from the soulless things. He whispered a prayer of thanks to God.

But what next? She had had a dose of the rays. Had she had enough of them to bring her back to normal life? Or had he been in time—had he gotten her out only to die?

Wayne gripped his hands in agony. She had had the rays. She might die and she might live. If she lived, would she be herself, or would she have lost her soul and be like the creatures?

In the warm yellow moonlight, she was like a sleeping sacred virgin. Her breasts rose and fell evenly with her breathing. A tender little smile seemed to linger around her lips . . .

On his knees, Wayne groaned prayers of sobbing agony while cold sweat formed on his brow and cheeks. What should he do? God help him, what should he do? Let her go on as she was and perhaps come back to life—and be a beast without a soul? Or kill her body and set free her soul to go to heaven?

Moment after moment he knelt there, while the sickness of despair tore at his vitals. His face was a black-gashed mask of horror as he turned to her again. She had the rays a long time. If she lived, she would have lost her soul . . .

He could not take the chance. He could not face the horror of the moment when her eyes would look up at him and blast his soul with their blank senseless gaze . . .

Kneeling beside her, Wayne gripped his hands around her throat—the soft, warm slender throat he had loved to kiss . . .

She stirred and smiled as she had used to smile when he touched her. Her lips seemed to move. They seemed to whisper, "Wayne, darling—!"

Wayne snatched his hands away. Sobbing, he threw himself down beside her, snatched her into his arms.

"I can't do it! I can't do it, even to save your soul!" he cried in his agony. "God forgive me, I can't do it—!"

With a gasping cry, Wayne pulled away from her, back up on to his knees.

And now, Nancy was moving—stirring—coming to life. She stretched her arms and yawned. She rubbed her eyes. Suddenly they opened. In the moonlight she sat up, looking at Wayne.

Wonder filled her gaze as she peered around at the trees and the moonlight, then at her own uncovered form. "Wayne, darling, where am I?" she whispered. "What's happened—?"

Tears of insane happiness streaming down his cheeks, Wayne leaned over and snatched her into his arms. "You have been in hell, darling—and you have come back again—back to heaven, for both of us," he whispered. "Crains' rays brought back your life, but they didn't kill your soul, because you never were really dead—"

He jumped up, stooped and gathered her, wondering, into his arms.

"The car is just a little way farther down the road," he said. "I'll tell you all about it while we're going home—!"

BRIDES FOR THE HALF-MEN

Chapter One

Half Man — Half ?

IF I HAD NOT BEEN so distracted by business worries I should have realized long before that Morton's Valley was no place for Elaine.

I had heard those whispered dark stories, suggestions of a whole village bewitched, and in my sophisticated way, had scorned them as back country nonsense. I didn't sense the fiendishness which was destined to make a horror out of our love till that midsummer dusk when all our surroundings combined to create a spell of macabre weirdness.

The late afternoon train that had left me, the sole passenger to alight at the little railroad station, had gone puffing along, its smoke a grey wisp against tumbling green hillsides. Not another soul was in sight.

The paper in my hand made thin cracklings as I read it for the tenth time. Elaine's telegram failed to tell what was the matter—but if stark terror ever breathed from written words, it did from hers when she begged me to cancel my business trip and hurry back home.

And now I couldn't understand why my wife hadn't driven down to meet me. Could anything have happened to her—already?

I wheeled to cross the platform and turn into the dirt road that wound into the hills. It was more than a mile to the village and there was nothing to do but walk it. I wanted to run!

A hundred yards from the station wilderness closed around me—as though something had pounced. The light died away in eerie gloom and over my head the hills flung their jagged rock masses.

Through the air moved a dull moaning, rising and falling like lament of a tormented soul. What it could be wailing back there in the hills I didn't know. I hurried faster. I didn't like the feel of this place!

And then I heard swift footsteps approaching. Around a turn appeared the one I longed most of all in the world to see—Elaine. She came almost running, her face a pallid blur in the dusk, hands reaching out to me.

"Tom! Oh, Tom, darling!" she panted, and the next instant she was in my arms.

I held my wife close, kissing her, soothing her quivering shoulders. "It's all right now, darling," I tried to calm her. "What was it? What happened to scare you?"

She looked up at me, laughed flutteringly—her eyes still clouded with terror. "Oh, I don't know!" she half cried. "I guess I was foolish. But it was so dark and I thought I heard something following me. The car broke down; that is why I had to come on foot. I was late—"

"You saw the big rocks and the shadows," I laughed. I looked at her more closely and saw—had I but realized it— ¬the first shadow of that ghastliness that was to sweep me over insanity's brink. My wife was young, gloriously lovely. But during the two weeks since I had last seen her, she had grown wan. She seemed, strangely—to have aged! But I didn't mention that puzzling circumstance to her then.

I slid my arm around her slim yielding waist and turned her around toward the village. I said only: "Why did you send me that wire? Tell me, what has been going wrong?"

She linked one rounded bare arm through mine. "Oh, Tom, something awful! Our cottage burned down. Nils Ekstrom took me in, no one else had any room." Her voice changed oddly. "And I'm—afraid—to be there at Ekstrom's."

"Our house burned down!" I exclaimed, breathlessly. "How did it happen? When was it?"

"Night before last. Ekstrom saw it and saved my life. He came through fire to get me. He was quite badly burned. But—" she shivered now as she repeated her exclamation—"

Oh, I'm afraid of that man!"

I stared at her. "Afraid of Ekstrom? I thought he was all right—"

Elaine looked at me significantly without answering. In that moment of silence I tried to adjust my thoughts to more than her peculiar remark about our neighbor—to the whole idea of this catastrophe which had arrived to make a difficult situation still more perplexing.

It had been a shoestring venture at best undertaken by Elaine, myself and our close friend Frank Morrison—that of trying to redeem from time itself this rural community hidden in the almost forgotten loveliness of New England hills.

Like scores of such little towns Morton's Valley had seen its last prosperity years ago and was now hardly more than a ghost town set in surroundings of jewel-like beauty. Morrison had never wearied of extolling its possibilities as a summer resort. Finally, Elaine and I had borrowed from him enough to eke out our own limited resources while we enlisted our friends—and they, still other nature-lovers—so that now on the slope of the hill rising behind the quarry we had a community of more than twenty vacationists in trim bungalows, as well as half a dozen hardy all year around residents.

The expenses of water and sewerage installations and other improvements, however, had exhausted our capital. This trip had been an effort to raise more money.

And now this! My heart ached at thought of Elaine's harrowing experience without me at her side. I felt deep gratitude toward Ekstrom, a native who was our next neighbor. He was a mildly uncouth character, that I knew. But I had considered him inoffensive. Why Elaine had manifested that loathing when she mentioned his name was beyond me.

I was about to ask her to tell me the whole story when she looked up—paled swiftly. Her hand fell tensely on mine. She whispered:

"Tom, listen. What is that dreadful noise?"

It was the sound I had heard before, now louder and

closer—a throaty yowling that rose to ululate banshee-like from wall to wall of the gorge. What sort of wild creature could be making it was hard to imagine—a panther perhaps, or a giant owl? But it possessed an eerie suggestion of humanness—of *half-humanness*—that tingled my nerves.

Elaine seemed stricken with a fear beyond reason. Her face became bloodless, eyes dark bottomless pools against the white of her face—as though that yell had conveyed to her the nearness of horrors. I took a step toward the roadside. Now I *had* to know what was in there.

At first I could make out only a maze of tree trunks and shadows. Then deep in that solitude something moved—and suddenly I was aware of a face peering out at us.

I rubbed my eyes and moved closer, my uncanny bewilderment mounting. For that face, limned in the sunset glow, seemed that of a young lad, weirdly beautiful as some Greek statue. Could it have been this sylvan Adonis who had let out that hellish caterwauling?

And then the hair bristled on the back of my neck and I too felt Elaine's terror. For as I looked at him he screamed again. His cherubic features twisted in a mask of utter malignity. Before I could move or speak he spun around and bounded out of sight into the forest.

I wheeled at the sound of Elaine's gasping cry. It had been a nerve-jolting experience for me as well, but the explanation seemed fairly obvious.

"It was only some half-witted native, turned into a wild man from wandering in the woods." I had heard of such cases. Yet that countenance of incredibly beautiful youth was a thing not accounted for by this theory. It had been my imagination, the uncertain light—that was the most obvious probability.

But my wife shook her head. She cried incoherently:

"No! No, Tom, that wasn't a wild man—not any kind of a man—just half man and half—" She shivered and whispered: "That is what Ekstrom is doing, why I sent for you to come home. Ekstrom and that thing are doing it together—"

I looked at her in bewilderment. "What do you mean? Ekstrom is doing what?" Then the natural thought came to me—I wondered if something could have unsettled her mind to cause her to speak seriously of such absurdities. I took her hand and started to draw her along. Gently I tried to get her to explain.

But there was no opportunity. We had taken only a few steps when from behind the screen of bushes that insensate screaming burst again. The creature appeared once more in an opening and now to my horror I saw that he clutched in his arms something struggling and white. It was a woman, utterly nude!

And then followed the most ghastly thing I had ever seen. For he flung her down on the ground. He leaped high in the air, fists clenched and teeth gnashing, to stamp on her with gnome-like ferocity. And now her agonized moaning could be heard.

I knew that I ought to rush in there and rescue her, beat the monster's brains out with a club. But my paralyzed limbs held me transfixed. Before I could move he had vanished again as swiftly as he had come. And then, despite the noisome surge of our fear, Elaine and I were both running into the bushes.

The girl came crawling to meet us. There was a reason why she could not walk, why she came grovelling on all fours, for her feet and her legs . . . All over her body too, her shoulders and breasts and her face . . . where hooks or claws or teeth—I couldn't tell—had been busy . . . till she was something horrible.

I stood there stricken, my brain knotting. "Red hair! Margery Ames had red hair!" Elaine's reedy scream gagged in her throat. She snatched at my wrist and I felt her terror in the force with which her fingernails dug into my skin.

Red hair—yes. My wife's most intimate chum had those gorgeous flame-colored tresses. That was the only way we could tell who she was, for there wasn't enough left of her face now to identify her. Only enough to reveal the added horror, inexplicable—mad.

Ten days ago Margery had been overflowing with youthful vitality, bubbling sheer joy of living. But the face we saw there now was that of a wizened hag who could have been a hundred years old!

I bent closer to stare in my incredulous horror. Did I actually see that or was I out of my senses? Not even through wasting disease could such a thing take place—a beautiful girl changed in a period of days into a hideous old woman! I had a vision of the countenance of unholily beautiful youth on the thing that had killed her and night's miasma worked under my scalp.

Common sense told me that there were no such things as supernatural powers. But that ghastliness, by whatever name I should call it, that had taken my wife's dearest friend—could take her as well!

There was nothing we could do for Margery. A moment later she died. That was the most merciful thing that could happen. With my arm half supporting my wife we started along. She clung to me sobbing like a terrified child. She had loved gay, red-headed Margery—we had all loved her.

I did my best to comfort her. But the woods still lay ahead of us and in the shadows under the trees that thing could be lurking. Waiting for her? Gooseflesh of primitive terror rolled on my spine. My fists clenched involuntarily at my sides. But we had to go through, there was no other way to get home.

Ten minutes might have passed while we hurried, clinging to one another. In my perplexity I wanted to question Elaine till she told me the whole story at which so far she'd only hinted. Mysteriously she had suggested Ekstrom's connection.

But I knew that now was no time to talk over horrors. She couldn't stand any more, she was on the verge of a crackup.

Presently to my relief the trees thinned away and fields with scattered, farm houses lined the road. A pair of figures could be seen coming toward us—living human beings. As they passed I recognized them as girls from the village.

Girls . . .? I half turned to stare at them while that uncanny tingling yanked at my nerves again.

For the impossible phenomenon which had visited Margery, was again evident! When I had gone away only a short time before, those two had been farmers' daughters in their teens. But now their cheeks were sagging and lined eyes hollowed, lips sunken. They gazed at me out of death's heads. In two weeks they had turned into old women!

That was what my eyes told me—yet in my leaping horror I tried to deny the evidence of my senses. I told myself that those girls from poverty-stricken families were under nourished, which gave them that appearance of age. The rest had been fancy, bred of the macabre light and my own horror-fraught nerves. That was the most reasonable explanation.

And then my weird terror rose, casting aside an explanation that failed to explain—when I thought about Margery. There could be no doubt about her. Something impelled me to peer at my wife. I had wondered before why she was wearing such unusually heavy makeup. Normally Elaine was sparing of cosmetics. On impulse I exclaimed:

"Elaine, stand still! Let me look at you!"

But she wouldn't allow me. She gasped faintly and turned her head—broke away from me, almost running.

I hurried along at her side, still trying to see her as she walked with face stubbornly averted—my soul stricken with a fear more chilling than any I'd yet experienced. Throughout this village youth seemed rushing to untimely gruesome senility—while death wore the cherubic visage of infancy. Was my darling already growing like the girls we had met— becoming like Margery? Was that why she wouldn't allow me to look at her?

But all I could see was the oval contour of her dear little head, the ringlets of hair nestled around her pink ears that I loved to kiss, the hectic rise and fall of her bosom.

In a few moments the lights of the village showed around a turn. And then the highway curved to skirt the rim of a huge cavity in the ground. Up till the time, five years ago, when the mysterious disappearance of old Amos Morton, the owner, had brought suspension of working, Morton's Valley had been a center of the marble industry. Amos had just walked out of his office one winter evening and never been seen again.

Nearly a mile across and in places three thousand feet deep, the abandoned quarry was an eerie sight now with its facades of sheer walls and purple shadows rolling into its depths. Legend said that it had mazes of side chasms and passages where a man might wander till he died without finding his way out—where the earth spirits, the cobalts and elves, would flock around him squeaking and gibbering till he became mad.

Up ahead the narrow streets of the village glimmered spectrally with their marble slab shanties. The natives gathered in their doorways to glower at us as we passed. As I gazed into hang-dog faces of flat-breasted women and seamed sullen countenances of the men—descendants of the mid-European laborers imported generations ago by the Mortons—I sensed their ignorance, their dangerous fanaticism. I knew that they resented the presence of city people among them and that most of all they hated me as manager and prime mover in the enterprise.

This Ekstrom, however, of whom my wife had spoken, was a superior type—something of a mystery as well. He lived with a housekeeper in a big place next to ours and though he had no occupation, seemed well supplied with money. He had been of the greatest help to us in smoothing over our contacts with the hostile villagers. Which made Elaine's accusation of him all the harder to understand.

All at once I saw the man coming toward us. "Here's Ekstrom now," I said. "Maybe he can tell us what it's all about."

Elaine stiffened, turned to me swiftly—paled again. "Tom, no!" she cried vehemently. She clutched my hand and muttered words whose utter terror bewildered me anew.

"Tom, don't let him know what we saw in the woods! Don't say a word about that to him—to anyone here—if you want us to live!"

Chapter Two

The Hunger of Half-Men

Ekstrom was almost up to us. I pressed my wife's arm and murmured: "Elaine—get hold of yourself!" I could only think that the horrors she had experienced had temporarily unbalanced her.

"Hello, Burnham, I'm glad to see you!" Ekstrom greeted me the next moment. He had a big square-boned figure from which his clothes hung loosely—wisps of light yellow hair and filmy pale eyes in a pasty face. He thrust out his hand. "Your wife got pretty nervous. I wouldn't have let her go down to meet you if I had known it." He inspected us narrowly and for the first time I realized how brightly red were his thin pitiless lips.

"It was perfectly all right," I told him. Then I thanked him for his services to Elaine at the fire. "Have you any idea how it started?"

He shook his head. "It was going too fast when I got there. Maybe a cigarette left around."

We went on up the hill, still discussing the fire. I couldn't deny now the tension of constraint in the air. Elaine stepped around to get me between her and Ekstrom. It didn't make me feel any better to realize that we had to go to his house—as his guests.

Arriving there shortly, I made excuses and took my wife, after a few moments, up to the room which he had placed at her disposal. I closed the door behind us—but it was she who crossed to turn the key in the lock. She wheeled to stand looking at me, breathing swiftly. She whispered a little cry and the next instant she was in my arms.

They say that being married dulls the edge of desire. Elaine and I had celebrated our third anniversary—and we were still sweethearts. She had a trim little figure, all entrancing curves and livewire energy. Her lips were trembling scarlet flames, her eyes like windows in heaven. And now with her soft warm body in my embrace I almost forgot the monstrous shape in the woods, the ghastly ruin it had left behind it. I pressed my wife closer while the spicy scent of her hair thrilled me and I knew heaven in the touch of her lips.

At last she partly freed herself—one hand reaching to draw my arm tighter around her and crush my fingers over her breast as she pulled me down at her side on the edge of the bed. "Tom, hold me tight!" she whispered tensely. "Oh, dear Tom, never let go of me!"

"Why were you frightened of Ekstrom?" I said. "Has he been bothering you?"

"Not that way," she murmured. She caught her breath. "Something even more awful. You saw those girls just now on the road, how they seemed unnaturally old? After you went away I found out that that had been going on for a long time. More than that, girls had been disappearing. And then they began coming back. And how they came back! You saw Margery . . ." Elaine shivered. She whispered:

"They say that thing we saw comes into their houses and takes them. He makes love to them—that's why they grow old. When he is through, he kills them—"

I made myself laugh. I patted her hand reassuringly. "Just back-country nonsense. There's nothing to be afraid of. It can't get into this house."

She turned sharply then, tense fingers clutching the bed cover. She exclaimed words which, unless I had deemed her distraught by fear, would have congealed me anew. "Tom, it has been in here! Ekstrom let it into this house!"

I drew her head to my shoulder, trying to calm her. "Elaine darling, you're dreaming. Ekstrom wouldn't let that creature—no sane man would—"

"Yes, he did!" she sobbed wildly. "I saw that boy's face out there in the hall. He was after me! Laura and Marian and Stella West—the young wives of our own friends—are growing old, too. Three of them have disappeared, besides Margery. I didn't tell you in the telegram, but the state police came and hunted everywhere."

I sank down on the bed, my legs suddenly limp. For the

first time then I was conscious of the full extent of our peril—felt terror pressing in from all sides, sickening me with its noisome presence. The spread of the horror among our friends was a catastrophe that threatened the ruin of all our hopes. And whether or not Elaine's charge against Ekstrom was true, the menace that had snatched her friends out of the world of the living could take her too. Take her at any time—

"I've seen Ekstrom at night, going into the woods," she breathed. "Coming back . . . His face in the moonlight—I watched through the window. His lips red as blood . . ."

For a moment I studied Elaine. Her story sounded incredible in a world ruled by reason. Was she telling the truth, or had something really happened to make her—abnormal?

Then before I had time to ask her anything more, footsteps sounded outside our door and a knock came.

It was our host, Ekstrom, who stood in the hall when I opened the door. Beside him was the gingham-clad form of a woman—his housekeeper. She was bearing a tray with refreshments. "I had Martha make some coffee and sandwiches," Ekstrom smiled hospitably. "If you are anything like me you get plenty hungry after a long train ride."

The least I could do in response to his graciousness was to ask them both in. The girl set the tray down on the table, set down a percolator and cups. At the moment I didn't see anything of which to be afraid, though it did occur to me that it was strange that a slavey domestic in this neck of the woods should be so heavily rouged.

Ekstrom accepted the cup of coffee that Elaine offered him—she had assumed the position of hostess—and I was frankly astonished when the servant also sank into a chair on the other side of the room, smoothing her apron primly over her knee. She was looking at me, and I felt, rather than saw, the fantical intensity of her gaze. As though she *desired* me . . .

For a short time we manufacture meaningless small talk. Then I disobeyed Elaine's warning. I told Ekstrom what we had seen—asked him candidly if he could offer any explanation of what had been going on.

He gazed at me oddly. "Your friend's body was found a short time ago," he murmured. "It has been taken care of. As for an explanation—you are a city man, Mr. Burnham, you are going to call this ridiculous. But the people here say that the earth spirits—the cobalts, the gnomes and the elves—became angry when their homes were torn open by the quarry excavations. In revenge, they attacked the workmen. You must have heard that during the time when the quarry was operating many laborers disappeared and were never heard of again. It was given out that they fell into deep pools of water. But the old people still say that the pixies made off with them."

He stirred his coffee with a thoughtful expression. "You must know too of the mystery of what happened to old Amos Morton. He dropped out of sight just about five years ago. The courts have been petitioned to pronounce him legally dead. But the old village crones will tell you that the earth spirits are still torturing him down there."

I was surreptitiously watching Elaine as I listened. Of course this was all utter nonsense . . . She had got out her vanity case and was daubing more makeup over her cheeks, though she was already heavily over-rouged. Her eyes shone with a crazy brightness.

Ekstrom's voice was droning on as he too watched her.

"The natives say that those earth-spirits cast a spell over those vanished men. They grow older and older and yet they can never die. They are fated to live on, half-human and half-supernatural. They believe that if they can know love of human girls—if they can drink their blood as they love them—they will become young and human again. Their leader is supposed to be a creature whose upper body is that of a lad irresistible in his allure over women. He entices the girls into the woods to be caught by the half-men. They give their youth to the old ones, becoming senile themselves." Ekstrom laughed shortly. "You can believe that or not."

I nodded. Of course this yarn belonged to the sorcery-ridden ignorance of the Dark Ages. I glanced toward Elaine. Her face even whiter if that were possible, she was gazing across at the girl Martha—with eyes in which terror was crawling. But the young servant was only scrubbing at her cheeks with the hem of her apron.

"How do the natives account for the girls who are growing old right in their own homes, without going into the woods?" I asked Ekstrom.

"They say that those girls steal away to meet the half-men in their revels before they quit home for good. And after they have been there they themselves become mad for the blood of young men—to restore the youth they are losing. They lust to kill the wives of those men, they hate them as rivals."

I wanted to pinch myself to make sure I was hearing aright. Earth-spirits, charms and love-slaves in the twentieth century! But there by the roadside I'd found evidence of something that wasn't imagination!

No one spoke for a moment. I was on the point of continuing my question when the sound of Elaine's voice in a choked exclamation brought my gaze back to her—from her to Ekstrom.

His strange eyes were fastened on hers, they seemed to possess a hypnotic quality. Her own eyes, lifted to his, grew rapt, dilated in terror. The next instant she had half stumbled up to her feet to move toward him as though entranced by some power he had.

I let out an oath and lunged in front of the man, shutting my wife from his gaze. "Damn you to hell, what are you up to?" I yelled. "Take your eyes off her!"

I was set to swing on him but he didn't give me the chance. He laughed curtly—mockingly—turned on his heel and strode from the room.

Then Elaine's shrilling cry rang and I knew that Ekstrom had left something with us—something diabolical.

The girl Martha had finished getting the rouge off her face. And now as I turned I saw revealed another countenance of noisome age, eyes sunken in lead-colored pits. Her eyes that fastened upon me with a gleam of terrible longing!

Then her gaze swerved toward Elaine. She screamed and came off her chair in a spring, face crazily working—one uplifted hand clutching a knife.

For an instant dismay sent me recoiling. And then as she clattered past, my fist flew. The blow caught her under the ear. She went spinning into a corner where she lay without moving.

Elaine came running to cling to me, slim figure shaking. "Tom, she wanted to kill me!" And then: "Remember what Ekstrom said? She's given her youth to the half men; she wanted to get it back through your love!"

"She won't do anything now, I knocked her out," I muttered inanely. I was too horror-stricken to think. God, that damnation I'd scoffed at was real! I said thickly: "What was the matter with you just before? What were you doing with Ekstrom?"

My wife murmured something inaudible. She turned her back.

I went over where Martha still lay unconscious, picked her up from the floor and carried her out into the hall. I laid her down not ungently on the floor and returned. I had no time now to play nurse! For black surmises were crawling like worms on my brain. And then my fear impelled me to an act of sheer cruelty to banish once for all the uncertainty I couldn't endure.

After turning the lights full on, I got a moist towel—held Elaine by an arm while I scrubbed her face clean. For an instant she fought me back frantically and then sagged limp in my clasp, her voice frozen, only her eyes sobbing her woe.

My arm dropped to my side. I had really known all along, but now my terror was photographed there in blasting reality. Elaine's dear cheeks that I had loved to kiss were like those of the farmer's girls on the road. That blight of hideous age! And those lips whose touch against mine had thrilled me to the core of my being . . .

Heedless of her heart-broken wail, I hooked my finger in the neck of her dress and yanked, ripping it to the waist. And there was the rest of it—evidence that Ekstrom's story was true. For on her lovely arms and her bosom were scars—that could have been made only by human teeth!

I groaned, my soul frozen—sickened desperately as though I had heard my death sentence pronounced. "Elaine, how did those get there?" I finally managed to croak. I gripped her bare arms till she winced with the pain. "Tell me where you went those nights when I wasn't here!"

She didn't move physically but all her life seemed to draw back from me, to shudder away in guilty consciousness while her face became snow-like. She wet her lips, husked out at last:

"I didn't go anywhere, Tom. Those marks—I don't know. I woke up in the morning. They were there—"

She stared at me pitifully while I remained silent. She sobbed: "Tom—you know I'm telling the truth? You believe me?"

I drew my hand over my eyes. Yes, I did believe that she wouldn't take part in such ghastliness—consciously. But what she might have done without knowing it, under influence of some awful spell . . .

Insane as it sounded, such a spell was what Margery must have felt when she left home to become the sweetheart of earth-creatures. And now Elaine my darling . . .

Chapter Three

Hours of Terror

I had no proof as to whether Ekstrom was really what Elaine had charged, the guiding brain of the awfulness, though it now seemed hard to doubt that. And my wife! Whether she had been guilty or not—whether she had been the sweetheart of monsters!—I still loved her. I had to save her from the ghastliness that had overtaken those others. I had to do something! And the first move was to get out of this house. When I had taken her to safety I'd come back and kill Ekstrom.

Martha was gone when Elaine and I stole soundlessly into the hall. Silence reigned in the lower part of the house. We concluded that Ekstrom must have gone out. Clasping one another's hands we almost ran down the stairs. Frank Morrison's bungalow was the nearest, only a short distance away.

Frank himself answered our knock. He led the way inside and listened silently while I gave him a brief story of what had taken place. Morrison was a tall, slender man with scholarly face and penetrating grey eyes. He was a man of few words—now that I look back on his memory after the horrors that followed, he seems the quietest, most restrained person I've ever known. He could face hell without flinching!

"My family left this afternoon—" his mother, father and sister, I knew he meant. Frank was unmarried— "and I've got plenty of room for you people."

Away from the poisonous aura of Ekstrom's house, Elaine's dreadful tautness had somewhat relaxed. We three settled down in Frank's cozy living room to try and talk some sense into the mysteries. He was my oldest friend— had known both Elaine and me before our marriage. In fact, he had almost taken her away from me. That was all past now, we could all laugh over it.

"This business of the young growing old and the old growing young—it's an ancient superstition," my friend pondered, his ascetic slim fingers turning his cigarette. "The sorcerers of the South Sea islands are said to do it with incantations. And I've heard my own grandmother say that if a boy or a girl sinned with a very old person the aged one would steal the strength from the young one. The people here are using the idea as a blind to cover some filthy stunt of sating their sex-hunger by victimizing the youth. But how they are doing it—"

I muttered. "The thing we saw in the woods, with the face of an angel and the voice of a fiend—what was that? Old Amos Morton turned into a wild man?"

Morrison shrugged. "It's my belief that the villagers threw

Amos into the quarry in vengeance for his having tried to make slaves out of them."

"Do you believe that Ekstrom can be behind it?" I questioned.

"Could be," he said. "Though what would make him want to—you know he's invested quite heavily with us. He stands to lose plenty if our gang stampedes. Seems more logical that it would be some of the folks in the village who hate us."

"But that doesn't tie in with their inflicting horrors upon their own people more than upon us," I objected.

Morrison nodded. "It certainly does not," he admitted.

We talked for a time longer. Frank revealed one more angle which only added to my worry. Our summer people were departing in numbers, demanding refunds on the advance payments they'd made—and who could blame them? Our treasury was empty. I could feel the shadow of ruin.

Finally Morrison excused himself. He was going to call on several of our people who were still hanging on to discuss forming a posse of vigilantes in an effort to stave off final disaster.

Elaine and I went to our room. I'd been intending to seek out Ekstrom and deal with him, but with Frank gone she wouldn't hear of being alone. Nor would I have left her. Almost timidly she came to me, stood gazing up into my eyes. "Tom—if you still love me—trust me." she whispered.

"Love you!" I groaned and took her into my arms. She clung to me as though only there in my embrace could she stop being afraid. "I know that nothing can happen if you only keep hold of me," she murmured. "Oh my darling, never let me out of your arms tonight!"

Some little time passed while we sat there close, not speaking, just thinking. Reason told me that here in Morrison's house she ought to be safe. Yet she wasn't safe! Perhaps from the physical attack of the monster I could protect her. But from that village as from a noisome half world there seemed to emanate a power against which my mortal strength and love were unavailing. I could feel its invisible tendrils twining around my darling, changing her, even while

she was in my arms, into a creature like Martha. God, now
could such things be possible? Moment by moment my sense
of helplessness grew, my numbing fear as I sat there—and
waited.

We were looking for Morrison to return. But minutes
stretched into an hour and he didn't show up. I wondered if
he would ever come—or if he had run into the thing in the
forest.

I extinguished the light and stood looking out of the window. Shadows cast by the moonlight peopled the hollows
under the pine trees. And now those inky swathes were coming alive. I saw flame colored eyes and crouched figures behind them. They emerged into light to surround the house in
a half circle. From their clothing they seemed like some of
the villagers. Yet I couldn't be certain if they were human
beings at all, those waspish forms of creatures of infinite age,
their long beards trailing over bodies sucked dry of life's
juices, their faces gnome-like in senile lust. Were they those
men doomed to grow forever older yet denied the surcease of
death, forever hungering for love of mortal girls to restore
them . . . coming now for Elaine?

"This is it!" I thought, and that cold cramping hit the pit of
my stomach. Tense on my toes I drew back from the window. If there was time to get a poker, a club—anything with
which to fight for her!

Half way through the motion I halted, my astonishment
stabbing. The figures had drawn back again. And now from
the dim shapes a familiar form had separated. It was crossing
the lawn toward the house. It was Morrison!

I was still completely bewildered when we heard his footsteps and then his knock on our door. What could he have
been doing with the horror-pack? I went to admit him—and
before I could ask him the question he burst out with what he
had to tell us.

The gist of it was that we had to get out of here in a
hurry—go now, on foot, without waiting. In the village he
had learned that the natives were planning to raid the sum-

mer colony. We would have to take to the woods and do our best to hide until morning.

Sudden suspicion came to me. Morrison didn't know that I had seen him talking with those figures outside. His sudden hurry to get us out of the house—where we would be at their mercy—sounded fishy. I remembered how he had courted Elaine before I had. Did he still long for her? Perhaps he secretly hated me, and was biding his time.

Whatever depths of infamy held sway in the village, those yokels couldn't have thought out its intricate details. Some shrewd and intelligent brain was bossing them for his own purposes. That boss could be—Morrison!

These thoughts raced hot and swift through my brain as I stared at him without answering. Yet that horrible guess might be unjust. His plan might be the only one that would save Elaine.

Then I became aware that her gaze had left his face to focus on a small object that projected out of his coat pocket. I saw three curved prongs which I knew belonged to a hand garden tool. They were covered with fresh dirt which adhered stickily as though underneath it was something *wet*.

Seeing our eyes on it, Morrison pulled it out with a short laugh. "I was weeding my zinnias this afternoon and forgot it," he muttered. "Just thought of it now as I was passing the bed."

I still looked at him without speaking; looked at Elaine—for her eyes, locked on the little implement, were dilating till it seemed they would burst from their pits. Her mouth opened—and then her hands flew to crush over her lips as though to choke back words that must not be uttered.

Morrison stiffened, made a motion to drop the tool back in his pocket. But not till I had seen what had convulsed Elaine. Clinging to the socket where the metal part fitted into the wooden handle was a wisp of long hair. Those threads were the flame color of Margery's tresses!

For a moment there was silence stark as a breaking heart. Morrison read our thoughts. A wry laugh escaped him. He muttered: "You utter fools!" He swung on his heel and left us alone.

Elaine and I stared at each other. Maybe we were fools, at that. Those who had murdered the lovely girl could have used Frank's instrument and then replaced it at the spot from which they had taken it. I felt appalled at the thought that I might have unjustly suspected my friend. Elaine and I both knew terror in the realization that those beasts from the village might come for us—anytime.

But still we did not take refuge in flight. Out in the woods were terrors unknown and unguessable. In here we had at least a chance to fight for our lives.

At last Elaine stretched out on the bed still dressed while I pulled a chair up to her side. I put out the light again; only the moonbeams streamed through the window to show my darling lying there in brightness and shadow. She moved restlessly, bringing her face into view, its dreadful pallor, its awful swift ageing.

Chapter Four

Things that Crawled . . .

I had vowed that I would never sleep again in this world. But at last weary nature assumed control. My eyes closed—and the next thing I knew Elaine was sitting up shaking my arm. "Tom, wake up!" she cried. "Wake up and listen—"

I rubbed my eyes, muttered incoherently—and then snapped into full tingling consciousness. Moonlight flooded the room with white witchery. A small wind had arisen, setting the leaves on the trees to whispering in their eerie soft voices.

Elaine's hand came groping for mine—sweat-cold in the night. She breathed in my ear: "There is some one walking around in the house. They tried to get in here. It wasn't Frank—"

Her voice died like a candle flame pinched between finger and thumb. I saw her eyes swerve to focus on the knob of the door which led into the hall. It was turning stealthily, sound-lessly. It halted, turned the other way. Repeated . . . And then I realized that those noises I'd taken for rustlings of tree leaves were voices! Eldrich pipings of—something—out there in the hall. I remembered what Ekstrom had said about earth spirits who came out of their midnight caves to snatch mortal women, and horror's fingers slid on my spine.

Stiff on my toes I pushed off the bed. I took a step toward the door and then Elaine was beside me, her face a pallid blur in the moonlight, frantic hands tugging me backward. "Tom, no!" she gasped. "Dear God, don't open that door!"

I put my arm around her. "They aren't—there can't be any such things," I tried to calm her. "It's the wind making the door hinges squeak." Both of us stood frozen and listening. The knob didn't move again. There wasn't a sound.

I stood the suspense as long as I could and then tiptoed over and unlocked the door—yanked it wide open. Not a soul was in sight.

"But some one *was* there!" Elaine murmured.

"Lock the door and stay in there," I said. "I'm going to see—"

"No!" her cry spurted. "I won't stay alone, Tom. I'm going with you."

With my arm tight around her we catfooted into the hall. For a moment nothing was to be seen or heard—only our heartbeats pounding our eardrums. We kept on going for a short distance. Then Elaine jumped. We had both stumbled against something that lay on the floor—yielded suddenly as our feet thudded into it. I struck a match then—I had to know.

God! It was Frank Morrison who lay here, face turned to-ward the ceiling. A crimson spider web spangled his throat and trailed down over his chest. The front of his shirt was a glistening blotch where the web ended.

The match died and darkness came leaping. I pulled Elaine away—it was useless to think of doing anything for Frank now. I had a sick emptiness in my stomach to think how we had misjudged our friend—what he had suffered trying to save us.

But the horrors were only beginning. They crowded up on us swiftly, after that—swiftly . . .

I knew that the things which had done that to Frank must be somewhere here close to us—close to Elaine. The only hope was to get her back to our room where I'd have a chance to defend her. I drew her a couple of steps and then between us and its door something started to—twitter is the only word to describe the voice of whatever it was that stood a yard away in pitch darkness.

Clutching one another's hands Elaine and I sagged against the wall. I had a vision of my darling like Margery; of Frank there close beside us—and stark terror twisted my throat till I couldn't breathe. Could those natives be right? Did science and knowledge mean nothing? Could the earth's caves send up among mortals things that—?

We stood there maybe a minute—it seemed an eternity. The voices didn't come again. But down the hall creaking footsteps approached. They could be the steps of the monster who was running this business—but even in that there was comfort, for I knew they were human. They became louder; and then suddenly a tall form glided past without seeing us. It was Ekstrom! Then we heard him talking softly. Was he muttering to himself or was he holding converse with those whom we had heard there before?

Presently he was gone. We didn't hear him depart. One moment he had been there and the next there was vacancy.

Elaine was tugging me along the hall in the direction that he had disappeared. "We've got to see what he does—and then go somewhere and telephone for the police!" she breathed tensely.

I went with her reluctantly. I didn't want to go there where Ekstrom had gone—into the darkness where *they* might be waiting.

Bang-bang-bang . . . At the farther end of the hall the open front door was slatting back and forth in the breeze. It filled the house with reverberations like beats of death's noisome heart. I got hold of the thing to stop its cursed noise and for an instant Elaine and I paused on the threshold to listen.

The only sound now was night's mysterious breathing, the shrill fiddling of its insect orchestras. We descended from the piazza and took three or four steps along the path. But I should have known that this was just a deceptive calm before terror's climax.

It was Elaine who pulled at my hand, halting me. I could feel her slim form going rigid. And then my wife screamed.

Ten feet away bushes had parted and in a ray of moonlight there appeared the face of the creature we had seen howling over Margery's body. It stood there motionless. And now I could see more clearly than before the upper part of its figure—a nude torso of muscular perfection such as would thrill a woman as tinglingly as the sight of a nude female provokes a man.

Uncanny wonder held me spellbound while I tried to figure who or what it really could be. The incarnate spirit of youth, it seemed, here where the motif of everything was the contradiction of dire age. But whatever it was or wasn't, it had a central part in the horrors, for I knew it had killed Margery. I moved a step toward it.

Heedless of my wife's wailing cry: "No, Tom, don't go over there! Don't leave me now!" I kept on going. For I thought that this was my chance to catch this demon and kill it—if mortal hands indeed could bring an end to its loathsomeness—put an end to the awfulness. I heard Elaine's desperate gasp. For to my dismay the thing ducked to one side, evading me, and then swerved to make a dash for my wife.

Spinning around, I flew at him. At my yell he halted to turn and face me, crouched and glaring. The next instant he came leaping, hooked fingers clawing.

I closed with him and for an instant we struggled. He must be mortal, I thought, for he possessed the strength of a viper. Finally I managed to clamp a headlock on him. I started dragging him along to the door. I had to get him inside and secured in some way till I could contact the authorities.

As I dragged him around he caught sight again of Elaine. He screamed, a high feral whine of beast-longing. He lunged backward with mad new strength. He was struggling to escape and get at her—as he'd attacked Margery!

"Elaine, get out of here! Go into the house!" I yelled. I heard her eerie cry, saw her retreat and stand crouching, hands crushed to her lips.

Something in the speechless new horror of her expression made me glance down at the thing I was fighting. What I saw registered in the back of my brain like a blow from a hammer. It will sound to you like insanity. But I *saw* . . .

The man I had grabbed hold of a minute before had been a weirdly beautiful youth. But the creature that now thrashed on spindling hairy legs was a fiend-like changeling who might have been a thousand years old. Those brown and mummified cheeks, bloodless lips pinched in a crease . . . His head was parchment stretched over a skull and over all a blueish glow dripped blobs of supernatural light.

Stricken, nerves jellied, I stared down at that vision. Revulsion sickened me, terror of the damned washed at my sanity. For now I had to accept Ekstrom's theory of the diabolical, had to believe the whole farrago of impossibilities. While I still clutched him, I had seen take place in this creature's body the transformation that was sweeping the village— youth following magically into age, a thing that could happen only through sorcery!

His gaze was locked on Elaine more hungrily than before—desiring her to bring back the youth that just now had flowed out of him. The sight of his lewd eyes defiling her stung me with fury. I applied pressure to the headlock. I'd crush in his skull.

He gave another terrific wrench and almost escaped me. Locked together we battled all over the place. God, I didn't know what I was fighting—man, half man or ghoul from the pit. His strength was too much for me. With a final jerk he got his head out from under my arm. He whirled to spring at me. Blindly I drove out my left—and by luck got him flush on the jaw. He dropped flat on his face and lay motionless.

I left him lying there while I ran over to where Elaine had slumped cold in a faint. Dropping on my knees at her side I loosened the front of her dress, rubbed her wrists—kissing her, whispering her name.

At last her eyes opened. She stared uncomprehendingly for an instant and then came erect with a scream. I tried to get her into my arms but she beat me away with her fists. She didn't know what she was doing! Finally I slapped her. She tottered a step and fell on my shoulder, her whole body vibrating with the tremors that swept it.

I remember that I was smoothing her bright golden hair and trying to get her to stop that awful hysterical moaning. It was just a whisper of sound that I heard behind me. I started to turn—got a glimpse of the creature I'd smashed still lying there inert on the ground—and then the house seemed to drop on my skull.

I went out like a light.

Chapter Five

The Valley of Tombs

The bed on which I lay was of stone.

The walls of the open-topped box which I felt as I stretched out my arms were of stone too. Six feet by two were the dimensions of my coffin hewn there in solid shale.

I rubbed my eyes. In my giddy weakness my surroundings reeled in a blur. Caverns of stone ... basalt and porphery shafts that lurched hundreds of feet into ghoulish light. Under the lofty roof harpy shapes wheeled in slow circles.

Damp with gelid sweat I pushed myself up to widen my circle of observation. In front, the floor of the valley sloped upward till it narrowed in V-shaped perspective at the foot of ramparts like those of hell's circle. Besides myself there was not a creature that lived, not a being that breathed, nothing that grew.

Was I dead, was this my eternal resting place? Then I saw that I wasn't alone, my companion lay at my side in another of the coffins excavated from stone. He lay flat on his back, glassy eyes fixed. A man who seemed the incarnation of age, dead and interred here like myself, yet through some unholy spell still retaining his bodily substance, not yet dissolved in putrefaction. Not yet food for maggots.

I gazed at him more intently. Had I seen him before? Was he the monster that I had battled at Morrison's? His macabre youth vanished, the picture of infinite weariness—lying there dead?

His eyelids fluttered. He sat erect and across the narrow space we stared at each other. Wildly I muttered: "Damn you—what have you done with my wife?" He did not answer. His hand reached out to fall upon mine. I felt its physical touch, the weight of its substance, but its stuff was not that of life but the clammy coldness of death.

I snatched my hand away. How could I tell if he were alive or if he were dead? Or if I myself . . . For what man has passed beyond that last frontier and returned to tell us what lies in its hidden bourne?

With a strangled yell I leaped to my feet, clambered out of my hole into the rocky floor, to go running wildly. And now I began to think that perhaps I might be really alive, for thoughts of Elaine came to torment me. What ghastliness had come to her during the time while I had lain there unconscious? Had she been taken away for the pleasure of half men—like Margery? Escape from this dungeon and get back to her somehow was what I must do. Get back there fast and pray to God there was time! Since I had come down here there must be a way back again.

Yet my despair mocked me, telling me that my fears were no proof that I lived. Perhaps even the wraiths of the Styx agonize for their dear living ones, yearn to return and aid them in danger.

For I wouldn't know how long I coursed through the maze of gulleys between dizzy cliff walls. In every direction I explored the vicinity and came to a standstill each time at the rim of a gulf in whose bottom an invisible river flowed with sepulchral gurglings. Leafless bushes thrust up spines like stabbing dead fingers from the edge of the abyss. Sprawled against a shelving bank, a skeleton grinned at me.

I retreated, to start running again in a circle—and presently found myself back in the valley of coffins. The old man advanced toward me. Others were with him—those I had seen surrounding Morrison's house. They came flocking around me, old with senility not of things mortal. Over their faces glimmered blue mold of putrefaction.

The tones of the leader came hollow and unreal, a voice in a dream. "These are men into whom the earth spirits have entered. They cannot live nor can they wholly die. You are doomed to become one of them, forever longing for the blood and love of the young to restore you."

Horror slid on my brain as I peered at them trying to make out who—what—they really were. Living men they must be—lepers—something within the compass of human reason. I to be like them! I heard madness whispering. Dear God, I had to keep sane to fight for Elaine!

In utter loathing I recoiled from them. But they had marked me their victim. In a rush they came leaping. Old though they were they possessed a viperish strength that I couldn't cope with so soon after the blow on my head. They swarmed over me like insects. One of them beat my legs out from under me and then I was down on my back.

Pinioning my spread-eagled legs and arms they held me out flat. Before my eyes there blazed fire, scorching of light that pierced to my brain. Through my chest lanced another fiery stab. And then suddenly my tormentors released me. They drew back to stand in a ring, their laughter like cackling of fiends. I struggled up to my feet to burst through their line and flee from their sight.

How long a time passed while I wandered alone through the maze of canyons I wouldn't know. I had lost the measure of time—if indeed time existed here in these shades! What eventually the old men would do with me I didn't know. I didn't care. I could think of only one thing, my darling Elaine. Somewhere down here she must be and I had to find her. Unless it was already too late to save her from those who'd killed Margery.

Hours—centuries—dragged while I searched fruitlessly. And now came hunger and burning thirst. Water was nowhere to be found in this desert. My tongue stuck to my jaws. I wept in my despair and my weakness.

Once again my evil genius, the old man, confronted me. He cacchinated reedy laughter. "You will see your wife soon—very soon if you are obedient. But meanwhile you must have food—"

A group of his comrades approached. Screams could be heard and then as the ring parted I saw the nude form of a girl. Sobbing in terror she cowered there, striving to cover herself with her crossed arms.

"You are like us now, you are a half man," the ancient intoned. "There is only one food upon which you can live—the blood of young women sipped as you love them. There is your first meal—go and take her."

The group pushed her closer and now I saw that she was Marian Frost, one of Elaine's and my friends! My fury burst as I beat my tempter aside with my fists. I started toward her to try and get her away from them. But already they had thrown her to the ground. They leaped—and then they were swarming all over her, lecher hands working, caressing, fondling—hideous teeth and lips busy . . .

"If you want to see your wife again, you must learn to do as you see them doing," the voice of the old man came through the blur of my horror. "Until you are ready she will be kept from you—for the rest of us to enjoy."

"Then she is here, damn you—you have brought Elaine down here!" I strode across to scream the words into his face. My hands flew for his throat but he twitched me off, went scuffing away.

Who can reckon the moments when time passes in intervals of torturing consciousness mingled with stretches of stupor? How many hours—or days—flowed across me as I roamed through that valley I never shall know.

Periods came when I was too exhausted to move, when I lay where my legs dropped me, murmuring Elaine's name through swollen black lips. And as my strength waned my terror mounted till it became fire fed by my helplessness. Elaine! Elaine my sweetheart, my wife! Somewhere she was, here or above on the mortal earth, suffering what hideousness while those fiends wove their enchantment about her?

For some reason that I didn't comprehend—then—my captors did not want me to die. Again they brought some of their own food to tempt me, another nude girl. When I turned from them revolted they did at last set bread, meat and water down at my side. Stood watching like vultures while I devoured it.

More time dragged away. They fed me again. And again . . . Awakening from another stretch of unconsciousness I lifted my hands to my face. When I had come to this place I had been young and smooth-cheeked. But now I wore inches long stubble. And beneath it I could feel my cheeks sunken in hollows. Through rents in my clothing I could see my legs wasted to pipe-stems, my withered arms.

Wildly I sprang to my feet. I started to run, now hobbling on stiffened limbs. Old! Old! Caught in this spell that was sweeping me into living death—without hope of death's final mercy. Doomed to wander here, never to see my darling again, never to know heaven in the touch of her flesh.

And with that terror came insidious temptation. They had told me there was only one hope, the love of a young woman—and her warm blood passing my lips as I possessed her. Crazy laughter spewed from me. There were plenty of young girls down here. I had seen the old men with them. I had to find one for myself. It was the only way to live and stay young till I found Elaine.

Animal-like now I wanted Elaine! Yet from a corner of my brain where a tiny flame of reason still flickered whispered terror of the thought that was driving me on to destroy the thing that I loved more than my life.

And then I found the victim whom they had placed out there for me. Utterly nude, her white figure crouched at the inky base of a cliff. I heard her terrified moan as I crept toward her. I croaked bestial laughter. She started to run—and I leaped from behind.

But in my weakness I couldn't catch her. She fled faster than my creaking legs could pursue. Her slim rosy outline disappeared in dark fastnesses leaving me panting, mouth drooling spittle.

I chuckled satyr-like exultation. The old men had been right! Even through desiring her I already felt stronger. I experienced the transient hot flushing which old age deludedly fancies the returning of youthful vigor. The next time I'd catch her. Her and also another, to sate myself till I was bursting with youth! But the one who would complete the rejuvenation, who would change me into a Sampson, would be—Elaine!

Licking my lips I prowled through the alleys in a mincing half human gait. I explored the narrow ravines, whispering in eerie companionship with the invisible things that seemed to chirp from the rock crannies. Somewhere here I'd find my prey—find Elaine.

Inhuman desire drove me on to hunt like an animal—while that vague terror, remnant of my decency and my love, grew to a black pall, freezing my soul.

But I didn't find her, or anyone. Only solitude where madness and despair were my comrades. My delusion of strength had faded now, I felt older than ever, more wearied, my face more hollowly graven, my legs trembling. Painfully I dragged myself over the stones, licking my parched lips, my whole being ablaze with one hideous craving.

A score, perhaps a hundred times, I had wandered to the brink of the abyss with the hidden river and found it impassible. But this time to my astonishment I could escape—for a bridge of planks had been laid across the ten-foot wide cleft in the stone.

Reeling in giddiness of sudden excitement, I almost lost my balance to topple into the depths as I staggered across.

On the other side was another wilderness of black shafts lurching into obscurity. And out from that place of stones—that Golgotha—quavered a shrilling cry.

An electric current stabbed through me. It was Elaine's voice sobbing there!

Chapter Six

Fiends at Play

In senile frenzy I tottered toward the spot from which that wailing had sounded. So! Now I would have her—love her—find in her death the end of my torment. I swung around the base of a cliff and then came to a standstill.

A fire built on the stones cast obscene lurid glow over the ring of old men. With its base wedged into a crevice stood a holy outline—a wooden cross. And trailing down from it as she half hung, half knelt with her arms tied to the cross pieces was Elaine.

They had undressed her; before the sadist pack she stood utterly nude. Her hair streaming down over her bosom outlined her little breasts. Her face, uplifted into moonlight, was a pallid agony mask. One of the torturers stood behind her. His whip whistled and fell to bring zigzags like red fingers clutching her shoulders.

For a moment the shock of that sight restored me to normal, swept me in my horror clean of beastly desire. With a curse I snatched a rock from the floor of the cavern and started to run.

The mob heard me and turned. The nearest one yelled and sprang. I hurled the rock at him, shouted relish as the stone pulped his face, and then I was dashing on toward Elaine.

For a moment the rest of them stood uncertain and during those few seconds I managed to get her out of the ropes. I swept her into my arms. "Elaine, darling, thank God!" I cried.

And then while I held her, casting my eyes desperately

around for way of escape, the man with the whip struck her again. Her moan undid my regeneration. The hiss of the whip was exquisite music. The scent of blood on her back and her quivering naked form in my arms sent my hunger surging in a wolf-like rush.

But the old men weren't going to let me take their prey away from them! They howled and came rushing. I let go of Elaine to whirl toward them—and the next instant was the center of a clawing and milling turmoil.

En masse they piled onto me, pummelling me with their blue-veined fists. Bleared red-shot eyes glared into mine. They charged into the melée with rocks and clubs. We fought one another with a fury more primitive than that of wild beasts after food. We were beings blighted with doom of half-life fighting for love and blood that would make us human again!

I was one against eight but my fury was a hundred times theirs. One by one I broke them and crippled them—drove them away. At last only Elaine was near me, a sobbing Niobe on the stones. I snarled triumph and stooped to clutch my fingers in her hair. Ape-like I dragged her up to her feet and snatched her into my clasp. At last!

She started to cry out her thankfulness at my coming—choked to stare at me, wondering. I saw her gaze, fixed on my brutalized face, grow terrified.

"Tom, no!" she gasped. "Let me go. Merciful God, what—" She struggled to free herself.

My rage flamed at sight of her loathing. I crushed her the tighter. Whispering my death-glee I stooped to sink my teeth in the curve of her throat beneath whose silken whiteness her life's blood coursed so sweet, so invitingly.

In another moment I would have killed her—when from somewhere came shouts, thudding of footsteps.

It was the sound of a pistol shot that froze me with lips touching her flesh— but it was the impact of a heavy slug in my shoulder that tore me away from her and spun me around. Before I could recover to get at her again, a trio of figures came rushing me backward. I glared into the faces of Ekstrom, Morrison and a spare grey-eyed man who I was to learn later was a constable from the town of Mountain View.

Ekstrom pushed his face close to stare at me unbelievingly. "Great God, its Tom Burnham!" he gasped. Still foggy in mind, I heard words flowing around me, disjointed explanations. "We had about given you up. When Morrison got over his slashing our posses searched the quarry—miles of caves where no one has been for ages—"

Ekstrom let out a cry and grabbed at my arm again. I had barked and tried to dodge past him to rush at Elaine! She sobbed and ran to stand trembling at the side of Frank Morrison. Ekstrom tried to hold me and I slashed my teeth at his throat. The constable came hurrying to help him. Morrison cried: "He's got it too! Tom Burnham is a raving maniac!"

Suddenly I quieted down, stood there apparently cowed, thinking craftily. Save for the leader, the old men had disappeared during the confusion. "There's the one who's at the bottom of it!" the constable strode across to grab his arm and drag him into the light. "One of the quarry hands was caught down here and lost till he went off his head. He had heard the stories about the earth-spirits and when he went mad he probably imagined that he was one of them. Those others are either more who were lost—or some from the village that he contact and made into a torture cult. They must have had some way of getting up to the top, though, for their food and their victims."

Morrison had put his coat over Elaine. She stood leaning against him, her eyes revolting from me—as though memory of my ghastliness would haunt her for the rest of her life. He put his arm around her, stooped to whisper comfortingly—intimately.

That sight set jealous fury ablaze in me. Elaine was saying to Ekstrom: "I owe you an apology, Mr. Ekstrom. For a while I almost imagined—that girl in your house, seeing you at Frank's just before—"

"At such times almost anyone is likely to be wrongly suspected," the big man replied. "Martha had got herself mixed up in the business, she was out of her senses. I went to Frank's to see how things were. I was afraid those devils would come after you."

"Yes, I can understand that now," Elaine answered. "But how can you or anyone explain about those people growing old so fast—and that thing that killed Margery?" She whispered a sob. "Explain what has happened to Tom—to my husband—"

They went on talking. I wasn't listening. The constable had let go of me. Now was my time when they had forgotten to watch me. Teeth showing through back-drawn lips I started gliding inch by inch from his side around behind Elaine and Morrison. I wanted to kill them both now!

And then there took place something amazing.

"Benny! Benny Morton!"

For the last few moments, the old man, ignored by all, had been gazing intently at Ekstrom. Over the vacancy of his face glimmered a ray of dawning memory. And then his voice came again:

"My nephew, Benny Morton, who kidnapped me and shut me down here! Didn't think I would know you again, did you, after all these years while you kept me shut up so that you could get hold of the quarry? But I could never forget my dear little Benny that used to fly kites with me and steal dimes from me."

Ekstrom whirled to stare at the old fellow. "The man's crazy!" he yelled. "I'm not any relation of his. I never saw him before in my life."

I heard what they said with half my brain only. I was looking across at Elaine. I tried to smile at her lovingly. If only I could coax her away from Morrison and a little nearer to me! "Elaine darling." I smirked. "Come here and kiss me—"

At my elbow I heard the constable talking. "Something damned funny about this, Ekstrom. Everyone around here knows that Amos Morton did drop out of sight five years ago—tied up the business while they hunted the world over for him."

"What of it?" the big man half shouted. His face had gone livid. The veins stood engorged on his temples. "Let's get back to the top. I'm sick of listening to idiot's drivel."

The country policeman had dragged the old fellow still nearer to the light and was peering into his face. "I knowed Amos Morton as good as I knowed my own phiz in a looking glass," he muttered tensely. "This here feller has been around hell but—I'd swear to it in any court." He wheeled dramatically. "This man is Amos Morton!"

To Ekstrom he cried: "You are his wastrel nephew Ben that I've heard of but that no one in these parts ever saw till you came here fours years ago to live under a false name— the old man's sole living relative. You kept him here to drive him insane so as you could let him come back after a while and have him sent to an asylum—get yourself appointed administrator of property wuth hundreds of thousands. You didn't quite have the nerve to kill him outright, this way would make a better story. I arrest ye in the name of the State o'—"

Ekstrom's hand flashed into his pocket. But the constable's gun whipped into sight first. "Make a funny move and I'll drop ye," he snapped.

Ekstrom shrugged and his hands dropped to his sides. He muttered sullenly: "All right. I know when I'm licked. I was a damned fool. I never let the old man see me till just now. I worked on him only in the dark, telling him he was one of the earth spirits. When it came to his sanity hearing the best evidence against him would be that he believed that, and had outraged the village girls. But I got careless. I figured he'd have forgotten me in five years."

"While you're at it, finish the story," the constable grated.

Ekstrom shrugged again. "Why not? The old stories about the youth-age business and the earth spirits made the whole thing a setup. The ones you saw down here were some of the natives I hired to work for me. They were plenty old anyhow. After they had had a couple drinks of drugged liquor they would believe anything—do anything. I enjoyed it myself too. I always watched and I loved to hear the girls screaming."

"God, what kind of a thing be ye?" the constable muttered. "And them girls that was torn into pieces—the thing that changed from a boy into a devil—How in heaven's—"

"Ask him! Ask that damned Satan Frank Morrison!" His face convulsed, Ekstrom stabbed his arm toward my. "He found out what I was doing. He had a game of his own to play here and he blackmailed me into taking him into partnership. After that he was boss—making me do things—"

"Morrison!" the officer scoffed. "You're lyin' to save yourself!" He glanced toward Frank—and what he saw caused him to yell and go rigid. Caused Elaine to shriek wildly, for the face that I knew was suddenly gone. We were all gazing into the fiendishly beautiful features of the demon that had ravaged Margery by the roadside!

For an instant that seemed endless we all stood there stricken and staring—incredulous. Once I'd seen this youth alter into a senile wreck—now I saw a man whom I'd known all my life assuming his form.

The constable cursed and lifted a shaking hand to cover Morrison with his gun. But the changeling jumped to catch hold of Elaine and sweep her in front of him. With his free hand he whipped his own gun out of his pocket.

The law man couldn't shoot then for fear of hitting Elaine! I heard his terrified cry the instant before Morrison's bullet tore through his heart. Ekstrom—or Morton—turned to run. But the second slug downed him.

Through a miasma of horror I heard Morrison addressing me alone—for his voice came suavely mocking from the countenance of the demon-lad.

"I'll just satisfy your curiosity, my dear Burnham, before I send you along with them. In a way it is rather sad, such an ending to our long friendship. If we had not both happened to love the same girl—jealousy is like a cancer, you know. It starts with a little sore and grows into a beast that devours you. God, how I've hated you, watching you kissing her, owning her! And when there is money too—"

It was the shooting that had finally jolted me back to my senses. My brain clearing suddenly I saw it all in ghoulish reality—the circle of cliffs, the dead men on the ground, my old friend a monster.

I stood there helpless and shaking. Terror more awful than that of death sent my thoughts leaping. I had to get Elaine away from him—before I saw her ravaged like Margery! But how? For his pistol was covering me.

"This hasn't worked out quite as I planned," Morrison's voice was continuing. "I never intended for Elaine to know my part in the business. I wanted her to come to me of her own free will. That was one of the reasons for killing the other girls. I had to break down her nerves with the terrors."

"And you figured that after that—when she had come down here and seen what a horror I was—that I had to be sent to an asylum—it wouldn't take much for her loneliness and gratitude at her rescue to take her into your arms!" I cut in.

"Exactly," Morrison nodded.

The callousness of the admission brought a loathing cry from Elaine. She twisted around within his arm that pinned her inescapably to stare horror-stricken into his face. Her in-effectual fists pounded his shoulders. To me she wailed de-spairingly:

"Tom, can't you get me away from him? Can't you do something!"

My hands grew into useless knots at my sides. I muttered desperately: "Yes, I'll get you away, darling. I'll do some-thing—"

Morrison only laughed. He tightened the clasp of his arm. He went on to me: "You must remember that you borrowed a lot of money from me to finance this business here. That was my other reason for killing those girls, to stampede the sum-mer colony. When you die and your estate can't cover your paper because the business is bankrupt, I'll gel the properly. After the terrors are over, people will start coming back again. It will be a damn profitable thing one of these days."

He paused and then went on:

"And again I wanted to be sure that Ekstrom was in deep enough to hang when I finally gave the cops evidence that he'd done the killings. With him out of the way I stood a good chance of even getting hold of the quarry itself."

"Had everything figured out, didn't you?" I whispered, dry-lipped. "And I suppose that face that you put off and on is only a mask—" For now the obvious truth had suddenly dawned on me.

Morrison chuckled and stripped away the fabrication so cleverly made that in dim light it could not be told from living flesh.

"While you were dragging me into the house after our fight in the yard I simply pulled off the cheater and threw it into the bushes without your noticing. The old man underneath was just me, made up. You know I used to go in a lot for amateur theatricals. The wounds on my throat were skin slashes. I did them myself to show the police. It was Ekstrom who brought you down here."

For a moment I simply stared at him, my faculties frozen. All this while Elaine had been fighting him more and more fiercely—while I watched and did nothing! Now he stooped to murmur to her:

"In a minute now I'm going to kill Tom. You won't miss him, for you're going to have me. I'll throw them all into the river where they will never be found. And then you and I, my darling . . . I've got a little house down here for you where I'll always know where to find you. Where I can love you and love you—hear you scream as I flog your beautiful white body . . ."

Elaine screamed then! Her slim figure writhed like a tortured white worm in his grip. In near frenzy she raked her fingernails into his eyes. He laughed . . .

My teeth showed through crooked lips as I started inching surreptitiously toward them. Dear God, I had to get over there! Get there and save her! But what price that with a gun trained on my heart?

The madman was starting now to drag her backward into

the maze of gulleys behind—where no human eyes would ever find her again. On hands and knees I followed, trying to work myself closer. If I could only get near enough to rush before he realized what I was doing . . . But that was hopeless. He saw me; halted his withdrawal and fired. Dust spurted into my eyes. I dodged to one side, he fired again.

In frantic zigzags I went stumbling on while he amused himself with target practice. Gelid sweat stood on me. In imagination I could feel those slugs driving into the pit of my stomach. Whether he killed me or not, they would be gone in a moment into those shades where my darling would live as his sadist prey till she too . . .

And then when in my madness I was about to rush on him to meet forgetfulness half way, I saw creep into sight behind him the one whom we had all forgotten in the excitement— old Amos Morton. Half concealed by a cliff flank he stood waiting, His uplifted hand clutched a rock. Through soundless lips he grimaced his vengeance-glee.

I froze where I was, waiting for him to strike—waiting for the bullet that would send me to eternity. Which would come first? Now Morrison, still backing away from me, was only a yard from the old man—still not suspecting his presence. Morton's arm rose and dropped with all his strength—in a blow yet so feeble that it did no more than partially stun Morrison. He spun around, gun lifting.

In an instant more he would have fired—save that coming up from behind I flung myself onto him, beating him down. Flattening him till he lay beneath me while I pounded. Pounded and pounded till my stone and I too were spattered with blood . . .

Even after I had saved Elaine we should never have made our way out of the quarry had we not, not been found soon after by another searching party.

My wife and I spent long weeks in a hospital and it was while we were there that the few remaining mysteries connected with the outrages were cleaned up.

The burning of our house was undoubtedly done by Morrison in order to get Elaine into Ekstrom's house where under his compulsion the big man carried on the program of terror to break down her nerves. The scars on her body always remained unexplained. Whether Ekstrom had drugged her and made them there with some instrument while she slept or whether while under narcotics she actually took part in the revels—that is something which we both try to forget.

Old Amos had seemed when rescued a hopeless lunatic. But modern experts can accomplish miracles. A year after the day of his rescue he sent for Elaine and me to tell us that he was going to reopen the quarries and wanted me as his assistant, later to become manager.

Now my wife and I live in Morton's Valley, a lovely modernized village, with hosts of our friends. We are blissfully happy, the shadows of those awful days have faded away. Save that when we walk past the quarry at sunset and see the purple shadows rolling into its depths and I feel her shudder against me—I know that she is hearing again the twittering of things that live in the rock crannies and feeling the teeth of a madman caressing her throat.

MERRY CHRISTMAS
FROM THE DEAD!

From the first I had suspected that it was a madman's party to which Rance Fuller had invited Marcia. And as we stood outside the house waiting for the doctor to get through so that we could go in to the injured man, I knew that I had been a fool to let her come.

The only excuse I have for letting her come at all, even under my escort, is that she needed the money so terribly, and that the danger I fancied seemed so bizarre, that I told myself my fears must be imagination.

If I could have guessed how close that imagination was to the hideous truth . . .

It was early dusk of a mid-winter day—the day before Christmas. The strangest day of all the year to visit the repellent old miser who, his life long, had scoffed at everything generous and kindly.

Fuller's house stood on the end of a long spit of sand which jutted out into the bay. Water surrounded it save for a narrow neck connecting it to the mainland.

It had been a winter of unseasonable warmth, and during the forenoon a storm of rain had set in. The downpour came in vicious shafts that drummed on the roof of the small summer house where we stood waiting. Across the yard, the old house sprawled gaunt and forbidding like the skull of some long-dead colossus.

We both wheeled as the door opened and the form of the doctor, case in hand, appeared on the piazza. Seeing us,' he came slopping through puddles toward the little shelter.

"How is Uncle Fuller?" Marcia asked. The old curmudgeon who lay at death's point in there was some distant relative of hers.

The doctor shook his head. His face wore an oddly unprofessional look of uneasiness.

"He won't last through the night. But there is no use of my staying—nothing more I can do for him." He hesitated, then added: "He has terrible brain lesions—they have affected his mind. And no wonder, seeing the kind of an auto wreck they pulled him from."

I didn't say anything. I had known before I came that old Fuller must be insane. That had been the only way to account for his letter. And what other tricks his brain might be scheming—crazy or sane, I was afraid of Rance Fuller.

The doctor pulled up his coat collar and turned toward the storm.

"You people had better hurry up with your business and get out of here," he called over his shoulder. "That bridge won't stand up much longer."

The bridge to which he referred was a decrepit structure across a break in the land spit, which made Fuller's house stand on an island, in fact. When Marcia and I had driven over it a few minutes before we had noticed how the abnormally high tide sucked and swirled against the sagging piles.

I took Marcia's arm and started her toward the house. "Let's hurry," I muttered.

In the dimly lighted hall, with its dingy furniture and motheaten carpets, we found the five others who had received letters identical to Marcia's. We read the same incredulity and distrust in their anxious faces that we felt. Would the old man go through with what he had promised, or was it a cruel hoax—a last sardonic gesture of mockery at the spirit of Christ which he had always flouted and scorned?

There was a moment of silence as we filed into the bedroom and got our first glimpse of the lean, emaciated form under the covers. Fuller's injuries were ghastly. Bandages half covered his face. The exposed portions were puffed in yellow and green bruises.

Only one thing about him was normal—the single black

eye that blazed from the network of white folds. It seemed to kindle in malevolent triumph as it traveled over us.

A raucous laugh cackled from under the bandages.

"So ye come, did ye? For two thousand dollars apiece ye came to see old Fuller on Christmas Eve?"

The voice fell. "Never mind—forget that. I didn't get ye down here to scold ye. I sent for ye to make ye happy."

Make us happy—perhaps. But I doubted it. Fuller was a money-lending Shylock who did business with poor devils who had nowhere else to turn. Marcia had borrowed from him to keep her worthless brother from going to prison. A young fellow just getting started, I hadn't been able to help her myself.

Neither of us had ever voiced the reason that we knew had lain behind Fuller's readiness to do business with her—but we knew she had a body of surpassing physical allure, a provocation to any man. I had heard plenty of rumors to prove that this old creature here was a sadist. Unsatisfied longing of sex-hunger flogged his senile carcass. Gazing at her loveliness had made him lend her the money—made him hope and plan . . .

And then, three days ago, the letter had come from him. In it he said that he had repented of his stern dealings with the debtors. He wished to do one kindly act before he passed on. If she would come to his house on the afternoon before Christmas, he would cancel her note and give her a release.

That was what had made me believe he was mad. In his right mind, Fuller wouldn't have paid a dollar for a cake of ice in the fires of hell—unless he could sell it again for two dollars.

He moved his head to catch the eye of two servants who hovered in the background. Old Mose and his wife, an ancient and ill-favored pair who had served him for decades.

Mose set a table bearing a pile of papers at his master's side. Fuller's lone orb roved over the faces before him while the old couple were making the preparations. His thin brown hands dry-washed one another, as though under the outward fair-seeming of his good deed, he amused himself with the contemplation of some ghoulish secret.

The arrangements completed, he extended claw-like fingers and picked up the two documents that lay on top. They made crackling sounds in the hush.

He called one of the debtors by name. A pale, middle-aged man stepped timidly forward. Fuller handed over the papers. One was his note. The other, we saw as he rejoined us, was a legal release from all obligations.

The old man sat, half laughing and half crying, wiping his eyes, while name after name was announced. Last of all, Marcia went up to the bedside to receive the precious documents that freed her from worry.

I saw how Fuller had leered at her, how his withered paw contrived to slide over her bare arm, to linger there an instant before she snatched her hand away.

She came back to my side. She wasn't looking at her two papers. She clutched them together, crumpled against her bosom. Her eyes were strangely dark in her white face as she looked up to me.

"John! Let's go now—let's get out of here!" she cried thinly.

I, too, was anxious to leave. Fuller, to be sure, had gone through with it. But in the scene just played there I had sensed a weird unreality. The old man had just given away more than ten thousand dollars, a thing that he would never have done save in madness—or in a still more dreadful sanity. Was he indeed out of his mind? Or was he shamming that? The way those lewd fingers had crawled on Marcia's arm . . .

The others were rising, too. We were all pressing around the bed to thank him before taking our departure. But the old man's uplifted hand stayed us.

"Hold on. I got sumthin' else," he chuckled. "It's Christmas Eve. I'm goin' to give ye a party. An' it'll be the fust real Christmas party I ever throwed."

We looked at one another in amazement. What was this?

Why was that scoffing old miser talking about a Christmas party? Was it just another quirk of his madness, or . . .

As if divining our thoughts, Fuller's voice came again, a cracked wheedling.

"Ye ain't goin' off and leave me, be ye—on Christmas Eve? When I'm a-go in' to die. When I've gone and got a party all ready?"

We hesitated. To desert him now, after what he had done for us, seemed heartlessly selfish. It was Marcia who finally settled it. She drew a breath and exclaimed:

"Yes, of course, Uncle Fuller. If you want us, we'll stay."

I listened to that—I felt a shadow of something malign and hideous—and still I allowed her to stay. If God can ever forgive me for that!

I won't take time to go through all the events of that party. Mose and Ella brought in another and larger table and set it up beside the dying man's bed. They laid it with dishes and gleaming silverware, flowers and a profusion of delicacies that would have done justice to an epicure's cuisine.

Candles shining from under pink shades cast softened lights upon the worn faces of the debtor-guests. There were even gifts for each of us—a cigarette case for me, a dainty compact with her initials set in tiny stones for Marcia, appropriate remembrances for the others.

But there was still that feeling of mockery about it all— like a feast set before those who were doomed to die. The only things that seemed genuine were the scream of the rising wind and the sinister light in Fuller's lone eye as it traveled over us—as it lingered on Marcia.

It gloated on her lush allure, on her round bare arms, on the deep V of her bosom revealed at the open neck of her blouse. And into it came again a gleam of desire. Sex-longing of a dying man which seemed to pierce through her clothes and shred them from her bit by bit, till he could see her utterly unclothed.

I saw her eyes drop, her face color painfully. She leaned over and whispered to me:

"It's late, John. We've got to be going—"

We were all rising then, when suddenly the door burst open and Mose, dripping, ran into the room. He panted:

"The bridge is gone! Tide's filled the gut level—runnin' a millrace. No one can git off'n here tonight onless he's got wings."

I felt a sudden click inside of me as my heart skipped a beat. Then this was it! The party had been a ruse to keep us here till the tide had had time to destroy the bridge. But what for? Granted that his soul hungered for Marcia, he must have known how futile was any hope that he, a dying man, could touch her with me here.

"There's plenty of room upstairs," the voice of old Ella broke in. She, too, seemed fired with a strange satisfaction. "Rooms enough for all. Come along and I'll show you."

There was nothing else to be done. We trailed behind her.

Ella distributed the others at various doors up and down the hall on the second floor and last of all assigned Marcia and me to a pair of adjoining rooms. Her angular figure cast skipping gargoyles of shadow against the walls as she strode away.

When she was out of sight, Marcia came to creep into my arms.

"Christmas Eve!" she shivered. "Here!"

We stood a moment wordless and listening. The wind shrieked with hooting of demons. Broadsides of rain battered the house like slaps of a gigantic hand.

"I'm afraid!" Marcia whispered. "I'm so terribly afraid!"

"It's not exactly what one would call a merry Christmas, but there isn't anything to be afraid of—how can there be?" I comforted her. "He just gave you two thousand dollars. He wouldn't have done that if he intended to hurt you, would he?"

I kissed her again and shortly afterward we separated to go to our rooms.

I lay down on the bed, but I didn't undress. I was oppressed by a foreboding that inhibited rest.

And then I summoned my reason and tried to tell myself

that I was a fool. Granted that the old man's party had been a trick to keep us here, it could have been prompted by nothing more sinister than a longing to have some one near him in the loneliness and storm of his night of death. The fact that he had given back the money seemed to preclude, as I had told Marcia, any thought that he could mean us harm.

These fears of mine were nothing but phantoms born of my over tense nerves.

I may have dozed off for a short while, and then suddenly I was awake again, sitting up in bed with a cold finger stabbing my spine.

Against the diapason of the gale, another sound had become audible. A wailing scream; a sound human—or animal? I couldn't tell. To my jittering fancies it sounded more like the screech of a damned soul driven upward on the yeasty blasts that suck from hell.

I swung my feet off the bed, got up and pawed my way through pitch blackness to the door. I got it open and felt my way out into the hall.

Not far away a window made a grey oblong against the gloom. I reached out and grasped the sill, trying to pierce the blackness of the storm that streamed against the window pane. For a brief instant I fancied that I saw down below a figure with an old-fashioned nightgown whipping around its knees, bent low as it struggled against the hurricane.

It was gone, and I was aware of steps at my side. I turned to feel Marcia there. Her hands groped for my arm. She clung to me, trembling. She whispered:

"What is it, John? That dreadful sound—who could have made it?"

I reached out to the wall switch and the light that sprang on revealed the others there. Like myself, not one of them had undressed. There was nothing in reason of which we should be afraid—only a dying old man. Yet we stood white-faced and spellbound.

"I'm going downstairs," I said after a moment. The rest of them trailed after me.

In the bedroom below we found a trio of figures standing huddled, whispering. Old Mose and Ella, and another man, not quite a stranger to me, for I had seen Steve Morgan, Fuller's only neighbor, once or twice before. He was a shiftless ne'er do well, a fisherman, generally believed feebleminded. He lived in a shack some few hundred yards away on the point.

I saw their eyes fixed on the bed. I looked—and I felt a swift prickling along my spine. For that bed was empty! Old Fuller was gone . . .

"Tide flooded me out o' my house," Morgan mumbled. "I come up here just as them two," —he gestured at Mose and Ella, "—was tryin' to hold him in bed. They couldn't do it. He'd went clean out of his head; he was crazy-strong. He got away from 'em and run out of the house."

I felt Marcia's hand grip mine, it was a hand of ice. Then that was the sound we had heard in the storm—Fuller's ravings.

"No use of you folks settin' up," Ella said after a moment. "We'll try to find him an' bring him in—ef we can."

We went. None of us wanted to stay in that room with the blood-stained empty bed—and Fuller likely to come raging back, any moment.

Huddled together, we climbed the stairs. For a short while, maybe three or four minutes; we all stood there, listening. We didn't want to separate. Fear gibbered in the storm's voices. Were they whoops of the wind—or old Fuller's shrieking? Was he still outside, or had he come back into the house? What was he roaming around for, what did he want? In his madness, what did he *think* that he wanted—

And then, all at once, some one let out a cry. The lights had gone out. A rushing torrent, darkness leaped to inundate the building from bottom to top. And at that same instant it seemed to me that I had heard the muffled thud of a closing door, somewhere below.

I moved over to feel for Marcia's hand. She had been only a short distance away. But I couldn't locate her now. I called:

"Marcia, where are you?"

There wasn't any answer. But the next instant I was aware of a new presence there in the darkness—a something that didn't belong to our party, that moved on feet which dragged with a cold scouring.

I fumbled in my pocket and dug out a match box. I struck a light and held it aloft. "Marcia—for God's sake where are you?" I yelled.

I saw a circle of white faces. But only five of them. For Marcia was gone.

"Where is she'? What happened to her?" I cried. "Did any of you see her go?"

They shook their heads. Their voices came as from mouths stuffed with cotton.

"We didn't see her. But some one was here—something was here—"

I whirled from them and went racing back into my room. I searched through the dark till I located a candle that I remembered having seen on a table. My fingers were wooden sticks that fumbled eternities till I at last got the flame going.

I spun around to the figures framing my doorway. I shouted:

"We've got to find her! We've got to find Marcia! Get busy and hunt for her! All over the house!"

Whether they heeded me or not, I didn't know, for the next moment I was beating my way through the blackness alone. The old house was a warren of echoing passages and vacant rooms. Door after door I yanked open and peered inside, to see only my own shadow clowning against the wall and to hear the storm hoot with its mocking voices.

I had covered all of that floor and had climbed to the next one above, I remember. I swung around a corner and froze in my tracks. For something was there on the floor—a shape that halted the swing of my foot with sudden resistance.

I stooped to hold down the candle and an iron hand wrenched at the pit of my stomach. The thing was Henry Ames, one of the debtors. I knew him by the gold-framed eye-glasses that dangled from a silk cord.

For the face that looked up at me wasn't Ames, it wasn't—
human. It was a crimson ruin where things long, sharp and
pointed had worried it into a gory pulp.

Something white protruded from between his clenched fingers. I parted them. It was the corner of a legal-looking
document—the release which Fuller had given him two
hours before. I forced myself to search through his clothing,
and his other paper, the note, was gone, too.

For an instant I stood there while I tried to figure out the
meaning of that. His debt had been released by Fuller two
hours ago and now the evidence of that release was taken
away—to compel him to pay the debt after all? But Ames
could never pay a debt now . . .

I muttered a curse and spun around as footsteps sounded
beside me. It was Steve Morgan. His moronic countenance
was the hue of paste. He looked at the thing on the floor and
was stung by a lash of horror.

I gripped his arm. "Have you seen Marcia—seen anything
of a girl?" I cried.

He shook his head. "I ain't seen her. But I heard a gal
screamin'—"

His voice broke in a note of stark terror. A blast of wind
swept my candle flame into oblivion. And with the down
sweeping of darkness came a cry—Marcia's voice in a thin
shrieking. It sounded from somewhere over my head.

I raced for a door which I found led up into the attic. What
happened to Morgan I didn't know. The last I saw of him he
was staring down at the dead man with spittle running out of
his mouth corners.

Up here under the roof, the gale flogged with screaming
whips. But over its tumult I could hear something moving—
feet whispering against the floor. A sound of struggling.
Panting and terror-fraught wails . . .

I didn't stop to try to make a light as I fought my way toward those noises. I stumbled over invisible hulks of furniture, tripped and went sprawling. Crazily I grabbed them and
flung them one side.

A dozen seconds—or eternities—got me over to the far corner. I halted. Pawing the dark, I choked out: "Marcia! Marcia, darling, where are you?"

She didn't answer. There was no sound—save the salvos of rain on the shingles.

To make short the agony of the next couple of minutes, I got my candle going at last and I searched that attic from end to end. She wasn't there. No one was there.

But in a corner I found a pile of feminine clothing—every article of Marcia's garments down to her underwear, shredded in ribbons and strewn on the floor. Garments some of which were sodden with still warm blood . . .

Just what happened in the next three or four minutes I wouldn't know. I have a dim recollection of clattering down the stairs from the attic, of storming through the house in a frenzy.

I didn't find Marcia, but I found two more of Fuller's guests. They lay in some of the empty rooms. They were dead—never mind how they were dead. I went through their clothes and in both cases I found no papers on them.

A conviction was growing on me then, a picture of horrors in answer to horrors. The injury to his head had driven Fuller insane—so mad that he had summoned his debtors to forgive them their debts. And then he had suddenly come to realize what he had done. He, miser Fuller, who worshipped Midas more than anything in heaven or hell, had given away ten thousand dollars!

How that thought must have tortured him as he lay listening to the storm and waiting to die! Till, in excess of madness—or in an interval of still more ghoulish sanity—he had got out of bed and started to undo what he had done! To vent his rage in those wounds while he took back what was his own! And in that paroxysm of dying energy to get hold of Marcia, for whom his body throbbed with untimely longing!

Somewhere in the hallways, I met the three of them—Mose, Ella, and the halfwit Steve Morgan. Their faces were bleeding from gashes where flesh hung in tatters.

"He tried to kill us! He tried to kill us all—and he is dead himself. *Old Fuller is dead—"* They gibbered.

I snarled as I shouldered past them. Fuller was dead and doing these things? We were all mad in this house tonight.

There was only one place which I hadn't searched yet—the cellar. I located the door opening out of the kitchen. At the foot of the steep flight of steps my candle revealed rows of barrels and packing cases, with vistas of crooked passages between.

For a short distance I felt my way along one of those alleys. And then suddenly, I extinguished my light with a cupped hand.

A dozen feet in front, a figure rose suddenly from stooping over something that lay between a couple of casks. It was old Fuller. Fuller with his bandages, his broken head—

I took a step forward and halted again, while my blood seemed to turn into individual droplets of ice. For that apparition wasn't a living man, it was a corpse! There was no mistaking the ashen hue of the exposed part of the face, the sightless glare of the single eye. A hand rose into sight. It had the macabre whiteness of a thing grown in a tomb.

I sagged against the flank of a packing case. I had deemed Fuller a maniac when he did what he had done. But now I myself was so crazed from supping with horrors that I imagined I saw a dead man standing there.

He had stooped toward something that lay hidden in shadows against the floor. He straightened and now in his grasp were papers that husked with thin cracklings. He chuckled and tucked them under his shirt.

Cold sweat clammed the palms of my hands. Once I had heard how Fuller had boasted that he would rise from the grave to collect a debt owing him . . .

The dead person from whom he had made this collection was, as I have said, out of my sight. And now a hideous question came to pluck at my brain. Was it—Marcia?

I started to steal toward him and then halted my motion. For at the same instant he had wheeled and moved away.

I followed soundlessly under cover of the big casks. I

passed the shape over which he had been stooping. It wasn't Marcia. It was another one of the debtor-guests.

Some distance ahead now, his candle turned and then passed out of sight. A moment more brought me to the place where it had veered to one side.

Another pair of steps I pressed forward. And then I halted, transfixed, while every thing inside of me seemed to drop into a bottomless void.

I was looking through the open door of a small storeroom. Another candle stuck into a niche spread a faint light over the dust-covered stone wall, over Fuller—over another shape that stood like a white Niobe in the gloom.

It was Marcia. Marcia—God!

He had stripped her stark nude. He had tethered her by the wrists to a hook in the wall. In that short time he had flogged her and burned her, too, with hot irons. The sweetish odor of scorched flesh hung in the air. I saw her shoulders and breasts, scored with livid weals . . .

I thought that he was going to resume the torture, for as he stood close to her, his hand strayed toward a whip in a corner.

But another temptation overcame him. He made an animal sound, he leaped toward her. He clutched her nude body and crushed it against him. He bent her back in his arms as he stepped to press his blue lips against her shrieking mouth.

His voice came, a sepulchral mumbling:

"The others are all dead. You will die, after you have been my bride in agony—bride of the dead!"

She struggled and kicked in his grip. She beat her ineffectual fists against his face. He laughed and clutched her tighter. From under his clothes he produced a three-pronged garden tool whose sharp points bore a dark stain. He drew the talons across her throat.

"You thought that you could get away with old Fuller's money?" he crooned. "The dead don't need money. I'm going to kill you with this. But first—"

He strained her closer to him. He bent above her while she

screamed thinly.

The sound of that agonized wailing broke the spell of horror that had held me transfixed, and the next instant I was lunging across there. I swung the heavy brass candlestick over my head. A candlestick as a weapon against the dead . . .

The figure dropped Marcia and whirled. It met my attack with a savage power that I couldn't match. Death had the strength of hell!

It snatched the candlestick out of my hand. We closed and for an instant we swayed, locked in a struggle of cracking bones and straining muscles.

I broke from it and let go my fist. I felt my knuckles slodge home on skin clammy as refrigerated meat. I smashed it again and then its hands clutched me around the throat.

I fought it but weakly, for my flesh crawled from its touch and horror drained my strength. The fingers found my windpipe and dug into it.

It was bending me backward until I felt my knuckles slodge home on skin bent over me and then I got its breath, effluvium of death and destruction.

I tripped and fell. The thing was on top of me. It had picked up the candlestick and was beating me. Blow after blow of the heavy base was cracking my skull.

I was almost gone. Bells of agony jangled inside my brain. I croaked in thin bubblings as my life ebbed away.

And then my hand, clawing in agony over the ground, touched something hard. It closed on the handle of the three pronged garden tool.

Like a tortured cat I twisted around in the thing's grip. And as I moved, I caught a glimpse of something that I hadn't seen before—Fuller's body, lying stark and motionless in a corner.

Fuller lying there dead . . . Fuller's corpse kneeling on my chest, pounding at me with his clubbed fists . . .

I screamed as I lashed up at him with the garden tool. Lashed and lashed again in a daze—till I came back to my senses at last, to find myself kneeling on the dirt floor and yelling like an ape while I hacked at the piece of pulped meat that lay before me.

I pitched the gory implement into a corner. I swabbed the sweat from my eyes and stooped to peer at the face on the floor. The face of the half-wit Steve Morgan, denuded now of the headpiece of false bandages which my fury had ripped from him . . .

I got Marcia out of her fastenings, led her upstairs and found her some clothes. Then I rounded up Mose and old Ella and worked on them for two hours till they finally cracked.

The whole business had been a scheme of Morgan's. His seeming stupidity had been to cover a cunning brain.

Fuller, it seemed, had been in need of more capital and had borrowed from Morgan—who had a sizable store of hoarded money. As security, Morgan had taken assignments on all the loans that Fuller had made with the funds obtained from him. And another thing that Marcia hadn't ever told me— whenever Fuller lent money, he always insisted on the debtor insuring his or her life in his favor, and for more than the amount of the loan. In Marcia's case it had been for three thousand dollars. Morgan figured that if he could bring about the deaths of these people he stood to cash in on their policies for more than if he just got his money back—for a total of fifteen thousand dollars.

He had first won over Mose and Ella by the payment of five hundred dollars each. Fuller hadn't been in any accident, as reported—Morgan had waylaid him and beaten him, not quite killing him.

Morgan, of course, had forged the letters to Marcia and the others. After the doctor had examined the almost senseless old loan-shark and gone, the three of them had hustled him out of his bed and out of sight. Morgan, his face heavily bandaged and painted to simulate bruises, had taken his place in the bed. There had been virtually no danger of detection, for the lights were low, the two men had some natural resemblance, and the bandages showed very little of his face.

Morgan had once been an actor. For more than an hour he had played the part of Fuller, giving out the releases and conducting the party. Later—after Mose had yelled outside the house to make it seem that Fuller had gone violently haywire—he had shut off the lights and then gone about his business of killing the guests and getting the papers back.

I had twice seen him in his own person while the slaughter was going on. His headpiece of bandages went on and off in a moment, and Mose had always been lurking in the background of darkness to hold it while he was talking to me. The injuries to the three of them, of course, had been self-inflicted.

Morgan had stolen Marcia, tied her and gagged her and hidden her in the attic. When I had heard her faint screaming and gone up there, he had slipped past me in stocking feet and taken her almost from under my face without being aware of his presence in the noise of the storm.

Taken her to the cellar—for he too was a sadist. He couldn't bear to kill her as he had the others—not till he had glutted his lust on her. The same quirk of perversion had led him to play the part of Fuller's corpse, painting his flesh with a chemical that made it deathly white—and deathly cold to the touch.

If he hadn't stooped to do that, if he had killed her promptly and disposed of his mask, there would have been nothing to prevent him from blaming the whole business on the now-dead Fuller, and collecting the fifteen thousand dollars.

Marcia and I got back to her mother's about noon the next day—after rowing across the tide gut in Morgan's boat and notifying the authorities.

It was afternoon of the same day when we decided not to wait till I had saved my five hundred dollars, but to be married at once.

"I can't be away from you another night—not another night ever," she whispered as she shivered close to me.

And I knew why—for fear that she might, in her dreams,

see the face of death bending over her again, feel his cold touch, without having my arms at her side, into which she could crawl.

RAMBLE HOUSE's

HARRY STEPHEN KEELER WEBWORK MYSTERIES

(RH) indicates the title is available ONLY in the RAMBLE HOUSE edition

The Ace of Spades Murder
The Affair of the Bottled Deuce (RH)
The Amazing Web
The Barking Clock
Behind That Mask
The Book with the Orange Leaves
The Bottle with the Green Wax Seal
The Box from Japan
The Case of the Canny Killer
The Case of the Crazy Corpse (RH)
The Case of the Flying Hands (RH)
The Case of the Ivory Arrow
The Case of the Jeweled Ragpicker
The Case of the Lavender Gripsack
The Case of the Mysterious Moll
The Case of the 16 Beans
The Case of the Transparent Nude (RH)
The Case of the Transposed Legs
The Case of the Two-Headed Idiot (RH)
The Case of the Two Strange Ladies
The Circus Stealers (RH)
Cleopatra's Tears
A Copy of Beowulf (RH)
The Crimson Cube (RH)
The Face of the Man From Saturn
Find the Clock
The Five Silver Buddhas
The 4th King
The Gallows Waits, My Lord! (RH)
The Green Jade Hand
Finger! Finger!
Hangman's Nights (RH)
I, Chameleon (RH)
I Killed Lincoln at 10:13! (RH)
The Iron Ring
The Man Who Changed His Skin (RH)
The Man with the Crimson Box
The Man with the Magic Eardrums
The Man with the Wooden Spectacles
The Marceau Case
The Matilda Hunter Murder

The Monocled Monster
The Murder of London Lew
The Murdered Mathematician
The Mysterious Card (RH)
The Mysterious Ivory Ball of Wong Shing Li (RH)
The Mystery of the Fiddling Cracksman
The Peacock Fan
The Photo of Lady X (RH)
The Portrait of Jirjohn Cobb
Report on Vanessa Hewstone (RH)
Riddle of the Travelling Skull
Riddle of the Wooden Parrakeet (RH)
The Scarlet Mummy (RH)
The Search for X-Y-Z
The Sharkskin Book
Sing Sing Nights
The Six From Nowhere (RH)
The Skull of the Waltzing Clown
The Spectacles of Mr. Cagliostro
Stand By—London Calling!
The Steeltown Strangler
The Stolen Gravestone (RH)
Strange Journey (RH)
The Strange Will
The Straw Hat Murders (RH)
The Street of 1000 Eyes (RH)
Thieves' Nights
Three Novellos (RH)
The Tiger Snake
The Trap (RH)
Vagabond Nights (Defrauded Yeggman)
Vagabond Nights 2 (10 Hours)
The Vanishing Gold Truck
The Voice of the Seven Sparrows
The Washington Square Enigma
When Thief Meets Thief
The White Circle (RH)
The Wonderful Scheme of Mr. Christopher Thorne
X. Jones—of Scotland Yard
Y. Cheung, Business Detective

Keeler Related Works

A To Izzard: A Harry Stephen Keeler Companion by Fender Tucker — Articles and stories about Harry, by Harry, and in his style. Included is a compleat bibliography.

Wild About Harry: Reviews of Keeler Novels — Edited by Richard Polt & Fender Tucker — 22 reviews of works by Harry Stephen Keeler from *Keeler News*. A perfect introduction to the author.

The Keeler Keyhole Collection: Annotated newsletter rants from Harry Stephen Keeler, edited by Francis M. Nevins. Over 400 pages of incredibly personal Keeleriana.

Fakealoo — Pastiches of the style of Harry Stephen Keeler by selected demented members of the HSK Society. Updated every year with the new winner.

Strands of the Web: Short Stories of Harry Stephen Keeler — 29 stories, just about all that Keeler wrote, are edited and introduced by Fred Cleaver.

RAMBLE HOUSE's LOON SANCTUARY

A Clear Path to Cross — Sharon Knowles short mystery stories by Ed Lynskey.
A Jimmy Starr Omnibus — Three 40s novels by Jimmy Starr.
A Niche in Time and Other Stories — Classic SF by William F. Temple
A Roland Daniel Double: The Signal and The Return of Wu Fang — Classic thrillers from the 30s.

A Shot Rang Out — Three decades of reviews and articles by today's Anthony Boucher, Jon Breen. An essential book for any mystery lover's library.

A Smell of Smoke — A 1951 English countryside thriller by Miles Burton.

A Snark Selection — Lewis Carroll's *The Hunting of the Snark* with two Snarkian chapters by Harry Stephen Keeler — Illustrated by Gavin L. O'Keefe.

A Young Man's Heart — A forgotten early classic by Cornell Woolrich.

Alexander Laing Novels — *The Motives of Nicholas Holtz* and *Dr. Scarlett*, stories of medical mayhem and intrigue from the 30s.

An Angel in the Street — Modern hardboiled noir by Peter Genovese.

Automaton — Brilliant treatise on robotics: 1928-style! By H. Stafford Hatfield.

Away From the Here and Now — Clare Winger Harris stories, collected by Richard A. Lupoff

Beast or Man? — A 1930 novel of racism and horror by Sean M'Guire. Introduced by John Pelan.

Black Hogan Strikes Again — Australia's Peter Renwick pens a tale of the 30s outback.

Black River Falls — Suspense from the master, Ed Gorman.

Blondy's Boy Friend — A snappy 1930 story by Philip Wylie, writing as Leatrice Homesley.

Blood in a Snap — The *Finnegan's Wake* of the 21st century, by Jim Weiler.

Blood Moon — The first of the Robert Payne series by Ed Gorman.

Bogart '48 — Hollywood action with Bogie by John Stanley and Kenn Davis

Calling Lou Largo! — Two Lou Largo novels by William Ard.

Cornucopia of Crime — Francis M. Nevins assembled this huge collection of his writings about crime literature and the people who write it. Essential for any serious mystery library.

Corpse Without Flesh — Strange novel of forensics by George Bruce

Crimson Clown Novels — By Johnston McCulley, author of the Zorro novels, *The Crimson Clown* and *The Crimson Clown Again*.

Dago Red — 22 tales of dark suspense by Bill Pronzini.

Dark Sanctuary — Weird Menace story by H. B. Gregory

David Hume Novels — *Corpses Never Argue, Cemetery First Stop, Make Way for the Mourners, Eternity Here I Come*. 1930s British hardboiled fiction with an attitude.

Dead Man Talks Too Much — Hollywood boozer by Weed Dickenson.

Death Leaves No Card — One of the most unusual murdered-in-the-tub mysteries you'll ever read. By Miles Burton.

Death March of the Dancing Dolls and Other Stories — Volume Three in the Day Keene in the Detective Pulps series. Introduced by Bill Crider.

Deep Space and other Stories — A collection of SF gems by Richard A. Lupoff.

Detective Duff Unravels It — Episodic mysteries by Harvey O'Higgins.

Diabolic Candelabra — Classic 30s mystery by E.R. Punshon

Dime Novels: Ramble House's 10-Cent Books — *Knife in the Dark* by Robert Leslie Bellem, *Hot Lead* and *Song of Death* by Ed Earl Repp, *A Hashish House in New York* by H.H. Kane, and five more.

Don Diablo: Book of a Lost Film — Two-volume treatment of a western by Paul Landres, with diagrams. Intro by Francis M. Nevins.

Dope and Swastikas — Two strange novels from 1922 by Edmund Snell

Dope Tales #1 — Two dope-riddled classics; *Dope Runners* by Gerald Grantham and *Death Takes the Joystick* by Phillip Condé.

Dope Tales #2 — Two more narco-classics; *The Invisible Hand* by Rex Dark and *The Smokers of Hashish* by Norman Berrow.

Dope Tales #3 — Two enchanting novels of opium by the master, Sax Rohmer. *Dope* and *The Yellow Claw*.

Double Hot — Two 60s softcore sex novels by Morris Hershman.

Dr. Odin — Douglas Newton's 1933 racial potboiler comes back to life.

Evangelical Cockroach — Jack Woodford writes about writing.

Evidence in Blue — 1938 mystery by E. Charles Vivian.

Fatal Accident — Murder by automobile, a 1936 mystery by Cecil M. Wills.

Fighting Mad — Todd Robbins' 1922 novel about boxing and life

Finger-prints Never Lie — A 1939 classic detective novel by John G. Brandon.

Freaks and Fantasies — Eerie tales by Tod Robbins, collaborator of Tod Browning on the film FREAKS.

Gadsby — A lipogram (a novel without the letter E). Ernest Vincent Wright's last work, published in 1939 right before his death.

Gelett Burgess Novels — *The Master of Mysteries, The White Cat, Two O'Clock Courage, Ladies in Boxes, Find the Woman, The Heart Line, The Picaroons* and *Lady Mechante*. Recently added is A Gelett Burgess Sampler, edited by Alfred Jan. All are introduced by Richard A. Lupoff.

Geronimo — S. M. Barrett's 1905 autobiography of a noble American.

Hake Talbot Novels — *Rim of the Pit, The Hangman's Handyman*. Classic locked room mysteries, with mapback covers by Gavin O'Keefe.

Hands Out of Hell and Other Stories — John H. Knox's eerie hallucinations

Hell is a City — William Ard's masterpiece.

Hollywood Dreams — A novel of Tinsel Town and the Depression by Richard O'Brien.

Hostesses in Hell and Other Stories — Russell Gray's most graphic stories

House of the Restless Dead — Strange and ominous tales by Hugh B. Cave

I Stole $16,000,000 — A true story by cracksman Herbert E. Wilson.

Inclination to Murder — 1966 thriller by New Zealand's Harriet Hunter.

Invaders from the Dark — Classic werewolf tale from Greye La Spina.

J. Poindexter, Colored — Classic satirical black novel by Irvin S. Cobb.

Jack Mann Novels — Strange murder in the English countryside. *Gees' First Case, Nightmare Farm, Grey Shapes, The Ninth Life, The Glass Too Many, Her Ways Are Death, The Kleinert Case* and *Maker of Shadows*.

Jake Hardy — A lusty western tale from Wesley Tallant.

Jim Harmon Double Novels — *Vixen Hollow/Celluloid Scandal, The Man Who Made Maniacs/Silent Siren, Ape Rape/Wanton Witch, Sex Burns Like Fire/Twist Session, Sudden Lust/Passion Strip, Sin Unlimited/Harlot Master, Twilight Girls/Sex Institution*. Written in the early 60s and never reprinted until now.

Joel Townsley Rogers Novels and Short Stories — By the author of *The Red Right Hand: Once In a Red Moon, Lady With the Dice, The Stopped Clock, Never Leave My Bed*. Also two short story collections: *Night of Horror* and *Killing Time*.

John Carstairs, Space Detective — Arboreal Sci-fi by Frank Belknap Long

Joseph Shallit Novels — *The Case of the Billion Dollar Body, Lady Don't Die on My Doorstep, Kiss the Killer, Yell Bloody Murder, Take Your Last Look*. One of America's best 50's authors and a favorite of author Bill Pronzini.

Keller Memento — 45 short stories of the amazing and weird by Dr. David Keller.

Killer's Caress — Cary Moran's 1936 hardboiled thriller.

Lady of the Yellow Death and Other Stories — More stories by Wyatt Blassingame.

League of the Grateful Dead and Other Stories — Volume One in the Day Keene in the Detective Pulps series.

Library of Death — Ghastly tale by Ronald S. L. Harding, introduced by John Pelan

Malcolm Jameson Novels and Short Stories — *Astonishing! Astounding!, Tarnished Bomb, The Alien Envoy and Other Stories* and *The Chariots of San Fernando and Other Stories*. All introduced and edited by John Pelan or Richard A. Lupoff.

Man Out of Hell and Other Stories — Volume II of the John H. Knox weird pulps collection.

Marblehead: A Novel of H.P. Lovecraft — A long-lost masterpiece from Richard A. Lupoff. This is the "director's cut", the long version that has never been published before.

Master of Souls — Mark Hansom's 1937 shocker is introduced by weirdologist John Pelan.

Max Afford Novels — *Owl of Darkness, Death's Mannikins, Blood on His Hands, The Dead Are Blind, The Sheep and the Wolves, Sinners in Paradise* and *Two Locked Room Mysteries and a Ripping Yarn* by one of Australia's finest mystery novelists

Money Brawl — Two books about the writing business by Jack Woodford and H. Bedford-Jones. Introduced by Richard A. Lupoff.

More Secret Adventures of Sherlock Holmes — Gary Lovisi's second collection of tales about the unknown sides of the great detective.

Muddled Mind: Complete Works of Ed Wood, Jr. — David Hayes and Hayden Davis deconstruct the life and works of the mad, but canny, genius.

Murder among the Nudists — A mystery from 1934 by Peter Hunt, featuring a naked Detective-Inspector going undercover in a nudist colony.

Murder in Black and White — 1931 classic tennis whodunit by Evelyn Elder.

Murder in Shawnee — Two novels of the Alleghenies by John Douglas: *Shawnee Alley Fire* and *Haunts*.

Murder in Silk — A 1937 Yellow Peril novel of the silk trade by Ralph Trevor.

My Deadly Angel — 1955 Cold War drama by John Chelton.

My First Time: The One Experience You Never Forget — Michael Birchwood — 64 true first-person narratives of how they lost it.

Mysterious Martin, the Master of Murder — Two versions of a strange 1912 novel by Tod Robbins about a man who writes books that can kill.

Norman Berrow Novels — *The Bishop's Sword, Ghost House, Don't Go Out After Dark, Claws of the Cougar, The Smokers of Hashish, The Secret Dancer, Don't Jump Mr. Boland!, The Footprints of Satan, Fingers for Ransom, The Three Tiers of Fantasy, The Spaniard's Thumb, The Eleventh Plague, Words Have Wings, One Thrilling Night, The Lady's in Danger, It Howls at Night, The Terror in the Fog, Oil Under the Window, Murder in the Melody, The Singing Room.* This is the complete Norman Berrow library of locked-room mysteries, several of which are masterpieces.

Old Faithful and Other Stories — SF classic tales by Raymond Z. Gallun

Old Times' Sake — Short stories by James Reasoner from Mike Shayne Magazine.

One Dreadful Night — A classic mystery by Ronald S. L. Harding

Pair O' Jacks — A mystery novel and a diatribe about publishing by Jack Woodford

Perfect .38 — Two early Timothy Dane novels by William Ard. More to come.

Prince Pax — Devilish intrigue by George Sylvester Viereck and Philip Eldridge

Prose Bowl — Futuristic satire of a world where hack writing has replaced football as our national obsession, by Bill Pronzini and Barry N. Malzberg.

Red Light — The history of legal prostitution in Shreveport Louisiana by Eric Brock. Includes wonderful photos of the houses and the ladies.

Researching American-Made Toy Soldiers — A 276-page collection of a lifetime of articles by toy soldier expert Richard O'Brien.

Reunion in Hell — Volume One of the John H. Knox series of weird stories from the pulps. Introduced by horror expert John Pelan.

Ripped from the Headlines! — The Jack the Ripper story as told in the newspaper articles in the *New York* and *London Times*.

Robert Randisi Novels — *No Exit to Brooklyn* and *The Dead of Brooklyn*. The first two Nick Delvecchio novels.

Rough Cut & New, Improved Murder — Ed Gorman's first two novels.

R.R. Ryan Novels — Freak Museum and The Subjugated Beast, two horror classics.

Ruled By Radio — 1925 futuristic novel by Robert L. Hadfield & Frank E. Farncombe.

Rupert Penny Novels — *Policeman's Holiday, Policeman's Evidence, Lucky Policeman, Policeman in Armour, Sealed Room Murder, Sweet Poison, The Talkative Policeman, She had to Have Gas* and *Cut and Run* (by Martin Tanner.) Rupert Penny is the pseudonym of Australian Charles Thornett, a master of the locked room, impossible crime plot.

Sacred Locomotive Flies — Richard A. Lupoff's psychedelic SF story.

Sam — Early gay novel by Lonnie Coleman.

Sand's Game — Spectacular hard-boiled noir from Ennis Willie, edited by Lynn Myers and Stephen Mertz, with contributions from Max Allan Collins, Bill Crider, Wayne Dundee, Bill Pronzini, Gary Lovisi and James Reasoner.

Sand's War — More violent fiction from the typewriter of Ennis Willie

Satan's Den Exposed — True crime in Truth or Consequences New Mexico — Award-winning journalism in the *Desert Journal*.

Satans of Saturn — Novellas from the pulps by Otis Adelbert Kline and E. H. Price

Satan's Sin House and Other Stories — Horrific gore by Wayne Rogers

Secrets of a Teenage Superhero — Graphic lit by Jonathan Sweet

Sex Slave — Potboiler of lust in the days of Cleopatra by Dion Leclerq, 1966.

Shadows' Edge — Two early novels by Wade Wright: *Shadows Don't Bleed* and *The Sharp Edge.*

Sideslip — 1968 SF masterpiece by Ted White and Dave Van Arnam.

Slammer Days — Two full-length prison memoirs: *Men into Beasts* (1952) by George Sylvester Viereck and *Home Away From Home* (1962) by Jack Woodford.

Slippery Staircase — 1930s whodunit from E.C.R. Lorac

Sorcerer's Chessmen — John Pelan introduces this 1939 classic by Mark Hansom.

Star Griffin — Michael Kurland's 1987 masterpiece of SF drollery is back.

Stakeout on Millennium Drive — Award-winning Indianapolis Noir by Ian Woollen.

Strands of the Web: Short Stories of Harry Stephen Keeler — Edited and Introduced by Fred Cleaver.

Summer Camp for Corpses and Other Stories — Weird Menace tales from Arthur Leo Zagat; introduced by John Pelan.

Suzy — A collection of comic strips by Richard O'Brien and Bob Vojtko from 1970.

Tales of the Macabre and Ordinary — Modern twisted horror by Chris Mikul, author of the *Bizarrism* series.

Tenebrae — Ernest G. Henham's 1898 horror tale brought back.

The Amorous Intrigues & Adventures of Aaron Burr — by Anonymous. Hot historical action about the man who almost became Emperor of Mexico.

The Anthony Boucher Chronicles — edited by Francis M. Nevins. Book reviews by Anthony Boucher written for the *San Francisco Chronicle, 1942 – 1947.* Essential and fascinating reading by the best book reviewer there ever was.

The Barclay Catalogs — Two essential books about toy soldier collecting by Richard O'Brien

The Basil Wells Omnibus — A collection of Wells' stories by Richard A. Lupoff

The Beautiful Dead and Other Stories — Dreadful tales from Donald Dale

The Best of 10-Story Book — edited by Chris Mikul, over 35 stories from the literary magazine Harry Stephen Keeler edited.

The Black Dark Murders — Vintage 50s college murder yarn by Milt Ozaki, writing as Robert O. Saber.

The Book of Time — The classic novel by H.G. Wells is joined by sequels by Wells himself and three stories by Richard A. Lupoff. Illustrated by Gavin L. O'Keefe.

The Case in the Clinic — One of E.C.R. Lorac's finest.

The Case of the Bearded Bride — #4 in the Day Keene in the Detective Pulps series

The Case of the Little Green Men — Mack Reynolds wrote this love song to sci-fi fans back in 1951 and it's now back in print.

The Case of the Withered Hand — 1936 potboiler by John G. Brandon.

The Charlie Chaplin Murder Mystery — A 2004 tribute by noted film scholar, Wes D. Gehring.

The Chinese Jar Mystery — Murder in the manor by John Stephen Strange, 1934.

The Compleat Calhoon — All of Fender Tucker's works: Includes *Totah Six-Pack, Weed, Women and Song* and *Tales from the Tower,* plus a CD of all of his songs.

The Compleat Ova Hamlet — Parodies of SF authors by Richard A. Lupoff. This is a brand new edition with more stories and more illustrations by Trina Robbins.

The Contested Earth and Other SF Stories — A never-before published space opera and seven short stories by Jim Harmon.

The Crimson Query — A 1929 thriller from Arlton Eadie. A perfect way to get introduced.

The Curse of Cantire — Classic 1939 novel of a family curse by Walter S. Masterman.

The Devil and the C.I.D. — Odd diabolic mystery by E.C.R. Lorac

The Devil Drives — An odd prison and lost treasure novel from 1932 by Virgil Markham.

The Devil's Mistress — A 1915 Scottish gothic tale by J. W. Brodie-Innes, a member of Aleister Crowley's Golden Dawn.

The Devil's Nightclub and Other Stories — John Pelan introduces some gruesome tales by Nat Schachner.

The Disentanglers — Episodic intrigue at the turn of last century by Andrew Lang

The Dumpling — Political murder from 1907 by Coulson Kernahan.

The End of It All and Other Stories — Ed Gorman selected his favorite short stories for this huge collection.

The Fangs of Suet Pudding — A 1944 novel of the German invasion by Adams Farr

The Ghost of Gaston Revere — From 1935, a novel of life and beyond by Mark Hansom, introduced by John Pelan.

The Girl in the Dark — A thriller from Roland Daniel

The Gold Star Line — Seaboard adventure from L.T. Reade and Robert Eustace.

The Golden Dagger — 1951 Scotland Yard yarn by E. R. Punshon.

The Great Orme Terror — Horror stories by Garnett Radcliffe from the pulps

The Hairbreadth Escapes of Major Mendax — Francis Blake Crofton's 1889 boys' book.

The House That Time Forgot and Other Stories — Insane pulpitude by Robert F. Young

The House of the Vampire — 1907 poetic thriller by George S. Viereck.

The Illustrious Corpse — Murder hijinx from Tiffany Thayer

The Incredible Adventures of Rowland Hern — Intriguing 1928 impossible crimes by Nicholas Olde.

The Julius Caesar Murder Case — A classic 1935 re-telling of the assassination by Wallace Irwin that's much more fun than the Shakespeare version.

The Koky Comics — A collection of all of the 1978-1981 Sunday and daily comic strips by Richard O'Brien and Mort Gerberg, in two volumes.

The Lady of the Terraces — 1925 missing race adventure by E. Charles Vivian.

The Lord of Terror — 1925 mystery with master-criminal, Fantômas.

The Melamare Mystery — A classic 1929 Arsene Lupin mystery by Maurice Leblanc

The Man Who Was Secrett — Epic SF stories from John Brunner

The Man Without a Planet — Science fiction tales by Richard Wilson

The N. R. De Mexico Novels — Robert Bragg, the real N.R. de Mexico, presents *Marijuana Girl, Madman on a Drum, Private Chauffeur* in one volume.

The Night Remembers — A 1991 Jack Walsh mystery from Ed Gorman.

The One After Snelling — Kickass modern noir from Richard O'Brien.

The Organ Reader — A huge compilation of just about everything published in the 1971-1972 radical bay-area newspaper, *THE ORGAN*. A coffee table book that points out the shallowness of the coffee table mindset.

The Poker Club — Three in one! Ed Gorman's ground-breaking novel, the short story it was based upon, and the screenplay of the film made from it.

The Private Journal & Diary of John H. Surratt — The memoirs of the man who conspired to assassinate President Lincoln.

The Secret Adventures of Sherlock Holmes — Three Sherlockian pastiches by the Brooklyn author/publisher, Gary Lovisi.

The Shadow on the House — Mark Hansom's 1934 masterpiece of horror is introduced by John Pelan.

The Sign of the Scorpion — A 1935 Edmund Snell tale of oriental evil.

The Singular Problem of the Stygian House-Boat — Two classic tales by John Kendrick Bangs about the denizens of Hades.

The Smiling Corpse — Philip Wylie and Bernard Bergman's odd 1935 novel.

The Spider: Satan's Murder Machines — A thesis about Iron Man

The Stench of Death: An Odoriferous Omnibus by Jack Moskovitz — Two complete novels and two novellas from 60's sleaze author, Jack Moskovitz.

The Story Writer and Other Stories — Classic SF from Richard Wilson

The Strange Case of the Antlered Man — 1935 dementia from Edwy Searles Brooks

The Strange Thirteen — Richard B. Gamon's odd stories about Raj India.

The Technique of the Mystery Story — Carolyn Wells' tips about writing.

The Threat of Nostalgia — A collection of his most obscure stories by Jon Breen

The Time Armada — Fox B. Holden's 1953 SF gem.

The Tongueless Horror and Other Stories — Volume One of the series of short stories from the weird pulps by Wyatt Blassingame.

The Tracer of Lost Persons — From 1906, an episodic novel that became a hit radio series in the 30s. Introduced by Richard A. Lupoff.

The Trail of the Cloven Hoof — Diabolical horror from 1935 by Arlton Eadie. Introduced by John Pelan.

The Triune Man — Mindscrambling science fiction from Richard A. Lupoff.

The Unholy Goddess and Other Stories — Wyatt Blassingame's first DTP compilation

The Universal Holmes — Richard A. Lupoff's 2007 collection of five Holmesian pastiches and a recipe for giant rat stew.

The Werewolf vs the Vampire Woman — Hard to believe ultraviolence by either Arthur M. Scarm or Arthur M. Scram.

The Whistling Ancestors — A 1936 classic of weirdness by Richard E. Goddard and introduced by John Pelan.

The White Owl — A vintage thriller from Edmund Snell

The White Peril in the Far East — Sidney Lewis Gulick's 1905 indictment of the West and assurance that Japan would never attack the U.S.

The Wizard of Berner's Abbey — A 1935 horror gem written by Mark Hansom and introduced by John Pelan.

The Wonderful Wizard of Oz — by L. Frank Baum and illustrated by Gavin L. O'Keefe

Through the Looking Glass — Lewis Carroll wrote it; Gavin L. O'Keefe illustrated it.

Time Line — Ramble House artist Gavin O'Keefe selects his most evocative art inspired by the twisted literature he reads and designs.

Tiresias — Psychotic modern horror novel by Jonathan M. Sweet.

Totah Six-Pack — Fender Tucker's six tales about Farmington in one sleek volume.

Trail of the Spirit Warrior — Roger Haley's historical saga of life in the Indian Territories.

Two Kinds of Bad — Two 50s novels by William Ard about Danny Fontaine

Two Suns of Morcali and Other Stories — Evelyn E. Smith's SF tour-de-force

Ultra-Boiled — 23 gut-wrenching tales by our Man in Brooklyn, Gary Lovisi.

Up Front From Behind — A 2011 satire of Wall Street by James B. Kobak.

Victims & Villains — Intriguing Sherlockiana from Derham Groves.

Wade Wright Novels — *Echo of Fear, Death At Nostalgia Street, It Leads to Murder* and *Shadows' Edge*, a double book featuring *Shadows Don't Bleed* and *The Sharp Edge.*

Walter S. Masterman Novels — *The Green Toad, The Flying Beast, The Yellow Mistletoe, The Wrong Verdict, The Perjured Alibi, The Border Line, The Bloodhounds Bay* and *The Curse of Cantire.* Masterman wrote horror and mystery, some introduced by John Pelan.

We Are the Dead and Other Stories — Volume Two in the Day Keene in the Detective Pulps series, introduced by Ed Gorman. When done, there may be as many as 11 in the series.

Welsh Rarebit Tales — Charming stories from 1902 by Harle Oren Cummins

West Texas War and Other Western Stories — by Gary Lovisi.

Whip Dodge: Man Hunter — Wesley Tallant's saga of a bounty hunter of the old West.

Win, Place and Die! — The first new mystery by Milt Ozaki in decades. The ultimate novel of 70s Reno.

You'll Die Laughing — Bruce Elliott's 1945 novel of murder at a practical joker's English countryside manor.

RAMBLE HOUSE
Fender Tucker, Prop.   Gavin L. O'Keefe, Graphics
www.ramblehouse.com   fender@ramblehouse.com
228-826-1783   10329 Sheephead Drive, Vancleave MS 39565